LOVE AND HIGH INTRIGUE IN FRANCES
PARKINSON KEYES' OWN NEW ORLEANS.

ORSON FOXWORTH
*The handsome president of a great
company, he was as unscrupulous with
women as he was with money.*

RUTH AVERY
*His beautiful niece from Washington came
to New Orleans in Carnival season to find the
romance which long had eluded her.*

RUSSELL ALDRIDGE
*The brilliant young archaeologist came
from Yucatan to find a staggering mystery
in the glowing city.*

AMÉLIE LALANDE
*The gorgeous widow would not be had by
Orson as easily as he anticipated.*

ODILE LALANDE
*The tragedy of Amélie's wistful daughter
forced the diners at Antoine's into shattering
appraisals of their own lives.*

Frances Parkinson Keyes

Dinner at Antoine's

AVON
PUBLISHERS OF
DISCUS • CAMELOT • BARD

To
ROY ALCIATORE
worthy successor
of
Antoine and Jules Alciatore
a great Restaurateur
a distinguished Orleanian
and
my very good friend

AVON BOOKS
A division of
The Hearst Corporation
959 Eighth Avenue
New York, New York 10019

First Avon Printing, January, 1968
Fourth Printing, October, 1970

AVON TRADEMARK REG. U.S. PAT. OFF. AND
FOREIGN COUNTRIES, REGISTERED TRADEMARK—
MARCA REGISTRADA, HECHO EN CHICAGO, U.S.A.

Printed in the U.S.A.

FOREWORD

Ever since 1936, the Forewords of my books have been lengthy and explanatory. This has been because the circumstances surrounding the books themselves have been consistently, though variously, extraordinary, and because I have felt that these circumstances demanded full and candid explanation. No mere list of acknowledgments to persons, places and reference books would, from my viewpoint, have been adequate in the way of introduction, clarification and expression of appreciation. So I have written the sort of Forewords which I hoped and believed would be thus adequate.

Almost without exception, so far as I can judge from fan mail and from verbal comment, these Forewords have given pleasure to my readers. But with nearly the same degree of uniformity they have been condemned as tedious and superfluous, or both, by reviewers. A desire to find favor with literary critics is natural to every author; therefore, it is with hope, not unmixed with apprehension, that I release the typescript of DINNER AT ANTOINE'S to the printers: hope that the critics may realize I have read, marked and inwardly digested their scathing remarks even if I have not previously appeared to do so; and apprehension lest they may be no more pleased than heretofore and that my readers may be disappointed.

However, honesty compels me to admit that there has been nothing extraordinary about the circumstances under which DINNER AT ANTOINE'S has been written. To be sure, I have lived a very secluded life and have kept very long working hours; but the seclusion has been a not unwelcome change from a hitherto hectic life and the working hours have been passed under about the pleasantest conditions imaginable. The greater part of the book has come into being in my study at Beauregard House in New Orleans—a study ideally located in the old slave quarters, at the rear of a pleasant patio dominated by an ancient fountain and surrounded with camellia bushes. The few chapters which have not been written there have been achieved in the equally pleasant, equally quiet, and still more spacious study of "Compensation," my house in Crowley.

I have not once gone hungry during the interval of writing —on the contrary, as is apt to be the case in this land of Creole gumbo and crayfish bisque, I have been almost too well nourished. I have not once been cold—and though that is not strange, since the temperature has ranged well above ninety much of the time, there is no possible choice, in my mind, between the icy chill of Normandy, which prevailed while I was writing CAME A CAVALIER and numerous other books, and the balmy warmth of Louisiana, which prevails at all times. I have not been obliged to learn any strange languages, to adapt myself to any unfamiliar customs or to travel under any trying conditions. I have not had to live without telephone service and mail delivery or to transport drinking water, as well as all foodstuffs, eight miles, under gas rationing, as I did at "The Cottage" while writing THE RIVER ROAD. I have not had to go halfway around the world in search of source material. I have had no long serious illnesses and have undergone no surgical operations, either major or minor. I have run into no wars, not even into any minor revolutions. In short, as I have remarked before, there is absolutely nothing to say about the conditions under which the book has been written except that they were very nearly ideal, and nothing to say about the elements which went into its making except that they were ready at hand for background and fictionizing.

In the way of acknowledgment, a little more should be said. Hermann B. Deutsch, Associate Editor of the *Item*, has again been my best editor adviser, as he was in the case of CRESCENT CARNIVAL, ALSO THE HILLS, THE RIVER ROAD and CAME A CAVALIER—only in this case the advice has been more constant and intensive and, now that the novel has reached finished form, represents a more integral part of the story. In fact, if I had my way, I should refer to him as a collaborator rather than as an adviser. But Hermann is one of those persons who likes to have his way and, as he says himself, there is no use in beating your head against a stone wall—it doesn't hurt the wall and it can do all sorts of painful things to your head. I have a wholesome respect for stone walls and I want to spare my head as much as possible. Hence my deference to the gentleman's wishes.

Thanks are also due to Franklin Hay, veteran police reporter of the *Item*, for his efficient and kindly help in those sections of the novel where his line of work made information especially valuable; and to Burdette Huggins, Society Editor of the *Item* for her help in tracing descriptions of the costumes worn by early queens of the Twelfth Night Revelers.

Marie Louise Miltonberger, Society Editor of the *New Orleans States,* also helped in the latter way. So did Mrs. Fernand Claiborne—the heroine of my book, ONCE ON ESPLANADE—and Mrs. Lucile Bohn Gillis of Biloxi, a sister of the "beautiful Leila Bohn" (the late Mrs. Edward A. Ferguson) who reigned as queen of both Momus and the Revelers.

I feel that I have been extremely fortunate in persuading Mrs. Hewitt Bouanchaud, whose songs of Louisiana interpret its characteristics with unique skill and deep feeling, to write both the words* and music of "Lady Levee," attibuted in this novel to Sabin Duplessis (see pages 334 and 335). I feel equally fortunate in having persuaded Mr. Joseph Donaldson, Jr., an assistant professor in the School of Architecture at Tulane University and an instructor in the McCrady School of Art, to furnish the drawings for the jacket, end papers, dedication page and chapter headings; while Mr. Donaldson's medium of interpretation is a different one from Mrs. Bouanchaud's, it has the same delicacy of feeling and skill of execution. The portrait sketch on the back of the jacket is based on photographs taken by Mr. Elemore Morgan, whose work is already pleasantly familiar to readers of my books.

Mr. Eberhard P. Deutsch gave immediate attention and authentic information in response to several appeals for the clarification of Louisiana law; and Dr. Robert C. Kelleher checked on the accuracy of the references made to various diseases. I am extremely grateful to both for their good offices.

My secretary, Geraldine Bullock, has shared my long laboring hours and has made a number of valuable suggestions in regard to the story. My housekeeper at Beauregard House, Clara E. Wilson, and my caretakers at "Compensation," Creacy and Beverly King, by their vigilance in safeguarding my seclusion and by their cooperative attitude, especially in regard to late and irregular meal hours, have also contributed to the comfort and speed with which it has been possible for me to work.

The United Press dispatch, noted on page 406 of the novel, is not imaginary. It appeared in the June 30, 1948, issue of the *New Orleans Item*. Doubtless other noteworthy newspapers carried it also. But if they did, I did not happen to see it in their pages, as I have been writing, rather than reading, during recent months. Besides, the staff members of other newspapers have not, in this instance, been acting as my guides, philosophers and friends. Perhaps, on some future occasion, they may be, in which case—whether it proves pleasing to reviewers or not!—I shall write a Foreword about them.

F. P. K.

Beauregard House, New Orleans, Louisiana
"Compensation," Crowley, Louisiana
December 1947-August 1948

---

* Mrs. Thekla Hollingsworth, who wrote the songs contained in some of my previous novels, made helpful suggestions concerning the adaptation of these to the printed page.

CONTENTS

DRAMATIS PERSONAE

ORSON FOXWORTH, President of the Great Blue Fleet
RUTH AVERY, his niece
RUSSELL ALDRIDGE, a wealthy young archeologist
AMÉLIE LALANDE, a beautiful widow, the object of
    FOXWORTH'S affections
CARESSE LALANDE, AMÉLIE'S younger daughter
ODILE LALANDE ST. AMANT, AMÉLIE'S elder daughter
LÉONCE ST. AMANT, ODILE'S husband
SABIN DUPLESSIS, ODILE'S former suitor
DOCTOR VANCE PERRAULT, the LALANDES' family physician
FRANCISCO DARCOA, principal stockholder in the Trans-Caribbean Fruit & Steamship Company
CLARINDA DARCOA, his daughter, a New Orleans belle
RICHARD HUNTINGTON, Assistant Secretary of State
JOE RACINA, successful writer on current events
JUDITH RACINA, his wife
JENNESS RACINA, their little daughter
PETER MACDONALD, Associate Editor of the *New York Enterprise*
MIRIAM HICKEY, representative of the Salon Superbe
DUTCH SCHAEFER, a soldier of fortune
DETECTIVE-CAPTAIN THEOPHILE MURPHY, member of the New Orleans Police Force
CAPTAIN REX BONHAM, member of the Fingerprint Bureau
DOCTOR KARL ALTGELD, Assistant Coroner
TOSSIE PRIDE, ODILE ST. AMANT'S personal maid
DOWNES
ELLEN } ORSON FOXWORTH'S English butler and parlormaid
Housekeeper and patients of DOCTOR PERRAULT
Servants in the LALANDE and DARCOA households
Etc., etc.

The above characters are entirely imaginary and any resemblance to real persons is wholly accidental.

DRAMATIS PERSONAE

continued

The following characters are real persons and their names are used with permission. The episodes with which they are connected in this story are, of course, wholly fictional, however.

ROY ALCIATORE, proprietor of Antoine's Restaurant

ANGELO ALCIATORE, his cousin and maître d'hôtel

AD GIVEN DAVIS, proprietor of the Bar-None Ranch, River Road

GIOVANNI PRAMMAGIORE, proprietor of Giovanni's Restaurant, New York

ANGELO CAFUERI, his maître d'hôtel

JOHN J. GROSCH, sheriff of the Criminal District Court, Parish of Orleans

DETECTIVE-CAPTAIN HARRY GREGSON } of the New Orleans
DETECTIVE FRANK CASSARD } police force
DETECTIVE JOHN MEREDITH

1

How Orson Foxworth gave a dinner at Antoine's on Friday—

January 2, 1948

"Isn't it *all* wonderful, darling? Would you ever have dreamed, back in Milwaukee, that it could be warm like this the second of January? Or that everything in New Orleans would be just ten times as cute and quaint as we thought it would be?"

The young man thus blithely addressed responded to his bride with becoming enthusiasm, muttering something to the effect that the weather and the sightseeing both suited him fine, but that this was mostly because she was along to enjoy them with him. Then, as if to assure her still more wholeheartedly of his unqualified pleasure, he brought his remarks to a close with a very intense kiss. For some moments, the two remained locked in each other's arms, utterly oblivious of their surroundings.

However, the rest of the motley queue, crowding the banquette from curb to wall on St. Louis Street, shuffled, complained, and shifted in the restless fashion of those who have come at weary last in sight of a long-sought goal. Now and again, as favored newcomers, who had secured advance reservations, by-passed the head of the line and gained admission at the century-old doorway of Antoine's Restaurant, murmurs of more active discontent became audible.

"It ought to be foist come foist soived," said a stocky corporal, his battle jacket bright with service ribbons and the silver-wreathed blue bar of the combat infantry.

"Sure it ought," agreed one of his uniformed companions placidly. "But you stood in line longer'n this for K-rations many's the time, soldier, di'n't you? Once you make the grade here, you anyway get something worth sinking your choppers in, so they tell me."

"I hope ya right. . . . Look, there goes another bunch of civvie brass, right in through that door. Say, I could go for that babe myself. But I bet you got to have a rezzavation for. . . ."

"Aw, lay off."

The queue inched forward as three couples left the glassed-in entrance and others were admitted in their stead. A steamer hooted hoarsely from the nearby river. Half a block away, on Bourbon Street, a night club doorway opened and a brief, tinny crash of music lost itself in a sudden confusion of motor horns as traffic jammed in the narrow street, stalled noisily, and then renewed its one-way flow.

In the one clear space along the curb, a shining black limousine slid to a halt. A yellow-capped taxi starter hastened to open its door.

"Go right in, Mr. Foxworth," he urged, stealing a swift glance at the queue to see whether the name created an adequate impression.

A tall man of spare, somewhat angular build, his thick, fiery hair sprinkled with neutralizing gray, alighted from the limousine and gave his hand to a pretty girl, whose carriage was as graceful as his was awkward, but whose features and coloring suggested a probable relationship. Then he turned and looked in amazement at the long queue waiting for admission.

"I wouldn't have believed it," he said to the taxi starter. "How long has this been going on?"

"Ever since the war."

"But that's been over for two and a half years!"

"I know. But they keep on coming just the same."

The girl touched the Foxworth sleeve. "Can't we go in, Uncle?" she whispered. "It bothers me to have all these people staring at us this way."

"It doesn't bother me. And if I'm any judge, you'll have to get used to arousing a certain amount of attention."

"But these people aren't curious. They're just angry. And I don't blame them, either. I wouldn't like to see someone whisked inside without a moment's wait if I'd been standing on the sidewalk for an hour."

"A sidewalk's still called a banquette down here. You'd better start learning the lingo right away."

"Well, a banquette then. But please . . . . That nice-looking young man won't be able to keep the crowd back much longer and still hold the door open for us."

14

Foxworth shrugged his shoulders and ushered his niece through the glass inclosure of the vestibule into the large plain dining room beyond. The nice-looking young man hastily relocked the door, and with a bow which became his bearing, smilingly greeted the magnate.

"We had a last minute cancellation in the Rex Room, Mr. Foxworth," he said. "And Roy thought perhaps you'd like to greet your guests and have the drinks in there before going on to the 1840 Room for dinner. It isn't so crowded, and besides—"

"And besides, Roy realized how much it would mean for a young visitor to see both those famous rooms on her first night in New Orleans. Well, that's like him. By the way, let me present you—my niece, Miss Avery. Ruth, this is Angelo Alciatore, the proprietor's cousin and maître d'hôtel."

Ruth extended her hand cordially as the nice-looking young man smiled and bowed again.

"It's a privilege to have you here, Miss Avery. And to welcome Mr. Foxworth back after such a long absence."

"Believe me, Antoine's doesn't look so bad after Central America," Foxworth remarked rather dryly. Then he added, "I hope the ducks got here all right?"

"Yes, indeed. Roy wanted me to tell you that he'd press them for your party himself."

"Good!"

Having settled this vital point, Foxworth was obviously disinclined to devote more time to amenities. Looking fixedly ahead, he strode along in the wake of a portly, sleek-haired waiter. Ruth, however, was intrigued by the large plain room; by the clean tiled floor and the big fans in the high ceiling; by the mirrors which paneled the walls, enhancing the general effect of spaciousness and simplicity; by the white tablecloths with their centerpieces of old-fashioned carafes; by the cashier's tall desk at the rear and the crayon enlargements which hung on the wall behind it. She was pleasantly familiar with France, and this room reminded her of restaurants in its more important provincial cities. Yet the atmosphere was individual rather than French. She had heard it said that the proprietor, Roy Alciatore, had been offered untold sums to open branches elsewhere, and that he had proudly replied, "There can be only one Antoine's." She understood what he meant. . . .

Suddenly the lights flicked out and the agreeable confusion of sound stopped abruptly. Puzzled, and slightly startled, Ruth saw a wavering thread of blue flame cascading from a lifted ladle into a bowl, and beyond the cascade, a waiter's

15

intent face and the gratified countenances of several guests. Ruth groped for her uncle's arm, whispering a question.

"Nothing but a bunch of tourists having their first *café brûlot* and getting a great kick out of it," he replied. "I wish the act could have been held up one more minute. Right now I want to get where I'm going and I can't see my way."

"But that blue flame's fascinating. And there's something weird about it. I'm sure the 'bunch of tourists' and I aren't the only persons who feel that way. Everyone stopped talking to watch it."

As suddenly as they had flicked out, the lights flashed on again, shining so brightly that Ruth blinked. The undistinguishable clatter of conversation was not resumed quite so quickly. Instead, an occasional voice with marked carrying quality rose above the subdued hum which followed the hush.

"I don't think so much of these Oysters Rockefeller. I don't see why we didn't order tomato soup instead."

"Well, about a million other people like them, even if you don't. Presidents and folks like that too! I give up, trying to suit you. Tomato soup, my eye! Who wants to eat tomato soup in New Orleans?"

". . . that was Orson Foxworth who just went by. You know—president of the Great Blue Fleet. The girl must be his niece from the East, come down for Carnival. I saw her picture on the society page of the *Item* this afternoon."

At first they had been only casually observed as they wove their way among the crowded tables. Now the susurrus of general recognition followed the two as the portly waiter led them into an immense annex where the walls were covered with autographed magazine articles, drawings and photographs. Basking in the obvious stir of recognition his entry evoked, Foxworth slackened his pace.

"This is the room where Roy staged the celebration of the restaurant's centennial," he told her. "And believe me, that *was* a party—an archbishop—supreme court judges—high ranking officers—all the big shots! And the champagne would have floated a freighter!"

Foxworth would not have been disinclined to enlarge on the subject; but the portly waiter persistently, though politely, indicated another door and guided his charges down a terrazzo-floored corridor. Then he stood aside to let them pass through a double portal into an imposing banquet hall. Ruth had a confused impression of recessed cabinets filled with glittering crowns, scepters, and other symbols of Carnival royalty; of exquisite camellias lavishly adorning the golden hair and white shoulders of three beautiful blonde women;

16

and of half-filled glasses, suggesting an exalted resemblance to old-fashioneds, in the hands of as many men. Then, as she stood hesitantly near the doorway, one of the women detached herself from the group and rushed forward, almost forestalling the embrace into which Foxworth quickly swept her.

"Well, at last!"

"What do you mean, at last? Isn't this my first chance?"

"Maybe the first chance since you got to New Orleans. But how about all the time you've stayed away?"

"Oh, we'll talk about that later! But don't let's start off with a quarrel. I never felt less like one in my life. It's grand, being with you again, Amélie! I swear, you look younger every time I see you!"

He held her off at arms' length, gazing at her with unconcealed admiration, then caught her to him again, more lightly this time, before beginning to greet the others who now crowded about him and clamored for attention. The impulsive lady was undeniably a beauty, Ruth reflected, quickly suppressing a mental qualification: "At least, if you like the siren type." But surely this fascinating creature could not be old enough to feel complimented by remarks on her apparent youthfulness! Her corn-colored hair lay in great coils above the soft ringlets which framed her radiant face. Her big blue eyes snapped and sparkled. Her delicately rouged lips parted over tiny white teeth. Her svelte figure triumphed over the exacting cut of her dress. She might possibly be thirty—admittedly a golden age for a woman. And why should any woman of thirty, who might well have the world at her feet—or at all events a large portion of its male population—set such store by the absence or presence of a man who would soon inevitably be classed as elderly? How could she invite his kisses, rebuke him for his neglect, and publicly demonstrate the degree of privilege to which she felt entitled? Amélie now linked her arm in Foxworth's, and her white fingers, sparkling with diamonds, were pressed against his sleeve. She had assumed the attitude of a friend so favored that she might take the role of hostess for granted. And no one seemed to marvel at her desire or question her right to do this. . . .

"May I introduce myself, Miss Avery? I'm Odile St. Amant. I'm afraid we've neglected you shamefully, leaving you alone by the door like this while we fell on your uncle's neck! But we're very fond of him, and it *is* a long time since we've seen him. Please believe we're not usually all that rude in New Orleans!"

17

The speaker smiled winningly and Ruth smiled back, murmuring that she quite understood, that it didn't matter in the least, that she was enjoying herself immensely, just looking on. As she spoke, she held out her hand with the same spontaneous friendliness which she had revealed in greeting Angelo Alciatore. Odile St. Amant, though still smiling, and resuming her pleasant apologies, did not instantly respond with the handclasp which Ruth had expected; and feeling slightly rebuffed, she withdrew her arm, only to find Odile's fingers at last touching hers, with a strange quivering motion. Greatly puzzled, she looked at the cordial stranger more closely; was it possible that Odile's eyesight was affected, that she had been groping for a hand that she could see only dimly, if at all? That first touch had suggested the tremulous searching of the blind. But she too had beautiful blue eyes, and though there were no siren glances here, the light in them was clear and bright. The shaking, which still continued, must be due to some other cause. And suddenly Ruth guessed that Odile was ashamed of it or troubled by it, that she would have avoided the handclasp if she could, in her hope of concealing an infirmity, oddly at variance with her fresh charm. For there was no doubt about it: this woman did not merely look young; she really was young, hardly more than a girl; and though she did not sparkle, she had a shining quality all her own.

"I thought of course that in a moment either *maman* or Mr. Foxworth would turn and present the others. But since they don't seem to be doing it—"

"Maman!"

The exclamation escaped Ruth before she could stop it. That siren the mother of a grown daughter! Odile answered with a pleasant little laugh.

"You'd never guess it, would you? I don't need to tell you that she married at seventeen. And ever since my father died we've been each other's closest companions. We're nearly always taken for sisters by strangers who haven't been told. I do have a sister here though. The girl in the jade green."

"Oh! Is that your sister? Yes, now you tell me, I can see the family resemblance. But she looks more like your mother than you do, I think."

The comment had no sting to it, either mental or verbal; but, as a matter of fact, Ruth thought Odile far more attractive than either of the others, and she had already observed the jade green dress with tempered admiration. She had always moved in circles where women wore smart and sophisticated clothes; but seldom, off the stage, had she seen

18

one as darking as this. She had been thinking—unoriginally—that perhaps a vogue which padded a girl's hips and covered her legs logically demanded a tightly banded waistline and a revealing décolletage. At all events, the heart-shaped bodice of the dress under observation did not even have shoestring straps over the shoulders, and was cut extremely low under the arms and across the breast; then it tapered down to a narrow point above a skirt of billowing tulle.

"She's the baby and the darling of the family," Odile continued, nodding in response to Ruth's remark about the resemblance. "Her name's Caresse."

"What a lovely name!" Ruth said, glad of the easy escape from saying, "What a lovely girl!"

"I think so," Odile replied. "And it suits her so well."

"The man standing beside her seems to feel the same way about it. Is he her fiancé?"

Odile laughed again, the same pleasant laugh as before. "No, only her brother-in-law. That's my husband, Léonce. . . . Come, I really must set you straight on all these puzzling relationships. I can't wait any longer for my host or my mother to do it."

She moved forward, adroitly giving the impression of taking Ruth with her, but, as Ruth did not fail to notice, managing to do this without actually touching her. They had advanced only a few steps when Foxworth, suddenly conscious of his negligence, wheeled sharply around.

"Oh, for the love of—excuse me, Ruthie! I'm just a victim of shock. My apologies to the rest of you, too." He grinned engagingly at the company casually grouped about him. "This is my niece, Ruth Avery, as all of you know anyhow. . . . My dear, the fascinating creature clinging to my arm is Amélie Lalande, the envy of all lesser charmers. I see that Odile's already made up for my negligence by introducing herself, and perhaps she's told you which is really her sister and which is really her husband. Yes? Well, I thought so. The Viking-looking chap on the other side of Caresse is Russ Aldridge—Russell Wainwright Aldridge, Ph. D.—a fast man with a hieroglyph, a drink, a samba and a back-to-back pair of Jacks, in the order named! And finally, Doctor Perrault, who painted tonsils for Odile and Caresse when they were only knee-high to a puddle duck. But they don't hold that against him and you needn't either. . . . Have you had a drink yet? As you see, some of our guests got desperate because we were so late and very wisely started in on Sazeracs."

"Only your *male* guests, Orson," Amélie corrected him coquettishly. "The Lalande family is better behaved than these Yankees and Cajuns. Naturally, Odile and Caresse and I waited for our host—and what a wait it's been!" Evidently she proposed to continue harping on Foxworth's tardiness, for she now glanced down at the diamond watch sparkling on her slim wrist, then looked archly up again. "Instead of being here to welcome us, as our host, you put us, as your guests, in the predicament of taking the initiative, you unmannered creature!" she went on. "Not that I couldn't have ordered for you—I'm sure you're still drinking that unimaginative Scotch and soda before, during, and after meals! I want a champagne cocktail, and Odile and Caresse never take anything but sherry."

"Got that, haven't you, Albert?" Foxworth inquired of a small, gray-haired man who had now appeared on the scene and stood solicitously awaiting instructions. And, as the man smiled with pleasure at Foxworth's instant recognition, the latter continued, "Refills for the gentlemen. And a Bacchus for my niece."

"A Bacchus? Why, I don't even know what that is! And nobody else seems to be drinking one."

"It's half and half Dubonnet and French vermouth, with a twist of lemon peel," Odile replied, again coming quickly to the visitor's rescue. "And I'm going to have one myself, instead of sherry. *Maman* didn't ask me what I wanted, you know, any more than your uncle asked you. So I'm merely changing her mind, and you can change *his*."

"All right, I think I will. I've always heard so much about Sazeracs. Are they as good here as they are at the famous bar?"

"You'll have to decide that for yourself on Mardi Gras," Aldridge informed her, coming forward. "The attitude of the Sazerac Bar is very ungallant—it admits women only one day in the year. But you and I have a date right now for that day. Will eleven suit you?"

"Better make it earlier, Russ. She ought to be at the Boston Club by then."

"I suppose she ought. And I can't say that the club does much better than the bar, when it comes to limiting ladies. However, it does open its sacred portals to them for six days instead of one, Miss Avery. So that gives you a little more leeway. You can afford to take time out for the bar. Would ten be too early for our date?"

"Well, as you've probably guessed, I never have taken a drink that early, but you make it sound very intriguing."

"That was the idea. I'm glad I succeeded. And eye openers won't be the only things you'll try out for the first time in

20

New Orleans. I hope you'll enjoy every last one of them. Well, here come the drinks. It's too bad you can't taste your first Sazerac on its native heath. But I think you'll find Oliver's done pretty well by these!"

Aldridge took one of the proffered glasses from Albert, whose rather wistful smile was changing to a broad grin, and handed it to her. Then he lifted his own glass in a toast. *He's very attractive,* Ruth thought, *much the most attractive man here. Of course, I can see that Léonce St. Amant could be just as fascinating in his way as his mother-in-law is in hers. But he's not my kind and I really believe this man is.* She sipped her drink, finding it delicious, and saying so. But she was glad that, while the others' conversation took on a swifter pace of give and take, Aldridge seemed content to keep their dialogue casual, enabling her to concentrate on mental observations rather than on small talk. She had been slightly overawed by the reference to hieroglyphs and a Ph. D.; somehow an archeologist did not seem to hold out much promise as a light-hearted squire for the Carnival season, and she knew it was part of the program that she should accept Aldridge in that role. She had also visualized him as patrician. Her first impression of his looks and bearing more than fulfilled that idea: he had a well-shaped head, sloping shoulders and a slim waist; his stiff collar shone immaculate against his bronzed skin and above his black tie; his beautifully tailored clothes were cut to show off his fine figure to best advantage. The other two male guests were both wearing soft shirts and dinner coats which suggested long use before long disuse. St. Amant was carefully shaved, but Ruth guessed he had to fight a "five o'clock shadow"; he was well-built, but stocky rather than slender, and it was obvious that before long he would have to watch his waistline. Perrault had a natural distinction which enabled him to carry off his careless dress without loss of dignity; his rather tired face revealed the experience and wisdom of devotion to his profession. But it lacked Aldridge's highbred look. Offhand, Ruth would have said she was likely to prefer it on that account; surprisingly, things had not worked out that way; she found Aldridge approachable, affable and—as she had previously reflected—outstandingly attractive. She glanced at him again and colored as she surmised that he was guessing much that was in her mind, but that his mild amusement was leavened with admiration.

"So they told you that I wasn't interested in anything less than a thousand years old," he said, his gray eyes twinkling. "Or that I spent most of my time prowling around jungles in

21

search of ruins, and that on rare occasions when I returned to civilization, I remained aloof, absorbed in the mighty tomes which I could not handily carry with me to Yucatan, Indo-China, Java and the Chaco. I shall devote the next few weeks to disproving these false rumors.... Incidentally, I hope that a card for the Twelfth Night Revels has been safely delivered to you?"

"Yes, thank you. In fact, three of them."

"One to get you inside the door at the Auditorium, one to get you as far as the floor committee, and one to get you past that august body into the call-out section instead of being sternly sent to the balcony," Aldridge explained, his eyes still twinkling. "I'm sure Caresse will go with you, if you like, and show you all the ropes. We'll talk to her about it a little later. She appears preoccupied at the moment." Ruth followed his quizzical glance, and saw that Caresse and Léonce St. Amant still seemed to be engrossed in each other, that Foxworth and Amélie were still sparring, and that Odile and Doctor Perrault were engaged in a conversation which appeared to be grave in character. "The Revels are among those features of New Orleans which I told you I hoped you would enjoy," Aldridge went on, "and incidentally, what about the burning of the greens at Kingsley House? Has anyone forestalled me with a suggestion you'd like to see that?"

"No one has forestalled you with anything."

"It's my good luck the Crescent got in so late last night that you weren't interested in coffee at the French Market. And that you slept so long this morning that you had brunch in your room while your uncle was out mapping new banana empire campaigns. And that the rest of your day has been devoted to unpacking and a hairdo and the antique shops."

"How did you happen to come to all those conclusions?"

"Well, the new hairdo and the happy results of the unpacking are both fairly obvious," Aldridge explained, his appreciative gaze shifting from Ruth's russet curls to her bouffant dress of creamy taffeta, brocaded in bright flowers. "And if it hadn't been for the fortunate fact that you are much more interested in antiques than I am, at this stage, I *would* have been forestalled. As I've said before, I've had great good luck. May I drop in tomorrow for a cocktail and set seriously to work mapping out a program for you?"

"I'd be delighted. But you guessed wrong about one thing. I wash my own hair and my curls aren't an assembly line job."

22

Ruth met the gray eyes with a lively look of her own. Then she was conscious of her uncle's hand on her arm.

"Who's remiss now?" he inquired, with the slight rasp in his voice, which she had learned to associate with annoyance. "I've been trying for the last five minutes to catch your eye and you've been too busy trying to vamp this king-size gravedigger. Come on, dinner's ready."

The conversation became general, with the recent Sugar Bowl Game, the impending election and the coming Carnival season as predominating topics, while the company passed through the double portal again, turning to the right this time and then doubling back through a series of small private rooms as unadorned as the great outer dining room, except for the framed menus and drawings which nearly covered the walls. The little square room in the corner was the one the well-known journalist, Joe Racina, liked best, Perrault whispered to Ruth. Well, as you might expect, there was Joe right now, with his wife and two special cronies—that smooth-looking New York publisher, who came down twice a year to ferret out local talent—he had a queer name, or nickname, or something, Perrault never could remember it—and Sally Sidwell, who was the most up-and-coming bookseller in New Orleans. Those stags, whooping it up in the next room, were a lot of gilded highbinders from the Cotton Exchange, giving a bachelor dinner in honor of "good old L. J." who was about to step off the deep end, rather unexpectedly—in fact, he had been one of the numerous lads with the habit of honking his horn in front of the Lalande manor on Richmond place. But, "good old L. J." hadn't been able to stand the competition in the Big League, so that left only eight or nine contestants still battling for the pennant. . . .

As if to prove that the doctor did not exaggerate, several of the stags rose quickly and gathered around Caresse, cutting her out of her company with practiced dexterity. The others did not wait for her. Another door was thrown open, and Ruth found herself on the threshold of a room whose individuality was rivaled only by its comfortable quaintness.

The walls, papered in Turkey red, were broken by niches where bronze statuettes were enshrined, and by a mantel of dark marble with glowing coals in the grate beneath. Bronze chandeliers, their lights shielded by Victorian glass globes, hung from the ceiling, and were reflected in the mirror above the mantel, which was flanked by two gilt-framed portraits, one representing a solemn bearded man, the other a comely woman of well-rounded proportions. Mahogany sideboards stood at either end of the room. On one rested a music box, its lid thrown back to reveal a pierced metal disc; on the other, a polished silver device that looked like something between an old-fashioned letter press and a small upright boiler, all mounted on sturdy, spraddled legs.

"Oh, how *charming!*" Ruth exclaimed. "Uncle, you only half prepared me—you told me the 1840 Room was a period piece, but you didn't tell me it was perfect!"

"No. I let you find that out for yourself. But I'm glad you appreciate it. . . . Sit down over there, my dear, between Russ and Léonce. . . . Amélie, I can't put you at the head of the table. Because, since we're eight, we'd have two men or two women together if I did. Personally, I'm glad I can't, as that gives me a chance to keep you beside me. I want you at my right and Caresse at my left—if she ever tears herself away from that Cotton Exchange crowd. Oh, there you are at last, you young hussy! Perrault, you take the other side of Amélie, between her and Odile. There, that does it, I think."

Very nice too, but that seating plan wasn't altogether haphazard, Ruth said to herself. *He makes it sound casual, but he must have thought it all out pretty carefully beforehand. Not that I blame him—of course half the success of a dinner party depends on the arrangement of the guests. But if he'd wanted Mrs. Lalande at the head of his table, he could have had ten guests instead of eight, just as well—the room's plenty big enough and he has no end of friends. And I wonder if—the way he said he couldn't have her for his hostess, but wanted her beside him . . . .*

The thoughts shuttled rapidly, and were dismissed almost as quickly. Determined not to invite a second reproof for allowing Aldridge to monopolize her attention, Ruth turned to St. Amant, with another enthusiastic comment on the charm of their surroundings. He answered adequately enough, but without much heartiness. He himself had been looking at Caresse when Ruth spoke to him, and somehow she felt that he had not expected her to do so quite so soon, that he had counted on her absorption with Aldridge, and that in some obscure way she had caught him unawares. She even thought she saw him make a furtive motion with his right hand, as if he were withdrawing it, as unobtrusively as possible, from another which he had been holding. And it was Caresse who was seated on his other side—Caresse, his wife's sister, whom Ruth had mistaken for his fiancé before dinner because of something in his attitude. That something was still there. Involuntarily, Ruth glanced across the table at Odile. She was trying to unfold her napkin and her fingers were shaking so badly that she could not do it.

"Here, let me handle that for you," Doctor Perrault said quietly. Then, having spread the napkin out, he looked up at the hovering waiter. "Ah—so there you are again, Albert! And Lord in the mountains! Don't tell me those are *huîtres Foch*!"

"I thought Antoine's oyster specialty was named for a financier, not a general," Ruth remarked, her genuine interest in the menu intensified by anything that diverted her attention from the shaking hand of Odile and the straying hand of Léonce.

"That's another specialty," Perrault replied. "There are any number of them. The term 'Rockefeller' was chosen merely to indicate richness—not richness in money, but ingredients! The term 'Foch' has a great deal more significance; back in '21, the Knights of Columbus feted General Foch at Antoine's. Roy's father, Jules, announced that he would create a special dish: Alsace-Lorraine had been redeemed by Papa Foch from the thrall of the hated Boche, and Jules had served his apprenticeship as a chef in Strasbourg. So he spread toast with *pâté de foie gras,* and heaped fried Louisiana oysters on top of that, and poured Madeira sauce over the whole thing. And did the Maréchal enjoy his *huîtres Foch*! As much as we're enjoying them now!"

"I wish France would send us another Foch," Foxworth said rather dryly, "instead of asking us to do all the sending."

"Not all of it. Burgundy's coming through again," Léonce remarked. He lifted his glass, turning it slowly, and the amber-colored liquid in it caught and reflected the light from the pendant globes above it. "A country that produces Montrachet and sends it over here for me to drink, gets my vote for whatever she wants in return," he said. "What about you, Caresse?"

"Well, it's all right, I guess. But you know I'm not supposed to know about anything except sherry and, confidentially, I like champagne best, especially if it isn't too dry," she added with a little tinkling laugh, as if she had made an amusing disclosure and was very much pleased with it.

"Then we'd better ask Mr. Foxworth if he won't tell Albert to serve two kinds, when we get that far. Sweet champagne! I'm ashamed of you, baby!"

He ought to be ashamed, Ruth thought, *but not because of sweet champagne. Because he's making a fool of her—and of himself. It's a crazy thing to do—a cruel thing.* She looked across the table at Odile, who was listening to something Aldridge was saying about the Mayas, her hands folded

25

quietly in her lap. She had hardly touched her *huîtres Foch* and her Montrachet was still untasted.

"... and they were living in palaces and temples and solving astronomical problems when your ancestors were a lot of savages Julius Caesar hadn't bothered to conquer yet," Aldridge was telling her, with his pleasant twinkle.

"But isn't the test of civilization endurance rather than age?" Odile asked thoughtfully. "The Mayas have almost disappeared, haven't they, except from Yucatan?"

"No. There are still some in Guatemala and some in Honduras. On my next trip. . . ."

She isn't really interested in the Mayas or in Aldridge's future explorations, Ruth said to herself. *She's just being a lady, pretending not to mind the barefaced flirtation her husband and her sister are carrying on, pretending that she does care how many Mayas are left on the Western Hemisphere and where Aldridge is going to seek them out.* Certainly the pretense was a good one. Odile St. Amant lacked the animation, as she lacked the coquettishness, of her mother and sister. But her expression was by far the sweetest and most intelligent of the three . . . .

The door opened and three women of indefinite age walked into the room with complete unconcern. Two were tall, and the impression of jutting corners suggested by their figures was in no wise softened by what was obviously their "Sunday best." The third was short and dumpy; her bulges had fared no better in the way of compensating garb than had the angularities of her companions.

The trio glanced casually at the diners, who had fallen silent in the face of this intrusion. Then the sightseers began a leisurely inspection of the trophies and curios with which the glass-enclosed cabinets along one wall were crowded: the ornate dress sword, left at Antoine's in 1870 by "a happy but forgetful U. S. officer"; the shaving mug that had once provided lather for the chin and jowl of Police Chief David Hennessy, who eventually fell dead beneath a rain of Mafia bullets; the baby shoe that Grandpère Antoine Alciatore had worn long before the bloody terror which gave the name of Bœuf Robespierre to the first of the many dishes on which his fame was founded . . . .

Suddenly another group of sightseers peered in at the door which the first intruders had left open. At that point Foxworth rose.

"Apparently you ladies don't realize this is a private room," he said in brittle tones, "and that you're interrupting a dinner party which isn't . . . ."

"Oh my stars!" gasped the short and dumpy sightseer. "We didn't know. Do please excuse us . . ."

"Hnfff!" sniffed one of her taller companions. "You needn't be so huffy about it. We paid cash money to eat in this place, same as you did, and I propose to see it real good."

But her actions were less valiant than her words. Inwardly she quailed before Foxworth's glare and cringed away from the small titters which swept about the table. It was she who led the trio as it retreated to the door. Foxworth jumped up, following close at the sightseers' heels and called loudly into the corridor beyond.

"Albert! See to it that we're not disturbed like this again. Evidently these people can't read or they haven't noticed the RESERVED sign."

Having punctuated this scathing remark by banging the door, he resumed his seat as Aldridge picked up the thread of conversation.

"I haven't decided yet whether I'll go by plane or boat," he was saying now. "Of course, there are advantages and disadvantages both ways, not only as far as my work is concerned, but my equipment, so it's hard to make up my mind. However, at least I don't have to consider anyone except myself, and that's a great help. There are no arguments." He glanced momentarily from Odile to Ruth, and she felt herself flushing again. Why should he flaunt his freedom like that? And why should she suddenly think that it would be a wonderful adventure to travel with him, no matter how or where he went, an experience which would enrich a woman's life and cause her to fulfill her destiny . . . .

"Well, at last! Here come the ducks! Keep quiet, all of you, while I watch Roy. I don't want to be disturbed. Remember it's four years since I've seen this."

Roy Alciatore had entered the room and was greeting the guests while his assistants kindled the flames beneath two chafing dishes. Over one of these, the breast filets of the ducks, which had been roasted and carved in the kitchen, were now set simmering. Over the other, a shallow copper skillet, silver-lined, was carefully heated while a lump of butter softened and melted. The gleaming silver device, part of which resembled a letter press, was now moved forward on the sideboard, and as the screw was turned to put more and more pressure on the chopped duck carcasses in its silver cylinder, the expressed juices were caught in a porcelain bowl. Roy skillfully blended these with various wines and spices over the flickering alcohol flame of his burner. Then he added cream and brandy, almost drop by drop; from a tiny pepper mill he dusted a few grains of freshly ground white pepper into the chocolate-colored sauce, just before this was decanted over the filets.

During the ritual, the guests had left the table and crowded about the masterpiece-in-preparation. Now they returned to their places murmuring their appreciation as the dish was served and the Château Nénin was poured.

"Uncle, it's scrumptious!" Ruth exclaimed. "I'm never going to eat duck any other way again, as long as I live."

"That's a large order. You haven't a duck press, for one thing."

" 'Yes, Virginia, there is a Santa Claus,' " quoted Aldridge sardonically.

"And I'll write Santa Claus to bring me one."

"Can't we concentrate on anything except food?" Amélie inquired. "First we had a long dissertation on *huîtres Foch*, and now we've had a professional demonstration of duck pressing. I wish—"

"Russ has been giving me some very illuminating information about the Mayas, darling," Odile said quietly. "I'm sure he'd be glad to make the discussion of archeology a little more general. Wouldn't you, Russ?"

"Certainly. Though I'll wager that isn't just what your mother had in mind. And I confess I'm rather astonished that she wanted to change the subject. Surely you haven't reached the point where you have to watch your figure, Amélie?"

"Of course not," she answered, almost sharply. "But just the same—"

"Just the same, Russ didn't hit so wide of the mark, and I'm not going to sit by and let you snap at him like that, Amélie," interposed Perrault. "Why, all that austerity they talked about in England last winter was wild indulgence compared to the way you've rationed yourself! A bad job, too. You'd do a great deal better to exercise."

"Now, there's a thought!" Foxworth exclaimed. "And I know just the time and place for it: the Blue Room at the Roosevelt, after this dinner. I hear the orchestra they've got there now really sends the cash customers, and dancing's the best exercise in the world."

"Orson, you gay and giddy creature! That's a marvelous idea."

"Darling, I don't think—" Odile began.

"Nonsense!" her mother said emphatically. "Of course, we'll go. It isn't every night one of my old beaux, who has deserted me for years, comes back to New Orleans."

"Why, darling, you and Caresse and the others go, by all means. But Léonce and I—"

"Oh, come on!" Léonce exclaimed impatiently. "You'd enjoy the floor show anyway. You don't need to dance if you don't want to, but you used to love dancing. I don't see why, lately—"

"I'd be proud to squire you myself, Odile," Doctor Perrault said quietly. "My dancing days are long since past, even if Orson's aren't. So you and I could pair off for the evening, and leave the youngsters, like him and your mother, to their shallow amusements."

"I'd really rather not, darling," Odile repeated, with quiet persistence.

"Well, all I can say is, you're acting like a stubborn child! And a selfish one! Just because you're in one of your moods, you spoil the evening for everyone—your husband, your mother, your sister, our new visitor—"

"But, Mrs. Lalande, I've had a wonderful evening already! As far as I'm concerned, it's complete with this dinner at Antoine's. I like to dance, but I can do that almost anywhere, almost any time. And just now, with all those Carnival balls ahead of me . . . .!"

Perhaps she had spoken too impetuously; perhaps, in endeavoring to soften Amélie's outburst, she had been discourteous herself. However, Ruth had felt impelled to retort. Odile's sweet expression had changed, not to one of stubbornness or selfishness, but to one of sadness; her lovely blue eyes were brimming with tears. She had been fingering her untouched wineglass when the dispute arose; now, in an effort to conceal the distress which her face betrayed, she tried to raise it to her lips. As she did so, the trembling of her hand became suddenly uncontrollable, and the Château Nénin, splashing over the brim of the shaken glass, spilled down the front of her dress, leaving a crimson stain on its snowy surface.

"Oh, for God's sake!" Léonce exclaimed, half-rising "What's the matter with you, Odile?"

"I really believe she did that on purpose," Amélie added accusingly, "to get out of going to the Blue Room. Of course, she can't go now. And, of course, Léonce will have to take her home and that means taking Caresse and me too. He can't keep commuting between here and Richmond Place all night!"

The murmured remark was addressed to Foxworth, but Perrault, on her other side, inevitably overheard it. In the

29

same quiet way with which he had unfolded Odile's napkin earlier in the evening, he came to her rescue now.

"Again I suggest that you keep a little closer to the facts, Amélie. You know Odile would never do a thing like that."

"Then this trembling of hers has reached a point where she ought to consult you professionally again," Amélie retorted. "I've been begging her, for a long time, to do it, and she's kept refusing. Will you give her an appointment for tomorrow, Vance?"

"Let's see. Tomorrow's Saturday. That means no office hours. And in the morning the Parish Medical Association is holding a committee meeting to decide whether or not we'll make an investigation into the professional conduct of one of our colleagues—he may or may not have been splitting fees with a certain optician here in the city. But I'll drop by the house, late in the afternoon, and have a friendly chat with you both. That is, if you don't mind, Odile?"

"Of course not, darling. I'd be very grateful to you for coming. Just as I am for everything else."

The red stain was still slowly spreading over the white surface of her dress. She rose, calmly, and again Ruth marvelled at the dignity of her speech and manner.

"If the rest of you will excuse me," she said, "I think I'll go to the *Toilette des Dames* and see what a little salt will do for this stain. I really haven't room for any dessert, after all the duck I've eaten. But I'll be back for coffee. If I don't have success with the salt, I'll get the jacket that belongs with this dress. I left it outside with my coat. And I can keep it on in the Blue Room. After all, almost no one goes in *costume de rigueur* any longer."

" 'Atta girl, Odile!"

For the first time that evening, there was a ring of pleasure in St. Amant's voice as he spoke to his wife. He rose with the other men, then put his arm around her waist and led her out of the room. Ruth heard her murmur, "Darling, you didn't need—" The rest of her words were swallowed up by distance. Foxworth gave an audible sigh of relief.

"Well, I'm glad that's over," he said. "I was afraid, for a moment, that we were going to have a scene, and I hate scenes like hell—you ought to remember that, Amélie. But now that everything's so nicely settled, we can round out the evening very pleasantly and profitably, I think. Isn't there something in the Bible itself about eating and drinking and making merry? Well, we're eating and drinking enough here at Antoine's—at least I am and I hope the rest of you are.

30

We'll see what we can scare up in the way of merriment at the Blue Room."

"And forget about the rest of the quotation?" Aldridge inquired. "It's all right with me, if you want to. Anyhow, we've all got to die some time. Tomorrow might be as good a day as any."

2

How Odile St. Amant and
Tossie Pride spent the night—

January 2—3, 1948

FROM THE TIME Odile had gone to her first party, her old mammy, Tossie Pride, had waited up for her. Occasionally, to be sure, Tossie herself went to the same party in a useful capacity. She had done so several times while Odile was still a child, when some little friend was celebrating a birthday; all the nursemaids employed in the circle of intimates were pressed into service, so that law and order might be preserved among their young charges. Later, Tossie was in great demand as an "accommodator" at debutante parties, and Odile, who was proud of her maid's skillful, gentle ways, was always delighted when another girl asked if Tossie could not take charge of a dressing room or help in the service of refreshments. There was something about the way Tossie said even such simple things as, "Res' yo' wraps, Miss Sally?" or "Cain' Ah freshen that fo' you, suh?" that sounded more eager to please and more capable of doing so than the same thing said by any other servant.

Tossie had enjoyed the birthday celebrations and the debutante teas quite as much as Odile herself; but the moment of supreme triumph, for Tossie as well as for her "chile," had come the night Odile reigned as Queen of the Pacifici. When the central door, leading from the foyer of the Auditorium into the call-out section, opened for Odile, Tossie was close behind her. And, as Odile advanced down the aisle, Tossie followed watchfully in her wake, straightening and smoothing her train of sapphire-colored velvet and shimmering silver cloth. Not until the King, waiting at the edge of the dance floor, had claimed his Queen, did Tossie turn back, after spreading the splendid train out to its full width; and, during the entire ball, she remained with folded arms at the rear of the call-out section, leaning against the side of the central door—an alien, almost a grotesque figure, in the midst of so much elegance. She was a tiny, taut woman, with closely braided gray hair, whose nearsighted eyes blinked behind large moonlike glasses. She was wearing, as usual, a conventional black uniform, relieved by an immaculate apron with matching cap, collar and cuffs. But the night was chilly, and at the last moment before leaving the Lalandes' house, she had snatched up a bedraggled old gray sweater and tied it round her shoulders by the sleeves. In the subsequent excitement, she had forgotten to remove this, and Odile had not even noticed it; throughout the ball, the sweater continued to dangle awkwardly around her thin shoulders.

No one interfered with her or rebuked her as she stood by the door. On the contrary, many of the committeemen, whom she had known since they were unruly little boys upsetting the decorum of birthday parties, made it a point to come and speak with her. Many of the favored girls in the call-out section, at whose debutante teas she had served, stopped to show her their presents on their way back to their seats after a dance. All assured her that not even the fabulous Stella Fontaine had been so beautiful a queen as her "chile." Tossie needed no such assurance; she knew this already. But the admiring words made music just the same.

For three hours she stood motionless, never once taking her adoring eyes from the gracious and glittering figure of the young queen, seated beside her king on a silver and sapphire throne, wielding a starry sceptre, inclining a crowned head. A fortnight later, Tossie's cup of joy, full to the brim already, overflowed completely: Joe Racina, one of the many who had watched the touching scene, wrote a story about it and this was featured in the magazine section of the *Times Picayune*, under the title of "Handmaiden to Her Majesty." Tossie all but exhausted the edition. Her innumerable relatives up and down the River Road, along Bayou LaFourche and on the plains below St. Francisville all received copies. Her own copy she kept, folded with her baptismal certificate, in her Bible.

There had been other triumphs for Tossie too, but to her lasting resentment, she did not number among them the occasions which most of her old cronies seemed to feel marked the most rewarding days of their servitude. She had dressed Odile for her wedding, and her "chile" had been even more beautiful as a bride than as a Carnival Queen. But Tossie had cried all the time she was arranging the priceless lace veil over the rich dress of white brocade; all the time

33

that she was sitting in a rear pew at the Church of the Holy Name of Jesus; all the time that champagne was being passed and wedding cake cut—hardest of all after Odile and Léonce had disappeared in a huge car decorated with streaming ribbons and telltale signs. She had not known a happy moment on her "chile's" wedding day, for she had hated the man Odile married from the time she first laid eyes on him; and she had been robbed of the one compensation for the luckless marriage on which she had counted: there had been no babies to nurse, no little boys and girls to tend. Moreover, from the beginning, Léonce St. Amant had made her feel like a nuisance and an interloper every time he saw her about the garden wing which had been set aside for him and Odile after their marriage.

If either Odile or her husband had succeeded in persuading Tossie that this attitude was due to a bridgegroom's overwhelming desire to be alone with his beloved, the old woman would not have resented it. She relished romance in all its forms, the more intimate the better; if she had been able to give her imagination free rein in visualizing ardent embraces, she would have vicariously enjoyed these, while awaiting their natural result with close attention to the calendar. But hardly had the newly-married pair returned from their honeymoon, than Tossie decided that the outlander was uncomfortable in her presence, less because she intruded upon his privacy than because personal maids, or even well-trained maids of any sort, had not formed part of the pattern in his mother's household. This conclusion, based primarily upon his uneasiness and incivility in her presence, was shortly confirmed by information which Tossie had no trouble in securing from reliable sources at her command: one huge Negress, who was an excellent cook but an indifferent chambermaid and waitress, and who was untidy both in her person and about her work, was the only servant regularly employed by Mrs. St. Amant, *mère*. The services of this sloven were supplemented, at intervals, by a relative of hers who did mountains of piled-up laundry work and a little alleged cleaning, generally designated as "passing the mop"; but there was no well organized household management as Tossie understood the term, and neither the mother nor the sister of Léonce employed anyone to care for their personal belongings or assist them with their toilettes. Like most servants of her type, Tossie was essentially a snob, and her regard for the St. Amants, which had never been high, sank lower and lower with each tidbit of backstairs gossip she secured about their slack ways. Sniffing, she relegated them to the unregenerate regions inhabited otherwise by Yankees, trades-people, and pass-for-whites.

In course of time, Tossie's grievance against Léonce changed in character, while increasing in volume: she suspected that he resented her watchful habits because they permitted her to observe his own too closely. When he came tiptoeing back to the garden wing in the wee small hours, instead of spending the evening with his wife, Tossie always knew it. Again she set her spies to work and presently she was able to form a fairly accurate picture of where he was going and what he was doing. He sensed this, and told his wife that he thought he had better move his belongings out of their bedroom: he could never get at his clothes when he needed them, with that troublesome nigger always underfoot; the bathroom was big enough to divide in two, giving him a dressing room of his own. Tossie could have shaken her "chile" when Odile pleasantly agreed that such an arrangement would probably be more convenient for him. Then, as the nervous trembling grew worse, Odile herself suggested to Léonce that perhaps he would prefer twin beds in their room to the big four-poster they had always shared. Tossie waited breathlessly for his answer. No, he said decisively; to his mind, twin beds had little to recommend them. They had all sorts of disadvantages and nothing to offset these, unless no extra room were available in case of illness, which, fortunately, was not so in this instance. Why not turn their small parlor into a second chamber for his temporary use, until Odile was better? He was sure she would be much more comfortable in the big four-poster than in a horrid little narrow bed, and he would be back and forth between the two rooms. For that matter, she would too. On the other hand, he would be out of the way when Odile needed Tossie and, of course, she really did need the old witch now that she was getting so helpless.

"De good Lawd knows she sho gittin' helpless," Tossie said to herself, as she listened, from the hallway, to the false, plausible words of Léonce. "She helpless in mah han's, jus' lak when she wuz a sho 'nuff baby. But de worstes' am she helpless to do nuthin' agin dis big beater she married to. But Ah still got stren'th to look after mah po' chile. Ain' nobody kin do fo' her lak Ah kin. Ain' nobody never comin' twix' me an' her."

As Odile's infirmity grew worse, this conviction became increasingly a solace to Tossie. Even more pathetically and completely than Odile was dependent on her, she was dependent upon Odile. She had served three generations of Lalandes now; she was very old and she was growing very feeble. Unless she husbanded her strength, it would not suffice for her daily tasks. But she did husband it and she cunningly concealed her fatigue. If she became short of breath while carrying a tray, she paused outside a door until she could breathe normally again. If her feet swelled and smarted from much standing, she unobtrusively changed her neat shoes for felt slippers. If her back ached from bending over, she managed to control all expression of pain as she straightened up. If her eyes hurt when she did fine sewing, she drew a little nearer to the light and sewed on. And she had her reward for all these sufferings. She still dried her "chile's" lovely body with soft towels as Odile stepped from the tub into which Tossie had stirred fragrant salts. She still laid out the fresh undergarments which she had previously washed and ironed and folded away with sprigs of vetiver. She still brushed and dressed the long shining hair which, but for her protests, would have been cut years before. And, with due care for the finished product of her skill as a coiffeuse, she still slipped an exquisite evening dress over her "chile's" shining head on the rare occasions when Odile now went to a party.

Tossie had her favorites among these dresses, just as Odile herself had. The one she liked best of all was the white satin which Odile chose to wear for the dinner Orson Foxworth gave at Antoine's the night after his return from Central America. Before Odile left her room, Tossie asked her to turn around slowly, so that she might be seen from every side.

"Ain' nobody at de party gwine to look beautiful lak mah chile," she murmured contentedly. "Ain' nobody *never never* look beautiful lak she do." And to herself, she added with swelling joy, "Effen hit wa'n't fo' Tossie, mah chile wouldn' look lak dat neither. Ain' nobody kin do her hair an' fix her dress an' pin on her flowers lak Ah kin."

Happy in the thought, she watched her white folks start off and then went from room to room, putting everything in order for the night. She was the only one of the servants who slept in, and the others had left earlier than usual, since none of the family would be home for dinner. As long as Ona, the cook, and Lop, the housemaid, were within hearing, Tossie grumbled that they were leaving her to finish up their work; actually, she was pleased to have the big house to herself, to feel that it was wholly her own domain. She lowered the lights, banked the fires, emptied the ashtrays, turned down

36

the beds and picked up the clothes which had been left lying about. Odile was naturally tidy in all her habits; but the others strewed their garments around as they discarded these, and again Tossie grumbled under her breath as she treed shoes, hung up coats, and put soiled linen into hampers.

"Mah chile, she diff'runt," Tossie told herself with pride. "Ah done teach her mahse'f to take keer her pretty clo'es. She don' never abuse dem lak her ma an' her sister an' dat no'count husban'."

As if to verify her own statement, Tossie opened the doors of Odie's armoire and laid fond fingers on the dresses that hung there, each on its padded and scented hanger. Then she closed the armoire carefully and went about the room giving it the little finishing touches by which she judged the work of the other servants: a swift brushing sweep of the gnarled old fingers to eliminate the suspicion of a wrinkle from a blanket, a more meticulous alignment of twin mantel ornaments. She took particular pleasure in arranging and rearranging two baby pillows of lace-covered blue satin on the chaise longue, because their presence was a continuing source of annoyance to Léonce.

"If the damned things were only *good* for something I wouldn't mind," he had grumbled to Odile, time and again. "But they make the sofa uncomfortable. I can't understand why you're so stubborn about getting rid of them."

Odile deferred to her husband's challenging demands in most matters with a docility that outraged Tossie; but she had never yielded to him in the matter of the two pillows. They had been made for her before she was born, by an aunt who lived in Paincourtville; her father's unmarried oldest sister, who had been sure the baby would be a boy—that was why the pillows were blue instead of pink. Odile had treasured them ever since she was old enough to recognize their beauty, and even more, later, when she could appreciate the tender thought and endless hours of needlework that had gone into their making. Nothing could change her mind about giving those pillows a place of honor in her room.

Tossie's eyes twinkled maliciously behind the moonlike lenses of her glasses as she adjusted them now, to make sure Léonce could not overlook their presence. Then she went to the kitchen to fill the thermos pitchers. When these had been placed on the nightstands, her evening's work was over. She reheated the shrimp gumbo which Ona had left in the icebox for her and helped herself liberally from the coffeepot which was always on the stove. After she had finished her simple

37

supper, she returned to Odile's room, and settled down contentedly in an old rocking-chair to await her idol's return.

She had left one light burning, and for a little while she read from the well-worn Bible where she kept the clippings about the Pacifici Ball and "Handmaiden to Her Majesty." But she preferred the Gospel as eloquently expounded by Elder J. J. Johnson, Pastor of Sunlight Christian Spiritual Mission African Baptist Church, to the printed word which was so hard on her poor old eyes. So she put the Bible away and picked up her knitting. However, that did not have much meaning for her either; the needles did not flash back and forth between her fingers; these moved slowly, especially when she was very tired. It was not as if there were babies in the house, requiring an endless supply of jacquettes, bonnets, bootees and carriage robes. Ladies did not wear shoulder throws and fascinators any more either, as they had when Tossie was young; even knitted afghans had been replaced by quilted comforts. Nowadays, knitting was only something to hold in her hands.

She felt it fall from her lap, as she sat waiting for Odile's return from the dinner at Antoine's, and realized drowsily that she must have let it slip away from her altogether. But she did not stoop to pick it up or bother to put it back in its bag. She was getting sleepy and it would do no harm to take a little nap. Her "chile" would not be back for hours yet. Long before that, she would have wakened, refreshed. Her shoulders sagged and her head dropped further and further down, first in short, jerky nods, then in a long, slow, comfortable movement. Tossie slept . . . .

She did not know whether it was the click of a switch or the sound of a sob which suddenly roused her. She leaped up, startled and confused, to see Odile standing inside the doorway, removing the jacket of her dinner dress. The light from the chandelier fell full on the girl's white-clad figure and, as the jacket parted, Tossie saw that a red stain covered one side of the bodice. She rushed forward, screaming.

"Sweet Jesus, do have mercy! Mah baby all covered wid blood!"

"Hush, Tossie! That's not blood. It's nothing but wine," Odile said soothingly, throwing the jacket down on the nearest chair.

"Ain' nothin' but wine! How come you cryin' den, effen you ain' bad hurt!"

"I'm not hurt at all. And I'm not crying—that is, not really. But I've had to keep this dirty old thing on for hours. I want to get out of it."

38

She tugged briefly at the zipper, but her shaking fingers made no headway. Still bewildered, but partially recovered from her fright, Tossie hastened to help.

"Don' you worry wid dat, honey. Jus' raise yo' arms over yo' head and Tossie have you out o' dat dirty ol' dress befo' you knows hit."

Obediently, almost eagerly, Odile lifted her arms and the next instant Tossie had whipped off the stained dress, as usual without disarranging the girl's beautiful hair. Her slip showed the same red stain, and feeling no need for further instructions, Tossie whipped this off too. Then she bent over, examining the bared breasts with anxious eyes and searching hands, making vague sounds as she did so.

"You see, there's nothing wrong," Odile said reassuringly. She reached for the dressing gown which lay at the foot of the bed, and disengaging herself gently, slipped into it. "Or you will as soon as I've had a bath—that stain will wash right off my skin."

"Ah'se gwine run de water fo' yo' bath in jus' a minute. But fust off, you 'splain all dis to me, Miss Odile. Seem to me lak dey's somethin' mos' might' queer 'bouten hit."

"There's nothing much to explain. I spilled some wine on my dress while we were having dinner at Antoine's. But all the others wanted to go dancing in the Blue Room at the Roosevelt afterwards, so I put on my jacket to cover up the stain and went along too."

"Wheah at all de others now?"

"They're still in the Blue Room. Except Doctor Perrault. He brought me home. But he's gone on. You know if there'd been anything really the matter, the others would have come home with me and Doctor Perrault would have brought me to my room and told you what to do for me."

"Mah min' got nothin' agin Doctuh Perrault. But Ah don' need him nor neither nobody else should tell me what to do fo' mah baby."

"No, not when I'm all right. But since I've had this trembling .... That's what I've got to make clear to you, Tossie. That's why I must try to talk to you some more."

"Don' you talk to me no mo' now. Ain' nothin' Ah needs to heah till Ah gits you in dat sof' warm bed. You set down on de edge of hit an' let me take off yo' shoes and stockin's."

Again Odile obeyed, almost eagerly. Kneeling, Tossie drew the silver slippers from the small arched feet, peeled the sheer stockings from the lovely slim legs and groped for the little feathered mules which she had ranged at the bedside

39

some hours earlier. Before she could slide these over Odile's insteps, however, the girl bent forward and putting her arms around Tossie's neck, began to cry convulsively.

"Now, now, mah precious lam'," Tossie murmured soothingly. "Di'n' you say yo' own se'f ain' nothin' real wrong? Co'se Tossie knows dey is. But nothin' ain' never bad lak hit seem."

"Oh, Tossie, you're such a comfort to me! More comfort than anyone else in the world! If I didn't have you—"

"What you mean, effen you di'n' have me? Ain' you allus had me?"

"Yes, always. As far back as I can remember, you've been there whenever I needed you. That's what makes it so terribly hard."

"You talkin' lak you don' have good knowledge, honey. Leastwise, Ah cain' make no sense outen what you say. But lak Ah tol' you befo', you hadn' ought to try to talk now. You lea' go o' me, Miss Odile, so's Ah kin run yo' bath water. Den, after you gits in yo' bed and Ah brings you a hot drink—"

"No, I want to tell you now, Tossie. It just gets harder to say every moment I put it off."

Odile rubbed her wet cheek against the old woman's and gave her a last lingering hug. Then she raised her head resolutely.

"I told you Doctor Perrault brought me home. He was at the party, so he saw me spill the wine. My hand shook and I couldn't help it. It had been shaking worse and worse all the evening and I knew he'd been watching it. He urged me to go on to the Blue Room with the others and he sat with me while they danced. He kept watching me all the while. Of course, he tried to keep me from realizing what he was doing. Part of the time we sat with other friends, and I'm sure they hadn't the least idea what was in his mind. But I knew. Before we left the table at Antoine's, *maman* had persuaded him to come here tomorrow—not as a friend, but as a doctor. You know she's been trying to make me consult him again for weeks and weeks. So he was just making as many observations as he could, beforehand."

"You uses awful long words, honey, when you gits started talkin' bouten somethin' lak dis. But so far, ain' nothin' Ah kin follow seem strange to me nor neither sad."

"I'm coming to that part. While we were driving home, Doctor Perrault told me he wasn't going to give me a comprehensive opinion until he'd examined me tomorrow— that is, he wouldn't be sure how badly off I was or in how

40

many different ways. But he said he was certain of one thing, even without examining me, and that perhaps he'd better prepare my mind for it right away. He said he was sure I needed more scientific care than I had been getting and more special treatments."

"Dere you go agin, honey, usin' dem long words yo' po ol' Tossie cain' understan'."

"I can put it more plainly, but it's going to hurt you terribly, Tossie."

"Shucks! Ain' nothin' gwine to hurt me dat bad, long as Ah has mah baby."

"That's just it, Tossie. Doctor Perrault says I've got to have a nurse."

Tossie had continued to crouch at Odile's feet all the time they had been talking. Now she clutched the girl's knees.

"A nuss! Ain' Ah ben yo' nuss ever since you come home wid yo' ma from de horsepittul wheah she birthed you? Doctuh Perrault done put you in mah arms his ve'y own se'f an' telled me he knowed Ah'd take good keer of you. An' Ah has took keer of you, 'ceptin' dose few times when you been back to de horsepittul to have yo' tonsils out an' de lak of dat."

"I know. He does too. But he says that this time, unless I'll consent to having a professional nurse in the house, I'll have to go back to the hospital again. And I can't bear the thought of doing that. Because it wouldn't be just for a few days, the way it has been before. It would be for a long time. So that I could be kept under observation. So I could have those treatments he's taking about."

"How come Ah cain' give you dem treatments?"

"That's what professional nurses are for—one of the things they're for, I mean. They do most of the observing and then they report to a doctor and he knows what to do to help the patient get well. And they're trained to give treatments. That's another thing they're for. You aren't trained."

"Ah could *git* me trained!"

"No, I'm afraid not. You see, the training's done at hospitals, at the same time the girls are taught lots of other things you couldn't learn. And hospitals don't take these girls in the first place unless they've been through high school, unless they're young and strong. You can just barely read and write, Tossie, you're old, you're getting feeble—"

Tossie loosened her hold on Odile's knees and rose, slowly and painfully. She wanted to deny, with all the vehemence she could summon, that her age mattered, to insist that she did not feel it. But she knew that her words would not carry

41

conviction to Odile, because she could not convince herself of their truth. Never had she been so pitifully aware that she was old, very old, that her waning strength was almost gone. Suddenly, she decided to change her tactics.

"An' you done tol' de doctuh he could sen' you one o' dem stuck-up white trash, do-less gals what won' eat in de kitchen cuz dey t'inks dey too good an' cain' eat in a dinin' room cuz day ain' mannersable, so someone got to tote dem trays all de time? Dem gals don' work only jus' so many hours, an' den dey stops to get dey hair frizz, or go out wid dey boy friends. Ona's daughter, she work in one o' dem beauty saloons, jus' right close by de horsepittul, an' she say hit's full o' nusses, gittin' deyselves fixed up, all hours. What's goin' to happen effen you took bad an' dis nuss out a-gaddin' round? What bouten dem treatments, tell me please?"

"Don't take on like that, Tossie. Those treatments are just massages at regular times and things of that sort. Anyway, Doctor Perrault only said—"

"Has you done tol' de doctuh he could sen' dat nuss o' his'n heah?"

"It isn't *his* nurse, Tossie. I mean it isn't any one special nurse. You see, he wants to get just the right person and that may take several days. He said he couldn't possibly send one tomorrow, for instance, even if he wanted to before he examined me. But he thought he ought to tell me about this general plan tonight, so I could tell you and so we could both get used to the idea."

"Maybe you git used to de idea, but not me. Ah ain' never gwine to let no strange white gal look after mah chile!"

Tossie folded her arms across her breast, and stood gazing at Odile through her moonlike glasses, no longer with tenderness, but with defiance. Odile made one more attempt to reason with her.

"But, Tossie, we have to do what the doctor says. I have to try to get well. And if he thinks—"

"Ah don' keer what he t'inks, ain' no strange gal comin' in dis heah room, interferin' wid me an' mah chile. Us gwine to be by ourselves long as us both alive. Ah rather be in de col' grave den see one o' dem womens tryin' to do fo' you lak Ah does. Ah rather see you in de col' grave yo' own se'f. Cuz Ah knows she couldn' ca' fo' you lak Ah kin. Cuz Ah knows you pine away an' die anyways effen ol' Tossie di'n' look after you."

"Good Lord, Odile, can't you and Tossie find anything more cheerful than cold graves to talk about at this hour of night?"

Odile had left the door ajar when she came into the room, and she and Tossie had been too absorbed in each other, and in their subject, to hear Léonce when he entered. He never knocked before doing so, and this lack of courtesy, trifling enough in itself, was one which Tossie had always greatly resented. Odile herself secretly considered it a sign of essential indelicacy. She was no prude, and if it had not been for the presence of Tossie, she would have unhesitatingly welcomed her husband, whatever her state of deshabille. But she felt that she should have the privilege of choice and of acquiescence. Belatedly, she thrust her feet into her mules, drew her dressing gown about her, and knotted it at her waist as she rose.

"We haven't been talking about them long, darling," she said pleasantly. "And Tossie didn't really mean what she said, anyway. It's just that her feelings are hurt because Doctor Perrault thinks that I ought to have a nurse."

"Damn good idea. A lot better than most of his. Too bad he didn't have it long ago, that's all. When's she coming?"

"Well, not before day after tomorrow at the earliest. He has to look around for the right person."

Léonce nodded understandingly. He was still in his evening clothes, which set off his high color, and now that his momentary irritation had passed, he had the satisfied, almost sleek look of the man who has eaten and drunk rather too well and who has also manged to wedge a pleasingly amorous interlude into the evening's entertainment. *He's been kissing Caresse again,* Odile said to herself with stabbing certainty. *Not just holding her close while he danced with her, but getting her off in a corner for some heavy petting. He's just come from her. How can he come to me straight from her? How dare he?* But she knew that he could, that he did dare, and—to her shamed realization—that if he wanted to stay she would let him: not because it was her wifely duty to do so, but because he still had power to rouse desire in her, when he chose to do this, instead of making her lack of assertive passion a pretext for his own philandering. *I wonder why it's always assumed husbands are unfaithful because their wives are unresponsive,* she asked herself miserably. *Doesn't it ever dawn on anyone that women want and need union too? Only, as a rule, they can't say so. Something curbs their speech even if it doesn't curb their feelings. And when they're ill—when they feel they've been rebuffed or supplanted, then it's harder still for them to express their yearning. At least it is for me. But if Léonce would only come back to me—if he wouldn't insist on regarding this wretched*

43

trembling of mine as aversion to himself—if it still wouldn't be too late for me to have a child—I could forgive him everything, even his advances to Caresse . . . . Aloud, all she said was, "I was just going to take a bath, darling. The stain of that wine I spilled went right through my clothes."

"So I see," Léonce observed, smiling. Odile followed his glance, and saw that, though she had knotted her dressing gown so closely around her waist, her bosom was still partially bare. She flushed and again tried to fasten the dressing gown more securely. Too late, the thought flashed through her mind that if she had not instinctively done so, her husband might have bent over and kissed the stain, and that if she had kissed him in return . . . . But by then her hand was trembling uncontrollably and because this filled her with shame and frustration, her lips began to tremble too. She knew that Léonce, like most men, shrank from the sight of tears almost as much as he shrank from the sight of infirmity in a woman who was young and who should have been alluring. She could not spare him in one way, but the feeling that she might have spared him in the other filled her with fresh distress.

"Well, I'll be getting along. I only dropped by to say good night, and you seem to be pretty much all in," Léonce observed. He did not speak disagreeably, but he did speak conclusively. "You ought to have climbed into your good warm bed as soon as you got home, instead of sitting around with next to nothing on, talking with Tossie about cold graves and chilly unpleasant things like that. No wonder you're shivering. I hope the new nurse will put some sense into you . . . . And I hope *you'll* have sense enough not to try to make trouble for her, you old witch," he added, turning suddenly to Tossie, who had been standing by in sullen silence. "If you do, you'll find yourself back in St. Francisville, or wherever it is you came from. If I'd had my way, you'd have been pensioned off and sent there long ago. You've made yourself a nuisance. Why, you've never given Miss Odile and me a chance to be more than half married!"

He looked fixedly at the old woman, to give his words added weight. Then, checked by the cold glitter of hate in her eyes, he turned back to Odile and kissed her. But it was not the long desirous kiss for which she had yearned, the one which would have begun at the stain and then gone slowly, searching upwards, until it rested on her trembling lips and sealed them. It was a casual kiss, as dispassionate as it was kindly, which caressed her cheek, but missed her mouth.

Before Odile could return it, Léonce was halfway across the room on his way to the door. He stopped before the chaise longue, however, glancing at the two blue baby pillows in a sudden access of fresh irritation.

"You're the same way about that old witch as you are about these damn pillows," he gibed, picking up one of them and gesticulating with it. "She's about as useful to you as they are, but because you've got the idea you have to have them around—oh, what's the use?" He turned and almost flung himself out of the door. It was not until he reached his own room that he noticed he was still clutching the little lace-trimmed cushion in his hand. He hurled it furiously into a corner and shrugged himself out of his dinner jacket. Meanwhile, the moment the door closed behind him, Odile sank back on her bed, weeping without restraint. But when Tossie tried once more to comfort her, Odile pushed her away.

"If you hadn't been here, he might have stayed," she sobbed. "You heard what he said—that he didn't feel more than half married with you around. I don't see why I didn't realize that before. Perhaps that's the reason——" She could not say, "Perhaps that's the reason he started going to other women." But Tossie knew what was in her heart. "And then, of course, I had to be sick too," Odile went on vehemently. "But maybe I'll get well when the new nurse comes. Maybe that's what I need—to have a young nurse instead of an old mammy. And she won't be here all the time—you said so yourself. I think Léonce is right. We ought to pension you off and send you back to St. Francisville, for a while anyway. You need a good long rest. I'll talk to *maman* about it the first thing in the morning."

3

*How Orson Foxworth
spent the night—*

January 2—3, 1948

UNDER MOST ORDINARY or even extraordinary circumstances, Orson Foxworth ate heartily and slept soundly. He looked down on men who picked at their food, or complained of insomnia, as weaklings. It was one of his boasts that he had been through five Central American revolutions without missing a meal or losing a night's rest. But he left the dinner at Antoine's feeling vexed and perturbed, and two hours of drinking and dancing in the Blue Room did nothing to assuage this agitation. Long after he had gone to bed, he tossed and turned, pounded his pillow, swore under his breath, and gulped drinks of water, all to no avail.

"I'll be counting sheep next," he told himself savagely. "Damned if I wouldn't take ten grains of barbital if I only had some of the stuff. I was a fool to refuse it when that scorpion latched on to me in the Olanchito Valley."

However, the sad fact remained that he had refused it, and an angry inspection of his bathroom cabinet revealed nothing in the way of a sedative. The tossing and turning, the pillow-pounding and water-drinking, went on until almost dawn. He could not get Amélie Lalande out of his mind.

She was just as desirable as when he had first suggested that she should meet him in Puerto de Oro, one of his Central American headquarters—and she had indignantly refused. The indignation was genuine enough; but its source was injured pride rather than outraged virtue, and Amélie was far too smart not to know that he realized this. He was attractive to her too, and he would have been the last to find this surprising; he had always had a way with women, and he was in no danger of losing it, even yet—of that he had abundant proof. But his attraction for Amélie was not so consuming that she would count the world well lost for his sake. She was very fond of the world, especially her own little world in New Orleans. She had no mind to abandon this for a hideaway in some mongrel port. Like Eugenie de Montijo, the famous beauty, to whom she claimed distant relationship, Amélie Lalande informed her imperious suitor that the only door into her bedroom led through the church. Like Napoleon III, Foxworth accepted the inevitable; and he knew that the church would have to be St. Louis Cathedral, the bed one of Seignoret's finest . . . .

He had not taken that first refusal very hard. But he had missed her, and longed for her, more than he would have believed possible, when he went back to Puerto de Oro without her; and the loneliness and the yearning had increased with the years, in spite of intervening distractions. He tried to console himself with the reflection that Amélie was not getting any younger, that no really formidable rival had appeared on the horizon, and that she had been permanently thwarted in the hope that she might someday reign as Queen of the Cressidian Ball. Perhaps, on his return, she might listen to reason . . . .

And she had not listened to reason. He had not meant to renew his suggestion the very first time he saw her, but she looked so lovely and seemed in so melting a mood, as they danced together, that he had whispered with almost collegiate impetuosity:

"This is mighty good, but we could have something a lot better."

"In New Orleans?" she murmured softly.

"I suppose it might be managed. But it would be a little awkward. After all, I've got Ruth with me now. And in your house we'd have three people to dodge, besides the servants. They're all bad enough, but that old witch, Tossie, sees everything."

Amélie did not answer. He waited a minute and then went on.

"Besides, I'm only going to be here a few weeks. I've promised Ruth I'd stay here with her for Mardi Gras; but I want to see her on the Crescent Limited when it pulls out for Washington on Ash Wednesday. There's a boat leaving for Puerto de Oro that same night and I want to be on it. I want you on the next one, Amélie. I wouldn't be satisfied with just a few hole-and-corner meetings, even if I thought we could get away with them. I want months alone with you, in a home of my own—of our own."

"Our own?"

"Yes. Yes. It would be your home too, Amélie. I can't seem to make you believe that, but it would."

He pressed her more closely to him and bent his head so that his lips almost touched her cheek as he went on, speaking gently and persuasively.

"You and I were meant to be lovers, Amélie," he said. "I know it and you know it, though you won't admit it yet. And if you put off the admission much longer, it'll come too late to do us any good. It isn't as if we were still youngsters, with the best part of our lives stretching out ahead of us. You know the old saying, 'It's later than you think.' It *is* later than you think, dearest. But it isn't too late."

"Yes, it is."

"I tell you it isn't. We could have at least ten glorious years. And when I say glorious, that's what I mean. Love can't be glorious when its fettered. Anyway, it couldn't be for us. We're free spirits, both of us. You think I've affronted you by not asking you to be my wife. The real affront would have been in doing it. I know you better than you know yourself. You need a chance to go your own way almost as much as I do. At least, you need to feel that you *can*."

"Men really want to be free, Orson. Women only say they do. What they want is the knowledge that they're needed and desired, that they'll be safeguarded and cherished."

"You are needed and desired. You will be safeguarded and cherished. Damn it, I'll prove it to you."

"What do you mean, you'll prove it to me?"

"I mean that if I can't do it any other way, I will marry you. I know you're wrong and I'm right, but you win. I've got to have you, so I'll take you on your own terms. Now that's settled, when do we have the wedding?"

For a moment Amélie stared at him, almost stupidly. Then she freed herself from his embrace, with no seeming abruptness or resentment, yet so decisively that he was startled.

"I've got to talk to you," she said. "And I can't do it while we're dancing. Let's sit out the rest of this, if you don't mind."

"I mind very much. Damn it, Amélie—"

Without turning, she walked on. He had no choice but to follow. Russ and Ruth, Léonce and Caresse were all dancing, and Perrault had taken Odile to join a group of mutual friends. But as Foxworth and Amélie passed the table next to their own, a strikingly beautiful girl detached herself from the group that was seated there, rising and coming forward with indolent grace.

"Good evening, Mrs. Lalande," she said. "How've you been?" She spoke in the same slow, pleasing way that she moved, and the stereotyped greeting was melodious as she pronounced it. "I can't help telling you how glad I am you're back, Mr. Foxworth," she went on. "You've been gone a long time and we've missed you a lot."

She nodded, with a smile that deepened the dimple in her chin, and reseated herself, apparently without expecting anything more than a passing asknowledgment of her greeting. Foxworth had failed to recognize her, and though his response had been civil enough, and he had not failed to be struck by her beauty, he was far too preoccupied at the moment to be curious about her identity, which Amélie did not take the trouble to disclose. He jerked out two chairs and flung himself into one of them. Amélie sat down quietly and clasped her hands together, midway across the table. Then she leaned forward.

"Listen," she said. "I've missed you too. I've missed you a lot. So much that I'd almost made up my mind—well, that if you asked me to go along with you again I wouldn't say no."

She paused, her voice sinking lower and lower.

"It wasn't an easy decision to make, Orson. I know you think I've been a flirt and I'll admit that. Why, I flirted with all Odile's beaux and they loved it! I could have stolen any one of them away from her, without lifting a finger, and she knew it. But I'm not that kind of a mother. I still flirt with the boys who come to see Caresse. I never let those boys get out of hand though. I haven't been—fast. If I'd come with you, it would have been the first time I'd done anything like that and—"

"I know it and it means a lot to me. But what makes you say '*if* you'd come, it *would* have been—'? Now that you've thought this thing through sanely at last, of course you're coming, and you'll never regret it, my dear, I promise you that I'll make you completely happy."

"You can't, Orson. It's too late, as I tried to tell you."

"Like hell it is!"

"Hush! Don't swear! It *is* too late. I can't leave Odile now. She's a hopeless, incurable invalid."

"You're crazy! She's let her nerves get the better of her, for some reason, and her right hand shakes a little. I've seen dozens of great husky men whose hands shook. It doesn't amount to anything."

"In this case I'm afraid it does. I'm not absolutely sure, because Odile's declined to see Vance Perrault, professionally, for months now. But he told me, a long time ago, that he was afraid she was developing what he called paralysis agitans. I didn't believe it, I suppose because I didn't want to. I kept telling myself she was just nervous, as you say. But when she upset that wineglass tonight and I saw the expression on Vance's face—"

"What the hell's paralysis agitans?"

"Look it up for yourself. Or ask Vance to tell you about it. But, meanwhile, take my word for it: the thing's incurable."

"Bring me a double Scotch and soda, will you?" Foxworth signaled a passing waiter. "And a pint of Mumm's Extra Dry for this lady." The waiter nodded, scribbled across his pad, and hurried off. Foxworth drummed on the table with his fingers.

"It doesn't sound too good, from the little you've told me," he admitted. "Does she suffer?"

"Only from her sense of disability. She can't do her own hair, or dress herself. Sometimes she even has difficulties with her bath. Of course, she had to give up driving a car, and all sports, and that sort of thing, some time ago. And she's growing worse very rapidly."

Amélie looked towards the table where Odile was sitting and Foxworth followed her glance. Odile's hands were concealed, purposely, or so he guessed; but he was suddenly struck by her marked slenderness and pallor.

"I couldn't desert her now," Amélie whispered. "She's terribly isolated already. Since she hasn't been able to do the things her friends are doing, she's been more and more cut off from them. Oh, they drop in to see her, out of sympathy, every now and then, and she does go out a little in a very quiet way. But that isn't as if she could drive out to the Yacht Club, or go to bridge parties, or do anything like that. And, the worst part of all is that, as far as Léonce is concerned—well, of course I can't talk about that."

The Scotch and the champagne arrived. Foxworth swallowed a stiff drink, while Amélie alternately sipped her wine and pressed a chiffon handkerchief lightly against her lips and eyes.

"If Odile had only had a baby before this happened, it wouldn't be quite so bad," Amélie murmured, behind the handkerchief. "It would have helped them both. She wouldn't have felt she'd failed him so completely as a wife. And perhaps Léonce wouldn't have felt—oh, you know what I mean! Perhaps he could have stood it a little better. Perhaps he would have made her feel it didn't matter if . . . . As it is, she's afraid she's losing him. In fact, she's almost certain she's lost him already. He couldn't stand continence any better than he could blindness."

Again Amélie looked away and again Foxworth followed her glance, this time towards the dance floor. The jade green dress would have made its wearer conspicuous, even if none of her other attributes had done so. But her blonde hair, her exquisite figure, the sprightly grace with which she moved, and her little tinkling laugh all served to intensify its effect. Caresse was laughing now, as she lifted her head so that Léonce could rest his chin against it, and the expression on his face was one of arrogant satisfaction.

"Good God!" Foxworth exclaimed. "Surely you don't think—"

"Hush!" Amélie said again, more warningly than before. "We must stop talking about this. That Darcoa girl keeps looking over here."

"What Darcoa girl?"

"Why, the one who got up and spoke to us as we went by! She told you how much she'd missed you. It would take her down a peg to find out you didn't even recognize her."

"You don't mean to say that knockout is Francisco Darcoa's daughter?"

"I wouldn't call her such a knockout. She isn't married yet and she's way along in her twenties. So evidently she isn't irresistible."

"Perhaps she's the one who hasn't found what she's looking for."

"Of course you're welcome to think so. I don't want to start an argument. But as I was saying, she keeps looking over towards our table. I know she can't hear us, with the orchestra blaring the way it is, but just the same she makes me uneasy. So let's not talk about Odile any more, *cher*. You do understand though, don't you, that I couldn't abandon her now? And not just on account of her helplessness, either. Of course, if I could stay on in New Orleans after you and I were married, that would be entirely different. A competent nurse could take physical charge of the poor child, under my supervision. I'm sure she'd consent very willingly to such an arrangement, if she thought she were adding to my happiness; and the other situation I could—dominate. But you're not willing to leave me behind. And if I went off to Central America with you, leaving her all alone, in her pitiful condition, to face a scandal between her husband and her sister— why, it would be kinder to kill her tomorrow and put her out of her misery!"

51

Amélie touched her eyes again with the filmy handkerchief and then tucked it into the bosom of her dress. Apparently she encountered some difficulty in finding just the right place for it, as the process was somewhat prolonged and, after her fumbling, ended with an even greater revelation of her charms than ever before. But finally she smiled bravely up at her companion.

"Let's dance again and not let anyone guess how sad we're feeling, *cher*," she said. "But don't forget. I do love you. I love you so much that I would have gone with you this time, on any terms—if it hadn't been for Odile."

This was the conversation which, in retrospect, so greatly disturbed Foxworth's rest. The more he considered the dilemma, the more hopeless he became of reaching any satisfactory solution. Suppose he did marry Amélie forthwith? When his sailing date came, she would use Odile's condition and the infatuation of Caresse and Léonce as pretexts for staying behind, whatever she might have promised to the contrary beforehand. And he would be worse off than ever—legally fettered, and still unaccompanied by the woman he desired. He had been sincere in saying he wanted her with him, not briefly, but indefinitely. Now it appeared he must still choose between having her on her own terms, or not having her at all. The realization was the more tantalizing because he had been so close to victory.

Finally he fell asleep, but his slumbers brought him no refreshment. He kept dreaming about Amélie, and in his dreams she lay, smiling and supine, in his arms, and he was about to possess her. Then suddenly his arms were empty again. The woman who seemed so quiescent, so responsive, herself so desirous, had somehow eluded him. Presently she reappeared, and he tightened his hold upon her, determined to prevent her escape, even if he had to use force. And still, before he could take her, she was mysteriously gone. She was no longer his destined mistress, his beloved mate, his joyous and yielding captive. She was only a bloodless wraith and at last only a distant voice, whispering, "If it hadn't been for Odile . . . ."

For a long time he himself was the prisoner of his dreams, rousing enough to recognize their unreality, but insufficiently to free himself from them. At last he succeeded in stumbling to his shower, and, with the shock of cold water, in regaining his sound senses. He rang for coffee, and drank it, as usual, in his room, glancing over the morning paper and running through his mail as he did so. Then he finished dressing and went down to the library, where he found Ruth bending over a great copper tray with a fluted brim, filled to overflowing with camellias, which had been set on a low table.

"Look!" she said excitedly. "These were brought in just a few minutes ago, just as they are, in this tray. I've never had such beautiful flowers sent to me before, or so many all at once!"

"Are eastern suitors stingy nowadays, or aren't any of them connoisseurs of camellias?" Foxworth inquired quizzically. "Oh, never mind! But whoever sent you this offering is plenty prodigal and plenty expert too. It costs a pile of money to raise flowers like that, and you can't walk into any florist's and order them offhand, either. That's a mighty fine display—very rare varieties arranged to the best possible advantage. Do you know the names of some of them?"

"Only Pink Perfection and Alba Plena."

Foxworth held up his hands in mock horror. "What? You can't recognize Adolph Audusson or Cardinal Richelieu or Governor Mouton or any of the other distinguished gentlemen in the camellia family? And speaking of distinguished gentlemen, did the one who sent you this collection do it anonymously, or did he reveal his name?"

"Oh, he revealed his name!" Ruth said laughing. "In fact, there wasn't anything at all mysterious about it. A very nice note from Russ Aldridge came with the flowers. He said he noticed that I seemed to be looking attentively at the camellias the other ladies in the party were wearing last night—it was kind of him not to say I was green with envy, because that's the truth! Anyway, he thought I might like some too. And he hoped I'd choose one of the kind I liked best to wear this afternoon."

"Which means that during the rest of your stay you'll have that kind to wear all the time," Foxworth remarked, in a gratified way. He was pleased because his niece had, obviously, made so favorable an impression on his most distinguished guest, and he knew no reason why she should not realize this. "I don't see how Aldridge has time to raise camellias on top of everything else he does," Foxworth went on, "especially when he's away from Louisiana so much. Of course, he has an excellent gardener—two or three of them, in fact. And the grounds of his place near Lacombe are something worth going a long way to see. Perhaps he'll ask us there for a week end—if there's time between balls. I gather you found him congenial?"

"Oh, very!"

Foxworth hesitated a moment. 'I haven't had a chance to

ask you what you thought of the party," he continued. "I hope you had a good time?"

"Of course I had a wonderful time. I'm sorry if I didn't tell you so before. I thought I did, when I was saying good night."

"Well, you were very enthusiastic about the 1840 Room and the pressed ducks. But you didn't say much about your fellow guests."

It was Ruth's turn to hesitate. "Perhaps I didn't," she confessed. "I'm sorry if that made me seem unappreciative. But I've just told you how much I like Russ Aldridge. I liked Doctor Perrault too. And I think Odile St. Amant is a lovely creature, even if she does call everyone 'darling' in that Hollywoodish way. I'm terribly sorry for her though. I think she must be very ill, or very unhappy, or both."

"She is, but I didn't know that myself until late last night, or I'd have warned you, so that it wouldn't come as a shock to you. Her mother confided in me while we were at the Blue Room. You and I'll talk about it later. But first I feel impelled to remind you that though you haven't said anything derogatory about anyone, there are some very conspicuous omissions in your comments."

Ruth colored. "Léonce St. Amant is one of the handsomest men I ever saw and he dances as if he had wings on his feet," she admitted.

"But—I'll say it before you do!"

"But he isn't exactly my type, that's all."

"Too much of a sensualist, eh?"

"I wouldn't have put it just like that. However, he certainly is a gourmand rather than a gourmet, to judge from the way he ate his dinner and drank his wine. And I wouldn't accept an invitation to go and see his etchings if his wife were out of town when he extended it."

"Oh, you'd still be well chaperoned! His mother-in-law and sister-in-law both live with him too—or rather, he lives with them." *Damn it, that was an unfortunate way to express it,* Foxworth added to himself. But obviously Ruth was not putting an undesired construction on his statement and he went on, "Lalande left his widow very well off, with a good deal of her property in real estate. She's always lived in a big house, and she likes that. But she and the two girls were just rattling around in that enormous house on Richmond Place, and as St. Amant had nothing much himself, it was natural for her to suggest that the bride and groom should stay with her and Caresse."

"Perfectly natural. Except that I think most young couples are happier by themselves, don't you?"

"Theoretically, and generally speaking. But not in this case. Amélie and Odile have always been very close to each other."

"Yes, Odile told me that herself."

"So I don't think she'd have been happy separated from her mother. She adores Amélie. Of course, it's mutual. They're more like sisters to each other than anything else. In fact, most strangers mistake them for sisters."

"Odile told me that too. And I could see the family resemblance. But, as I told *her*, I think it's stronger between Mrs. Lalande and Caresse than between Mrs. Lalande and Odile, or Caresse and Odile."

"Which is a nice way of saying you liked Odile much better than either her mother or sister."

"Well, yes. But I thought they were all lovely-looking. And probably I have a very feminine viewpoint, slightly tinged with subconscious jealousy, because Mrs. Lalande and Caresse are both so much more intriguing than I could ever be. I'm sure if I were a man—"

Foxworth tapped his front teeth thoughtfully with his thumbnail. "I'm sorry your first impression of Orleanians wasn't a hundred per cent favorable," he said. "Or at least more than fifty per cent. I ought to have given you a wider choice by having a bigger party. For instance, there's a nice young fellow named Sabin Duplessis who'd have fitted in finely. He's a great friend of the Lalande family, and for awhile everyone thought that Odile would marry him instead of Léonce. As a matter of fact, when Léonce first started going to the Lalandes' house, the general impression was that he was after Amélie. Not that she ever would have married him; but he's not so much younger than she is as to make the idea altogether fantastic from that point of view. And Sabin would have been better suited to Odile in lots of ways—less earthy, more of an idealist. Talented fellow too—paints and plays the piano—all that sort of thing. Lives in a studio apartment and has it crammed full of treasures he's collected here, there, and everywhere—musical instruments, primitive paintings, fancy firearms, illuminated missals—I don't know what all. Keeps Chinese servants and gives parties like nobody else's. He's no panty-waist though—he was a captain in the ATC during the war, and was always starting off casually from Newark for Karachi, or some such place. Had all kinds of decorations before he got through and has been offered every sort of inducement to go into commercial aviation. But he says if he never flies another plane that'll be too soon for him .... Well, we'll get hold of him some other time—he'd be another good date for you. As I just said, perhaps I ought to have asked him last night. But I couldn't think of just the right extra woman to make up ten."

And besides, Ruth said to herself, *if you'd had ten, Amélie Lalande would have been at the head of your table. And that was what you intended to avoid, as I figured out before. It's what I believe you still intend to avoid. But I wonder—*

"Then there's Joe Racina," Foxworth went on. "I might have asked him. You'd have been sure to like Joe. Most people do."

"You mean the war correspondent whom Doctor Perrault pointed out while we were on our way from the Rex Room to the 1840 Room?"

"That's the man. He's famous now, but he started out as a cub reporter on the *Item,* like a whole bunch of other famous people. Most of them were outsiders, but Joe was born right here in New Orleans, on Erato Street. Father was a baker, rented half a double-barreled shotgun house and brought up five children on twelve-fifty a week. Well, that's neither here nor there. The point is that, after Joe had made good on the *Item,* he went up to Washington and made good on the *Bulletin*; then he got sent all over the world by his paper. So finally he started writing books, the way all those fellows do and made a mint of money. He's back in New Orleans because he'd rather live here than anywhere else in the world. Married a New Englander, Judith Somebody, about five years ago, and I hear he's just as crazy about her now as he was then—never goes anywhere without her. I like her, myself, and Amélie could go for Joe in a big way, if he'd give her any encouragement. But she's never taken to Judith. Anyhow, as you just said, they were dining with someone else last night, in that little back room."

"Yes," Ruth answered briefly. But she went on thinking. *They were dining with someone else, but perhaps they wouldn't have been if Uncle had taken the trouble to ask them far enough ahead. I'm not surprised that Amélie Lalande hasn't "taken" to Judith Racina, and if I'm not terribly mistaken, Judith Racina hasn't "taken" to Amélie Lalande either. However, the real reason Uncle didn't ask the Racinas was the same one that kept him from asking Sabin Duplessis and an extra woman—he didn't want Amélie at the head of his table. But he does want ....*

"Mrs. Lalande is on the telephone, sir. She says it's very urgent," the butler announced, bowing in the doorway.

4

How Odile St. Amant and Sabin
Duplessis spent the afternoon—

January 3, 1948

"ORSON, I KNOW you don't like to have me 'phone you. But I just had to."

"All right. Why?"

"Oh, don't take me up that way! When you're so terribly brusque, you drive every thought straight out of my head. And don't go on to say that wouldn't leave it any emptier than it was already, either."

"I wasn't going to. But I may, if you don't come to the point pretty soon."

"Well, the point is, Vance s meeting was over much earlier than he expected it would be. He was in a perfect state about it, too. Said the others on the committee were a bunch of fee-splitting old windbags, who voted not to go into the charges without hearing half of what he had to say, when the man was plainly guilty of . . . ."

"I cheerfully concede that Vance Perrault is an honorable physician, devoted to the principles of his profession. But I don't suppose you called me up just to prove it to me."

"Of course not. Whatever gave you such an idea? All I've been telling you was that, since Vance's meeting adjourned so much earlier than he had expected, he came here this morning, instead of waiting until this evening. In fact he's just left, still muttering to himself about the species of beasts who would not even consider disciplining a practitioner who had been guilty of all sorts of . . . ."

"Amélie, please! Must you really?"

"I'm sorry, Orson. But I'm so upset I hardly know what I'm saying. Because, of course, Vance came out and told Odile, in my presence, that her case was hopeless. Oh, not brutally, the way you might have done it. You know perfect-

57

ly well how you are. He was gentle enough, but he was positive. Said it was better to face reality than kindle false hopes. That she would become increasingly helpless, and there was nothing anyone could do about it, because that type of paralysis or palsy was one of the afflictions for which no one could find a cure. But she mustn't be despondent. She must go on to make herself a full, rich life in every way she could, and there were many such ways."

"Um-m-m. That's pretty rugged, all right. But, of course, there's always the chance Perrault might be mistaken."

"Not in this case. He told me afterwards he had gone over the situation with some of the finest and best-informed doctors in the city, and they all agreed with him."

"Did he give you any idea of how long it would be until—that is—well, whether it would be a slow, lingering illness, or whether . . . ."

"Not in so many words. But I gathered that this wasn't something in itself—oh, I don't know just how to say it—that it wasn't the kind of thing people die of. It just makes them completely helpless and dependent, and she might live to be an old, old woman just as any normal person might, unless. . . ."

"Yes, unless—?"

"Well, unless she contracted some sickness like pneumonia, that perfectly healthy people die of, or had an accident, just the same as any other person. It's too utterly heart-breaking, a lovely young girl like that, looking forward to all those years of being helpless, unable to do a thing . . . ."

The last sentence ended in a sob. Foxworth disregarded it to ask a practical question.

"How many extension telephones are there in your house?"

"Two. But you needn't worry. Odile can't be listening in. She's gone out with Sabin Duplessis. He's almost the only one of her old friends that the still sees regularly. They used to have an early tête-à-tête luncheon together every Saturday when he was courting her, besides their other dates, of course. About six months ago, he asked Léonce if there'd be any objection to resuming the luncheon dates, and Léonce said, 'Hell, no!' You know he's never given Sabin the credit for much masculinity, and anyway the character of the luncheons has changed—they're held in Sabin s studio, served by his Chinese house boy, and there are always other guests present—Caresse and I have been included in the group several times. But Sabin still calls for Odile and takes her downtown in his car. This morning Vance was just leaving when Sabin arrived. As her physician he persuaded Odile to go right ahead. He practically ordered her to do it. Said it would be the best thing in the world to take her mind off the bad news. It wasn't easy, getting her to go, but finally she did. That's the reason I called you now. I could be sure she wouldn't hear any of this. Oh, Orson, you see that everything I said to you last night was true! Only I didn't make it sound half bad enough! As it is—"

"Where's Caresse?" Foxworth inquired, again interrupting abruptly.

"Why, she's downtown. Didn't you know Caresse had a job? No, I guess I hadn't told you that yet—there were so many more important things for you and me to discuss." Amélie paused, waiting for an interruption, but this time none came. "Three times a week she broadcasts at WWL," she continued. "It's for that new dress shop, The Fashion Plate, and it's all about the origin of styles, and old recipes, and who was the first girl to wear a hoop skirt. You wouldn't believe the number of people who seem to listen to her."

"What the devil's she know about things like that?"

"Oh, she doesn't know anything. One of the men at the studio does the writing for her. But they all rave about her voice. They say it mikes like a temple gong, whatever that's supposed to mean. And she does know how to use it. They pay her frightfully well, considering, and give her the most unbelievable bargains in the dresses and things she buys for herself, and you know how crazy she is about clothes, although I do say to her, 'Caresse, if only your taste didn't run to such extremes, you could be the . . . .'"

"Oh, for God's sake, Amélie! Let's stick to the important thing that concerns us. Have you told Léonce what Vance said?"

"No. I'm just starting downtown and I thought I'd stop in at Voisin-Caprelle's on my way to Solari's and—"

"What's Léonce doing at Voisin-Caprelle's?"

"Is that another thing I haven't told you? He's been made manager of their used car department. I suppose you wouldn't think much of him as a salesman, and less as an executive, but he's done a lot towards making Voisin-Caprelle's the swankiest automobile agency in New Orleans and adding to the demand for the Fremond Eight. After all, his social standing and other qualities he has—"

"I know all about those 'other qualities' and I'm not much impressed by his social standing. What you mean is that almost anything on four wheels can be sold right now, and besides, the popular-priced makes have gone so high that a lot of people, with money burning holes in their pockets anyway, are willing to pay a few hundred dollars extra in order to have the smug satisfaction of driving a luxury car."

"Well, let's not argue about that. Who's dragging out this conversation now? I started to say, very briefly, that I was going to stop in to see Léonce because I thought he ought to know about Odile as soon as possible, and it's always easier to break bad news in person than over the telephone. But, as far as you were concerned, the telephone seemed the only way, because, of course, I couldn't come to your house. As I reminded you yesterday, I've never failed to observe *les convenances*. I'm not going to begin now just because I'm overwhelmed with this terrible tragedy. But I had to talk to you."

"I'm glad you did." The statement, though somewhat tardy, did not lack heartiness. "And I think we'd better try to meet, as soon as we can. With Ruth here, I certainly don't see why you shouldn't come to the house. I've got to go to the office for a little while. After all, I'm supposed to be in New Orleans to discuss a proposed consolidation with the Trans-Carib crowd. But I can get back here by two and we can have a late lunch. Afterwards, I'll drive you home. No place like an automobile for a quiet conversation that no one can overhear or interrupt. I wouldn't like to leave Ruth for all day, until she gets going under her own steam; but she has a date of her own for this afternoon, and she won't miss us. In fact, I think she'll be mighty glad to have the house to herself, unless I've misread all the signals."

Ruth was still bending ecstatically over the camellias when Foxworth returned to the library after leaving the telephone. She did not ask about the "urgent matter" which he had been summoned to discuss, and he decided that she did not feel any more curiosity than she revealed. He told her, briefly, that Mrs. Lalande was going to drop in for luncheon, as both her daughters and her son-in-law were out, and she would be downtown shopping, in any case. He had set the luncheon hour rather late, as he really must get down to the office for an hour or so, and tell that bunch of stuffed shirts from the Trans-Caribbean how little chance they had of holding up the Blue Fleet in any merger deal. With this information, he departed, and when he returned, Amélie had already arrived, and she and Ruth were conversing amicably, if rather aimlessly. The same type of small talk continued during the luncheon hour, with no reference to Doctor Perrault's morning visit at the Lalande house. Coffee and brandy were served at the table, and Amélie offered to show Ruth how to

60

"make a little private *brûlot* of her own." Then she put sugar in her spoon, poured brandy carefully over it, and lighting it, watched the mixture carmelize under the little blue flame before stirring it very slowly into the coffee itself.

"You see, it's quite easy," she said in an encouraging voice. "You try it too, while I fix another cup for Orson."

Ruth did try it, with fair success, and they sat sipping and chatting, in a leisurely way, for some minutes longer. Then Foxworth glanced at his wrist watch, and sprang up with an exclamation of mock horror.

"Four o'clock!" he said. "And I had an uptown appointment at three-thirty! I didn't dream it was so late! But I'll have to ask you both to excuse me now. Perhaps I can give you a lift, Amélie? I'm going right by Richmond Place and I'd be mighty glad of your company. Unless you've got your own car here, of course."

No, she had walked downtown, Mrs. Lalande replied. She often walked downtown, partly because she really enjoyed the exercise, in spite of Doctor Perrault's slanders, and partly because Léonce usually had one of the family cars and Caresse the other. She'd be very grateful for a lift, because otherwise she'd have to take a taxi. After all, enough was enough, as far as exercise was concerned, just as it was with everything else. She drew a wisp of pink veiling, which had been folded back over the brim of her hat while she was eating lunch, down over her face again, securing it neatly in the rear with a hairpin, which she extracted from the golden coils of her hair; and when the veil was in place, she looked even younger and more alluring than before. Pink was certainly a very kind color, Ruth reflected, while she watched the departing guest draw on her spotless gloves; and a veil of almost any sort the most flattering of accessories. But the thought had no rancor in it; on the whole, Mrs. Lalande had impressed her more favorably than the night before. She stood at the window, watching her uncle and his lovely guest as they crossed the courtyard and got into his car; and, as if they were conscious of her presence, they both glanced up and waved. Then they were gone, and for a few minutes Ruth continued to stand looking across to Toulouse Street: at the quaint antique shop whose heterogeneous wares overflowed from its crowded interior to the sidewalk—oh no, the banquette!—before it; at the smart perfume shop whose gracious bay window displayed a tempting array of bottled fragrance on glass shelves; at the quaint story-and-a-half house with the closed shutters between the two shops. She considered the possibility of crossing the street to buy perfume and poke around among the antiques, but dismissed the idea. After all, it was late already. She would rather put her time into changing her dress, so that she would be fresh and poised when Russ Aldridge arrived, giving the effect of a lady of leisure, waiting unhurriedly for an expected caller. That would certainly be better than to risk having to rush in, disheveled and hasty, after he arrived. There was always the chance that he might come early . . . .

Since this was exactly what he did do, she was doubly glad that she had not followed her first impulse. She was still standing at the library window when Downes, the butler, came to tell her that Mr. Aldridge was on the telephone; and chagrined at the degree of her apprehension lest the message might announce some change of plan, she hastened across the room. When she heard Aldridge's words of reassurance, she was almost equally chagrined at her relief.

"Hello there! Glad to find you in. I called to ask whether you'd mind if I came early?"

"Not in the least," she replied, proud of her understatement. "About what time?"

"Well, straight off, if that would be all right. I've been lunching at Sabin Duplessis' studio, and the party is about over. I live on Felicity Street, and it seems silly to go uptown and then come back again, after the manner of the King of France and his ten thousand men. But of course, I can always go over to International House."

"Oh, don't do that! I'd really be delighted if you came here," Ruth said, speaking less temperately than before.

"Well, I'd be delighted to do it, so that makes it mutual. I'll be with you in about five minutes."

So there would not be time to change her dress after all. Well, it really did not matter much—the thing that mattered was that he was coming, that she had not been disappointed, as she feared she might be. She seated herself on the sofa which faced the low coffee table where she had placed the camellias, and drawing two of them from the copper tray, tucked them into her russet curls. Then she sat down, looking at the other flowers, and listening for the doorbell, feeling curiously content and relaxed. But when the ring came, a little quiver of excitement zigzagged through her contentment; and when Aldridge entered the room and took her hand, an unfamiliar feeling of joy welled up in her heart.

"Well, as I live and breathe, Lady Hume's Blush!" he exclaimed without preamble. Then, as Ruth looked at him in bewilderment, blushing herself, he laughed, indicating the flowers in her hair.

"Is that really their name?" she asked, touching them lightly and laughing too. "Uncle gave me a terrific ribbing when he found the only camellias I knew by name were Pink Perfections and Alba Plenas. But that doesn't mean I don't appreciate the beauty of all the others you gave me or that I don't want to learn more about them."

"All right, let's have the first lesson right now. Lady Hume's Blush is a very rare variety, generally considered a collector's item. A shy bloomer when planted in the shade. Does not flower as freely as some, but under really favorable conditions achieves great splendor. Here endeth chapter one of Aldridge on the care and feeding of camellias. Remarks: tutor hopes pupil gathered why he wanted her to put that kind in her hair." Seeing that she was blushing again, he added, more gravely, "Was it really all right for me to telephone and ask if I might come early? You see, this wasn't just a case of a party breaking up; it was a case of suddenly realizing that two persons, who cared a great deal for each other, wanted and needed to be by themselves."

Russell Aldridge had not misread the signals when he decided that Sabin Duplessis and Odile St. Amant wanted to be alone.

The fourth member of the studio party had been Nancy Hopkins, the brisk, efficient young assistant to the director of one of the top-flight advertising agencies. Soon after her arrival, she had announced that, to her regret, she would have to go back to her office that afternoon—not that she usually did, on Saturdays, but that slave driver, Cliff Saucier, had insisted they had to rough out the promotion campaign for Dash-o-Fire pepper sauce, so that he could put in a bid for a new account. Several times during luncheon she had looked at her watch, and while the others were still drinking coffee, she left, almost abruptly. Sabin remonstrated with her: the understanding had been that they were to play bridge; if she left that would break up the foursome; he did not know of anyone he could call in at a moment's notice on a Saturday afternoon. Nancy replied, rather tartly, that she would rather break up a foursome than lose her job any day, including Saturday. Then she was gone, leaving the others at loose ends.

Conscientiously, Sabin made two or three efforts to fill her place. But, as he had predicted, these attempts were fruitless. There were only a few persons with whom Odile was willing to play, now that her hand shook so badly, and none of these was available. Presently, conversation lagged a little, and Odile found it increasingly difficult to conceal her nervousness and depression. Sabin went to the concert grand piano and began to play snatches of Lehar's music, beginning with *"Du hast mein ganzes Herz"* and winding up with the "Merry Widow Waltz," but even these tuneful selections did not seem to ease the atmosphere. Aldridge was aware that Sabin brought Odile to these studio gatherings and took her home again in his car. Therefore, it was indicated that he should leave first in any case. And when Sabin said he had promised to show Odile the most recent additions to his collection of firearms—some remarkably fine pieces that had just come in, after a long delay, from Spain—Aldridge remarked that, no doubt these were extraordinary, but that they were not quite down an archeologist's alley and, if the others would be good enough to excuse him . . . . Then he, in his turn, went to the telephone, and immediately afterwards took his departure.

An antique Chinese bed, with a framework of red lacquer and coverings of black satin embroidered in gold, served as a divan in Sabin's studio; and ever since lunch, Odile had been sitting on this, leaning back against its welter of small pillows, and taking no part in the discussion about Nancy's inopportune work. She said goodbye to Aldridge listlessly, as if his presence nor his absence made any difference; and when Sabin came back to the divan, after speeding his parting guest, she seemed to be greatly preoccupied with one of the pillows. She had drawn it into her lap, and was pulling at its silken tassels with one hand, while she traced the pattern of its embroidery with the other. Her fingers were shaking badly, but she seemed to feel no self-consciousness about this, now that no one was about except Sabin. He stood silently beside her, waiting for her to speak first, and at last she looked up at him with questioning eyes.

"Have you really had a shipment from Spain, darling?" she asked.

"Yes, of course. Wednesday, on the *David J. Hill*. Did I ever lie in order to be alone with you?"

"No-o. But even if you weren't lying, you were using the arms as a pretext. And you made Russ feel as if he were terribly in the way."

"I gave him a chance to take a hint, that's all. And, if I'm not very much mistaken, he wasn't at all sorry to use the arms as a pretext himself."

"Sabin, you're begging the question. You know we haven't any right to create chances to be alone, and it isn't very much better to do it with a pretext than it would be to do it with a lie."

"Very well. I'll stop begging the question. I think we do have a right to be alone, and if I hadn't been able to create the chance in one way, I'd have done it in another."

"It was understood, when I started coming to these luncheons—"

"Correct. It was. But I'm not talking about any past understandings. I'm talking about today. I want to know what Perrault told you this morning that upset you so. You were still trying to choke down sobs when I got to the house. I know you'd been crying hard. It was all you could do to get hold of yourself and come along with me, and you were still too shaken to be coherent while we were in the car. By the time you'd calmed down, we were almost here. I couldn't start a heart-to-heart talk with you then, or while Nancy and Russ were around. But I can now and that's what I propose to do."

Without answering, Odile looked down at the pillow again, resuming her tracery and her tassel-pulling. Sabin came nearer and placed his hands over hers.

"Don't you think I have a right to, Odile?" he asked. "Hasn't any man such a right when the woman he loves is unhappy and—unsolaced?"

"No. Not if she's married to someone else."

"Even when the husband who's sworn to love and cherish her is neglecting her, even if he's—"

"Hush, darling. I said we mustn't. Unless you're really going to show me that Spanish shipment, you'll have to take me home."

She drew away her hands and put the pillow aside, rising as she did so. Without further insistence, Sabin walked over to a chest of beautifully tooled leather, upheld by a stand of wrought-iron, which stood on the opposite side of the room, and lifted its lid.

"Most of this is old Toledo ware," he said. "I don't think I ever saw a finer set of swords. They came from the Serreno collection. In case you don't know, the Serreno family was one of the most prominent in Spain for centuries. But it's practically extinct now. Gabriel de Serreno, who was Archbishop of Granada, died during the revolution, and his younger brother, Sebastian, went into exile after the horrible murder of his wife and daughters. I suppose there was no one left to look after these things, and, by fair means or foul, they landed in the antique shop where I found them. But there's no doubt about their authenticity or their value."

Sabin began to take the swords from the chest one by one, passing them to Odile, who had followed him across the room, and almost reverently calling her attention to the fine texture of their blades and the delicate inlay on their hilts. She examined each with care, expressing appropriate enthusiasm, and then laid it down with precision on a small teakwood table that stood nearby. Eventually, Sabin looked up from the chest empty-handed.

"There are no more swords," he said. "The rest of the Toledo ware doesn't amount to much—just the usual sort of stuff that you have to take in order to get the really good things along with it. But some of those Serrenos must have gone in for defending their honor in a large way. There was almost every kind of duelling weapon I ever saw, in that collection. Take a look at these pistols!"

He reached into the chest again, and drew from it a small rosewood case, with a gesture which indicated that he expected Odile to open it herself. She unclasped the cover, disclosing a pair of small, silver-mounted pistols embedded in purple velvet, which glowed with the patina of age. This time there was nothing studied or forced about her admiring exclamation.

"Oh, *darling,* how beautiful!" she cried. "Why, they don't seem like firearms at all! They seem like—well, some sort of an exquisite ornament. I'm sure there's a story connected with them—a romantic one. Isn't there?"

"Well, there might be some kind of family legend."

"Tell it to me, won't you, Sabin?"

"I don't know all the details. But it seems one of the Serrenos was very much in love with a lady he couldn't marry."

"Why not?"

"She married someone else while he was fighting in Peru," Sabin said, "though, of course, she had promised by the Holy Cross to wait for him, and all that. Finally he came back and found that Doña Otilla—yes, that was her name, Doña Otilla—was extremely unhappy. But she had scruples about being unfaithful to her husband, though she hadn't had any about being unfaithful to her betrothed. So Serreno took matters into his own hands. He found a pretext—apparently he was more adroit about that than some other people—for calling the lady's husband out and killing him. This death made her a virtuous widow, so after a decent interval, she and Serreno were married and lived happily ever after."

"Sabin, that isn't an old Spanish legend. It's a story you made up as you went along."

"Well, you asked for a romantic tale, so I told you one. I'm sorry it didn't please you. I thought it was pretty good myself .... Anyway, I'm glad you appreciate the pistols. They're as fine a collector's item as I've seen in a long time. I'd like very much to give them to you. Perhaps if you put them where you could look at them, every so often, they'd remind you of my story and it would have more weight with you, the more you thought it over."

"I don't want to be reminded of your story."

"You don't want to be or you don't need to be?"

"All right, I don't need to be. And I don't want to spoil your collection. If you separated the swords and the pistols, the collection would be incomplete. Then it would lose most of its importance."

"All right, let me give you the swords too."

"You know I couldn't accept such a valuable present. And anyway, what on earth would I do with the swords? Where on earth could I even put them, as far as that goes? We haven't a gun room or anything that corresponds to it in our house—you know that perfectly well. And *maman* doesn't like anything disarranged—she wants to keep everything unchanged in the elegant, ultra-feminine surroundings to which she's accustomed. I could tuck away that rosewood case somewhere, I suppose, but—"

"Well, take it then, without the swords. That's what I suggested in the first place."

While they were talking, Odile had laid the pistols down beside the swords on the teakwood table. Now Sabin picked up the case, and tried, without success, to put it into her hands.

"Darling, I just told you, I don't want to spoil your collection."

"Nonsense! You don't want to be reminded of my story, you're not willing to accept a present from me—"

He was speaking heatedly again, as he had when he asked her if he did not have a right to know what was troubling her. For the second time, Odile answered him soothingly.

"Hush, darling. Of course, I'm willing to accept a present from you. Not the pistols, that's all."

"I suppose you mean that I can send you a pound of chocolates, or half a dozen red carnations or something of that sort?"

"I didn't mean anything of the kind and you know it. I think it's very unfair of you to say so."

"Well, what did you mean?"

"I didn't have anything specific in mind. But since you've

pinned me down—" She hesitated for a moment and then went on in a lowered voice. "I'd like something that's connected with you, rather than a bargain you happened to pick up in a shop. Something you got overseas. I don't know whether you'll believe it or not, but I'm awfully proud of your war record."

"Is that why you married a four-effer while I was ferrying stuff across the Hump from Calcutta to Kunming?"

"Darling, please . . . . I can't bear it when you talk to me like that. You know I'm—troubled already; do you have to make me still more unhappy by reproaching me? Don't you suppose I reproach myself, every day of my life, as it is?"

Her lips were trembling now, as well as her hands. "When I heard you were killed, I wanted to die too," she whispered. "And afterwards—when we learned the first report was false, that you'd had an almost miraculous escape and covered yourself with glory—why then, I nearly died with *joy*! But you don't know the effect Léonce has on a girl—practically any girl. It's almost like mesmerism. Ruth Avery is the only one I've seen in a long while who didn't fall under the spell of it. I did say no to him, over and over again. But he came to the house all the time. And when I thought it might be *maman* he wanted instead of me—of course, Caresse was just a child then—I was jealous for the first time in my life. I didn't want him to take her out for long rides along the River Road. I didn't like it when he laughed with her in a knowing way over little secrets they shared. I couldn't bear to see him look at her as if—well, as if she didn't have many clothes on, and as if he thought the less she wore, the more beautiful she was. That's the way Léonce does look at a woman, Sabin."

"Don't I know it?"

"I suppose so . . . . And when he touched her, or Caresse, it—it did something to me. I don't mean that he acted exactly like a lover towards either of them. He just put his arms around them casually and kissed them once in awhile. I don't know why it should have seemed any different than when other men, who came to the house, did the same thing. But it did. Perhaps because Léonce seemed to take it for granted that he could fondle them, and because they seemed to take it for granted that he would. Oh, I don't know! But I couldn't stand it! I wanted him to put his arms around me; I wanted him to kiss me. And I couldn't have let him do it casually. I really have to care. Well, you know that. So, at last, I said, all right, I would be engaged to him, and he said, 'hell no.' I'd be *married* to him, because he knew he'd never really get anywhere with me until I was. So we *were* married, almost immediately. Before I half realized why I was doing it, before I had time to think what it would do to you."

Sabin put down the rosewood case, moving the swords slightly to make room for it. "Well, it did plenty," he said briefly. "I'd say it had done plenty to you too. I don't see why women never seem to learn that marriage isn't any cure for men who are casual about caresses. But are you taking it all that hard, because Léonce hasn't changed his spots? Do you still care so much for him? Is that what's causing this state you're in?"

"I don't care for him the way I did at first, of course. That's part of the trouble. But I'm terribly humiliated, and I know it's my fault, as much as his, that he isn't a better husband. Another thing I didn't realize, beforehand, was what marriage would be like. Don't look at me that way, Sabin! Of course, I knew it wasn't just a spiritual relationship; I didn't want it to be. I've just confessed to you that, physically, I once found Léonce irresistible. There are—moments when I still . . . ." She paused, flooded with fresh humiliation at the thought of the previous night. "But I didn't think marriage would mean just one thing to him," she went on, "or that there wouldn't be any tenderness and devotion mingled with the vehemence. Or that, if I didn't have children right off, he'd feel I was a failure as a woman, just as he felt I was a failure as a wife when I wasn't responsive to him. And I am a failure, Sabin—a terrible failure. I've been married over four years now, and I've never had even the hope of a child. And this last year—"

"This last year you've been ill. You're very ill. Anyone can see that. You've got to tell me about this illness, Odile, just as you've told me about the rest. You've got to let me help you."

"I've told you a great deal too much already. No wife ought to talk about her husband the way I've talked to you about Léonce. And you can't help me. No one can."

"You're wrong, I can help you. I may have to take desperate measures to do it, but it can be done."

Odile shook her head, but because she had finally unburdened her soul, at least in part, she was able to smile faintly as she did so.

"I don't want you, or anyone else, to take 'desperate measures,' or even to talk about them," she said. "But you might do what I asked you to before you sidetracked me like this. You might give me a little present to take home with me. I mustn't come here again, after what's happened today. But if I did have something connected with your war record, it would mean a lot to me."

"Well, there's another pistol," Sabin answered, as briefly as he had spoken before. Evidently he did not mean to argue with her any longer, or to coerce her into telling him more than she had already. Odile gave a little sigh of relief, and Sabin went on quietly, "It isn't a beauty, like that pair of Serrenos. And it isn't part of a collection, so you couldn't object to it on that ground or on the ground of any essential value. It's of no use to me whatsoever, because I can't get ammunition for it in this country, and there are only two or three of its own cartridges left. But it does have a connection with my war service. Wait a second, I'll get it for you."

He went into the small bedroom, leading off the studio, and shut the door after him. Odile closed the lid of the chest, and sat down on it. She was glad that Sabin had shut the door, because, when it was open, she could hardly help seeing into the room beyond and she did not like to do so, for it had always seemed to hold out a tacit rebuke. It was scarcely more than a slit in the wall, and it contained nothing but an army cot covered with a honeycomb spread, a chest of drawers with two military brushes lying stiffly on top of it, and one straight-backed chair. That was not the kind of room it was natural for Sabin, who loved space and luxury and beauty, to sleep in. He was doing it as a protest, perhaps an unconscious one, but nevertheless a protest.

Odile closed her eyes, trying not to see the sort of bedroom she and Sabin would have shared if they had been married, and then opened them again, so that they might dwell fondly on every costly and exotic detail of the studio which Sabin had planned and equipped for her reception, and which was so different from the bare narrow chamber to which he had withdrawn alone: the primitive paintings, with their golden backgrounds for haloed saints and angels; the rugs from Isfahan, with the tree of life forming the center for their jewel-colored pattern; the Syrian silks which covered the great armchairs; the carved Peruvian *armarios*, in which Sabin kept his collections of strange musical instruments and gorgeous illuminated missals. No one else could have achieved such harmony from things so alien to each other, or created such a homelike atmosphere with museum pieces. Her mother's house had never seemed like home to Odile, since her marriage. As she had told Sabin, Amélie Lalande wanted to keep everything unchanged; and she herself had missed the bride's prerogative of choosing her own dwelling place and furnishing it in her own way. Odile slept in the same room she had occupied as a girl, and which seemed to her singularly inappropriate now; she still ate from her mother's china and received her guests in her mother's drawing room. Her mother did the housekeeping, planned the meals, supervised the servants. Only old Tossie, who had been her mammy when she was a baby, took orders from her by preference; and if she had left, Tossie would have come with her to this house, which she and Sabin had chosen together long ago, and which did seem like home to her. Of course, she had not selected the furnishings for it, but that was not Sabin's fault. He had not accepted what was already provided, like Léonce, indifferent as to the settings, as long as he could have a surfeit of rich food and rare wine at the table, and take his unbridled, voluptuous way night after night. Sabin had done the selecting for her, more wisely, more tastefully, and more appropriately than she could have done it herself. This room seemed doubly hers because it bespoke all that tenderness, all that devotion, which she had missed so woefully and with which Sabin would have so prodigally surrounded her if she had married him. She looked down at the Spanish chest of tooled leather, sturdy and capacious and magnificent, and knew that it had been meant to hold the outfit of a bride. She looked over towards the great divan, its red lacquer and gold embroidery gleaming through the early dusk of the January day, and knew that it must have been a bridal bed . . . .

When Sabin returned, he was holding a snubby, flat and vicious-looking little pistol in one hand, while he wiped it free of the heavy grease with which it was covered. Odile looked up with a start.

"Was—was that the one you carried when you were in the Army?" she asked.

"No, I got this off an Arab."

Odile looked up from the gun, obviously disappointed.

"But I was hoping it wouldn't be something you bought or . . . ."

"I didn't say I bought it. I got it because if I hadn't, it would have got me, but good. And by that time the Arab wasn't in any position to bargain. He was very dead."

"You mean you—killed him?"

"Well, after all, that was part of the job, wasn't it? And in this case it was a particularly good thing, too. It happened while we were at Sfax, long before the surrender at Bizerte. But Staff was already piling up material for the Sicily show,

71

which was top of the top when it came to being secret. We'd all noticed some of the natives losing their way accidentally on purpose, and turning up where they'd no business to be, and this night I got to worrying about my plane which was due to take a fast trip to London in the morning, and went out to check things. Then I stumbled over this bum, and that was it. I'd still like to know how he got hold of this made-in-Germany number though. It's what they used to call a Kamerad-gun. Small enough to hold in your palm when you raised your hands, and potent enough to get you out of a tight place at close quarters."

While he talked, Sabin had been shifting the pistol lightly about on his fingers. When he said, "Now that *is* a true story!" he tossed it up, caught it again, and held it out to Odile. This time she accepted his offering without hesitation, and, in her turn, attempted to toy with the pistol, though the trembling of her hand made this almost impossible.

"Wait a minute, my dear," Sabin interrupted hastily. "Let me fix this baby so there can't be any accidents."

He took the gun, pressed a catch beside the checkered hard-rubber grip, and slid the magazine from it. He worked the barrel action to make sure no cartridge was left in the chamber.

"Now she's harmless," he announced, examining the flat little magazine of blued steel. "The three shells in this thing are probably the only ones in this country that'd fit it, and as long as you keep gun and magazine apart, the way I've got them now, there can't be any accidents. You won't forget, will you?"

"I shan't forget. I don't forget anything, Sabin."

"Don't you?"

"No."

It was not only her hands and her lips that were shaking now. She was trembling all over. Sabin took the pistol from her unresisting fingers and laid it on the little table.

"Just leave it there until you're ready to go home," he said quietly. "Since you've got such a good memory, you won't be likely to forget it. If you do, I'll remind you of it. I want you to have it. But you're not ready to go home yet, are you, dearest?"

She tried to answer and could not. But she bowed her head and Sabin understood.

"And I'm not ready to let you. Not until I've told you again how much I love you. Not until you've said that you still love me."

72

However, neither of them said anything more for a long while. Because he had put his arm around her and bent his head. Then she had lifted her face to receive his kiss and there was no more need for words.

5

How Caresse Lalande and Léonce
St. Amant spent the afternoon—

January 3, 1948

"LADIES AND gentlemen, you have been listening to Caresse Lalande's nostalgic report on the fashions of yesteryear, brought to you by The Fashion Plate Dress Shop, for whose clients distinction in dress is more difficult to avoid than to achieve. Miss Lalande will return to you at this same hour next Tuesday, with a continuation of her unique tri-weekly broadcasts." A gong sounded and the announcer continued, "Two P. M., and time to remember that Zoot, the soo-oo-oothing laxative is compounded like . . . ."

Instinctively, Caresse always shied away from the line about the soothing laxative. Nevertheless, she left the studio in great good humor, with the pleasing comments on her voice, from the newscaster who was to follow her, still ringing in her ears. She smiled engagingly at her fellow passengers in the elevator, and stopped to joke and chat with Cary Emery—one of the young brokers who had waylaid her at Antoine's the evening before—when she chanced upon him in the Roosevelt lobby. Léonce was to call for her at two-fifteen. It had required very little persuasion on his part, in the course of the Foxworth dinner, to convince her that they might drive out into the country on Saturday. After all, Odile had a date with Sabin Duplessis every Saturday; why shouldn't Caresse herself have one with Léonce? Not that she supposed Odile or their mother would feel that way about it; so at home she had said she would have to remain at the studio, after her broadcast, to rehearse her Tuesday script. But even when Cary Emery insisted on accompanying her to the Baronne Street entrance, she had no twinges of self-consciousness. It was certainly natural that her brother-in-law should call for her . . . .

"Isn't that Léonce honking for you now?" her impromptu escort inquired, interrupting a lively bit of repartee.

"No, his car's maroon," she answered nonchalantly. Then, realizing that the blue sedan to which Cary Emery had called her attention was blocking traffic, she looked at it more carefully.

"Why, it *is*!" she exclaimed. "So long, Cary. See you tomorrow at the Sulloways' cocktail party." Then, as she sprang lightly into the blue sedan, she inquired rather pettishly, "How did you expect me to recognize you on the double when you drove up in this poor ramshackle bus, Léonce? You might have told me beforehand, instead of making all that racket. What's happened to your own jalopy, anyway?"

"Nothing's happened to it. I just decided it might be better if I took one of the cars from the lot for our little outing today. So I said I was going to show it to a prospect."

"Why? That is, why did you think it would be better to take a car from the lot?"

"If you can't guess, I'll tell you as soon as I get out of this traffic jam. Right now, I've got to keep my mind on my driving."

"Well, I didn't realize that a simple little question like that—"

"Oh, hush your mouth, can't you, Caresse?"

Obviously, Léonce was in a very bad temper. Without the least idea of what had caused this, Caresse began to feel irritated herself. Her mood of bright banter darkened, and she lapsed into rather sullen silence.

"Your mother stopped in at the agency, awhile back," Léonce finally volunteered, after they had crossed the Industrial Canal and were heading out St. Claude Avenue. "That holier-than-thou pain in the neck, Perrault, came to the house this morning, after all. His medical Kaffeeklatsch didn't last as long as he thought it would. So he filled in the spare time by telling Odile her case was hopeless. And, of course, your mother felt she ought to hurry right along and bring me the good news."

"What do you mean, hopeless?"

"I mean she's going to be an invalid all her life. And her life's going to be a long one. Cheerful prospect all around, isn't it?"

"I'll say it is. Why, Léonce, I don't see how we can stand it—any of us! Odile's so depressed anyway that, if she gets to dwelling on endless invalidism, she'll lapse into melancholia. The first thing we know, she'll be a mental case."

"She's pretty nearly that already. Anyway, there isn't much of the physical left to her."

"You don't need to be quite so crude about it, do you?"

"I'm not so sure. After all, you asked me why I thought it might be better to use a dealer's car for our little expedition."

"But we're just going out for a ride in the country. Anyone can go for a ride in the country."

"Yeah. And anyone can stop at a tourist camp and rest for a couple of hours, if they get tired while they're out riding in the country. I thought we might, so I picked out a used car one of our customers brought in from Biloxi. It's got a Mississippi license plate on it. And, just in case the operator of the camp decided to eke out his rental income with a spot of minor blackmail, it might be darned handy if—"

"Léonce, you know you never said—"

"Oh, I know I never said! My God, you *do* need everything spelled out for you! You're crazy about me, at least you've been saying you were for the last couple of months now, and I'm crazy about you, and I'm married and my wife's going to live forever. So what? You don't want me to kill her, do you, so I can marry you? And you don't want to kill her yourself, I suppose, so you can marry me? And divorce doesn't enter the picture because we're all good practicing Catholics—not that it wouldn't be a dirty trick to trump up excuses for a divorce from a sick woman, even if you were a Baptist or something like that. But what she doesn't know won't hurt her. She'll never know about this, Caresse."

"About what?"

"About this afternoon."

They had left the city streets behind them now, and were well out on the Pointe à la Hâche road. As they approached the Pakenham Oaks, Léonce steered the blue sedan to the side of the road and shut off the motor.

"Listen," he said, "I've tried to stick this thing out. As long as I thought there was a chance Odile might get well, I tried to be faithful to her—reasonably faithful, at least. Now that I know she may live to be ninety, I don't see the slightest use in trying, because I'd know from the beginning that I was licked. I'm only thirty-five. I might live to be ninety myself. Did you ever hear of a normal man living a continent life for fifty-five years?"

"Well, priests and—"

"Oh hell, don't let's get on the subject of priests! You know I wasn't talking about them anyway. I don't see why you have to drag them in. And I don't want to keep on jawing about this thing. I want to *do* something about it. If you want to turn around and go home right now, I'll take you. But I give you my word that if I do, I'll be out this evening with some other date who isn't quite so squeamish."

"I'm not squeamish, but—"

"You can't prove it to me, just by telling me so. And I'm not going to sit around, holding Odile's hand and saying how sorry I am for her. That's probably what Sabin's doing right now—hand-holding is right in his line, and he does it a lot better than I do. Probably, because it's as far as he ever goes, except maybe for one chaste kiss on the brow, so he has to concentrate on it. When Odile gets home, she'll be exhausted from the strain of accepting such tender proofs of eternal devotion, and she'll go straight to bed. Then, Tossie'll bring her a cup of Ovaltine to quiet her nerves and she'll settle down for the night. I won't enter the picture at all and God knows I won't want to. I'll want to get the hell out of there, unless something's made me feel a lot better beforehand than I do now."

There was no doubt about it, Léonce meant what he said. For a long while, Caresse had harbored an envious resentment against her sister because Odile had the right of way, as far as Léonce was concerned; but never before had she been tortured by the sharp thrusts of jealousy which now pierced her through and through. It was one thing to endure with bad grace, but some compensation, a situation of long standing; it was something else again deliberately to provoke another which she realized it would be impossible to endure with any grace at all, and for which there would be no compensations. The threat Léonce had made of a night's outing in other company was bad enough in itself; but it might well lead, directly or indirectly, to a more lasting intrigue. If he became really infatuated with some shutter-girl, that could mean the end of those secret embraces which had become a stealthy habit between him and Caresse, and to which she looked forward more and more avidly. And a shutter-girl was not her only menace. There was Ruth Avery, for instance, whose uncle had more millions than he knew what to do with, but which Léonce could find all sorts of ways to spend, if he could get his hands on them. And, unfortunately, Ruth Avery had other intriguing attributes in addition to the millions. Her figure was altogether too good, for one thing, and her coloring was the kind that made men sit up and take notice. Caresse had not failed to observe the way Léonce looked her over the night before, or the obvious pleasure he had derived from dancing with her . . . .

"Well, do you want to go home?" he inquired. He had guessed, without much difficulty, what was passing in the mind of Caresse, and was eminently satisfied with the results of his warning. "Just so there won't be any misunderstanding later, I'll add one thing more—if we do go on, it isn't going to be merely a jaunt to look at the scenery. It's got to be the real McCoy or nothing this time, Caresse."

He still spoke derisively. But, as he finished speaking, he slid his arm around her, digging his fingers into her slim waist, and with his free hand tilted up her face and pressed his mouth hard against hers. Again, a fierce pang shot through her, not of jealousy this time, but of ecstasy. She could make no immediate answer, because he had so effectually sealed her lips; indeed, she could hardly breathe in his vehement embrace. But long before he released her, he knew that she would not withstand his insistence, because she no longer had either the power or the will to do so.

He finally let her go and looked down at her. She nodded, almost imperceptibly and without speaking. But he smiled broadly and indulgently as he flipped the ignition switch and fumbled with his foot for the unfamiliarly placed starter. A moment later the car throbbed noisily into life, and still smiling, Léonce swung about the fenced-in walls whose ragged brickwork constituted all that remained of a beautiful and historic house. He did not need any answer now, and the satisfaction over the success of his methods, together with his anticipation of the interlude at the tourist camp, had entirely restored his good humor. After all, this was no minor victory. In spite of that long succession of secret embraces, he knew that Caresse was no light-of-love. Today would mark her first complete capitulation, and his conquest of her would do much more than appease mere sensual craving. It would gratify his pride, it would assure him a permanent source of pleasure, and it would endow him with power. No other man had broken down her defenses; but his virility had triumphed where theirs had failed. She was very beautiful, and the possession of such beauty would represent untold delights. Best of all, this would be no transitory or elusive relationship, but an enduring mastery. Once he had taken Caresse, he could have her again whenever he wanted her. She would not dare deny him; it would be too easy for him to give her away, to say she had thrown herself at his head, and that, in a weak moment, he had yielded to her. A tourist camp would do now, for an expedient. But he would not have to bother with

78

expedients very often. Not with Odile increasingly handicapped by invalidism, not with Caresse in the same house . . . .

He settled back in his seat, driving faster and faster. As he crossed the highway and swung into a side road, leading through reed-grown swamps, he narrowly escaped collision with a passing farm truck and Caresse was unable to stifle a frightened protest.

"For heaven's sake, Léonce, take it easy! Can't you look where you're going? Do you *know* where you're going anyway? I never saw this road before—if you can call it a road."

"You bet it's a road. It's the cutoff from Chalmette to Gentilly. And we're heading for that tourist camp I've been talking about. Only, instead of approaching it from the New Orleans' side, we'll be coming from the east, in a car with a Mississippi license, as though we'd driven over to New Orleans from somewhere along the Gulf Coast."

In spite of herself, Caresse felt impelled to make an indiscreet comment. She knew, even as she did so, that Léonce would resent it, but she could not bite back her words.

"Apparently, you've been to this out-of-the-way place before."

Léonce, who was now paying more attention to the rough road, did not answer.

"Have you?"

"Oh, for God's sake! Of course I have!"

"Did you go there alone?"

"No, I didn't go there alone. Anything else you'd like to know?"

"Yes, I'd like to know what you meant when you said, a few minutes ago, that as long as you thought there was a chance Odile might get well, you'd been faithful to her."

"I said, *reasonably* faithful. I supposed you'd understand what I meant by that. I thought we'd always understand each other, Caresse. You aren't going to disappoint me, are you?"

So such a secret expedition, with its stolen delights, was not a glorious adventure, poignant in its fulfillment, as far as Léonce was concerned; it was only a commonplace of his existence. Suddenly, Caresse saw herself as one in a soiled and sordid company of flashily over-dressed girls, reeking of cheap perfume; among them perhaps a young wife, seeking escape from the household drudgery of a degenerated romance; or perhaps an elderly and wealthy woman, her face grotesquely made up, seeking to recapture long-vanished ecstasy . . . .

79

Jealous as she was of her sister, eager as she was to possess Léonce, Caresse tardily realized that she could not join this shabby procession. Even if she lost him to others in a tawdry guild, even if the fires he had kindled remained unquenched, the company in which he had classified her was too cheap, the cost of capitulation was too high. She spoke with abrupt decision.

"Léonce, please turn this car around. I want to go home after all."

Again he glanced at her with amusement, less tinged by indulgence than before she began to question him, but still with the tolerance of a man of the world, to whom such a temporary turn of affairs was no novelty.

"You don't really want to, honey," he said easily. "That's just a passing whim. In a minute you'll have another."

"No, I won't. Because it isn't a whim. It's a resolution."

"Stuff and nonsense. You're a little worried, the way girls usually are the first time. But you don't need to be. Everything's going to be all right."

"I know it is. And I'm not worried. There isn't going to be anything to worry about."

Léonce took one hand from the wheel and slid it along the back of the seat, cupping her right shoulder. "That's what I'm trying to tell you, *chère*," he said, still more soothingly. "And afterwards—afterwards you'll be glad it's happened. You won't be sorry or ashamed. All the talk about that is a lot of bunk."

She wrenched herself away from him. "We don't seem to mean quite the same thing when we say there's nothing to worry about," she said tartly. "And the rest of your line's pretty old stuff. Presently, you'll be telling me it's a long walk back to town. Doesn't that usually come next?"

"Maybe it does. Anyway, it's a thought. You don't suppose I'd let you or anyone else tease me along like this, do you, without—"

His amusement was gone now and his tolerance. He took his eyes from the road to glare at her in sudden fury.

"Léonce! Watch out!"

Too late he saw the heavy van and the whipping red markers, set out to warn approaching vehicles that it was stalled. Desperately he jammed clutch and brake pedals down to the floor board and felt something snap, as the old car plunged forward once more. In a final effort to avert disaster he tried to twist the sedan onto the soft shoulder of the road. Caresse was still screaming when the car slued crazily side-

wise into the heavy corrugated housing of the parked truck.
. . .

The fog that enveloped him began to lift and he heard a deep, rumbling voice in whose speech he could not at once identify words. Then he caught the thread of the sentence.

". . . . about him. His kind always manages to get off easy. It's always the other guy gets killed. Yeah! And if I hadn't jumped the hell away, there wouldn't 'a' been nothing left of me outside of a mess in the morgue and maybe a pitcher in the paper tomorrow."

Léonce sat up. The left side of his face felt oddly stiff. He put his fingers up to it, found it warm and slippery, brought them away, saw the oozing red and felt his stomach kick within him at the realization that this was blood. As his blurred vision focused, he saw standing above him a huge man, clad in muddy overalls of blue and white ticked denim, a visored cap pushed far back on his head.

"What I by God and by rights ought to do," the apparition boomed down at him, "I ought to take and beat the living bejeezus out of you. In broad daylight, mind you, with my markers out a good fifty yards behind where I'm changing a tire, and a road as wide as a football field on the other side, but still and all a dopey bastard like you has to plow into me!"

"I'm bleeding," mumbled Léonce.

"Aw, get your can off that road. There ain't nothing wrong with you outside of a bump 'longside the head. I seen that when I picked you out of that jalopy."

In a gingerly way, Léonce picked himself off the road, vaguely surprised to find that he could move without difficulty or even discomfort. As he rose, he saw Caresse, her lips and chin hidden by a wadded red cloth. Again he felt the thump and tug of inner recoil, until he realized that this was a bandanna and that its red color was not due to blood.

"Are you all right?" he asked.

She nodded, mumbling. His faculties were clearing, and he turned to the truck driver.

"I can't tell you how sorry I am this happened, old man," he said. "If you'll see us out to the highway, when you get squared away, I'll make it right with you."

"You'll make all hell right with me, you will," growled the driver. "Besides, your car'll run. How d'you reckon it got back on the road, anyway? I drove it back out. But you better let the young lady drive into town. You ain't fit to be at the wheel of no car."

81

"But the damage . . . ."

"You got insurance, ain't you?"

"Yes, of course . . . . er, that is to say, no. Not on this car, I mean . . . . No, I haven't any insurance. But whatever the damage is, I can pay you now, or send . . . ."

"Aw, there ain't all that much damage. Ten bucks to one of the boys at the refrigeration plant to take the dents out of the back housing where you hit ought to fix it."

Léonce brought out a cordovan wallet from his hip pocket, ran a zipper back along its upper edge, and then looked towards Caresse.

"I'm dreadfully sorry, *chère*," he said. "But—but I don't seem to have more than about six dollars and a little change with me. Could you—that is, if you'll be good enough . . . ."

Disdainfully Caresse passed him her smart afternoon bag. As she took down the wadded bandanna, he saw that her lip was bruised, but she turned away before he could make any reference to her hurt. He fumbled through a miscellany of keys, handkerchiefs, cigarettes, matches, and cosmetics until he found a small bulging purse. The ten dollar bill he extracted from it was only one of many crisp banknotes, some of large denominations, and the humiliating thought flashed through his mind that Caresse earned more from her broadcasts than he did from his sales. *He had only just enough money with him to pay for that room*, she was thinking contemptuously at the same moment. *I suppose two dollars apiece would be a normal charge at a respectable tourist camp. But probably the place where we were going runs a regular racket, at special prices, and Léonce allowed for that. He didn't allow for anything else though. It was going to be a pretty cheap outing, in more ways than one. He thought he could get me for six dollars. That's the sort of price he puts on what he calls love. It ought to be a free gift if it's the real thing. And a night on the town must come a good deal higher than six dollars. Wouldn't you know it would be a cheapskate like that I'd want so?*

She did not speak to him when he climbed into the car beside her, or turn to look at the truck driver, who was still standing in the middle of the road, fingering his ten dollar bill and grinning derisively. For some moments they rode along in defensive silence, each avoiding the unalluring sight of the other, and each privately classifying the other as a poor sport. At last Caresse asked a scornful question.

"Did you have some brilliant idea for our next plan of action?"

"I never have any brilliant ideas, and I don't quite follow you about a plan of action."

"Well, after all, we both came downtown in family cars. If we go home separately, someone's sure to ask us how we happened to get banged up in pretty much the same way."

"I suppose you're right. Any suggestions?"

"Nice of you to ask. I don't think it's going to be too easy to keep altogether in the clear, whatever we do. But I think maybe the best plan would be to take this beat-up wreck back to Voisin-Caprelle's first. While you're telling any kind of a story you can dream up, I'll go to the parking lot and get my car. Then I'll come back for you. When we get home you can say that you had engine trouble on your way to the agency this morning, so you left your car in the shop for repairs and telephoned me at the broadcasting station, asking for a lift. Which, of course, I was delighted to give my dear brother-in-law."

"Well, that still wouldn't explain our battered condition," he retorted, smarting under the sarcasm of her tone.

"I'm coming to that. It just isn't your lucky day—"

"Are you telling me?"

"Hush your mouth, as you tenderly said to me a while back. On our way up St. Charles Avenue we were struck by a hit-and-run driver and when we came to we were still too much dazed to know just what had happened."

"And, of course, St. Charles Avenue is so completely deserted early of a Saturday evening that no one else would have seen the accident or have any idea of how it happened either!"

"Well then, let's say right out we took a drive in the country. It was such a pretty day, and we knew *maman* and Odile were both having fun and so we thought—"

"It doesn't sound too good, but it might get by."

"Can you think of a better story?"

Léonce did not succeed in doing this and again he took refuge in defensive silence. But this time a continuing thread began to shuttle back and forth through the pattern of his thoughts. Caresse had never appeared less desirable than she did at this moment, with her bright hair disheveled and her beautiful lips bruised, her smart dress rumpled and stained. But that was beyond the point. The point was that, reasonably or not, he still did inordinately desire her; moreover he had intended to have her, and he did not propose to be balked in his purpose. And he intended to have *Caresse,* not any hussy that he could take out on the town. No one else would do now. No one else, under the present circumstances, could assuage his injured pride or satisfy his thwarted passion.

Therein lay the great difficulty. He had been within an ace of getting her, that afternoon. If she had not annoyed him with her prying questions—if he had not taken his eyes off the road—if it had not been for that damned truck—if friction had not corroded their mutual yearning, she would have accepted the tourist camp, in spite of all its sordid connotations and, by now, she would have been his. But never again would she deliberately embark on such a scurvy adventure. She would hold out for the narrow band—preferably diamond set—and the center aisle. She was even more truly her mother's daughter than Odile, when it came to showy externals. It would have been unthinkable, in the first place, to ask for Odile in terms other than marriage. But it was the sacrament, not the pageant, which mattered to her. Caresse would demand that Society—spelled with a capital S—be on her side.

Caresse was silent too, but her thoughts were very different: this mortifying retreat, bolstered by a framework of lies, was surely a sorry ending to an adventure designed to sound a high note of reciprocal passion! But striking through her humiliation and her resentment were still those sharp thrusts of jealousy which had pierced her earlier in the afternoon. If it had not been for Odile, Léonce would never have tried to seduce her; he would have asked her to marry him. Indirectly, everything was Odile's fault. She hated Odile, that nasty-nice, prunes-and-prisms sister of hers, who was so terribly, terribly sweet that everyone was darling to her . . . .

As she finally slowed her car to a halt in front of the Lalande house on Richmond Place, Caresse saw that another automobile was parked directly in front of the driveway. A street light slanted across the rear license plate, revealing the caduceus which proclaimed it a physician's. She gave a quick exclamation.

"Doctor Perrault's here again, Léonce. Something must have happened while we were gone."

"I'd say plenty happened while we were gone."

"I mean something must have happened *here*."

"Well, didn't I tell you Odile would come home in a state of collapse? Your mother's probably sent for Perrault again. It would come in mighty handy if she had, at that. This eye of mine hurts like the devil. There might even be glass in it."

"My lip doesn't feel so good either. I suppose you wouldn't think about me."

84

"I don't know how you feel, but I can see how you look all right."

They crossed the sidewalk and went up the steps with an increasing sense of rebellious dissatisfaction. While Léonce was still fumbling for his latchkey, the front door was thrown open and Tossie sprang towards them. Ordinarily, in spite of her nearsightedness, very little escaped her, as Foxworth had reminded Amélie. But if she noticed the battered condition of the couple whom she now confronted, nothing in her manner or words indicated this.

"Mah baby ben took bad," she wailed. "When Mistuh Sabin brung her home, a while back, he had to carry her into de house and straight to her room. She couldn' walk no mo'n if she'd been a sho 'nuff baby. She couldn' stan' on her po' li'l feets. She done shake an' shake an' cry an' cry. Even after Mistuh Sabin done leff de room, an' Ah taken off her clo'es an' gits her into her bed, she go right on a-shakin' an' a-cryin' 'til de doctuh gits heah."

"Well, is she still shaking and crying?" Léonce demanded, brushing past Tossie and flinging his hat on the rack by the door.

"No, de doctuh, he done give her somethin' to make her stop. But she still a-moanin'! Please, Mistuh Léonce, go to de do' an' tell de doctuh he got to let you in. He won' let Miss Amélie in, he won' let me in, but you Miss Odile's husban'. He boun' to let you in. Ah'se scared of what's happenin' to mah baby."

"Keep quiet, Tossie, and give Miss Amélie a chance to tell us about this."

Amélie was coming down the stairs. The ubiquitous chiffon handkerchief had been called into play, but, in contrast to Tossie, she was comparatively calm. Unlike the old servant, she did notice that something was amiss in the appearance of her daughter and her son-in-law. However, it obviously caused her only passing curiosity and no concern.

"Have you two been in some kind of accident?" she inquired. "Well, it's a good thing Vance is here—he can patch you both up .... As Tossie seems to have been telling you, Odile's gone all to pieces. She frightened Sabin almost to death. He refused to leave the house until Vance got here and gave an opinion. Vance reassured him—said all she needed was complete rest and he'd see that she got it. He's given her a strong sdative and is going to stay with her until he's sure that it's taken effect. Then he'll come back again, around midnight, to check on her condition. Meanwhile, of course, he doesn't want her disturbed. If Léonce or anyone else went barging in on her now, that would undo all the good work of the sedative."

"Hit ain' no medicine she need," Tossie broke in, scornfully and impudently. "Hit be's comfort. Effen none of her kinnery gwine to her, Ah is!" She charged towards the rear of the hall, in the same desperate way that, a few minutes earlier, she had charged towards the front door. Léonce caught her by the shoulder, roughly pulling her back.

"Don't you try to go another step," he said, "or I'll shake the daylights out of you. Listen! If Miss Odile were still moaning you could hear her, if you'd only keep still yourself. And there isn't a sound."

He clapped his free hand over Tossie's mouth to silence her outcry. For a moment, she continued to struggle in his grasp. Then she subsided, spent by the effort, and stood listening, like the others.

Léonce was right. The moaning had ceased. The heavy silence of the house engulfed them all.

6

How Russell Aldridge and Ruth Avery spent the evening—

January 3, 1948

RUTH AVERY had made no immediate answer when Russell Aldridge told her he had left Sabin's studio, not merely because a party was breaking up, but because he suddenly realized that two persons, who cared a great deal for each other, wanted and needed to be by themselves. She did not automatically connect Odile St. Amant with this luncheon; in reporting Amélie Lalande's telephone conversation to his niece, Foxworth had merely said that both Mrs. Lalande's daughters and her son-in-law had engagements for that noon, and Ruth had more or less taken it for granted that they were all lunching together. Even if she had identified the studio group, she would have given this no special thought; the casual information that Sabin had once been Odile's suitor had been followed by the suggestion that he might now become her own; nothing had given her the idea that he was a one-woman man, or that Odile was the type of wife who permitted attentions from anyone except her husband. Indeed, in the latter case, Ruth would have dismissed the idea of such a possibility almost indignantly. The same delicacy which precluded her from a deliberate attempt to draw mental conclusions also prevented her from asking any questions, and no apt comment came quickly to her mind. But Aldridge did not permit the pause to become awkward, or even marked. Only a moment elapsed before he himself picked up the thread of conversation.

"Besides, I was really looking for an excuse to prolong the cocktail hour," he said easily. "As I thought the matter over, I didn't believe we'd have enough time to map out the program we spoke of—at least, if we were to have any left over for other subjects. And I wanted to talk to you about all sorts of things."

"For instance?" Ruth inquired, sitting down on the sofa and lighting a cigarette.

"Well, in the first place, I'd like to ask a number of leading questions. You were given a comprehensive, if somewhat misleading, dossier on me. I wasn't told anything about you except that you were Orson Foxworth's niece and—"

"And that he'd appreciate it if you'd look after me during Carnival?"

"Something of the sort," Aldridge admitted imperturbably.

"Weren't you afraid of such a blind date?"

"On the contrary. What could be more appropriate for an explorer? Isn't he always deliberately seeking the unknown? And, believe it or not, he has relatively few disappointments."

"This might have been one of them."

"Not a chance. I knew that whatever else she was, no niece of Orson Foxworth's would be dull company. And I happen to be one of those men, theoretically non-existent, whose main requirement in a woman is that she should have something between the ears. Of course, if russet curls are added to her equipment, it's all to the good. And I took that pleasant possibility into consideration also. After all, family resemblances aren't, as a rule, wholly mental."

"So you think we're alike?"

"Engagingly so, in some respects. The gray matter and its auburn camouflage both came up to expectations. But, if you'll permit me to say so, on such short acquaintance, there are some other qualities that far exceed these—a somewhat different and decidedly higher set of standards, for instance. I wouldn't mention that if I didn't know your uncle would admit the same thing, not only freely, but proudly. He can't be bothered with too many scruples—never would have got where he is today if he had been, either."

"And is that the only difference between us?"

"By no means. Again you may think I'm rather rushing the season, but I haven't been able to help noticing that you're not built like him physically, any more than you are ethically."

He looked at her with the same merry appreciation as when he had paid her his first compliment, the evening before, and though the quick color came into her face again, she found herself involuntarily making a pleasant comparison. *I'm glad he thinks I have a good figure,* she told herself,

88

*just as I'm glad he thinks I have a good mind and good
principles. His admiration wouldn't be complete unless he
did—something would be lacking in his tribute to me, coming
from a young man to a young woman. I'm glad it is complete—it means a great deal to me that he feels that way.
But if Léonce St. Amant had said what Russell Aldridge
did, it would have sounded offensive; if Léonce had looked
at me as Russell did, I'd have felt ashamed.* Ruth could not
guess that, almost at this same moment, Odile St. Amant
was whispering wretchedly to Sabin Duplessis, "I couldn't bear to
see him look at her as if—well, as if she didn't have any
clothes on, and as if he thought the less she wore, the more
beautiful she was. That's the way Léonce does look at a
woman, Sabin . . . ."

Downes, the butler, entered the room with a well-laden
tray and set it down in front of Ruth, moving the camellias
slightly in order to make room for it. Then, after putting
more wood on the cheerful fire, and turning on a few
well-shaded lamps, he withdrew as quickly as he had come
in. Ruth lifted the cocktail mixer.

"These seem to be Dry Martinis. Would you rather have
something else?"

"Heaven forbid! Downes makes the best Dry Martinis in
New Orleans, and for that I'm ready to forgive your uncle
for keeping a stiff old English butler instead of a sociable
Negro houseman. I hope you don't appreciate as fully as I do
the drinks he learned to make during his novitiate at New-
port and Palm Beach, because all these expressions of opinion have delayed the recital of your life history."

"There really isn't much to tell you. Of course, you know
that my uncle isn't a native Orleanian, that he came here
from a little midwestern town, with hardly a cent in his
pockets, when he was just a boy. My mother, Muriel
Foxworth, was his only sister. She was ambitious too, and she
must have been very pretty—in fact, she still is. Anyway, 'she
married very well,' in the usual sense of the word."

"Meaning the most outstanding citizen in the little mid-
western town?"

"Yes."

"And eventually his appreciative fellow-citizens sent him to
represent them in Congress?"

"No. He died, leaving my mother extremely well off, while
she was still very young and attractive. Just as Mrs. Lalande's
husband left her. Only the rest of the story is different."

"I'd especially like to hear that part."

"She went to Washington by herself. At least, she took me

along, but I wasn't old enough to be much of an impediment. Haven't you learned, somewhere in the course of your vast research, that heading for Washington is a favorite pastime of rich, mid-western widows? It's a happy hunting ground for them. They really have much more scope than Congressmen's wives."

"Yes, I can see that they might have."

"You mustn't think I'm speaking disrespectfully of my mother, Russ. I admire her very much. But it's just as you said about my uncle—if she hadn't had lots of—initiative, she wouldn't be where she is today and she'd tell you the same thing herself. She's very proud of what she's made of her life and the way she's done it."

"Don't worry. I understand all that. So your mother—"

"My mother married again before I was five years old. My stepfather's in the Foreign Service. Of course, that means we've lived abroad a great deal. But Father came from Fairfax County, just over the District Line, and he's always kept up 'Tradition,' the old family place. He and Mother are living there now. It's within easy commuting distance of Washington, and, at present, he's attached to the State Department."

"You've left out his name, somewhere along the way."

"I didn't intend to, because I'm very proud of it. I just hadn't got to it yet, that's all. His name's Richard Huntington."

"You don't mean the Assistant Secretary of State?"

"Yes, I do."

"Well, that's New Orleans for you! To gloat over the fact that you're Orson Foxworth's niece, and never mention that you're Richard Huntington's stepdaughter!"

"I wondered myself why nobody spoke about it. He's a wonderful person, Russ."

"I'll say he is, from all I hear of him. If we only had more men like him in public life, the national picture would be a different one. So that's where—"

So that's where you got your standards—from this stepfather of yours who belongs to the landed gentry of Virginia, and who's a great scholar and a great statesman. Who seems like your own father because you've never known any other and who's brought you up like his own daughter because he never had any. Well, no wonder you seem more like his daughter than you do like your uncle's niece, in some ways. No wonder you speak of him with more affection and more respect than you do of your mother .... These, Ruth felt sure, were Aldridge's unspoken thoughts, and with the con-

90

viction came a guilty sense of having been disloyal to her own kith and kin. She interrupted hurriedly.

"He's wonderful, but he's simple, almost severe, in his tastes, and do you know, really shy, inside? He'd much rather have gone on living quietly at 'Tradition,' with horses and dogs and books, and his county neighbors for company, than to have entered public life. It was a real sacrifice for him to do that. But he honestly felt it was the way he could serve his country best. And when he fell in love with my mother, naturally he wanted her to have the kind of life she craved, he wanted her to be happy. She has been too. She's loved every moment she's spent in Washington and London and Paris. Some of father's other posts—the out-of-the-way places —didn't appeal to her so much, though he and I both loved them; and she began to be afraid he might turn me into a bookworm, that I might be a recluse by preference eventually, like him. We both told her not to worry, that there wasn't any danger, but she did. So I gave up college and came out, in Washington, to please her. She wants me to 'advance' too, and she doesn't think I have much 'initiative.' You know how some people are—they always feel they have to do things for other people's good, no matter what happens to the other people in the process!"

"I do indeed. Especially women. That's one of the reasons I'm still single."

"Well, I have to admit that I did have a grand whirl," Ruth went on, without commenting on his final remark. "But none of my rushes turned into romances, and then she began to worry about *that*! So she wrote to Uncle, telling him how concerned she was about me, and he cabled back that I'd better meet him here for Carnival. So, here I am. And that's all."

"Oh, no, it isn't! But it'll do very well for a starter. And, incidentally, I'd like to finish the sentence I'd just begun when you interrupted me. I'm a little afraid, from the way you've talked since, that you were mistaken about what I was going to say next, just as I was mistaken about the assembly line curls. I started to make the sage remark, 'So that's where your uncle's close connection with our Embassy in Honduras comes in—through his brother-in-law.' " Mentally, Aldridge added, *and that's Huntington's only weakness, from what I hear. He can't say no to anything his relatives and friends want. And he's a man of such integrity himself that he's slow to suspect double-dealing in others.* This time Ruth, slightly startled because he had divined her previous surmise, made a conscious effort not to guess what was passing in his mind,

91

and he went on, "Not that it matters. Would you give me still another cocktail? I think they're even better than usual this evening. Thanks . . . . Well, about that program of ours— I'm afraid there isn't enough of a week end left now to make the trip worthwhile, but how about trying to go down to Lacombe next Friday? Since I've found out that you like the country so much . . . ."

Downes came in again, coughing a little behind his hand, put more wood on the fire, turned on a few more lights and, before picking up the cocktail tray, paused in front of Ruth.

"I beg your pardon, miss," he said politely. "But Mr. Foxworth asked me to tell you that he has retired for the night, completely exhausted. He has been suffering from a severe headache all day and he found the meeting this afternoon extremely taxing."

"Oh, I'm terribly sorry! I'll go to his room right away and see if there isn't something I can do for him! You'll excuse me, won't you, Russ?"

"Of course. Or rather, I must ask you to excuse *me*. I've stayed on and on. I didn't mean to wear out my welcome like this, but—"

Respectfully, Downes raised an objecting hand. "If you please, miss. If you please, sir. Mr. Foxworth did not wish to discuss his indisposition. That is why he did not come into the library himself. And he feels that complete rest will be the best remedy for him. He asked me to say that he was not to be disturbed on any account. On the other hand, he thought that, perhaps, since he couldn't offer any special entertainment for the evening . . . . Shall I bring some fresh cocktails, miss? And will you be dining at home with—er—guests?"

"You will stay, won't you, Russ? It's been so pleasant—"

"I'll say it has. But if you're really at loose ends, wouldn't you come out and have dinner with me? You've been in the house all day, haven't you? I'm sure, by this time, you must need air and exercise."

"It sounds very nice. But—"

"But what? We'll walk over to the Court of the Two Sisters and have dinner. Then, we'll go over to Stormy's place and dance for a while. Afterwards, we'll do whatever the occasion offers. Run along and powder your nose, like a good girl—you don't need to dress for this sort of an outing. I'll meet you downstairs in five minutes."

Five hours later they were seated at one of the small

modernistic tables in the Café du Monde at the old French Market, companionably dunking hot, sugared doughnuts in steaming coffee. Russ had tried to find two vacant stools at the square marble counter in the center of the room, where truck drivers, train crews, and revelers like themselves were congenially foregathered. But the shifting crowd of customers had nowhere left two adjoining places, so they went to a corner table, where a white-jacketed waiter took their order.

"Do you know, I like this better than any place we've been yet," Ruth observed thoughtfully, as she licked sugar off her fingers. "I love to dance, and when Uncle said you were a fast man with a samba, he didn't begin to do you justice. But after all, night clubs are pretty much the same whatever part of the country you're in, and you can always find a good floor and good music. This Café du Monde couldn't be anywhere except in New Orleans, like Antoine's and Mardi Gras. And it isn't only unique. It's—it's *real*. Not like those so-called 'quaint' tea shoppes for lady tourists—oh, you know what I mean!"

"Yes, I do."

"Besides," Ruth went on, dunking again. "I like the feeling of living in day-before-yesterday and day-after-tomorrow at the same time. Nothing could be more modern than those neon signs just outside on Decatur Street, or the traffic tearing past between us and Jackson Square. But the square itself must look exactly the same tonight as it did a hundred years ago and, while we were passing it, I could imagine all sorts of ghosts wandering around, under the palm trees."

"Sure that wasn't because an old crescent moon was just spilling silver on the Cathedral spires when we came by? Moonlight can play queer tricks on almost anyone who's in a receptive mood."

"Yes, but after all, this wouldn't be the first time the moon got in my eyes. It's only that I never felt this way about a place before. I could just see those old-time French brides getting off a sailing ship with their little dowry trunks and walking across the square, and the Ursuline nuns shepherding them along, and all the rest of it."

"You'll have my fish creeping in a minute, and that's going some for an archeologist who's always laughed at ghost stories. But, speaking of apparitions, look who's here! You remember Joe Racina, don't you, Ruth?"

She nodded, though as a matter of fact, she would not have instantly recognized the tall man who was now charging in their direction, after pausing a moment in the doorway for a swift survey of the motley crowd in the café. She had caught only a glimpse of him the night before, and then he had been seated at a table, leaning forward over his folded arms, and grinning in appreciation of the story his publisher was telling. Now she saw that he was built on much longer lines than she had thought, and his manner, instead of being relaxed and merry, was purposeful, almost grim. He wore a thin overcoat with an upturned collar and a dilapidated hat slanted low over his forehead. As he approached the corner where Ruth and Aldridge were sitting, he pulled off his hat, revealing a keen sallow face and searching black eyes with dark circles underneath them.

"Don't get up," he said with friendly abruptness. "Hiya, Russ. Had an idea I'd find you and Miss Avery here. Hiya, Miss Avery. Glad to get to meet you. Of course, I've known you by sight for a long time, but naturally you wouldn't have known me from Adam if I hadn't been pointed out to you last night as the local boy who made good. I never caught up with your crowd in Washington." Momentarily his somber face lighted, and Ruth saw that when this happened, it was singularly attractive. "Mind if I join you?" he inquired.

"Of course not," Ruth said pleasantly, while Aldridge murmured something civil, though less cordial, under his breath.

"Coffee for me—no doughnuts," Joe instructed a passing waiter, lowering himself sectionally into one of the tubular-legged chairs. He turned down the collar of his overcoat and threw it open. Then he fumbled for a cigarette and flipped flame from a small lighter. "Now that I have met you, Miss Avery, I wish I could take time to make a good impression, because I came here on purpose to ask a favor of you. Of course, I ought to do it very tactfully and delicately. But in the first place I wouldn't know how and in the second place I'm in too much of a hurry."

Ruth laughed. *Here's another man I can't help liking right off*, she told herself. *That makes two in two days, so I'm doing pretty well in New Orleans.* Aloud, she said, "It doesn't necessarily take much time to make an impression, does it? Anyway, I'd be glad to have you tell me what I can do for you."

"You can tell me, if you have any idea, where I can find your uncle."

"Why, that's not much of a favor to ask! It's easy enough to tell you where he is—at home, in bed. But that isn't saying you could get to him. I don't believe he'd see the President himself at this time of night."

"Five will get you forty of my own personal sweat-stained dollars he's not at home and hasn't been for the last four hours at least."

"You'd be betting against a cinch this time, Joe," Aldridge assured him. "Mr. Foxworth came home around seven, and sent in word to the library that he was completely bushed, that he was off to bed, and that he didn't want to be disturbed by anyone for any reason. That's how I happened to have the great good luck of getting Miss Avery to do the town with me. We'd been having cocktails, and when this message came in, I suggested—"

"Orson Foxworth bushed?" interrupted Joe derisively. "The answer to that is quote nuts exclamation point unquote."

"But it's the truth, Mr. Racina."

"My dear young lady, I know perfectly well you think it's the truth. You couldn't lie if you tried, even if you have been raised in topflight diplomatic circles. I don't know you, but I do know your type. That's why I tried to get hold of you when I couldn't reach the boss man. I thought you might know something and that if you did you might tell me what it was, if I could convince you there was some good reason why I should find out. And believe me, there is. So, when the butler reluctantly informed me, under pressure, that you were out with the Blond Beast here, I figured you'd wind up at the French Market sometime during the night. I've been dodging in and out of this place and the Morning Call for the last hour or so."

His tone and manner had become increasingly earnest. Ruth found his urgency contagious. Aldridge, less susceptible to swift impressions, asked a cautious question.

"Do you mind telling us what the good reason is?" he inquired.

"No. At least, I don't mind telling you enough so that you won't think I'm reverting to type, trying to follow up something that's half-hint and half-hunch, like any cub reporter. But, as I told you in the beginning, I'm in a hurry. And besides, I wouldn't say this was the best place for a confidential talk."

He looked over his shoulder at some fishermen who had just come in, and who showed signs of choosing an adjacent table, hitherto vacant. But they finally wedged their way to the central counter, and no one else moved forward.

"You know that *This Month* has a mania for sending me off to write pieces about out-of-the-way places, when I'd much rather stay in New Orleans," Joe began, reassured. "But I can use the money, and afterwards Brooks and Bernstein publish those pieces in books, which bring in money that I can also use. So I keep on going. That's by way of bringing out that I've knocked around Central America quite a bit."

"I ought to know," Aldridge said rather dryly. "I've bumped into you myself enough times down there and I've even read some of the pieces."

"All right, all right. I'm talking to Miss Avery, anyway. She may not believe it, but I've made lots of friends in those countries. One of them is a fellow named Pepe Villanova, who lives in Llorando. Two-three weeks back, I got a letter from him, asking me to let him know anything I could about certain things that seemed to be in the making."

"What kind of things?" Aldridge inquired warily, looking around in his turn. "I wish you'd be a little more definite."

"If Orson Foxworth is at home—and remember, I'm betting he isn't—there'd be no point in giving you a blueprint on what's worrying Pepe. Of course, if he isn't . . . ."

"That's easily settled," Russ interrupted. "And you've got a bet, *compadre*. Ruth and I were going to call it a night, anyway, when we finished our second cup of coffee and our third doughnut. Then you turned up. If it's all right with her, come along with us now. When we get to 784 Toulouse, she can slip up to her uncle's room. She'll come down and tell us that he's there. Then you'll pay over forty bucks, make an apology of sorts, and go home. All right with you, Ruth?"

"Of course it's all right for Mr. Racina to go home with us. But suppose he won't believe me when I tell him Uncle's sound asleep in bed?"

"Don't you fret about that," Joe said easily. "You couldn't lie to me; not and get away with it." Joe rose, giving the same impression of doing so sectionally as when he had lowered himself into his tubular-legged chair. "Besides," he added, jamming on his hat and turning up the collar of his overcoat, "you wouldn't, as I said before. You'd lie to save someone possible embarrassment, like you did when you pretended to recognize me. But not for forty bucks. Let's go."

The pleasant tranquillity of a well-ordered establishment, prepared for the reception of late comers, pervaded the house on Toulouse Street when Ruth opened the door with her latchkey. The shaded lamps still shed a soft light over their surroundings and the remains of the fire still glowed on the library hearth. Whiskey and soda were set out on one side of the low table adorned by the camellias, and a plate of sandwiches on the other. Ruth removed the damp napkin which had been carefully folded over these and laid her wrap over the back of the sofa.

"Make yourselves comfortable, won't you?" she said hospitably. "I won't be gone more than a few minutes. But meanwhile, perhaps you'd build up the fire and pour yourselves some drinks."

She was gone, her slippers tapping quickly up the stairway. Then the house was quiet again. Aldridge poked the embers, and laid more wood over them. It kindled briskly with a crackling sound which somehow seemed very cheerful. Joe poured Bourbon and siphoned soda into one of the glasses. The gurgle of the whiskey, the hiss of the soda were also pleasantly suggestive of welcome. He paused before filling the second glass.

"Bourbon for you too?"

"No, make mine Scotch. Half and half."

Joe followed instructions with meticulous care. Then, with his characteristic gesture, he fumbled for a cigarette and set his lighter into action before walking over to the fire and leaning against the mantel. Aldridge wandered up and down the room, here and there inspecting a book or a picture with special appreciation. The quiet was companionable. Joe's cigarette was hardly more than a butt and neither man had spoken when the light tapping sounded again on the stairs. The footsteps were even quicker than before and almost instantly Ruth flung open the portieres.

"Uncle isn't in this room," she said breathlessly. Though her voice betrayed more bewilderment than fright, she was unquestionably startled. Joe threw the butt of his cigarette into the fireplace and walked across the room again.

"I told you that's how it would be," he said quietly. "Also that you wouldn't lie about it. Don't worry. He'll be all right. Only . . . ."

"Only you want your five dollars," grinned Russ Aldridge, extracting a bill from his wallet. "A bet's a bet. Here you are, Lucky."

"No, that wasn't what I was thinking of," said Joe, pocketing the bill absently. "What I was getting at was that now it's more important than ever to find out what really is going on. Sure you haven't any idea where your uncle might be, Miss Avery?"

"No, I haven't. And really, if I had, I don't think I would tell. After all, Mr. Racina . . . ."

"Joe, to you."

". . . . is it any business of yours what my uncle is doing?"

"So far as I'm concerned, it doesn't interest me. But Pepe Villanova's a good egg, and I owe him a day in harvest for some favors he's done me."

"And how would Mr. Foxworth's whereabouts concern him?" Aldridge demanded.

"Wouldn't it simplify things if we all sat down, and Mr. Racina told us what this is all about? I can't help worrying. This isn't like Uncle. He's the most direct person in the world."

"Believe me, it's nothing to worry about. I'll give you a short rundown on it, if you'd like. And if you don't mind, I'd rather stand. I think better on my feet." He took a pull at his drink and fumbled out a fresh cigarette. "I can keep this from being an eight-installment serial if you'll sort of take my word for some of these things, without asking me how I know them. Not that I couldn't answer. But it would take hours."

Russ Aldridge looked questioningly at Ruth. She nodded.

"I'm going to stay up now anyway, till Uncle gets back," she said, crossing to one of the fireplace settees and settling herself comfortably.

"Well, your uncle's Blue Fleet has been trying to take over the Trans-Caribbean Fruit and Steamship Company," Joe began.

"That's a secret everybody's in on," interrupted Aldridge. "Why, there's been talk about that ever since the Maritime Commission turned back the fruit ships to their owners after the war."

"But T. C. has been—well, let's say coy. And with the in they have down yonder, they can afford to hold up anybody that wants to buy them. They've got the administration down in Llorando sewed up, but good."

"So?" prompted Aldridge.

"So the answer would be to put some other administration into the palace at Llorando, and it wouldn't be the first time Orson Foxworth had a hand in something like that."

"Don't forget we're talking about tonight."

"I'm coming to that. Dutch Schaefer is in town. Ever hear of him, either of you?"

Both shook their heads in denial.

"Quite a character. Sabin knows him. They were in ATC together. Used to run into each other at Karachi one week and maybe in Reykjavik the next. Dutch had an idea about buying surplus army transport planes after the war and selling 'em where he could get a good price for them, with another good price for arming them, too. Wanted Sabin to

98

go in with him and make a pile of dough. There's been some of that going on, anyway. The FBI arrested a couple of fliers in Miami not long ago .... Said they were flying just such a deal to Haiti or somewhere. I had a hunch Dutch might have been in on that one."

"And you think Mr. Foxworth could be mixed up in something like that?"

"Hell, no! Not directly. But if you think he'd be above using somebody like Dutch ...." He turned quickly and almost apologetically to Ruth. "You understand there's nothing personal in this, don't you?"

"I'm afraid I don't understand any of it very well, so far. Do you think my uncle is with this man now, and is trying to keep it a secret?"

"Probably not. But I do know Dutch is in town. I saw him duck into the Blue Fleet building this morning, and got to him before he could get an elevator, but he wasn't talking. Just the same, I had this letter from Pepe Villanova, and all of a sudden both your uncle and Dutch Schaefer are here at once. And so I went around to a certain furniture store on Poydras Street, where most of the Tropical Tramps hang out, figuring I'd catch Dutch there and buy him a couple of drinks, and he'd come through. And, believe it or not, none of the gang so much as knew Dutch was in New Orleans."

"And that all adds up to exactly what?"

"Any time Dutch Schaefer is keeping himself hidden out so that nobody, even at Izzy's, knows he's around, there's a big hen on. That's why I looked up Diego Gonzalez—he's in the sisal import racket; any time anybody in Llorando has a headache Diego knows it before they've sent for aspirin. And Diego's not to be found anywhere. Neither are a couple of other parties. And by that time I decide I'd better ask Orson Foxworth himself what the score is. He's a straight shooter, and I think he'd trust me to keep my nose clean. And by gollies, I'm told he's retired for the night and can't be disturbed."

Joe shook his head as if in wonderment.

"Dutch Schaefer, Diego Gonzalez, Jerry Coleman and certain others all in New Orleans together, all very much not in evidence anywhere, and I'm supposed to believe that Orson Foxworth, who has been trying to take over Trans-Caribbean, has peacefully gone to bed at eight P.M., and doesn't want to be disturbed. Why, a child of six would know better! And if O. F. of Blue Fleet has gone to all this much trouble to provide an alibi for where he's been or whatever he's doing tonight, then it's a cinch the chips are down."

Ruth leaned forward, clasping and unclasping her hands a little nervously. "And this means he's doing something—well, almost dishonorable?" she asked.

"Dishonorable? Certainly not," Joe answered decisively. "As I said before, he shoots square—even if he isn't—well—squeamish in going after what he's made up his mind to get. But he'd be a fool—and he's certainly not that—to let anybody link him up with whatever Dutch might pull on his end of the deal. And, as I also said before, my only interest in it is in letting Pepe know what's in the wind. I owe him that much."

"But what is in the wind?"

"I couldn't say, yet. But something is, and it will be pulled off soon. So would you mind very much if I got off a cable to Pepe over your phone? . . . I know that sounds like a dopey question; but look at it this way. I can leave here and get off a cable from the nearest pay telephone. If I do it from your house, you can hear every word I'm sending, and you can tell your uncle about it later, if you care to."

"Well, I rather think I shall," she said thoughtfully. "But, of course, you're more than welcome to use the telephone. It's right outside, in the hall."

Joe reached to lift the telephone from its cradle and, as he did so, its bell shrilled out a summons that was startling in its abruptness. Almost mechanically he answered. Ruth and Aldridge had come into the hall at the ring.

"I'm sorry, he's not in," they heard Joe say. "No . . . . I don't believe he said when . . . . No, this is Joe Racina, Mrs. Lalande . . . Please, Mrs. Lalande, it's hard for me to understand . . . . Oh, good God! . . . . Please, Mrs. Lalande! *Please!* . . . . Have you sent for Vance Perrault? . . . . Oh, I know how all of you must feel, but it won't do any good to take on . . . . Did you say it was Tossie? . . . . No, Mr. Foxworth didn't leave word where he could be reached, but I'll tell Miss Avery . . . . Can you read me the note? . . . . Yes—yes—oh, my God! . . . . I'll come right up. I don't suppose there's anything I can do . . . . No, no. I'll take care of that. I'll see you as soon as I can get out there."

He cradled the telephone and turned to Ruth.

"I've got some pretty grim news," he said. "No—not about your uncle. Odile St. Amant is dead."

"Dead!" Ruth and Aldridge exclaimed together in horror.

"Yes. She's shot herself."

"Oh, no! Why, only last night—"

"I know. But here's what happened, as nearly as I can

100

make out from what Mrs. Lalande was saying, very hysterically: Odile collapsed late this afternoon. Vance Perrault was called and gave her a sedative, saying she mustn't be disturbed by anyone. But he went back to check on her condition, around ten, and reported that it was satisfactory. However, Tossie, her old mammy, kept right on worrying, and a little while ago she crept into the room. There was Odile, shot through the heart and lying on the floor in a pool of blood. The pistol was on the floor beside her. And now a note's been found, propped up against the lamp on the bedside table."

"A note! What kind of a note?"

"Only a few words, scrawled in Odile's shaking hand. It said, 'Darling—I have tried to be a good daughter and a good wife, but I can't take this any longer. I love you. Odile.' "

7

How the police came to the Lalandes' house at one-thirty in the morning—

January 4, 1948

"AMÉLIE! I beg of you! You must make more of an effort to control yourself. Any moment now—"

Sobbing more and more convulsively, Amélie Lalande slipped further down among the great brocaded cushions of her sofa and buried her face in one of them. Vance Perrault, who, for some moments, had been patiently trying to calm her, pressed his lips together and shook his head. In spite of his concern for her, he could not suppress the thought that she embodied a strange medley of contradictions. He had often said she was the only woman he knew to whom tears were actually becoming, and hitherto the remark had been meant as a compliment. Now the contrast between the abandonment of her behavior and the elegance of her accoutrements seemed to him almost grotesque. The suppleness of her figure permitted her to fling herself about without loss of grace; in fact, Perrault had never seen this shown to better advantage than at the moment. The sculptured lines of her purple velvet robe suggested a hostess dress, selected to impress privileged guests, rather than a negligee flung over a nightgown in a dreadful emergency. Its color, as well as its cut, was more indicative of regality than of mourning; moreover, it enhanced the luster of the wearer's neck and arms. Even Amélie's beautiful blond braids and ringlets showed no signs of dishevelment. Tossie, who now knelt beside her, endeavoring to press a handkerchief, drenched in eau de cologne, against her temples, was an accomplished hairdresser and, as far as appearances went, her mistress might have just come from the skillful hands of this faithful coiffeuse. Her face, to be sure, was hidden at the moment;

102

but Perrault could have sworn that, unless it had taken on an appealing degree of pallor, this too would be unmarred.

He found the sight of Caresse infinitely more affecting. She had on the red wool dress which she had worn for her broadcast and her drive in the country, and, in a grief-stricken house, it seemed glaringly inappropriate. Apparently, she had been wearing it when she rushed off to bed, almost immediately after reaching home, and had snatched it up hastily, when she was called, because it was the nearest thing at hand; indeed, Perrault recalled seeing it flung down on a slipper chair, when he had gone to her room to examine her injuries. It was beautifully cut, as all her clothes were; however, it had been torn and stained in her motor accident, and it had received no attention since. Her hair revealed the same negligence; the page boy bob, which was so becoming to her when it was smooth and shining, obviously had not been combed for hours. The girl was standing with her back to the room, by a long window; one hand was laid lightly against its draperies, as if she were on the point of drawing them further back; but she had not stirred since Perrault came into the room. Her slender form, silhouetted against the cold glass, was almost uncannily motionless. She had not spoken either. Finally her silence and her immobility became unbearable. Perrault felt impelled to put an end to them.

"Caresse, please come and see if you can't comfort your mother. As I started to say, the police will be coming any moment now and—"

"Dear God, the police!" wailed Amélie. Momentarily, she raised her head, and Perrault saw that, as he expected, her face was completely unravaged, though tears were streaming down her cheeks. "Why, in the name of heaven, are the police coming here? Haven't we enough to bear without that? Oh, my precious Odile, my sweet . . . ." The rest of her words were muffled, for she buried her face in the pillow again. Caresse had still neither stirred nor spoken. But Léonce, who had been prowling sullenly around the dimly lighted room, came to an almost abrupt stop beside the center table and rapped out an angry question.

"Have you actually sent for the police already?"

"Of course. I tried to explain to your mother-in-law, though she wouldn't listen to me, that I had no option in the matter. You don't need any such explanation. You know perfectly well that, as soon as I found Odile was dead, I had to notify the police, since, obviously, she had not died a natural death. It's not only a question of law. It's a question of ethics."

"And with the police will come the reporters, I suppose," Léonce growled, still more angrily. "Couldn't you have forgotten your damn code of ethics for once, and spared us all the ghastly notoriety that'll mean? I suppose not. I suppose we've got to be smeared by every filthy scandal sheet in the country now. And all so you can have the satisfaction of saying, 'Lord, what an honorable guy I am! Even if I drag my best friends through the mud, I won't sacrifice my scruples!' If you ask me, I'd say you're—"

"But I didn't ask you, Léonce. It's a matter of complete indifference to me, what you think. I'm only concerned because I can't spare Caresse and her mother this added anguish. However, I'll shield them as much as I can. I'll—"

"How can you talk about sparing us or even shielding us, Vance, when you've already called the police? Just as Léonce says, this is simply too much to bear! It's too dreadful! It's too hideous! It's—"

Amélie's fresh outburst of stormy grief was punctuated by the sound of muted chimes. Caresse at last turned from the window.

"The police are here," she said coldly. "Go to the door, Tossie."

Tossie tucked the wet handkerchief under the nearest pillow, wiped her nose with the back of her hand, and smoothing the purple negligee into still more becoming folds, struggled painfully up from her knees. But she showed no disposition to hurry. The muted chimes sounded again before she had shuffled halfway across the room.

"I told you to go to the door, Tossie," Caresse repeated.

"Ah'se a-gwine, Miss Caresse, fas' as ever Ah kin."

Still sniffling and shuffling, she disappeared through the portieres. A moment later the front door opened and closed, and the murmur of unfamiliar voices filled the hallway. Then five or six strangers shouldered their way awkwardly into the room, in the wake of a dapper little man who wore eyeglasses and carried a black medical kitbag. While the others remained unobtrusively in the background, this newcomer advanced with some sprightliness and greeted his fellow practitioner in a chirping voice.

"Evening, Perrault. Don't know whether you remember me. Altgeld, assistant coroner."

"Yes, of course," Perrault replied courteously, holding out his hand. "I've seen you at any number of Parish meetings. Doctor Altgeld, Mrs. Lalande—Miss Lalande—Mr. St Amant."

Even the sprightly little man could hardly express pleasure

104

over a meeting which took place under such circumstances; but he nodded, in turn, towards the sofa, the window, and the center table, eliciting no response from any of these quarters. Then, motioning in the general direction of the men who had accompanied him, he introduced the two who came forward to Doctor Perrault.

"This is Detective Captain Theophile Murphy," he said, indicating the taller and heavier of the pair. "And this," he added, presenting a stocky, sallow man, "is Captain Bonham of the Fingerprint Bureau. The other boys—well, they're on my staff." He made a vague gesture in the direction of the men who still remained in the background, and afterwards glanced in some embarrassment towards the purple-clad figure reclining, with hidden face, on the sofa. "Dreadful, dreadful," he murmured, lowering his chirp to a whisper. "But these things do happen, more's the pity."

The note of false cheer trailed away into silence. As this became increasingly painful, Doctor Altgeld made a conscientious effort to lighten it.

"I don't suppose I really needed to introduce Captain Murphy," he said. "Most of you must have known him as 'Toe' Murphy when he was All-American tackle at LSU. Since then, he's been through the FBI School at Washington. We're all very proud to think he represents the type of police official the department now attracts to its service and—"

"Skip it, Doctor," the big detective interrupted, rather brusquely. "No need to make polite conversation. We're here on a job, and the sooner we do it and leave, the better these distressed people will like it." He turned to Perrault. "You've already made some sort of examination, I take it. Suppose you show us to the scene, Doctor."

Doctor Perrault shot a questioning glance towards Amélie, but her face was still hidden in the brocade pillow. He then looked towards Léonce.

"Well, you know Father Kessells is still in there," Léonce said.

"That's right. I'd forgotten about him for the moment . . . . Of course, the Lalandes sent for their parish priest at the same time they did for me," he told Murphy. "He's remained to say the usual prayers. But I believe he'll understand—"

"No doubt of it. So do I. I might remind you I'm a Catholic of sorts myself. Father Kessells and I won't make any trouble for each other. We both know our own jobs and stick to them."

"Then, as you've said, the sooner we get this over with—"

Motioning to the officials and their retinue that they

should follow him, Perrault led the way from the room. Once the sound of their retreating footsteps had died away in the distance, Amélie sat up, arranging the folds of her robe with one hand, while she continued to press her chiffon handkerchief against her eyes with the other.

"There are so many terrible things staring us in the face, I don't know what to do first," she said with a deep sigh, ending in a sob. "But I suppose we have to start somewhere. First of all, about the funeral—"

"Perrault can take care of that," Léonce said abruptly.

"I don't know whether he can or not. You know how Father Kessells reminded us, in that heartless way, when he came in, that if this were a suicide, we couldn't have the usual church service."

"He was just being practical. And Perrault will be practical too. He knows all the ropes—there's nothing new about any of this to him. If the meddling old busybody only hadn't called in the police! It wouldn't have hurt him a damn bit to overlook a thing like this just once. He could have explained it easily enough." Less harshly, he added, "Well, it's too late to worry about that now. And you two have got to keep up your strength, you know. I better tell Tossie to make some coffee, hadn't I? Or what about a drink?"

Caresse continued to stare out of the window without answering. Amélie began to wail again.

"Heavens above, how could I swallow a thing, with that poor child lying there and those strange men staring at her and prying around! I'll never get over it! I won't have another happy momnt as long as I live! When I think how Odile must have suffered before she could bring herself to write that note to me, it's more than I can bear!"

"To you?" Léonce interrupted sharply. "What makes you think she wrote that note to you? She always had been a good daughter; there wasn't any reason why she should feel she'd failed you. But she was worried because—oh, don't look so shocked! You know what I mean! She was writing as a sick wife to a healthy husband!"

"Odile called everyone darling," Caresse said suddenly. It was the first time she had spoken since she told Tossie to admit the police, and there was something in her voice which startled both her mother and her brother-in-law, something which had never been there before. "That note might have been meant for me. I wish to God I could be sure it wasn't!"

"Why, of course, you can be sure! There wasn't anything

about being a good sister in those lines about being a good wife and a good daughter, now was there?"

"No. But there was another line about not being able to 'take this' any longer. I'd like to know what she meant by 'this.' And I bet Léonce would too. Anyway, he'd better give some thought to it. Odile *was* a good wife—she was a damn sight too good for him. There's a lot more to being a good wife than going to bed with a man or having a baby every year. Besides, she may not have been thinking about her health at all when she wrote that she couldn't 'take this' any longer. She may have been thinking of something entirely different. That letter didn't say anything about a good husband any more than it did about a good sister."

The startling quality in her voice was now swallowed up in its scorn. Amélie, who had no idea of permitting her grief to be marred by a scene which was not of her making, and who preferred to dismiss certain insidious doubts as to the cause and character of the afternoon's motoring accident, made such a genuine effort to speak soothingly that she neglected to sob.

"For pity's sake, don't let's quarrel at a time like this! After all, we can't prove anything about the note and it's unworthy of that dear, dead girl to wrangle over it, especially while those dreadful men .... Léonce, it's all very well to talk about having Vance make the arrangements for us, but, as I reminded you before, we're helpless about making plans until we know what Father Kessells is going to decide. And anyway, Vance can't buy our mourning and until we have that, we can't appear at a funeral. You know that neither Caresse nor I ever wears black and we haven't a thing .... Then, we've got to send telegrams right away, or all our relatives will read the awful stories in the papers before they hear the truth from us and imagine .... But we can't send telegrams until we know when the funeral will be. Oh, it's all a vicious circle! And there ought to be candles lighted already and flowers on the door and .... Léonce, can't you do something about getting flowers on the door straight off?"

"At two in the morning? How many florists do you suppose are open for business now? But I reckon I'd better go to the door just the same. I don't know where the hell Tossie's keeping herself, and someone else is ringing the bell. More police, no doubt, as if we hadn't a brigade of them here already."

"It isn't more police," Caresse remarked in her new cold way. "It's Joe Racina. I saw him coming up the walk."

"Well, why didn't you say so?"

"I didn't have a chance, with you and *maman* doing so much talking. But I'd be glad to let him in myself."

In her turn, Caresse disappeared through the portieres and again there was a subdued murmur of voices in the hallway. Then Joe Racina came into the living room, with his arm around the girl's slim waist. He had known her since her childhood, and the clasp indicated nothing more than the spontaneous and sympathetic gesture of an old friend. But as Léonce looked at the two, his sullen resentment flamed into sudden fury. *She won't let me come near her with a nine-foot pole,* he raged inwardly. *She won't even speak to me. And it isn't so long ago that the only thing she minded was my technique. But it's all right for that wop to maul her over as much as he likes. Damn it, he's got a wife too. Why doesn't Caresse turn prissy on him?*

With the same unconcern for Léonce that Vance Perrault had expressed, Joe gave him a casual greeting, and drawing Caresse down with him, seated himself on the sofa between her and her mother and put his free arm around Amélie's shoulders.

"I can't begin to tell you how shocked I am, Mrs. Lalande," he said earnestly. "I know there's nothing I can say or do that will really make this any easier for you. But please believe me when I tell you I wish there were .... And that if there's the slightest thing that would help .... That's right, go ahead and cry. You'll feel better when you get all the tears out of your system."

"Oh, Joe, you *are* a dear! And it *is* a help, just having you here. I'm so thankful you've come! Everyone else has acted so unfeeling, but you—well, you seem to understand how a mother feels. Almost as if you were one. Of course, that's a silly thing to say, but—"

"If Joe really wants to help, there is something he can do," Léonce interrupted.

"Sure. What's on your mind?"

"Well, if there were any way you could keep this out of the newspapers .... After all, you must know all those chaps pretty well and they'd listen to you, if you put it to them the right way. You could get on the telephone and—"

And you could take that long lean arm of yours off from around my girl's waist, he added mentally, wishing he dared say it aloud. Meanwhile, Joe had settled back more firmly on the sofa, shaking his head.

"I wouldn't even try to shut 'those chaps' up," he said easily. "It would be about the worst possible thing I could do, from the standpoint of helping. The surest way to give

108

them the idea that there's more to this than meets the eye would be to make an effort to cover it up. It's a terribly tragic, terribly personal thing to all of us. But it's just a routine item to them. They'll give it a few lines and a small head, along with the rest of the obits; but you can rest assured there'll be no big headline. Forget it. I realize how repugnant the announcement that Odile committed suicide will be to you—I suppose there's no doubt that she did? But, by week after next, no one you care about will be giving it a thought, even if tongues do wag for a day or two now."

"Perrault could have settled the whole thing without anybody ever being the wiser," Léonce burst out angrily. "But no! That damn ethical pill peddler had to notify the police. It was his duty, and God forbid that any sense of friendship or even decency should interfere with his duty!"

Joe looked up sharply.

"Have the police been here already?" he asked.

"Been here? Hell, they're in the garden wing now, with some clown from the coroner's office and fingerprinters and God knows what all! The place is absolutely crawling with them; and Perrault is holier-than-thou-ing it all over the shop out there too."

He was still spitting out vituperation when Tossie came shuffling back, carrying a tray, and Amélie, looking more than ever like a tragedy queen, rose and went to a small coffee table. This left Joe and Caresse in sole possession of the sofa and added to the rising wrath of Léonce, though, actually, at the moment, Joe was hardly conscious of the girl at all. His active mind was preoccupied by his aversion to Léonce, whom he had always disliked, but whom he had not actually detested until that moment; by a vague sense of disaster which, for no logical reason, seemed to be taking possession of him; and by inconsequential thoughts about the unsuitability of the Lalande drawing room as a setting for tragedy. A life-size portrait of Amélie, attired in full evening dress and adorned with all her jewels, hung over the mantel, completely dominating its surroundings. Other paintings of her, at different ages and in various costumes, were lighted with equal care and displayed with almost equal prominence; and these, in turn, were supplemented by a clutter of large photographs, mostly depicting the two daughters of the house on such decorative occasions as First Communions, garden parties, weddings, and Carnival balls. The regalia which Odile had worn as Queen of the Pacifici completely filled a glass-walled cabinet; and several similar cabinets were crowded with Dresden china, Dutch silver,

109

snuff boxes, and other miscellaneous bric-a-brac. A series of antique fans, encased in frames which followed their shape, and a set of bisque figurines, representing amorous shepherds and coy shepherdesses, added to the general effect of artificiality and uselessness. Even the table at which Amélie now seated herself was a teetering affair of carved and gilded wood, its unstable top encircled by medallions painted with the simpering faces and bared bosoms of court favorites. With thankfulness, Joe bethought himself of the restful, book-lined room where he and Judith spent their free evenings, wishing that he were at home with his wife now. Then, tardily and rather remorsefully, he turned back to Caresse, only to realize that footsteps were approaching from the direction of the hallway which led to the garden wing. He withdrew his arm and rose from the couch.

"Would you rather I'd leave you folks alone till these men go?" he asked quietly. "It might be you wouldn't want any one outside of the family to know everything that could be coming up."

"Of course not!" Amélie whispered. "I'd feel much better and much—safer, somehow, if you stayed. Please don't go."

"All right, just as you say," Joe answered briefly, looking toward the official group. Doctor Altgeld, who led the way, was no longer merely fussy. There was in his bearing a sort of pompous gravity oddly at variance with his almost diminutive stature. Captain Murphy's expression, which had been one of studied friendliness, was now rather heavily impassive. And, though Doctor Perrault kept his eyes averted, and seemed to be staring fixedly at the tips of his shoes, it was obvious he was laboring under some sort of a strain. Captain Murphy's glance had passed over Joe Racina without apparent recognition, until the latter's casual, "Hiya, Toe," drew a noncommittal nod from him.

"How do you happen to be drawing cards here?" he asked. "You're not with any of the papers any more—or are you?"

"Nope," replied Joe briefly. "Friend of the family."

"Let me do the talking, then."

Joe shrugged. "Have it your own way, pal," he conceded. Then, with a startled glance at the detective, he gave a smothered exclamation, and, after hesitating for a moment, crossed the room to an obscure corner to which a rather shabby looking chair, that seemed to offer a reasonable degree of comfort, had been relegated. Settling back in this, he lighted a cigarette, prepared to withdraw as far as possible from the proceedings, while still following them attentively. Amélie continued to sit behind her elaborate silver service and, from time to time, she lifted the coffeepot, indicating her readiness to serve. But, for the most part, the gesture went unheeded.

"Father Kessells said to tell you he was going to stay where he was for the present," began Murphy, addressing no one in particular. "He'll be in a little later. Meanwhile, there are a couple of points to clear up. First off, was that Mrs. St. Amant's own gun, and if so, where did she get it?"

"As far as I know, she never had a gun in her life," Léonce replied. "Now that you mention it, it seems strange none of us thought of that."

"How about the rest of you? Did any of you ever know her to have a gun? Or see her with one?"

"Certainly not!" declared Amélie. Murphy looked inquiringly at Caresse, who shook her head. Then, as if she too preferred to withdraw from the discussion, she pulled a small straight chair up beside Joe's, and leaned over to accept a light from him.

"I don't know about other guns," Murphy went on. "But I'd take an oath she hadn't had this particular gun long . . . . Does it belong to any of you? To anyone in this room?" A chorus of denial answered him.

"Well, do any of you know who does own it?"

The plainly discernible bewilderment of Amélie, Caresse, and Léonce was eloquent and convincing. Abruptly, Murphy wheeled toward the door. "Put that down and come back here," he ordered Tossie, who had been, unobtrusively, making her way out of the room with the coffeepot. "Doctor Perrault said you had been Mrs. St. Amant's nurse, and later her maid, ever since she was born. Did you ever see her have a gun?"

Standing in the doorway, still clutching the coffeepot, her face set in its wizened, masklike lines, Tossie answered. "Never befo' dis day."

"When was the first time you saw it?"

"When Ah foun' mah po' li'l baby daid on de flo' by de window. Hit a-layin' by de side o' her."

"You never saw the gun before that time?"

"Nor neither no other one."

"You took care of Mrs. St. Amant?"

"Ah sho' did. Me an' not nobody else."

"Cleaned up her room, put away her clothes, kept everything in order and all such as that?"

"Hit's de God's own troof you's speakin'."

111

"And at no time did you ever see any gun in her room?"

"Not never at no time."

"If Mrs. St. Amant had kept a gun somewhere in her room for any length of time, even if she had tried to keep it hidden, would you have seen it or known about it, do you think?"

"Sholy. Sholy. Wa'n't no drawer nor neither nor box Ah di'n' rid up fo' de po' li'l angel."

"And you believe she never had a gun there?"

"Believe ain' nothin'. Ah knows hit."

"Okay, Auntie. And if you won't put that coffeepot down, take it wherever you were going with it. But come right back. There might be something else I'd want to ask you."

"Ah was aimin' to anyway. Ah was only gwine to git some fresh coffee. De doctuh, he got de lastes' dey is."

Rather thoughtfully Murphy watched her out of sight. Then he turned to Vance Perrault, who had indeed belatedly accepted a cup of coffee and was standing beside Amélie as he drank it. "You were her physician, and, as far as anyone knows, the last person to see Mrs. St. Amant alive," the detective went on. "That was exactly when?"

"As I told you when we were in the other room, at ten o'clock or a little after."

"Just for the record, Doctor, will you go over the details of that visit again, leaving out nothing, however trivial?"

"To give you the full story, I'll have to go back to an hour or so before noon, when I came here to the house, by appointment, to see Mrs. St. Amant about an—an affliction, an illness: to be explicit, about a palsy that was steadily growing worse. Since I was under the painful necessity of telling her that her condition was hopeless, that no cure, in the commonly accepted sense of the word, for paralysis agitans was known, I thought it might be better to tell her this in her own home, where she could have the comforting presence of her family in the event the shock of such a disclosure brought on a pronounced nervous reaction."

"And did it?"

"Not to the degree I had anticipated. The poor girl was upset, of course, and dreadfully depressed. But I did my best to encourage and reassure her. Without building up false hopes of a recovery, which would have been dishonest, to say the least, I tried to show her that, even as an invalid, many fields of pleasant and enjoyable activity would remain open to her. After some persuasion from me, she finally agreed to keep a luncheon engagement at the studio of one of her great friends, Sabin Duplessis."

"Who else was at this luncheon?"

"As to that, I couldn't say. Perhaps Mrs. Lalande—?"

"I think Russ Aldridge said something at the Blue Room last night about having lunch at Sabin's today, but I couldn't be positive," Amélie remarked. "Or maybe I should say yesterday. Anyway, it's after midnight, so this is really Sunday morning, isn't it? But everyone knows what I mean." Tossie had returned with the fresh coffee and before pouring some for herself, Amélie moved the cups aimlessly about on her tray. "I suppose there might have been others at Sabin's luncheon," she went on, thoughtlessly taking two lumps of sugar, "but Odile was in no condition to tell me about it, so I'm afraid I can't help you. However, if it's of any real importance, why not ring up Sabin?"

"That won't be necessary for the moment," Murphy decided. "Later on, if it is indicated . . . . But no matter. Suppose Doctor Perrault finishes his part of the picture we're trying to reconstruct."

"I can only tell you that sometime in the late afternoon Mrs. Lalande telephoned me, expressing great alarm about her daughter's state, and asking me to come to her as soon as possible. I did so at once. Then I learned that Odile had returned from the studio luncheon in a state of hysterical collapse."

"Who brought her home?"

"Sabin. Her host. He had to carry her into the house," Amélie replied. "The poor child couldn't walk or talk. She was trembling very violently, and crying incessantly. And any questions merely made her cry the harder. That is when I called Doctor Perrault."

"And this chap Duplessis carried her to her room?"

"Where Tossie and I undressed her and put her to bed. That's where she was when Doctor Perrault arrived."

"And then?"

"I found her completely hysterical and took measures to relieve her extreme tension," Perrault continued. "I thought perhaps an ordinary soporific would suffice, and tried to give her an amytal tablet, but she could or would not listen to me, so I finally administered an eighth-grain of morphine hypodermically. Within a few minutes that took effect, and she became quiet. Since that was the first requisite, I left without further effort to learn what might have brought on the hysterical condition, and cautioned the others in the house that no one was to enter Odile's room, that the house was to be kept completely quiet. Odile's husband was on no account to disturb her. He and Caresse had sustained some minor

113

bruises in an automobile accident of some sort. I examined these, but no treatment was necessary. Then I left, promising to return about midnight to check on Odile's condition."

"But you returned earlier than that. At ten o'clock, I think you said. Wasn't that unusual?"

"I had been called to another home in this part of the city. Besides, I felt a good deal of concern over Odile's condition. After all, I was not only her physician, but a friend who had known her from the moment I spanked her into drawing her first breath. And being in the neighborhood earlier than I had anticipated, tonight, I stopped to reassure myself that all was as well as could be expected."

"And when you arrived at ten o'clock, Mrs. St. Amant was alive?"

"Not only alive, but actually up and about. I admit I was vexed, less at her than at myself. Obviously, in her generally over-stimulated condition, the effect of the eighth-grain of morphine I had administered was much less potent than would otherwise have been the case. When I got into the room she seemed to be on the point of dressing, as if to go out. I tried to reason with her, but she grew very angry with me, which was not at all like her, but was probably part of the after-effect of the drug. She insisted she would not go back to bed, and when I told her as firmly as I could that she was very sick, and would have to do what I said if she ever expected to get well, she reminded me that I had already told her she never would get well anyway. She pleaded with me to leave her alone, but naturally that was out of the question, and when she saw I was not to be put off, she once more became very hysterical, said she had nothing left to live for, and that every one of her family and her friends, as well as she herself, would be better off it she were dead. I tried to calm her, but this only seemed to make her extreme nervousness more marked, so I administered another and somewhat stronger hypodermic. When she relapsed into drugged sleep, I left, once more emphasizing to the members of the household the importance of quiet, and directing that, under no circumstances, should she be disturbed."

"But some one did enter the room later." The statement was almost a challenge.

"A little before one o'clock, I am told."

"Can you tell us about it, Mrs. Lalande?"

Amélie put down the current coffee cup. "Only that all of us were startled by Tossie's screaming," she said, "and rushed in to find her kneeling beside—beside—oh, I can't stand this!

114

Isn't it enough the poor child's dead? Does everything about her have to be dragged about in this disgraceful way?"

"I'm afraid so. Tossie, why did you go into Miss Odile's room when the doctor had said you mustn't?"

"Wa'n't nobody takin' keer o' mah baby, mah po' li'l baby," retorted the old Negress. "Ah wa'n't gwine to wake her, not me. Ah was jus' gwine creep to de side o' de bed an' lay me down on de sof' rug, so's she'd have somebody what loved her close by. An' effen Ah'd did it soon as ever my heart tol' me to, she'd be alive dis good minute. Ah's tellin' you what God loves—de troof."

"And how did you find Mrs. St. Amant when you did go into the room?"

"De light was burnin'. How could Ah help but see de po' angel?"

"I mean, where was she and what did she look like?"

"She was a-layin' on de flo' by de window, an' de blood was all aroun'. Yes, Lawd. Mah angel honey baby done daid, an' de gun was a-layin' by de side o' her, an' she all col' an' still." A rapt expression came into the old servant's eyes, as these rolled upward behind her large-lensed glasses. "De angel o' death come into de room an' took mah baby wid him. Bless de name o' God in Heab'm. She gone to Beulah Lan' now in a gol' chariot. De po' li'l gal's body col' an' daid, but de sperrit shinin' an' bright on de yonder side o' Jordan. Do, Lawd, took keer mah baby, cuz Tossie cain' took keer o' her no mo', no mo'!"

"One other thing. Was the window you found her beside open or closed?"

"Hit was open. Ah see de shade stirrin' in de col' night wind wheah mah baby daid."

"That'll do, Auntie." Captain Murphy turned from Tossie to Léonce, who had resumed his restless pacing up and down the room, stopping every now and then to glower in the direction of the corner where Joe and Caresse still sat silently smoking. "You're familiar with this garden wing, of course, Mr. St. Amant?" the detective inquired.

"Well, naturally. It was turned over to my wife and myself when we came back from our honeymoon, and we've occupied it ever since."

"Just what do you mean by 'occupied'? Did you and your wife share a bedroom?"

"We did until fairly recently. But after she had this nervous breakdown, she imagined that she disturbed me. Since then, I've been sleeping in what was originally our private sitting room. As you must have noticed, both rooms lead off a small hall and the bath's between them."

"Yes, I did notice. Now, to get all the facts straight: the window beside which Mrs. St. Amant's body was found opens onto some sort of gallery or courtyard, I believe."

"Onto a screened-in patio that is part of a little walled garden. During warm and pleasant weather we used to eat breakfast there. Since the little garden is walled in, the patio is just as private as any other room."

"And in addition to the window, there is also a door from the bedroom to this patio, I believe."

"Yes."

"Well, so far so good. Now we come to the note Doctor Perrault told us about when we were in the bedroom. I should like to see that note, please."

Amélie gave an exclamation of surprise. "Why, it was left in the room, of course. At least, after I read it, I put it back on the nightstand beside the bed. That was where it had been propped, against the base of the reading lamp, when we .... When Tossie .... " She buried her eyes in her handkerchief. "And Doctor Perrault had said nothing must be touched," she ended in muffled tones.

"It was on the nightstand the last time I saw it too," Léonce announced.

Murphy looked inquiringly at Caresse. "I did not have it at any time," she said. "I heard Mother read it. Perhaps Tossie put it away."

"Ah ain' never touch nuthin' in de room, me," Tossie burst out vehemently.

"Well, it isn't there now. But it will turn up sooner or later, I'm sure. To whom was it addressed?"

"It was not addressed to any one by name," Caresse explained. She rose from her small straight chair and came forward, and, after a moment, Joe rose too and joined her. "It was merely headed 'Darling.' And my sister called everyone that. *Maman*, Léonce, Doctor Perrault, me—everyone was 'darling' to her."

"But the text of the note should have given some indication of the person to whom it was written."

"I feel certain it was meant for me," Amélie declared emphatically. "It was only a few words long. It said: 'Darling, I have tried to be a good daughter and a good wife, but I can't take this any longer. I love you. Odile.' That was all there was to it. And she had been a good daughter and a good wife. She was good to everyone. If ever there was an

116

angel on earth .... And to think that she was given such a heavy cross that she couldn't bear it!"

"Would you mind if I asked you to repeat what you just said? I mean your daughter's exact words. They're important. That's why we'll have to find the note. But, meanwhile, please do as I ask."

The detective's manner, like his words, was still completely courteous and impersonal. Nevertheless, Amélie looked at him as if in sudden apprehension.

"I'm afraid I don't understand. As far as I can remember, it was just as I told you. 'Darling, I have tried to be a good daughter and a good wife, but I can't take this any longer. I love you. Odile.' Only those few words. If I don't remember them exactly as they were, or if Léonce prefers to think they were addressed to him instead of me, what difference can it make now?"

"A great deal, I'm afraid."

"For that matter," Doctor Perrault interposed, "it might have been written to me. As Caresse indicated, Odile invariably addressed me as 'darling,' just as she did everyone else of whom she happened to be fond. And her statement that she couldn't take this any longer could refer only to what I had told her earlier that day, that she was doomed to be a lifelong invalid. There was no other harsh fate for her to flee from. Except for that oncoming paralysis, her life was beautiful and happy."

"You said it might have been addressed to you, likewise, didn't you?" Murphy asked directly of Caresse.

"I said she called me 'darling,' just as she did everyone else. So it might have been."

"Was there any circumstance in which both you and she were involved that might prompt her to say she 'couldn't take this any longer'? Saying that to her mother, or to her husband, or even to her physician is understandable enough, since they were all directly concerned in her illness and its effects. But how could this have included you, rather than one of the others?"

"I don't know that it did. I merely said it might have been addressed to me."

"And you didn't answer my question, either. I asked you whether there had been anything that involved both you and your sister to such an extent that she would have made it her last earthly act to tell you she couldn't take it any longer?"

"Actually, there wasn't. But she might have thought there was."

117

"Such as?"

"She might have thought her husband was paying more attention to me than he should have." Caresse still spoke with cold detachment.

Léonce glared at her. "What she means is this," he broke in hastily. "My wife was inordinately sensitive on the subject of her growing helplessness, which inevitably affected our—our—relationship. She was suspicious of every other woman to whom I spoke a pleasant word. That is why I feel sure the note was addressed to me. Undoubtedly, the conviction was implanted in her poor, sick mind by Doctor Perrault"—this with a malevolent glance at the physician—"that she would be increasingly incapable of—of—well, of living with me in the way husband and wife normally live with each other. I am convinced that was what she meant when she said there was something she couldn't take any longer."

"Perhaps Léonce is right, after all," Amélie said, with something like eagerness. "At first, I couldn't see it that way, but now I do. I merely thought that she had turned to me, her mother, because she was troubled, just as she had always done ever since she was a baby, and wanted me to forgive her for what she was about to do. But I must confess that what Léonce says sounds as if it might be the real explanation."

"Well, we'll let it go at that for the present . . . . Which of you, or how many of you, saw that note and read it?"

"I did," Léonce and Amélie said in unison.

"And how about you, Doctor?"

Doctor Perrault hesitated for a moment. "Yes, I saw the note and read it," he said with apparent reluctance. "But before you go on to any further questions about its possible meaning, let me make it plain that anything a patient says to a physician must be regarded as a confidence which he is sworn to keep."

"I understand that quite well, Doctor. My only other question—at least right now—is one you need have no scruples about. I take it you are all familiar with Mrs. St. Amant's handwriting. Could there be the slightest doubt in the mind of any of you as to whether or not she wrote that note herself?"

Again Léonce and Amélie answered almost simultaneously. But the detective's next question was addressed pointedly to Odile's mother.

"What makes you so very sure, Mrs. Lalande?"

"Don't you think I know my own child's handwriting? Why—why I've been seeing it for nearly twenty years. I taught her to write myself when she was just a tiny little girl."

"You couldn't possibly be mistaken? After all, her right hand shook very badly, according to Doctor Perrault."

"Of course, I couldn't be mistaken!" Amélie's voice had become increasingly shrill. Instead of sobbing and sighing, she was very close to shrieking. "Odile's hand did shake. But I knew exactly how she wrote every letter of the alphabet, just the same. Nobody could know her handwriting any better."

"I'll grant you that, Mrs. Lalande. I'd even grant that you knew it so well you might possibly be able to produce a pretty fair imitation of it yourself."

Amélie leaped up, screaming. "Get out of this house!" she cried shrilly. "If you haven't any respect for me, you might at least have respect for the dead. Joe—Vance—"

She turned imploringly from one to the other. To her horror, she saw that Racina's normally kind, keen face was wholly without expression. Perrault laid a steadying hand upon her arm, appalled to see that the ravages which grief had failed to make in her beauty had now been made by fury.

"Amélie, Captain Murphy didn't mean—" he managed to say.

"Never you mind what I meant or didn't mean. I'm quite capable of speaking for myself," snapped Captain Murphy. "I didn't necessarily mean that Mrs. Lalande had written that note. But I did mean, and I do mean, that the dead girl at the other end of the hall didn't write it. And while I don't yet know who did, I propose to find out. Because Odile St. Amant didn't commit suicide. She was murdered!"

8

How Captain Theophile Murphy made
an arrest before Mass on
Sunday Morning—

January 4, 1948

As Captain Murphy put it later, in describing the scene to Dan Gallian, one of his cronies at the Detective Bureau, the reaction to his announcement that Odile St. Amant had been murdered was "rugged."

"The mother—and if you ask me she's a lot better stacked than that daughter of hers—flung a sure enough hissie right then and there," he related. "Next thing you know, the old mammy is down on her knees, walling her eyes behind those big glasses till you couldn't see anything but the whites, raising her skinny old arms over her head, and knocking off the hallelujahs sixty to the acre. St. Amant was stomping and cussing and goin' on till I had more'n half a mind to take him to the bathroom and show him the goldfish. Only the daughter and this Racina character kept their heads, but the way that gal gave St. Amant the poison eye, with her face a kind of toad-belly white, I'd rather have seen her throw fits like the rest of them. Racina, of course, is still a newspaperman in his heart, and every one of those birds feels he's got to act as if he'd already seen everything at least twice, and was bored stiff with it both times. Hell, you know how they are."

"Don't I though?" agreed Dan sympathetically, biting off the end of a cigar.

"Coming back to this girl, I noticed another thing for the book—she's the kind that ordinarily would be dressed up to the nines; but not this night. It's a red dress made out of some fuzzy kind of woolen stuff. And there are spots along the front of it. Not a lot, but enough to notice. Usually that girl would sooner be caught with a live bat in her hair than with a dress that wasn't clean. More to draw her out than anything else, I ask her how come she spilled gravy on her dress; and you could have knocked me down with a sledge hammer when she says, cold as a penguin's heel, that it's not gravy, it's blood. Then she realizes what she's said, you understand, and goes on about some automobile accident that afternoon, and how she came out of it with a bump on the nose that made it bleed. 'And you're still wearing the same dress?' I ask her. 'Not still; again,' she comes back. It seems she's badly shaken up by this accident and goes right to bed when she gets in, dropping her clothes wherever she was standing when she stepped out of them. Then, when the screaming and commotion wake her up, she puts on the nearest thing that comes to hand, which is still this dress. And just between you and me and the bulletin board, Dan, I'm not overlooking the idea that there might be more blood on that dress than you'd get from a bump on the nose."

Dan nodded sagely, as Captain Murphy continued. "Well, the old doctor—Perrault, I mean—was going from one to the other, trying to get them quieted down some, and he'd no more'n bring one of them halfway out of the screaming meemies when one of the others would start a fresh one.

"Right smack in the middle of this Operation Bedlam, in walks a tall, gangling beanpole of a guy with hair that was still trying to stay red, if you know what I mean, and that was no less than Orson Foxworth, the Number One Guy of the Blue Fleet outfit. I hadn't heard any doorbell, you understand. And I pegged that right away. Ordinarily, I'd figure it was his business if he had a latchkey and what you don't talk about don't get you any kicks in the teeth, either. But here's Mister Big Shot letting himself into a house where there'd just been a murder, so naturally, I make a note to ask him how come."

"I coulda told you," Dan remarked with a wink.

"Too bad you weren't there then. Anyway, when he showed up, Mamma flung herself at him in a brand-new sample of collywobbles. This one made everything that had been shown up to that time look like a summer evening's calm. But it didn't last. She acted just like, as long as he was around, everything was bound to come all right. I didn't miss that part of it either. And so I made me another little note to see what gives. Meanwhile, Rex Bonham says he thinks there are fingerprints on the gun, but he can't be sure; and he and Doc Altgeld between them have found the fatal bullet. So I told Rex to go dusting down to his bureau and develop the fingerprints, and if any of them were plain, to bring them here; likewise to check on the landmarks of the bullet to see if it was fired from the gun. That was just for the trial, of course. There wasn't any doubt about what gun that bullet had come from, but it don't hurt to have all the loose ends tied up."

"You bet it don't," agreed Dan, puffing away at his cigar.

"By that time Doc Altgeld's boys had carried the girl's body outside in their morgue basket; and the priest who'd been saying the Prayers for the Dead had gone too, after telling me on the q.t. to pass along the word, whenever I got the chance, that if I were sure this was a murder and not a suicide there could be a real funeral with all the trimmings. He'd tried to say this himself, but none of them would give him a chance, they were taking on so, and it was almost time for him to say early Mass. I wanted to get to Mass myself; but I knew I had to keep all hands right where they were till Rex made his report; so I figured to let them whoop and holler till they got tired. It was one way to pass the time. But this Foxworth is a sharp number. Between him and Perrault, they got those lunatics quieted down. He even had Aunt Tossie back out in the kitchen hustling up another vat of coffee. It's funny about some people. They've got something everybody seems to recognize. Authority. Foxworth is like that. I could've talked myself black in the face, and they'd only flung fits faster. But he comes in there, says a half a dozen words, and they break their ankles to do what he tells 'em to. I give you my word he even defrosted that Caresse icicle. First thing you know, she was crying, quiet-like. No storm scene like her mother had put on. But when the Léonce boy walked over and tried to pat her shoulder, she froze up again, and gave him a look that would've chilled a beef. So by and by . . . ."

"Suppose we get at this thing like reasonable people," Foxworth suggested. "I mean from A to B and then from B to C and so on. As I understand it, Captain, you state, unequivocally, that Odile was murdered. Why are you so positive?"

"No powder burns," the officer replied briefly.

"And that means?"

"The gun was at least eight feet away from her when it was fired. Her arm wasn't eight feet long, so she couldn't have fired it. If the gun had been pressed up against her

122

breast the way it would have been if she had fired it, the skin around the wound would have been burned and blackened by the flash. And it wasn't. Neither was her nightdress." He turned to Doctor Perrault as if for confirmation. "Right, Doctor?"

Perrault nodded agreement, without speaking.

"But is there no other way the gun could have been set to fire? Is the possibility of accidental discharge excluded?" Foxworth persisted.

"Certainly it could have been set. But if Mrs. St. Amant had done that, she couldn't have destroyed the set-up after killing herself. No such set-up was found. The gun was on the floor close beside her body."

"You have only Tossie's word for that, I believe."

"So?"

"She was excited. In any case, she's senile. Hardly a very trustworthy witness, do you think?"

"I'm thinking, all right. It isn't along any lines of that girl's death being a suicide, though. She was murdered."

"But that note was certainly in her handwriting."

"In a handwriting that couldn't be told from hers," Murphy said firmly. "Four people, all of them in a position to know, identified it as hers. But she didn't write it."

For the first time since Foxworth's arrival, Amélie addressed the detective directly.

"I tell you again, she did. No one else could have written that note! No one!"

"Somebody else did," Murphy replied placidly. "And as neat a bit of forgery as I've ever seen. Neither her mother, her husband, her sister nor her doctor had any idea the handwriting wasn't hers, and that means that at least three of them—possibly all four—were taken in by it."

Joe Racina straightened up in his chair, as if to speak, then seemed to think better of it, fumbled out a cigarette, lit it, and subsided.

"When you say at least three of the four people you mention were taken in by what you insist was a forgery," said Foxworth, "you imply that perhaps one of the four knew it had not been written by Odile."

"I said possibly," Murphy reminded him. "Don't get the idea I'm jumping to conclusions. I'm not. But I'm not overlooking any bets, either. And it's possible any one of the four people I mentioned could have written the supposed suicide note. Which doesn't alter the fact that it was good enough to fool the other three into accepting it, without question, as genuine. Which is why I'm not particularly interested in the note, even though it seems to have disappeared. If it was that good, there wouldn't be any chance of my finding out who wrote it, and using that approach to get to who did the killing. If any of you have that note, or know where it is, you're welcome to keep it or destroy it, for all of me."

"Now look here," Léonce burst out angrily. "I'm getting a bit fed up with these insinuations. Apparently, you don't or won't realize you're in a house of mourning . . . ."

"Oh, drop it, Léonce," Doctor Perrault interrupted. "Captain Murphy has a job to do. Let me say that I don't agree with his theory that Odile was murdered, even if the absence of powder burns is still to be explained. No one knows better than I do the despair that must have taken hold of that poor girl yesterday, and how much reason she had to—to feel that she was justified in ending all the dark doubts that clouded her mind."

"Nobody knows any *better* than you do. But I know just as well."

The remark was addressed to Perrault. But, as she made it, Amélie buried her face against the rough, homespun fabric of Foxworth's coat and gave way to a feverish paroxysm of weeping.

"My baby, my poor, poor baby!" she sobbed. "When I think of what she went through and how sharply I spoke to her these last few days! Maybe that's why she did it. She might have thought none of us loved her any more, that she was only in the way . . . . Oh, I can't bear it! If I could only tell her . . . . If I could only ask her to forgive me . . . ."

"There, there, my dear," Foxworth said soothingly. "You haven't a thing to reproach yourself for. Why, just Friday night—" He checked himself, tardily conscious that his manner towards Amélie had attracted Murphy's critical attention. "We'll all feel better about this in a few days," he concluded, rather awkwardly. "Meanwhile, we mustn't lose our sense of perspective. Look, here's Tossie back again. Let's have some good hot coffee. For that matter, it isn't too soon to begin to think about breakfast. What time does Ona get here, Amélie?"

"Not until nine, on Sundays. But of course Tossie can scramble eggs and make toast right now, if anyone's hungry."

She looked inquiringly about her. Almost simultaneously, Perrault and Foxworth commended the idea, while Caresse and Joe shook their heads. Léonce, who had kept on pacing restlessly back and forth, made no direct answer to his mother-in-law's suggestion. But he slackened his pace and then halted.

"You know," he began slowly, "it just occurs to me that Odile and Tossie were quarrelling pretty violently when I came in Friday from the Blue Room. I distinctly remember hearing Tossie say something to the effect that she'd rather see Odile dead than to see a strange nurse taking care of her. If Odile was murdered . . . ."

Tossie straightened her spare frame. "Hit wa'n't me po' li'l Miss Odile was cryin' bout Friday night, nor neither lots of other nights," she charged. "An' hit wa'n't me left de blessed sweet angel lonesome an' sick whilst Ah went night-walkin' round till de po' lamb's heart busted plumb in two. No, Lawd. Not me."

She looked fixedly at Léonce and again he was aware, as he had been on Friday night, of the cold glitter of hate in the eyes behind the moonlike glasses. But this time, it did not check him. Instead, he gave a violent exclamation and made a threatening gesture. Suddenly, Caresse spoke from her corner, in that new voice of hers which had such a strange carrying quality.

"Don't be a bigger sap than you can help, Léonce," she said. "Tossie worshipped Odile, and you know it. In fact, you've complained about it ever since you came here to live."

"If you think I'm going to let her or anyone else say I drove my own wife to suicide, you're crazy," Léonce retorted furiously. But he lowered his arm and unclenched his fingers. The cold voice affected him quite as poignantly as the cold stare, though in a different way. "I tell you again I heard that old witch say she'd rather see Odile dead than see a strange nurse around her," he repeated, less furiously, but still more emphatically than before.

"Sho' Ah say dat, an' had Ah did what mah min' tol' me to do, an' stayed wid de po' grievin' chile lak Ah wanted to, she still be wid us."

"It's all right, Tossie. Everything's all right," Foxworth assured her, speaking almost as soothingly as he had in addressing Amélie. "Mr. Léonce didn't mean anything by what he said. And none of us believes you'd have harmed Miss Odile for the world . . . . This sort of bickering gets us nowhere," he went on, addressing the others as a group. "I think it was Léonce who said, a few minutes ago, that this was a house of mourning. We can't very well ask others to bear that in mind when we seem to lose sight of it ourselves."

"Good for you, Orson!" Perrault exclaimed. "And, as far as I'm concerned, I shall continue to believe Odile took her own life, until and unless it's conclusively proved that she didn't. And now, I think I'll take my leave. There isn't anything more I can do here, I've had a terrific twenty-four hours, and I've got a full schedule for tomorrow—for today, that is. When it comes to that, all of us ought to get some rest. And this applies especially to you and Caresse, Amélie."

He nodded towards the girl, who still sat on the small straight chair in the corner, and to her mother, who was again ensconced behind the coffee table. Then he started towards the door. Murphy's voice stopped him.

"Sorry, Doctor. I don't like to go against your professional advice to your patients, and as far as you're concerned, of course it's just a formality. But I'm asking everyone to stay right here until I get word from Rex Bonham. That should be fairly soon. And there are still quite a few questions to which I need answers. Because, whatever Doctor Perrault says to the contrary, Mrs. St. Amant didn't die by her own hand. Someone killed her. Quite possibly someone in this very room."

"Oh come now, Captain Murphy, that's carrying things a bit too far!" Foxworth said sharply. "You aren't talking to a lot of characters you've rounded up in a series of Tenderloin raids. And before you adopt any high-handed procedure, let me remind you that there's a difference between subjecting the usual run of police suspects to a grilling, and dealing with persons of some standing and consequence in the community."

Murphy grinned wryly.

"The next line of that routine is that if I'm not careful, you'll have me broken or get my badge. I know both verses and the chorus of that one," he said. "I haven't charged anybody with anything. But a murder's been committed, right down the hall here. Remember? It's up to me to find out who did it. And it's up to all of you to help me. Just to put it right out into the open, I'm holding all of you, for the time being, as material witnesses."

"Meaning me, too?" Joe Racina asked from his corner.

"Why not?"

"Because it would make you look pretty silly. I didn't get here till after you did, and can account for everywhere I was between ten o'clock last night and two this morning, when I did get here."

Murphy seemed to consider this briefly. "That lets you out,

126

then," he conceded. "You're not a material witness, and if you want to go, there'll be no objection."

Joe shook his head. "I just wanted to know where I stood," he said. "Mrs. Lalande asked me to stay, I haven't got a full day ahead of me, my wife has long since quit worrying about what might happen to me, and there's no telling what I might learn by keeping my ears open and my mouth shut."

"Suit yourself," Murphy told him. "As long as it's all right with Mrs. Lalande, it's all right with me, if you stay." He looked slowly from one to another in the cluttered drawing room. "You know, I haven't got Idea One as yet on who might have killed that girl, but it's not going to be too hard to get the right answer," he explained thoughtfully. "In the first place, whoever it was, he—or she—was a rank amateur. A professional wouldn't have forgotten about powder burns, after planting this as a supposed-to-be suicide. Anybody who would make a mistake like that will be bound to have made plenty of others. So this won't be much of a trick."

"Unless it turns out to be a suicide, as Doctor Perrault suggested," Foxworth countered. "Incidentally, I'm inclined to agree with him."

"That's your privilege, Mr. Foxworth. But me, I've got to stick to the facts. You know, finding out who did a killing, especially an amateur killing like this one, isn't a matter of reading up on strange poisons or analyzing cigarette ashes or looking for secret panels in the wall. It's a routine. First you list everybody that had an opportunity to do the job, then you find which one of those who could have done it had a motive for doing it. By that time, you've got your field narrowed down to where you figure out which of those who had both the opportunity and the motive was the last one to see the victim alive. Because that's who did the killing, of course."

"But look here," Perrault protested, smiling a little. "If that's what you meant when you said I was the last one to see Odile alive . . . ."

"Take it easy, Doctor," counseled Murphy. "You're only the last one we're sure about. We go on from there. So far as I know, you couldn't have any motive. In that case, it would be up to us to find out who could have seen her after you did. Now on the question of opportunity, anybody who lived in this house had that. Mrs. Lalande, Miss Lalande, Mr. St. Amant, and Tossie—any one of them could have gone to that room. Just to play no favorites, so could you, Doctor Perrault—you were in there twice by your own account of

127

what happened since that afternoon—and so could Mr. Foxworth."

"What's that you're saying?" The question fairly crackled across the room as Foxworth jumped up.

"No use getting angry, Mr. Foxworth. We're not playing parlor games. Somebody's been killed. When you came in, you didn't ring—or at least I didn't hear you; and no one left this room to let you in. That suggests the possibility that you may have a latchkey to this house."

"It wouldn't, to anyone with a decend mind. It's an insult to Mrs. Lalande to make such a suggestion—an insult I won't tolerate. But I'll take that up later. Meanwhile, just for the record, I did ring. But probably all this confusion prevented anyone from hearing me. Anyway, nobody came to the door, so I tried it. I found it unlocked and walked in."

"Well, that explanation doesn't satisfy me either. It certainly isn't customary to leave a front door unlocked, at night, in this part of town."

"It certainly isn't. So I relocked it. It's my opinion that somebody must have been mighty careless."

"That's my opinion too. But I don't know who or why. So there's one more thing for me to look into. If it was unlocked for any length of time, you could have come and gone without anyone being the wiser. And that has to be tallied with the rest of the facts."

Murphy waved aside Foxworth's further angry protests before the latter had time to utter them. But, meanwhile, Joe had risen from the shabby chair, where he had so long been slouched as if he were sitting on the back of his neck, and had begun to prowl around the room, apparently in futile search of some practical receptacle into which he could empty his overflowing ashtray. His movements permitted him to get a clear view of Foxworth, who was making a visible effort to control his anger and recapture his composure. *The great man is sure in a hell of a jam,* Joe said to himself. *He went to a lot of trouble to have him a fancy though phony alibi for his whereabouts from seven* P. M. *until two* A. M. *—which takes in the period when Odile was killed. But if I'm right in my hunch that during this time he was in a huddle to overthrow the government at Llorando, he can't say so without letting himself in for a federal charge and a term in federal prison. On the other hand, my guess about Dutch Schaefer and the rest of the boys may be completely wild. The real reason Foxworth was pretending to be incommunicado in his quarters could have been to screen a cozy little call at 84 Richmond Place. And, in that case ....*

Murphy's next retort to Foxworth interrupted Joe's train of thought.

"Yes, I know. You'll have me broken for this. That's twice you didn't quite say it, but wanted to," the detective was saying. "And before you blow a gasket, let me tell you there's some one else who's going to have to show where he was this night and what he was doing there. That's the lad who brought Mrs. St. Amant home last evening—Duplessis. After Doctor Perrault told us that, apparently, something which happened late yesterday afternoon upset Mrs. St. Amant so that she became hysterical, and touched off the events that ended in her bedroom tonight, I gave orders to have Mr. Duplessis brought here. I want him to fill in on the part of the story that comes before Doctor Perrault took over."

"Sabin Duplessis? You've had him arrested? Oh, no—that would be too ghastly!" Amélie wailed. "What on earth will people say when they find out about it? All that scandal and gossip about a poor girl who never harmed a soul in her life!"

"Not arrested, Mrs. Lalande. I just sent a radio message to the squad car nearest his apartment, with orders that they were to ask him to come here. Better that way than at an inquest, you know, and no publicity, either. But—and this is the part I wanted to bring up, really—Duplessis isn't at his residence and, apparently, hasn't been there since leaving here. So the boys are waiting for him yet. I only mention that to show he'll have to account for his whereabouts, too. Meanwhile, there's still one other angle to talk about while we're waiting. The gun."

"Do we have to go through all that again?" Léonce demanded impatiently. "Everybody knows Odile never had a gun. Even that black witch says she'd never seen one in the room before."

"But somebody brought it there," Murphy reasoned. "Somebody who had access to that room. And I know how it was brought—though not by whom or when."

The announcement was made with deliberate dramatic emphasis; but beyond the glances of bewildered inquiry which all but Foxworth and Joe Racina turned on the detective, there was no indication of startled surprise or alarm. He waited for a moment, and then nodded with something like approval.

"If that gun was used by somebody in this room, score one for whoever it was," he admitted ungrudgingly. "Seeing as how this was an amateur job, I thought maybe—but never mind. Skip it. Let's get back to the gun. It's an unusual one.

You don't run across many like it. Too hard to get ammunition for them in this country. 'Kamerad guns' they're called. It's a small job that can pretty nearly be concealed in the palm of a man's hand. The Germans used them in the First World War. The idea was that you could have one of them when you raised your hands in surrender, and maybe use it to kill your captor, and have a chance to get away. So I'd like to know if any one in this house, including Mrs. St. Amant, had any close friends who were in the Army during the war, and saw service abroad. Because only some former G. I. would have had this particular gun."

"Hold on a minute," Joe Racina protested. "Maybe I'm not supposed to stick out my neck, but anybody who really wants to do it can get hold of almost any kind of a war souvenir. The boys brought 'em back in batches—guns, bayonets, helmets, belt buckles, and Lord knows what all. Bet you anything you like that I can put a want-ad in tomorrow's *Item* and have two or three of those same guns offered to me for a price by night."

"Oh?"

"Well—I mean about it being a service man. That ain't necessarily so."

"Nice going, Joe. Only this gun still had traces of cosmoline on it. The kind of grease the Army uses to protect guns from rust and dust. Looked like whoever brought it here had wiped if off in a hurry, and hadn't removed all the cosmoline."

"But, even so . . . ."

"I'll take it from here," Murphy said sharply. "This is my side of the street."

Joe nodded, returned to his chair, and jackknifed himself sectionally down into it.

"And there was cosmoline on the paper the gun was wrapped in," Murphy was continuing. "A gift-wrapped gun, no less." He drew a flat packet of neatly folded tissue paper from his pocket, and a length of tinsel-edged blue ribbon. Then, he took a step toward Tossie. "Ever see anything like this before?" he asked.

Behind her moonlike glasses, Tossie's eyes were staring as if transfixed. The cords in her skinny old neck worked convulsively, but for a moment her lips made no sound.

"Oh, Lawd, ha' mercy!" she moaned at last. "Dat present was de gun what kill mah baby!"

"What present?"

"De present Mistuh Sabin brung wid him when he carry Miss Odile to de bed las' evenin'! Wid mah own two eyes Ah

130

seed him lay hit down an' never knowed hit was de gun what'd make her daid. Oh Lawd God in Heab'm, why'n' you lea' me to know hit was a gun de man was totin'?"

"By God, that fits in with everything!" Léonce interrupted. "Sabin was in the Army, you know. And he's a gun crank. His studio is full of weapons—old ones, new ones, rifles, shotguns, duelling pistols, everything. It's a regular museum."

Murphy silenced him with an impatient gesture, and looked intently at Tossie.

"Now listen to me, Auntie," he said urgently. "Listen to me real good. I want you to tell me just what you saw when the man brought this into Miss Odile's room."

"Ah ain' saw nuthin', Cap'n," wailed the old Negress. "Dat's de mis'ry Ah got to carry wid me de rest of mah days. Mistuh Sabin carry Miss Odile to de room an' lay her down on de bed, whilst she a-cryin' an' goin' on somethin' dreffle to heah. Miss Am'lie was a-cryin' too, an' say she gwine foam de doctuh, an' run out de room to wheah de foam at. Ah done mah bes' to get de po' chile's clo'es off to make her mo' easy, but she takin' on so Ah couldn't do a thing wid her, not me. Mistuh Sabin, he started out de do' when Miss Am'lie lef' but direckly he come back an' say he forgot to lea' Miss Odile's present what he had in his pocket, an' he lay de debblish thing on de dresser-table, all wrop up in tissue paper wid de blue ribbon 'round hit. Ah never studied 'bout hit bein' nuthin' out de way. Miss Odile was all de time gittin' presents, suh. All kin's of presents, an' de mos' of dem wrop up jus' lak dishere one, in tissue paper wid silk ribbons 'round. So wid all de goin's on Ah never paid no mo' mind to hit in dis worl' after Mistuh Sabin laid hit down on de dresser-table. Oh, if only de good Lawd above had of lea' me know hit was de somethin' dat would kill mah po' li'l angel col' an' daid! Do, Miss Odile, f'give ol' Tossie fo' lettin' dem do you lak dey done! Look down f'm yonnuh up in de sky an' . . . ."

The double note of the door chimes punctuated the old Negress' quavering lament.

"We heard the bell all right that time," Murphy observed, as Tossie went to answer it. "That'll be Bonham, I expect. Well, it looks as if we couldn't go much further along until we have this chap, Duplessis, among those present. In view of the fact that there's been no report on him, it may be necessary to send out an all-station message, and . . . . Okay, Rex. Any news?"

The stocky, sallow identification expert nodded noncommittally to the group he had left some time earlier and laid on the nearest table the large flat package and the small wooden case he had been carrying.

"Yeah," he said to Murphy. "They've got your boy friend Duplessis under glass at the Third Precinct. Drunk, fighting, disturbing the peace, reviling the police, resisting arrest—they can throw the whole book at him if they've a mind to, after he sobers up enough to appear in court."

"What time was he arrested?"

"Not more'n twenty minutes before I left headquarters to come out here."

"Where?"

"At the Diamond Horseshoe—Dave King's trap on Dauphine Street."

"How long had he been there?"

"I thought about that, of course. That's why I stopped by there to ask, because the arrest report didn't show. He got to the joint just after the midnight show—him and some other guy came in together. The fellow with him was a stranger to the people in the barroom—short, thick-set, heavy shoulders; they've got his description at the Third Precinct. The two of them seemed to be pretty well oiled up by the time they got there. Anyway, they flocked to themselves down at one end of the bar, putting straight whiskey down the hatch. Some of those B-girls tried to cut in on 'em, but they gave 'em the quick brush. Finally they got to quarreling, and one thing led to another till they started swinging at each other. One of the bouncers jumped in to stop the fight, and then this Duplessis started to clean out the joint single-handed—barkeeper, bouncers, customers, and all. About this time the other guy, the short one, took it on the lam and got away, but Duplessis went right ahead. The way Dave told it, the fight was a lulu. It was all the beat man and two of the boys in a cruiser car could do to bring him in. Clancy, the desk sergeant at the Third, got his name off one of these identity bracelets the guy was wearing. He remembered your message about bringing him out here, so he telephoned headquarters to let you know. That's that. But I guarantee you nobody'll get anything out of him till he gets rid of one super-special eight-cylinder hangover. Boy! What a head he'll have when the swallows come back to Capistrano!"

"Ummm. And that's a bum break," Murphy fretted. "Maybe he's not such a dumb pigeon at that. He wouldn't be the first one to claim he was too lit up to remember what happened or where he was—and with everybody in the Diamond Horseshoe and in the Third Precinct to bear him out, too. Well, time enough to worry about that when we have to. How'd you make out on the prints?"

"Aces and eights. The ballistic check can't miss. No possible doubt about that being the gun that fired the fatal bullet. The landmarks on it and on the test-bullet were identical, right to a gnat's whisker."

"And the fingerprints?"

"Got three fair partials, and one beaut." His stumpy fingers fumbled with the wrapping of the flat packet he had brought in with him. Discarding the crackling outer paper, he brought out two large gray desk blotters, between which a sheet of photographic enlarging paper, still moist, was pressed. He held this up with a craftsman's pride.

"Ain't that a honey?" he asked.

Murphy nodded. "Might as well check to see if anybody here has one to match it," he said.

Bonham threw back the hinged lid of the wooden case, revealing an inked slab and a small roller. "No use messing up everybody," he proposed. "This whorl-and-arch pattern is so plain that I can tell just by looking at the fingers if they're likely to check. That way we can eliminate some of them."

"That's all right, for a starter," agreed Murphy. "Of course, if nobody's prints match this one from the gun, there's still this Duplessis to check, and . . . ."

"Nope," Bonham said. "I forgot to tell you. I checked him at the station. He was dead to the world, but he didn't have to be sober for me to take his prints. And you can take it to the bank and borrow money on it that this print wasn't one of his."

"Even so, if you don't find a match we might have to take prints of everybody here—everybody but Racina, that is— just to be able to say we didn't overlook any bets, in case it's ever brought up. But take it your own way first."

Bonham had already extended his hand for Orson Foxworth's fingers. He subjected first one set and then the other to quick scrutiny, shook his head, and went on to examine Amélie Lalande's. Again he shook his head in negation, and approached Léonce.

The latter seemed on the point of objecting, but apparently thought better of it. He extended his hands, palm upward. Bonham studied the tips of the proffered fingers.

"Do you mind stepping over here to the light?" he asked, indicating a silk-shaded table lamp.

"Yes, I do mind," Léonce protested. "But there's nothing I can do about it at the moment. The idea of treating reputable people as if they were . . . ."

"Yassuh, he de one!" Tossie burst out with startling shrillness. "He de knivin'-hearted one dat tried to broke mah baby's po' heart, an' couldn' wait fo' her to grieve herse'f to death. Ah kotched him mah ownse'f dis ve'y night a-sneakin' down de hall after de doctuh done lef'. On'y when he see me, he mumble cuss-words and turn back to de parlor wheah he suppose to be sleeping. Ah seed him wid dese two eyes!"

Léonce leaped toward the old woman. "By God, I've had enough of this!" he shouted. "I don't have to . . . ." But he lunged into the solid bulk of Captain Murphy, who had somehow moved around the table behind which he had been standing, in time to interpose himself between the lunging Léonce and Tossie. "Pipe down, Buster," he said without raising his voice. "We'll do all the handling that needs to be done around here. Go on over to that lamp where Captain Bonham's waiting for you."

"I'm not going to stand here and let that old black bitch lie about me," Léonce raged. "I tell you I heard her say to my wife last night she'd sooner see her dead than have another nurse in. How come she should be the one to discover Odile's death? She's the only one we all know went to Odile's room after the doctor said nobody was to go in there. I demand that you arrest her."

"Too bad about you and your demands. I demand you go over to Captain Bonham, and now."

Turning away sullenly, Léonce returned to the waiting officer, and held his hands under the flooding light that poured down beneath the lamp shade. Bonham held the shaking fingers to steady them, peered at the contours intently, studying each patterned finger tip.

"I guess we'll have to check the print of this forefinger," he said at last. "It's the same general type, right enough. If you'll just go over there to the table and wait."

Muttering under his breath, Léonce complied. "Now if you'll step over here, miss," Bonham said to Caresse. But he gave her slim fingers little more than a glance. "This isn't it," he said, looking up. "All right, Auntie."

"What y'al want wid me, Cap'n?" Tossie pleaded. "Ah got no time fo' such stuff. Dat's white folks bizness."

"Just go on over and let him look at your fingers," Murphy urged her, pleasantly.

"Cap'n, please suh, don' mak me do dat. Hit ain' fitten fo' me," she demurred.

"Tossie!" Amélie spoke sharply. "Do as you're told."

"Effen you says so, Miss Am'lie."

Bonham peered closely at the gnarled old fingers.

"Hmmm. Got a whorl-and-arch here too," he decided. "Well, might as well take the prints and check them. Come on over here to the table with me." He passed the roller back and forth across the inking slab, took hold of Léonce's right index finger, pressed it against the inked surface with a rolling movement, and then repeated the maneuver with Léonce's finger pressed against a small square of stiff white cardboard. "And now you, Auntie," he directed.

From a compartment in the wooden case, he removed a small, folding lens mount, and examined first one card and then the other. He passed the magnifying glass to Captain Murphy, and with the point of a nickeled pencil indicated two or three spots on one of the newly-made prints. Captain Murphy nodded in obviously complete agreement.

"Can't miss!" he said. He threw back his shoulders, and, speaking to the room at large rather than to any one individual, he added, "This isn't pleasant for me. I'm only doing what I have to. Aunt Tossie, I arrest you for the murder of Odile St. Amant."

9

How Caresse Lalande confided in both Ruth Avery and Joe Racina—

January 5, 1948

JOE RACINA left Foxworth's house immediately after receiving the telephone message about Odile. But Russ Aldridge stayed on with Ruth while she awaited her uncle's return. She was very tired by that time, and she did not try to talk much. Russ did not seem to mind; he did not talk much either. And the silence between them was not strained; it was companionable. Ruth had learned, through Richard Huntington, that when silence between two persons was companionable, this meant that there was also harmony. She marveled that such harmony should exist between herself and Russell Aldridge, so soon. But her surprise was not disturbing; it was comforting.

At last she heard a latchkey turn in the lock of the front door and the sound of footsteps mounting the stairs. She waited a moment, hoping that her uncle would come into the library of his own accord, and voluntarily explain his astonishing absence. But the footsteps went steadily, almost stealthily on. She called from the entrance of the library.

"Uncle! I've waited up for you. I had to. Something terrible's happened."

The footsteps ceased to retreat, but they did not begin to approach. Russ took Ruth's hand and pressed it, as if in reassurance. Then he too called into the darkness, more compellingly than she had.

"You're badly needed, Foxworth. Amélie Lalande telephoned. Odile has shot herself."

The effect of these words was instantaneous. Foxworth plunged down the upper flight of stairs and hurled a few questions at his niece and his friend. Then he flung himself out of the house. The question of where he had been and why he

136

had given Downes a misleading message was not even raised, much less answered.

Aldridge had continued to hold Ruth's hand while the brief colloquy took place. He went on holding it as he said good night.

"I'm not on as intimate a footing with the Lalandes as Joe and your uncle. I'd be intruding rather than helping if I went to their house. But I'll keep informed. And I'll call you in the morning—I mean I'll call you later *this* morning. Do you generally go to church?"

"Yes, generally—always when I'm home, because Father likes to have me go with him. He's a vestryman at Christ Church in Alexandria."

"Following in the tradition of George Washington and Robert E. Lee? Well, why not? . . . . If you'd like to go to the Episcopal Cathedral here, I'd be pleased to take you. But I've been thinking . . . . We might drive out to Lacombe after all. We can do it in less than two hours. I have an idea your uncle may be somewhat preoccupied. So I doubt if he'd be free to go with us. However, I have some friends, the Herbert Morrisons, who'd be simply delighted to have us lunch at their place, which is just down the road from mine. Think it over, and let me know when I call you up. Meanwhile, don't dwell on the thought of Odile any more than you can help. I'm afraid she's been pretty unhappy, but if so, she's out of her misery now. Think of that, if you have to think about her. But try to get some sleep."

His handclasp tightened again. It was firm, it was friendly, it was warm, it was—or did she imagine it?—something more than that. Long after he had gone, Ruth still seemed to feel his fingers enfolding her palm. And surprisingly, she was able to sleep. Her slumbers were so profound that Ellen, the maid who had been assigned to her, was obliged to come very close to the bed and twitch the sheet, before Ruth sat up with a start, rubbing her eyes.

"Mr. Aldridge has called twice, miss. He left his number and asked if you would call him back, as soon as you conveniently could. And Mr. Foxworth would like to see you immediately. He's sorry to disturb you, but it's very urgent."

Ellen had added the part about being sorry on her own initiative, feeling that her master's message to his niece lacked the requisite courtesy. But when Ruth replied that she would be down in ten minutes, the maid reluctantly shook her head.

"I think he meant he'd like to see you here, without waiting at all, miss. I'm sorry, but he does seem very much

137

upset. I suppose it's natural—that poor young lady! Would you like me to give you a bed jacket, miss? I know right where I put them, in the second drawer."

The bed jacket was hardly adjusted, when Orson Foxworth knocked imperatively and strode into his niece's room. He had now spent two successive nights with practically no sleep, and this alone would have tended to make him irritable; but the underlying causes for this wakefulness had gone from bad to worse, and, as Ellen told Downes in the pantry, he was now "almost fit to be tied." He berated rather than addressed his niece.

"I decided you were going to sleep all day, and I've got to get back to the Lalandes', so I had to wake you up. They must be wondering what's become of me. I said I'd be gone only long enough to shower and shave and change and have some breakfast. And I've been hanging around doing nothing for the last hour or so."

"I'm terribly sorry, Uncle. And I can't understand why I slept so soundly. Can you take time to tell me what's happened?"

Jerkily and impatiently, he gave her an account of the scene in the Lalandes' drawing room. "For myself," he concluded, "I agree a hundred percent with Perrault in the view that Odile committed suicide. There's only one good thing about the line Murphy's taken. In the light of it, Father Kessells consented to let arrangements for the funeral go forward. It's to take place tomorrow—not until noon though, to allow time for buying mourning beforehand. That connection Caresse has with The Fashion Plate Dress Shop is certainly a help at a time like this. It would be pretty hard getting the necessary things together on such short notice if it weren't for that. Everything's difficult to manage on a Monday. But I advised against waiting over another day. No use prolonging the agony."

"You'd like me to go to the funeral, wouldn't you, Uncle?" Ruth inquired, wishing she did not feel so critical of the undue importance apparently attached to mourning, and wishing still more that she did not feel there was something vaguely sinister about so much haste.

"Well, naturally," Foxworth replied crisply. "The family would consider it an affront if you didn't. For that matter, so should I." He hesitated and then went on, "This isn't the moment I'd choose to tell you, but it isn't exactly a matter of choice any more. I've been urging Mrs. Lalande to marry me and go back to Puerto de Oro with me on Ash Wednesday. I think it might be a good plan if I could persuade her to leave sooner than that—get her away from everything connected with Odile's death as quickly as possible. Of course, under the circumstances, we'd have to be married very quietly, but that would suit me better than a showy wedding anyhow. I'd be sorry to disappoint you, Ruth, about Carnival. However—"

"Why, Uncle, you mustn't give that a thought, at a time like this! I've been wondering if perhaps it wouldn't make too long a visit anyway, if I stayed six weeks. And please let me say I hope you and Mrs. Lalande will be very happy. If there's anything I can do to help about the funeral—or the wedding, you'll tell me, won't you?" It seemed incongruous, even a little gruesome, to mention the two in the same breath, though, apparently, there was no help for it, and Ruth could not suppress an intrusive thought. *I was so sure, just Friday night, that he didn't want to marry her, that he didn't mean to. And this is only Sunday morning. I must have been mistaken. Or else something suddenly happened that made him change his mind. I wonder ....* Aloud, she added, "Do you think Mrs. Lalande would like to have me call on her today? I'd be glad to, if you do." But Ruth knew that though she would be willing to help, her heart would not be in such a visit. She wanted desperately to go to the country with Russ Aldridge, to leave all the ghastly details of the Lalande tragedy behind her. She was worrying for fear it might be so late by the time she returned Aldridge's telephone call that he would have already made other plans; and she could hardly suppress a sigh of relief when Foxworth said shortly, "No, everything's too upset, right now. As a matter of fact, I hope Amélie and Caresse are both finally resting. And after they wake up, there's bound to be a lot of confusion, though Perrault and I will spare them everything we can. That's why I'm going back to their house—to take charge. Not that I'm looking forward to it. I could do with some sleep myself."

"I'm sure you could. And, of course, I wouldn't want to intrude. But if there's anything I can do to be helpful—"

"Well, I think that tomorrow morning, before the casket's closed, Amélie would like to have you come and look at Odile. She's going to be buried in her wedding dress. Of course the bullet wound won't show and she'll look—well, beautiful, I suppose. Except for her hair. Amélie's grieving terribly about her hair. Tossie's always dressed that and no one else can do it the way she did. But now, thanks to that so-and-so, Murphy,—"

In spite of herself, Ruth could not control a shudder. When she spoke of being helpful, she had thought of answering the telephone, sending and receiving telegrams, arranging flowers. It had not occurred to her that she would be invited, much less required, to stare at the defenseless girl in her coffin, and to Ruth there was something ghoulish in the idea. Equally repugnant was the vision of Amélie, wailing because her dead daughter's hair was not becomingly dressed—surely a mother overcome with deep and genuine grief would hardly be conscious of such a detail! Foxworth noticed the involuntary shiver and spoke even more sharply than before.

"Creoles still make quite a cult of their mourning. I hope you'll respect their customs and not betray the fact if any of these are strange to you. It would hurt Amélie's feelings terribly if you did, and it would also put me in an extremely awkward position. Incidentally, I've already ordered flowers sent in your name—a large spray of white lilies to supplement the white orchids I'm sending myself. I might add that I probably won't be home until late and that I hope you won't feel you have to sit up for me this time. If the day offers anything in the way of diversion, you'd better take advantage of it. Naturally, I won't be able to do anything for you myself."

As abruptly as he had entered the room, he strode out of it, leaving Ruth with the feeling that she had not only been rebuked like an unmannered child, but relegated to the position of an unwelcome guest. There was no extension telephone in her room, so she had to wait until she had bathed and dressed before calling Aldridge, and, in the meantime, she had begun to consider the advisability of consulting train and plane schedules between New Orleans and Washington. But she changed her mind on the latter point as soon as she heard Aldridge's voice.

"Hello there! I'm glad you took my advice and had you a good long snooze. We'll get to the Cathedral next Sunday."

"I'm sorry about church. But I did say Father's favorite morning prayer; 'In the Name of the Father and of the Son and of the Holy Ghost I begin this day.' He says that's helped him to meet almost every difficulty he's encountered with calmness and assurance."

"It's beautiful—and meaningful. I think I'll adopt it myself."

"I'll tell him so. He'll be pleased and touched to know it's 'meaningful' to a great archeologist. But to go back . . . . I haven't been sleeping all this time. Uncle's been in my room, talking to me about the Lalandes."

"Well, we'll have to compare versions of that story then, because I've been getting one from Joe, and I doubt if the

two are identical .... How soon can you be ready to start for Lacombe?"

"Why, I'm ready now—that is, I haven't had anything to eat yet. But Uncle wants me to go to the funeral tomorrow morning and before that—"

"Yes, I know. I'm afraid it'll be pretty hard for you. But as I said before, don't keep dwelling on the thought of Odile. We can still get to Lacombe for two o'clock dinner at the Morrisons'. And there'll be enough daylight left for a tour of my garden after dinner. I shan't be satisfied until I've seen you standing between the two biggest bushes of Lady Hume's Blush. But, for heaven's sake, eat a good hearty breakfast before we start! It'll take me at least fifteen minutes to get to Toulouse Street. And you've got a long cold drive ahead of you. Be sure to wrap up well!"

She was already waiting for him in the courtyard when he came swinging into it, a jaunty little gray hat confining her russet curls, her beautifully tailored gray suit topped with a sling cape of silver blue mink. He grinned his appreciation as he helped her into his car.

"I see you bettered my instructions, at least in one respect. You're not only wrapped up well, but magnificently. I've read about that fur in advertisements, but this is the first time I've actually seen it in the skin. I hope you did as well by your breakfast as you did by your outfit."

"I did indeed. I ate a fluffy ham omelette and two English muffins dripping with butter and orange marmalade and washed them down with three cups of coffee."

"Well, that ought to hold you until we get to the Morrisons'. As a matter of fact, I hope it won't quite. I want you to be hungry when we arrive. Because you'll have all kinds of wonderful things for dinner."

That prophecy was amply fulfilled. Among the other dishes that were later set before them was a vast bowl of fluffy golden spoon bread, and a chicken-parlow that had been a personal triumph for The Old Soul—the burnt-sienna genius who presided over the Morrisons' spacious kitchen. And the cream that was served with the season's first strawberries from nearby Tangipahoa Parish was too thick to be poured; it had to be spooned from the pitcher a bit at a time.

Meanwhile, the journey had been a series of surprises. Russ had spoken of his place as "across the lake." But Ruth had not realized that they would literally go over Lake Pontchartrain on a six-mile bridge which spanned it at its narrowest point; nor had she ever seen anything like the trappers' cabins they passed as they crossed the wide roseau marsh fringing the lake, cabins thatched with palmetto leaves, spread shingle-wise over the frames, each hut with its own drying rack from which countless muskrat skins were suspended on wire stretchers to cure in the sun and await the visits of the fur-buyers.

"The trappers come here in November and they stay until February," Russ explained. "Don't get any wrong notions because they live in these shacks throughout the season. Just look at the automobiles that are parked under those lean-to sheds! During good times, like now, some of those trappers make a lot more in a year than your stepfather does. Of course, these folks are lucky, in a way, because they can get to civilization any time they want to. But you take the ones who trap the deep marshes in Vermilion or Terrebonne Parish, along the Gulf Coast, and they live in houseboats out along the edge of absolutely nowhere at all, right through the winter. That's why there are places where they celebrate Christmas in February—with trees, and presents and Santa Claus and all, mind you. They couldn't do it in Christmas week, you see. So they put if off till after the trapping season closes."

Ruth realized that Russ was making a deliberate effort to divert her mind from Odile, but after all, he was succeeding wonderfully well. Once across the bridge they entered the piney woods country, slowing to a more sedate pace as they passed through the placid little town of Slidell which, Russ, said, had begun its municipal existence as a brickyard. Then they turned west to follow the northern rim of the lake. Throughout the drive Russ kept up a merry round of descriptive talk about the countryside.

"See that little plot at the left enclosed in a white wall with a gate?" He indicated the enclosure set back a short distance from the road. "That's no less than a one-man cemetery. Well, sir, the old recluse, who built it, didn't want company even after death. That's why it's surrounded with those no-trespass and keep-out notices. The popular tradition is that the whole place is planted with bear traps, too. Apparently, no one has even ventured to put that theory to the test."

They finally turned off from the highway at a fork, slowing their pace as they entered a graveled country road, and went from this through an ornamental arched gateway along a private drive, bordered by clipped boxwood hedges. Beyond these were stately groupings of camellias and massed azaleas already in a light foam of lavender, scarlet, white, and shrimp-color, promising still more abundant bloom. But be-

142

fore Ruth could fully voice her delight over the breath-taking beauty with which they were surrounded on every side, they had drawn up before a rambling, gray-shingled house, and were greeted by Tip and Peg Morrison—their tweed-clad, ruddy-faced hosts—a miscellany of bird dogs, and The Old Soul, whose statuesque proportions seemed oddly at variance with the cigarette held between her grinning lips.

Dinner was a long leisurely meal; the spoon bread, the chicken-parlow, and the strawberries took time to consume; the conversation, in which camellia culture and duck hunting were the major topics, was unhurried and expansive. In the course of it, Tip interrupted a glowing account of his latest experiences in the Pecan Island marshes to ask a question.

"Speaking of hunting trips, when are you dashing off into the jungle again, Russ? Seems to me you've stayed put longer than usual, since you got back from the Peten this last time."

"I have," Aldridge said, rather ruefully. "The Foundation has insisted I've got to get out my last notes for their publishers, so they can have something to show for the money they put behind the Peten job. As far as I was concerned, the report I wrote for the American Society covered all that's really notable. But they want something on slick paper, with loads of photographs and a snazzy binding—you know, like a glorified piece for the *National Geographic*."

"How much longer will that keep you tied down here?"

"I can't answer that one. I'm not one of those glib chaps who can dash off adventurous pieces about the romance of exploration, which is what the Foundation really wants, worse luck. I have to take my romance and my exploration separately." Aldridge paused, for no obvious reason, but somehow the halt seemed significant, and no one broke in on him. "I've been wishing I could get the damn book out of the way," he went on. "Guy Welburn's got it all fixed for us to make a real trek through some caves on the Island of Roatan, off the North coast of Honduras. He's heard rumors that one of those caves has great stone tables and benches and urns in it. Lord, when I think what it would mean to run into a real treasure trove like that, where the Mayas may have hid their codices to keep them away from Cortez and his gang! And, instead of starting off to find out whether it's really there, I have to hang around New Orleans until I finish that flossy book for the Foundation! .... Not that there haven't been compensations."

The final remark mitigated the show of impatience revealed by the earlier part of his speech; but before he made

143

it his voice had betrayed both his excitement over the possible cache on Roatan and his real resentment over the delay in his departure. Again a brief silence followed his outburst. Tip nodded as if he could understand his friend's disappointment, but did not seem to feel that any comment on it was necessary; indeed, after a moment he resumed his own interrupted narrative about the marshes. Peg's silence was wholly accidental; she was absorbed in feeding tidbits from the table to the bird dogs. But Ruth was not talking because she was thinking with great intentness of what Aldridge had said during the dinner at Antoine's: *I haven't decided yet whether I'll go by plane or boat. I don't have to consider anyone except myself and that's a great help.* She had been annoyed then because he seemed to be flaunting his freedom; now she was more than annoyed: she was puzzled, she was offended, she was, beyond all reason, hurt. She recalled something else Aldridge had said at Antoine's: *I shall devote the next few weeks to disproving false rumors to the effect that I spend all my time prowling around ruins or that I'm not interested in anything less than a thousand years old.* She had understood him to mean that he was interested in her, that he wanted to devote himself to her. And she could have sworn that their subsequent meetings had meant as much to him as to her. Now he talked as if he were unwillingly biding his time, as if he could hardly wait to be off to another jungle . . . .

No one else seemed aware that her happiness was clouded and, eventually, Russ said that if they were going to see his garden, they must really get going; so, accompanied by the bird dogs, they all strolled over the smooth lawn towards the boxwood hedge and entered the adjoining grounds through a small iron gate. On the further side of this, the wide expanse between the hedge and the house was dotted with camellia trees of every conceivable size and kind; and Ruth's attempts to digest her host's rapid-fire information about the different varieties soon ended in a state of hopeless confusion.

"Remember this is only Lesson Number Two!" she protested at last, laughing. "You've got to leave something for the rest of the course." *Unless it's going to be cut short,* she added, fearfully to herself. To her relief, Aldridge answered as if nothing could be further from her mind.

"That's right, so I have. Well, come and be photographed. Then we'll forget about camellias for awhile. You must be fed up with them by how, anyway."

Again Ruth protested, but this time Aldridge would not listen; and after she had posed between two prize specimens of Lady Hume's Blush, he said they would leave his house for another time too, but that they must have a look at Bayou Lacombe before they left. So they went through a grove of pecan trees, festooned with gray pennons of Spanish moss, and came down to the bayou's edge. The black water went slipping silently lakeward, the banks were edged with iris blades, and beyond were wild azalea trees and dogwood. As the group watched, a gorgeous wood duck drake came whistling down to the water, settled, and began to paddle shoreward in a purposeful way; then, noticing the intruders, he took off with a shrill, discordant call.

"A disturber of the peace, isn't he?" Russ asked. "Now you know why they're called squealers."

"I'm afraid we disturbed *him*. But he seemed to belong, like everything else."

"You do like it here, don't you?"

"Like it!"

There was no mistaking the sincerity of the exclamation. But, with obvious reluctance, Ruth declined the Morrisons' urgent invitation to remain for a late supper. It had all been heavenly, she said. However, under the circumstances, she felt she should be getting home to see what had happened during her absence; and, through the early dusk of the January day, she and Russ drove back across the lake. The thatched cabins were lamp-lit now, and again Russ talked to Ruth about the trappers and their ways. But, on the whole, he was less communicative than during the morning's drive; and though the periods of silence had much the same companionable quality as those of the previous evening, they were marred for Ruth by the memory of the announcement Russ had made concerning his plans. She was tempted to refer to it, to question him about his brochure and his expedition; but she resisted the temptation. After all, he had said nothing to her on the subject of his own accord; if Tip had not made his disturbing inquiry, she would never have heard about the Peten and Roatan. She tried to forget about them, to persuade herself that she had imagined Aldridge's eagerness and impatience and, to a remarkable degree, she succeeded. But she resisted the further temptation to ask him in for another quiet hour before the library fire.

There was no sign of Orson Foxworth about the house when Ruth reached there and no message from him; but she was too full of fresh air and good food and new impressions to worry about the omission. After a light and early supper she tumbled into bed and again slept soundly until Ellen called her. Ellen was very grave, as became an old retainer on the day of a funeral in the family circle and, without awaiting instructions, she laid out a black ensemble for Ruth to wear. Orson Foxworth was also very grave when Ruth went downstairs to join him, and his attire was more suggestive to his niece of a bereaved widower in some Latin country than of a prospective American bridegroom. But his ill humor had passed, and as the day progressed, he seemed to take a subdued satisfaction in the major role he was playing. He himself ushered Ruth in for that last inevitable look at Odile which his niece had so greatly dreaded; he sat with her in the pew directly behind the one occupied by Amélie, Caresse, and Léonce at the funeral; and after the services at the cemetery were over, he assisted the weeping mother into the first car and got in beside her. Ruth rode back to the house with some distant relative, whose exact connection with the Lalandes was never clearly defined, but who also wept unrestrainedly all the way from Metairie to Richmond Place, and whose mourning was almost as heavy as that worn by Mrs. Lalande. However, the grieving relative brightened perceptibly at the sight of the copious luncheon which had been prepared for the benefit of those who, like herself, had come from a distance, and which Orson Foxworth capably directed. And when the last of these out-of-town visitors had departed, he offered suggestions amounting to instructions to the remaining members of the group.

"Léonce, you'd better take your mother and sister home and sit with them awhile. This has been a strain on them also .... Amélie, my dear, please go and lie down. I promise you I won't leave the house. I'll be waiting for you, right here, when you come back .... Caresse, you'd better go to your room too. You've been very helpful, very efficient. But there's absolutely nothing more you can do at the moment .... Ruth, the car's waiting. I'm sorry to leave you to your own devices another evening, but there's still a lot to be done here."

Neither of the first two persons thus addressed appeared to resent these directions in the least. Léonce, whose black clothes were extremely becoming to him, immediately prepared to shepherd Mrs. St. Amant and Miss St. Amant from the drawing room, where the usual oppressiveness of the atmosphere was enhanced by the heavy perfume of too many sweet-scented white flowers. They were both rather fragile, futile-looking women, entirely lacking in the ruddy forcefulness of Léonce, and they followed meekly in his wake, after enfolding Amélie in one last tearful embrace. Amélie herself trailed from the room, leaning upon Foxworth for support. He glanced back at Caresse.

"I haven't the least idea of going to lie down," she said, with a terseness worthy of his own. "I'm not going to stay here and stifle, either. I'm going for a walk . . . . Would you care to go with me?" she added, suddenly addressing Ruth.

"Why, yes, if you'd like to have me," Ruth replied, slightly startled by the unexpectedness of this approach.

"All right. My things are out in the hall. I'll just pick them up as we go along."

The Fashion Plate Dress Shop had certainly done extremely well by Caresse, Ruth reflected, as she watched the other girl adjust her black halo hat above her blond bang, and buckle the belt of the black coat which fitted closely above the waist, and flared widely below this. As far as that went, Caresse did extremely well by The Fashion Plate; she was far and away the smartest looking girl Ruth had seen in New Orleans. She walked rapidly down Richmond Place, her taffeta petticoat rustling pleasantly as she went, the suede handbag, which matched her suede gloves and her suede shoes, tucked securely under one graceful arm. When they reached St. Charles Avenue, she paused.

"Do you care which way we go from here?" she inquired.

"Not in the least. This is all new to me, you know, and there seem to be beautiful streets and beautiful houses in every direction. Besides, the main idea is to get air and exercise, isn't it?"

"It's one of the ideas. But I've a letter I'd like to show you, if you don't mind. I want to ask your advice about it, and I knew I'd smother if I didn't get away from all those gardenias and Creole lilies. I thought we could go to Audubon Park and sit on a bench. That is, if you're willing."

"Of course I'm willing. I'd be glad to do anything you feel like doing, Caresse."

"That's mighty white of you. Especially as you took such a dislike to me, almost the moment you met me. Not that I blame you."

Ruth opened her lips to protest, but decided against it and closed them again. Caresse turned right and went uptown, past the looming red brick of Loyola and gray, ivy-clad Tulane. Then they crossed the broad double roadway and the neutral ground of the avenue to the ornamental gate of Audubon Park. Presently they came to the shore of a winding little lake, grown to huge water lilies, and found a bench screened by a planting of striped bamboo. Caresse immediately opened her smart suede handbag and took from it a commercial-sized envelope.

"This came in by airmail special early this morning," she said. "It's a wonder I got it, in the midst of all the hullabaloo. But Lop thought it probably had something to do with the funeral and brought it straight to me. I read it while I was drinking my coffee .... Haas and Hector is a pretty big department store, isn't it?"

"Yes, one of the biggest in New York. And one of the most important. Not just in size either. It's got lots of class."

"That's what I thought. All right, go ahead and read the letter, will you?"

Ruth unfolded the crackling sheets. Underneath the imposing letterhead, the neatly typed paragraphs covered more than a page.

HAAS AND HECTOR

NEW YORK 22, N. Y.

Phone SMith 3-1948

NEW YORK, N. Y.
CHICAGO, ILL.
BEVERLY HILLS, CAL.
MIAMI BEACH, FLA.
HYANNIS, MASS.

SALON SUPERBE

January 3, 1948

Miss Caresse Lalande
84 Richmond Place
New Orleans, Louisiana

My dear Miss Lalande:

Your tri-weekly radio program, broadcast under the auspices of The Fashion Plate Dress Shop, has been called to our attention by our representative, Miss Miriam Hickey. Miss Hickey is in New Orleans for the purpose of studying old portraits in the Cabildo collection and others, with a view towards adapting old Creole costumes for a special showing in our Salon Superbe. Quite by chance, she happened to tune in on one of your broadcasts and was so delighted with it that she listened to others. Then she created an opportunity

148

to have you pointed out to her and since then has seen you on several occasions.

Miss Hickey feels that the local experience you have already had, combined with the unusual effectiveness of your voice and the charm of your personality, might qualify you for a position which we have long been considering as an adjunct to the many unique services offered to our distinguished and discriminating clientele, which extends from coast to coast. Without being prepared to go into details at this point, I may say that such a position would not be dissimilar in character to your connection with The Fashion Plate Dress Shop in New Orleans. It would, however, be much wider in scope, much more productive of opportunity and—we believe—much more remunerative. It would, of course, entail your residence in New York City.

If this tentative offer sounds attractive to you, as I hope it will, I suggest that you contact Miss Hickey, who is staying at the St. Charles Hotel, and make an appointment with her for a personal interview at some time in the near future convenient to yourself. Should such an interview take place, and should it prove mutually satisfactory, we hope you will feel inclined to accompany her when she returns to New York, in order that a supplementary interview may be arranged with Madame Micheline, the director of our Salon Superbe, and other officials of this establishment, including myself. Such a trip would, of course, be made entirely at our expense, both as to transportation to and from New York and as to hotel accommodations during your stay here. A member of our staff would also be placed at your disposal to accompany you to the theatre and on any sightseeing and shopping trips which you might care to undertake, though, as far as the latter are concerned, we believe we could meet your every requirement in our own establishment.

Hoping for an early and favorable reply, we remain

Respectfully yours,
HAAS AND HECTOR

Per Annabella Avila, Assistant Director
SALON SUPERBE

Ruth put down the crackling sheets to find Caresse looking at her with questioning eagerness. "Why, I think that's a perfectly wonderful letter!" she said sincerely. "And I should think you'd be awfully proud to feel that you'd done so well, by a small shop on a local station, that a huge store like Haas and Hector would consider you for a national hook-up."

149

"Is that really what this means? A national hook-up?"

"Well, I may be mistaken, but that's the way it sounds to me. You see the letter stresses the fact that the 'distinguished and discriminating clientele' is scattered all the way from coast to coast. And a connection like that would mean all kinds of opportunities, Caresse, besides meaning a lot of money—just as the letter says. Only it *would* mean living in New York. I suppose that would be the catch. I suppose you wouldn't want to leave New Orleans."

"Yes, I would. I'm crazy to leave New Orleans. I'd leave tomorrow if I could."

It must be imagination, Ruth said to herself. *But when Caresse said that she sounded to me just the same way Uncle did, when he told me he'd like to push off for Central America before Ash Wednesday.* Aloud, she remarked, "If you feel that way about it, why don't you telephone Miss Hickey the first thing in the morning?"

"I've already telephoned Miss Hickey. I did it while—while the rest of you were in the garden wing. Of course, I'd been there already." She spoke with undisguised revulsion, and Ruth had no trouble in gathering that however right her uncle might be in regard to a cult of the dead, as far as Amélie was concerned, he was mistaken about Caresse. "I have an appointment with Miss Hickey at ten o'clock tomorrow morning," the girl concluded. "She sounded awfully pleased at hearing from me so promptly."

"I'm sure she is pleased. The fact that Annabella Avila wrote you on her recommendation shows that her opinion's very highly regarded. Anyone likes to have proof of that."

"Do you really think I could make good? You know the kind of people this Annabella calls a 'distinguished and discriminating clientele'—women who spend thousands and thousands of dollars on their clothes all the time, instead of scrimping and saving in other ways so that they can make a good showing at weddings and Carnival balls and times like that. I don't know that kind of people. I only know our own little set here in New Orleans. Why, I bet the clothes you're wearing right now cost twice as much as my entire winter outfit! And you had on an ermine coat the other night!"

"Well, yes," Ruth answered, hoping that Caresse had not heard that this was only one of several fur coats she had with her and that among them was a silver blue mink. "But you've got no end of style, Caresse. You make your clothes look as if they cost a lot because you wear them so well. Your appearance would be a credit to any store. That is," she added honestly, "they might ask you not to go in for fashions that are too extreme, like—like that jade green dress you wore to the dinner at Antoine's. Haas and Hector are rather on the conservative side. But those details are just minor matters. Of course, I haven't heard you broadcast, but your voice does have wonderful carrying qualities and—"

"Oh, do you really think so? Because I really am crazy to go. But I'd hate like hell to have to come slinking home again. I'd hate to have everyone saying that I thought I was really good, when actually . . . . I'd hate to have people make fun of me behind my back. I'd hate—oh, I'd hate it all so that I couldn't bear it! I'd rather not go at all than have that happen!"

Her voice was not merely eager any more. It was desperate. Ruth tried to speak both soothingly and encouragingly.

"My stepfather always says that the surest way to succeed is to keep telling yourself you can't fail," she said. "Why don't you do that, Caresse? I've got lots of confidence in you. I believe you could make good, when you want to so much. But I honestly don't know that I'm qualified to advise you. I do understand about nice clothes, but there are lots of other things . . . . Isn't there someone else you can ask, someone you've confidence in? What about Joe Racina? I should think you could trust his judgment in a case like this."

"Of course I could! I don't see why I didn't think of him myself! Let's go to his house and ask him, right away. You haven't met Judith, have you? Well, she doesn't like me any better than you do—any better than you did at first. But she's another grand person. I think we can catch them both at home right now. They almost always spend the latter part of the afternoon with the children."

"It's all right for you, I think it's a fine idea. But do you suppose I ought to burst in on the Racinas, just like that? After all, I've only met Joe once and I don't know Judith at all, as you say."

"Of course I think it's all right. Come on, they live just a little way from here."

Ruth had the feeling of being pulled bodily from the bench. Then Caresse hastened along a cinder-covered bridle path in the opposite direction from the gate by which they had entered the park. As they passed a large Italian Renaissance house, she paused briefly and looked up at the cream-colored façade.

"That's where Dorothy Dix lives," she announced. "Maybe I ought to stop and ask her for advice. But I really think Joe's a better bet."

She was in such a hurry that only once again did she

slacken her pace to give Ruth a piece of indicated information. "You may think Judith's a little stiff," she said. "She isn't really. But she was injured by a bomb, or something, during the war and she has to wear high-necked dresses and do her hair just a certain way, in order to hide the scars. Believe it or not, Joe dreamed up the kind of clothes she wears and the hairdo for her."

Ruth would have liked to know more about Judith, especially how she happened to be injured by a bomb, but Caresse hurried on and eventually ran up the steps of an unpretentious but pleasant looking Queen Anne house on Henry Clay Avenue. Joe, very casually dressed and holding a pipe in one hand, opened the door for them himself.

"Well, this is a pleasant surprise!" he remarked cordially. "How are you, Ruth? Everything all right, Caresse? Judith will be down in a minute. She's just getting the kids off to bed. I was helping, but my part's done now. I hope you've come to supper. Meanwhile, what about a drink?"

He ushered them into a book-lined room where the prevailing color was a warm shade of brown, and shoved a couple of chairs, which proved to be deeply comfortable, a little nearer to a cheerful grate fire. Then he disappeared, to return shortly afterwards with well-filled glasses and some cheese-crackers on a small tray.

"I told Judith you were here," he said. "She said, of course you're to stay. She'll be right along."

"Naturally, I want to see Judith too," Caresse informed him, accepting her drink. "But I really came to consult you. I've had a very important letter. I showed it to Ruth, and she gave me some good advice. But she suggested that I show it to you too. So we came right over."

"Glad you did," Joe answered. There was nothing in his manner to suggest he thought it in the least strange that she should be preoccupied with an important letter on the very day of her sister's funeral. "Got it there? Let's have a look at it."

Caresse handed him the letter and watched him breathlessly while he read it. He put it down with much the same sort of comment that Ruth had made.

"Why, that's great!" he exclaimed. "Of course you ought to have a try at it, Caresse, and I haven't the least doubt you'll make a go of it. Not just with the broadcasting either; you could be a topflight model along with your other work. This Zaragoza woman—no, beg pardon, Avila—probably has that in mind herself, from what Hickey's told her. And besides, they'll cash in on your name. Caresse Lalande—hell, it's made

152

to order! The first thing you know, Haas and Hector will be putting out a full new line of Caresse perfumes, Caresse face powder, Caresse lipstick, and what have you!"

"Do you really think so? Or are you just trying to kid me along, Joe?"

"I wouldn't kid you along, not at a time like this," he said seriously. "Why, it's a natural!"

"It's come in the nick of time, too," Caresse went on swiftly. "I'm almost sure *maman*'s decided . . . . Anyway, probably you know Mr. Foxworth's been trying for years to persuade her and I think that now—"

"Well, of course I'd heard rumors and I saw the clinch and the master-of-the-house act Saturday night," Joe replied, permitting himself a slight grin. "Naturally, they'd do everything they could to make you feel welcome, but I don't suppose you'd really care about tagging along to Central America with them. And as for staying on at Richmond Place with that brother-in-law of yours—"

He stopped abruptly. Then he jumped up. "Here comes Judith now!" he said, his voice filled with sudden warmth. "Judith, Caresse's brought us some wonderful news. And this is the Ruth Avery I was telling you about."

"I'm awfully glad to see you both. Can I hear the wonderful news right away, before I get involved with supper?"

She shook hands with both girls and then, declining a chair for herself, sat down on the arm of Joe's. Ruth had a chance to study her while Judith, in turn, read the letter. *I can see what Caresse meant,* she said to herself, *and I'm glad I had that warning about the clothes and the hairdo. I might have thought they were a little queer if I hadn't. But I never would have thought Judith herself was stiff. She's lovely. She may have been rather reserved, when she was younger. She isn't any more though. She's too happy.* Ruth looked around the brown, book-lined room, at the fire and at Joe and Judith, together in the big chair. No one was speaking, and through the stillness came the sound of a child, singing himself to sleep. *No wonder she's happy,* Ruth thought. *I'd be happy too, if I had all this. Of course, I'm happy as it is. But not the way Judith Racina is.* And, as an afterthought, came the conviction, *This is the way Father would have liked to live. This is what he's tried to make me see was so important. He's missed it himself, but he doesn't want me to miss it too . . . .*

Judith looked up from the letter. "Why, this *is* wonderful!" she said. "Have you any idea when you could start, Caresse?"

"I've already got my appointment with Miss Hickey. I could leave tomorrow on the Crescent if she could."

The desperation had crept into her voice again. This time Ruth was sure she was not mistaken, for Joe noticed it too.

"Oh, I wouldn't try to crowd things all that much!" he said easily. "Better find out your mother's plans first, hadn't you, and then dovetail yours into hers? What I mean is, if she is planning to be married, you'd want to be here, of course. But the wedding wouldn't be right away. You probably could make this trial trip and then get back here to wave good-bye to the newly-wedded couple and sort of wind things up."

"I don't care a damn about being here for my mother's marriage," Caresse said in a stifled way.

"Oh yes, you do! You're upset right now—terribly upset and on top of that terribly excited. You're not seeing straight. When you've had a chance to think things through you'll realize that, of course, you'll want to be on hand for that."

"No, I won't," Caresse insisted stubbornly.

"Well, we won't argue about it. But since you're so bent on dashing off, perhaps I'll have to remind you of something else, though Lord knows I hate to. You can't think of leaving town until the mystery of Odile's death has been fully solved."

"Why, Captain Murphy's already arrested Tossie! She's in jail right now!"

"Of course he's arrested Tossie. Of course she's in jail right now. But you know damn well she didn't kill Odile. You told Léonce off in short order when he tried to pull a fast one about that."

"But that was before Captain Bonham took those finger-prints! And besides . . . ."

"Yes? And besides?"

"Well, it may not mean a thing, of course. But two little baby pillows, blue ones, lace-covered, have disappeared from Odile's room. Odile was so attached to them that *maman* wanted to put them in—in the coffin—with her. But they were nowhere to be found."

"And what can that have to do with Tossie?"

"Nothing, perhaps, except that she's always made it a point to flaunt those pillows in the face of Léonce, because he hated them. He had begged Odile to get rid of them, and it was one of the few things in which she wouldn't give in to him. An aunt of ours had made them for her before she was born, and Odile vowed she would always keep them. But neither one of them was to be found."

"But what of it? Suppose Tossie *has* hidden them as a keepsake of her darling Odile—perhaps to prevent Léonce getting his hands on them now that Odile is no longer there to stop him?"

"But Tossie couldn't have hidden them afterwards. They were already gone when we came rushing in there—I mean, after Tossie's screaming roused us. I'm as sure of that as I can be. Somebody was in that room between the time Odile was brought there and the time Tossie found her dead; somebody who took those pillows away. I missed them right off—the queer way you do notice some insignificant thing when any number of other things are a lot more important."

Caresse spoke with increasing vehemence. But Joe's answer revealed that he felt less strongly about the matter.

"I'm afraid you can't be sure of what was or wasn't in that room, with all the excitement going on at the time. Remember the suicide note? That disappeared too, and hasn't turned up yet. But let's say you're right, and whoever went into that room that nobody was supposed to enter, took two pillows some time before Tossie found Odile dead on the floor by the window. Isn't that all the more proof that it wasn't Tossie?" Joe paused for a moment, and then continued with increasing scorn. "And as for those fingerprints, I know all about them. Toe showed them to me himself, so that I could see they matched to the last little detail. But that doesn't prove a thing. Tossie probably moved the gun, without even noticing what she was doing, when she found Odile and knelt beside her. Tossie's arrest was—a gag of some sort. I don't know just what Toe Murphy's up to, but he knows just as well as you do, and just as well as I do, that Tossie didn't kill Odile."

"How?"

The question had almost the quality of a shot. Joe answered it quietly.

"Because, while Tossie might conceivably have fired the gun, she couldn't possibly have written the suicide note."

10

How Joe Racina's line of reasoning led to a compromising question—

January 7, 1948

AGAIN SILENCE fell upon the pleasant room, not gradually and naturally, as it had before, but with abnormal suddenness and again, through the silence, came the sound of a little child singing, more drowsily this time.

"As far as anyone knows yet," Joe said at last, speaking very slowly and distinctly, "if that note was genuine—and it may have been, in spite of Toe's theory—Odile committed suicide. And Perrault, who ought to know as much about this as anyone, isn't convinced that she didn't. On the other hand, if Toe was right about one thing, and Odile was murdered, the note was a magnificent forgery."

He paused, but no one interrupted him. The child's voice trailed away to the last sleepy note.

"So I can't help wondering all the time," Joe went on, "to whom that note was addressed, if it was genuine. And if it was forged, who could have been shrewd enough to phrase it so no one could know for whom it was meant .... But come on, don't let's talk about this any more. Supper's ready, isn't it, Judith?"

"Almost," Judith said and went to put the finishing touches to the table, while Joe explained that they had only a part-time maid, besides the sitter who came to stay with the children when they went out in the evening. "We wouldn't have a regular servant at all, if I didn't insist," Joe continued. "Judith was raised on a farm, and she was a nurse in a small country hospital before she was one in North Africa. She insists that, with all the gadgets we have now, she could do every bit of work in this house with one hand tied behind her. I don't know but what I'd just as well let her, at that. She's a born scrubber and I don't need to tell you that most hired help isn't. If she does leave Elvira in charge, she tacks up little notices in different places, labeled, 'Clean thoroughly.' After she comes home again, she sniffs around, and if she can't smell enough soap, she scrubs all over again herself. When we were first married, I had an awful time with her because I could see her fingers were just itching to tidy up my desk. But she loved me so much that she didn't, which was the supreme test. I might add that I loved her so much I wouldn't have greatly minded if she had. We only had one room then, in a boarding house in Alexandria, and she was mighty good about putting up with it—and me. We didn't have anything like this until a good deal later."

He looked around the library with an expression of deep contentment and went on. "About Judith. She isn't a bad cook, either, as you'll see. Of course, I had to convince her that you mustn't use rice to make puddings—in fact, that the best way to use it is with red beans, cooked with a hambone and seasoned with enough red pepper to start a holocaust. She had an entirely different idea about beans too. She thought they should be white ones, cooked with molasses and served with brown bread and fish balls. So, after considerable argument, we compromised: one week end we have beans her way and the next week end we have them my way. It's worked out very well. Probably arguing over silly things like that has kept us from quarreling over more serious things. Incidentally, I'm in a position to argue about food. I'm not such a bad cook myself."

Just then Judith called from the dining room and they all went in together. The supper was excellent and in spite of the disturbing questions about Odile's death which Joe had momentarily raised, the atmosphere continued to be both calm and cheerful. They lingered for some time over their coffee and Camembert. Eventually, Joe said he would take both girls home, Ruth first; the extra drive would do Caresse good. Well, it was nice of him to think of it, Caresse replied quickly. But after all, she'd been playing hooky. She thought she ought to go back to school before the truant officer chased her up. Joe assured her that he could take care of a truant officer, if one appeared, and it was evident to Ruth that there was something he wished to say to Caresse privately. But it was equally evident that she did not welcome the idea of a heart-to-heart talk, and Joe did not press the point. They made their first stop at Richmond Place, and, as the two girls said good night to each other, it was agreed that Caresse would let Ruth know the results of the interview with Miss Hickey as soon as this had taken place.

Caresse came to Toulouse Street late the next morning to give her report in person. She would have been there sooner, she explained, but she had stopped in at the jail on her way downtown to see poor old Tossie, and that had taken much longer than she expected. In the first place, she had gone to the wrong entrance, and then there had been no end of argument; she was told there wouldn't be any use going to the other side of the block, because it wasn't visitors' day, and as she wasn't Tossie's attorney, she wouldn't be allowed to see her. But Caresse had kept right on insisting, and finally a grumbling old guard had taken her to Sheriff Grosch, who was just as nice as he could be, and, incidentally, quite young-looking. Then things really started moving at last. He had Tossie brought into his office and told Caresse to stay and talk with her as long as she liked.

"The poor old woman must have been pathetically glad to see you," Ruth said, as Caresse paused in her recital.

"Yes, she was. So glad that she cried. She's not so much frightened as bewildered; she can't understand what it's all about, why she should be in this strange cold jail instead of in the only home she's ever had. And it's hard for her to be idle. Of course she hasn't done any real work for a long time. But she's used to puttering around among Odile's things, and now she just sits in her cell with her hands folded and thinks and thinks about her baby . . . ."

Caresse paused again, and Ruth realized that the other girl could not help thinking about Odile too, that the scene in the jail with Tossie had brought back that other tragic scene, in all its dreadful implications. But after a moment Caresse pulled herself together and began to talk about Miss Hickey, who had been simply grand to her. Apparently, there were no obstacles at all, though they could not leave that night, as Caresse had hoped they might, because Miss Hickey had not quite finished at the Cabildo. However, as far as she was concerned, they could do so by the end of the week, and in spite of what Joe had said, Caresse was determined . . . . Anyway, she was going to talk over the whole plan with *parrain* first, she explained, referring to Foxworth in a way that had long been natural to her, though he was not actually her godfather. She felt sure he would approve of it, and put it to her mother better than she could herself; she was going up to his office right off. But first she wanted to tell Ruth that she, Caresse, hadn't forgotten Twelfth Night was coming up. She had wanted to have Ona bake a cake to bring along with her, the kind they always had at home, with a ring and a thimble and a coin in it, but *maman* had thought that the very day after the funeral . . . .

This time Caresse had an unmistakable catch in her voice. Ruth hastened to cover it.

"It was dear of you to think of it. But I *have* a cake like that already. Sabin Duplessis sent me one, in a perfectly beautiful box with a perfectly beautiful note."

"He did! Well, I don't know why I should be surprised. That's exactly the sort of thing he specializes in. He never forgets birthdays or anniversaries or anything like that, the way most men do; and what's more, he comes across with something about ten times as original and attractive as any other man can dream up. I always thought Sabin was pretty exciting myself. I wouldn't wonder if you did too, when you have a chance to find out. He's not a highbrow, like Russ Aldridge, but he sure has what it takes. Of course, you won't be seeing him running on all cylinders, right now. He's had a knockout blow himself."

There was no use trying to avoid it; they kept reverting, directly or indirectly, to Odile. But Ruth made another valiant effort to keep the conversation casual.

"Naturally I haven't met him yet. The note went into that—not at much length, but very deftly. I guess you know how he would do it. I could tell, just from reading it, that he is the exciting type."

Caresse nodded. "I'm sure if he *were* running on all cylinders he'd start rushing you right away. Not that it would mean anything serious—just the same, if he couldn't give you a thrill, no one could. He might do it anyway, with his trick presents and his deft notes and what have you, even though he doesn't take you out on the town. All that's sort of second nature to him, as I just said. And when it comes to technique, I don't know a man who can touch him. The only trouble is, he's a little on the thirsty side. But as long as he's sober, or even half sober—well, you'll handle that all right . . . . I really must cruise along. But I started to say, when we got switched off talking about Sabin and his cake and all the rest of it, that Clarinda Darcoa would be coming for you tonight, as long as I can't."

"Clarinda Darcoa?"

"Yes. She's just the girl to take you to the Revels. She's still one of the greatest belles in New Orleans, though she must be at least twenty-five. Incidentally, your uncle's her *beau idéal*. She's been following his career from afar and she thinks he's the man of the hour if not of the century. So she's delighted to do something, indirectly, for him. I've got everything all fixed up with her. She'll be along early enough to make sure you have seats in the front of the call-out section and show you the ropes. You're bound to have a good time."

And Ruth did have a good time. So good that it was above all the memory of it which caused her to snuggle down among her pillows the next morning, living it all over again. It began when she went down to the library where Clarinda Darcoa was waiting for her, and at last beheld the lovely embodiment of a "typical Creole beauty" as she had imagined this beforehand. The Lalandes had all been too blonde to verify her vision, Amélie and Caresse too ultra-smart in their dress; Judith Racina was unmistakably a New Englander; Peg Morrison the wholesome, tweedy sort no more characteristic of Louisiana than of the Hunt Country in Virginia or the North Shore in Massachusetts. But Clarinda had creamy skin and a heart-shaped face and a dimple in her chin; her large dark eyes were dreamy, like her smile; her glossy black hair was arranged in two great coils just above the nape of her neck, and in the center of each coil nestled a pink camellia. The four ruffles of her pink tulle dress were caught up with other matching camellias and even the fan which she held was studded with them. Her perfume was a scent strange to Ruth, elusive but very sweet, and she spoke in a soft, almost hesitant voice.

"This is a great privilege for me, Miss Avery. I'm grieved that Caresse should be deprived of it and for such a tragic reason. But I suppose if poor Odile was so hopelessly ill, her death may be a blessing in disguise. I believe Mrs. Lalande really feels that way about it." And as Ruth looked her surprise, Clarinda explained, "I was in the Blue Room, dancing, Friday night, and my date and I sat down, for a few minutes, at the table next to the one she and Mr. Foxworth had. There was one of those sudden hushes between loud pieces and I overheard Mrs. Lalande say that it would really be better if Odile could—that is, if she were—oh, of course it was just one of those things people do say when someone they love is sick and suffering, usually without meaning them seriously! But when I heard Odile had died so suddenly I hoped that her mother actually could look at it that way."

"Yes, I hope she can too," Ruth said, rather slowly and thoughtfully.

"Well, we mustn't talk or even think about that now. What I started to say was, I can't be sorry I'm having a chance to take you to your first Carnival ball. I'm sure it seems queer to you not to have a male escort. But you see, our future partners are at the Auditorium already, disguised as chefs in charge of our Twelfth Night cake. And we're not supposed to penetrate the disguise."

"Yes, I understand about that. And I'd much rather go to my first Carnival ball with you than with any male escort I can think of."

A few days earlier, this would have been entirely true. Now Ruth suddenly realized that it was not. But as Clarinda answered only with her slow, charming smile and an understanding look from her dreamy eyes, Ruth did not contradict herself. Instead, she asked, "Do you have a coach and four waiting outside? Nothing else would be worthy of that dress!" Then, feeling vaguely disloyal to Russ, she added, "And I can't help telling you that you've made me appreciate the full beauty of camellias for the first time."

"Thank you—I like them better myself on a dress than on a tree . . . ." She touched one of the pink ruffles lightly, fluffing it out where the camellias caught it, and Ruth saw that she moved her hands with the same slow grace that she did everything else, that her white fingers were tapering and her pink nails exquisite ovals. "Your dress is lovely too," she said, tacitly acknowledging the perfection of her own at the same time she paid her pleasant compliment.

"I'm glad you like it. I'm very fond of brocades. And when I saw this one, I couldn't resist it, the old gold's such a wonderful color."

"And so exactly right with your hair . . . . About the coach and four—I'm sorry I have only a limousine. But we'll pretend it's a coach. That's one of the nicest things about Carnival, I think—pretending. You have your cards, haven't you? Then, shall we go? I came early, as Caresse told you I would, so that we'd be sure to have seats in the very front row."

It did not take them five minutes to reach the Auditorium, and the doors were just opening as they went swiftly up the steps. They were by no means the only early arrivals; a throng of other beautifully dressed girls and some handsome older women were hurriedly entering at the same time. But Clarinda, without discourtesy or apparent haste, managed to press forward, and presently she and Ruth were safely seated at the side of the section reserved for the debutantes, in the front row of the call-out section. This occupied the entire space under the balcony and was filling rapidly; while beyond it, across the cleared floor, a group of little boys, dressed like miniature chefs, came joyously charging, their arms full of programs, which they distributed with many bows and

161

smiles. Clarinda glanced casually at her program, but Ruth studied hers with eager attention. The text was framed by an arbor-like design which harmonized, in miniature, with the huge clusters of grapes and the rich hangings of green and purple with which the Auditorium was decorated; and supplementing the greeting of the Twelfth Night Revelers to their guests and the invitation to attend "A Grape Festival in a Persian Vineyard," appeared a quotation from Omar Khayyam:

> "Better be jocund with the fruitful grape
> Than sadden after none or bitter fruit."

Suddenly the music took a livelier turn and there were other signs that activities were impending. Vague sounds began to drift in from the foyer and some kind of a stir seemed to be taking place outside. Then a door opened and a procession of beautiful girls entered the hall and advanced with dignity across the floor.

"That's the '47 Court," Clarinda told Ruth. "The King's guard will escort them to the royal box. It's a sort of preliminary rite. The real celebration begins afterwards."

Ruth nodded, her eyes on the girls who had just been seated with such ceremony. But almost immediately she was diverted. Another door opened and a bevy of "chefs" appeared, marshalling an enormous cake, surmounted by glittering candles; and having wheeled this to the middle of the floor, they capered gaily about it. In their wake came a second group of maskers, dressed in Oriental costumes of purple and green; and at almost the same moment, the curtains of the stage parted, to reveal the King seated on a resplendent throne, his Dukes about him, in the midst of a trellised garden.

"Do you like to have me explain as this goes along, or would you rather just watch?" Clarinda asked, noticing that Ruth looked a little puzzled, as the 1947 Queen, who only a few minutes earlier had been conducted to the royal box, was now led with even more ceremony to the throne.

"I love to have you explain. I can watch while I listen."

"Well, last year's Queen will continue to reign until the first call-out's over and the Cake March is held. Then the new Queen will take her place. Look! They're starting now."

The "chefs" and the "Persians" were already romping across the floor, beckoning to the debutantes to join them; and presently the Revelers and their partners were clustered

162

around the cake together, the maskers thrusting their hands into it and drawing out tiny boxes which they offered to the debutantes.

"One of those boxes has a gold bean in it," Clarinda whispered to Ruth. "The girl who gets that will be the Queen. Then six other boxes have silver beans in them. The girls who get those will be her Maids. It's supposed to be all a matter of chance at this ball—that's why the Queen isn't in her royal robes already. But, actually, everything's been carefully planned. The boxes with the beans in them have been marked and they'll be given to the girls who were chosen weeks ago. Unless there's a slip-up. Sometimes there is. But I hope there won't be tonight, because if rumors are true, the Queen's one of the loveliest girls in New Orleans."

Again Ruth merely nodded, as by this time she was almost too enthralled for speech. Obviously there was no mishap, for the atmosphere of the ball had become one of released anticipation ending in delight. A sceptre of purple orchids was handed to the new Queen; then her silver mantle, edged with purple velvet, was fastened to her shoulders, and her glittering crown, bedecked with one tall white feather, set upon her head. In turn, her Maids were given baskets of grapes and capes of ruffled tarlatan, grape trimmed. They gathered about their Queen; the cortege made its way around the hall and finally the King and Queen mounted to their joint throne in the "Persian Vineyard."

"It'll be our turn now. The first dance is just for the debutantes. But afterwards it's a free-for-all."

"I don't suppose I'll be dancing much. You see I hardly know anyone in New Orleans. And I really shan't mind if I don't. I'm enjoying everything so much, just watching."

Again Ruth realized that she had not spoken the whole truth, that though it did not matter whether she had a whirl or not, she would be bitterly disappointed if she did not have two or three dances with Russ. And again Clarinda looked at her out of those dreamy eyes which saw so much more than they betrayed, her lips curving in that slow charming smile. At the same moment, the black-coated committeemen began to call out names.

"Miss Mary Bond—Miss Cornelia Sheldon—Mrs. Charles Valliat—Miss Ruth Avery!"

Clarinda gave her a little shove. "Stand up, so the committeemen can see you and then edge over to the aisle. Your masker's right there waiting for you."

Obediently, Ruth rose, assenting to the nearest committeeman's repetition of her name, which he pronounced this time like a question. He offered her his arm and she took it; but almost immediately a tall masker claimed her and led her rather slowly and formally towards the throne, where he stopped, releasing her long enough to make a deep bow while she curtsied. Then he put his arm around her and they began to dance. Ruth did not try to "penetrate his disguise"; it was quite unnecessary. And he did not make trivial talk or ask superfluous questions; he did not need to be assured that the spectacle she was witnessing for the first time intrigued and charmed her. Once more, she was aware of harmony which brought happiness with it, and realized that this feeling far transcended the superficial enjoyment of a pleasant dance; and once more the vision of the dark caves of Roatan rose to menace her gladness . . . .

A whistle blew, and her partner took his arm from her waist, slowly, as if he were as loath to let her go as she was to have him. Then, as they reached the aisle nearest her seat, he plunged his hand into the white bag which was slung over his shoulder and drew from it a small box which was wrapped in tissue paper and tied with blue ribbon.

"I hope you will often drink to the health of the Revelers, Miss Avery," he said, with a bow as low as the one he had made to the Queen. Then he turned away and was swallowed up in the throng.

Ruth sat down and untied her package excitedly. It proved to contain a tiny silver goblet, marked with the letters T. N. R. and the numerals 1948. She looked towards Clarinda, who had evidently just reseated herself too, and who was untying a similar package.

"This year's official favor," Clarinda explained. "Pretty, isn't it? If you got enough of them, they'd make a nice liqueur set. And, of course, there'll be lots of other favors too."

"But I don't expect to get any more. And this is charming just by itself. I'll keep it for—"

The committeemen were calling again.

"Miss Margery LeBoeuf—Miss Elaine Caldwell—Miss Ruth Avery—"

Once more she was on her feet, back in the aisle, back on the dance floor, back before the throne. She was dancing, more gaily and unrestrainedly than the first time; she was opening another package. And before she could replace it in its tissue paper nest, she was answering another summons. She was dancing with tall chefs and short chefs, chefs who were strikingly slender, chefs who were pleasantly plump. Some of them chatted incessantly, some paid her extravagant compliments, some had obviously dined well rather than wisely. But each in his own way added to the thrill of the evening; and each suffered somewhat by comparison with the special chef for whose intermittent return she eagerly waited.

By the time the ball was over, her favors were heaped all around her, and Clarinda, instead of saying, "I told you so!" was smiling more and more charmingly. She had plenty of favors herself; but Ruth felt sure, that even if this had not been the case, there would have been no envy in Clarinda's heart-shaped, dimpled face.

"I want to come and help christen the liqueur set," she told Ruth, as the limousine finally turned into the courtyard. "You'll let me, won't you? And I want you to come to my house too. I don't suppose Mr. Foxworth has time for dinner parties?"

"No, I'm afraid not. He's terribly busy. And besides—"

Ruth checked herself. Probably her uncle's connection with the Lalandes was an open secret; even so, she had no right to refer to it. But once more Clarinda smiled understandingly.

"Well, let's not add to all the other complications he has on his hands. But I'd like to give a little luncheon for you anyway—just girls—so that some of my friends can meet you. Then we can make plans for all the rest of Carnival. You're going to stay through Mardi Gras, of course."

"I meant to, when I came, but now I'm not sure. I'm afraid my uncle may have to change his schedule, for business reasons."

"Afraid" was the right word. She would not have minded, before, but now she knew that she wanted to go to more and more balls, she wanted to see Carnival through to the end. She would not have believed that the spirit of it would be so contagious. She was ready to admit her mistake.

"Well, that would be too bad, of course, but don't let it affect your schedule. I'd love to have you as my house guest. We'll talk about that too, at the luncheon. I'll call you up tomorrow and fix a date. Good night, Ruth."

"Good night, Clarinda. And thanks a million for everything."

Well, it must be getting very late. She really should stop lying there, daydreaming. If she didn't, Ellen would be forestalling her ring again, knocking respectfully, but persistently, looking grave, speaking in a serious tone of voice. Ruth sat up in bed, straightened her tumbled pillows and touched her bell. Ellen appeared promptly, bearing a tray adorned with some fine specimens of Lady Hume's Blush. A note lay

165

underneath the delicate shell pink blossoms. Ruth tore it open and read:

Wednesday Morning.

Dear Ruth:

    I did so enjoy meeting you Monday night that I do want to see you again, and Joe does too. As far as either of us knows, there is no great gala event going on tonight, and if you're free, we'd love to have you dine with us at Antoine's. (This is one of the nights we have a sitter, and I don't like to ask you to take potluck with us so soon again!) It won't be a magnificent party, in the 1840 Room, the way Mr. Foxworth's was, just a very quiet little dinner in the small back room Joe likes best—the part of the restaurant where the old mushroom cellar used to be. We aren't asking any one else except Sabin Duplessis, who is pretty low in his mind right now, and needs cheering up. We're sure you can help us do this.

    Unless we hear from you that you can't come, we'll call for you around seven. But if you'd rather go to some other restaurant, don't hesitate to say so. I suggest Antoine's because it's Joe's favorite, and because I can't believe you feel that Mr. Foxworth's party had any direct connection with what happened afterward to poor Odile. However, there are lots of other good places to eat, so if you do have any feeling, please say so quite candidly.

    Hoping to see you soon, and with kind regards, in which Joe joins me,

> *Cordially yours,*
> *Judith Farnham Racina.*

Judith was right in assuming that Ruth had no feeling that her uncle's dinner was in any way responsible for the subsequent tragedy, and she had no other plans for the evening. Russ had told her he was tied up with some sort of a scientific meeting; he had not mentioned Roatan again, but she guessed that the appointment might have some connection with the expedition, and was glad of a chance to do something herself which would divert her thoughts from the possible consequences of this gathering. Her uncle seemed to have so completely dismissed her from his plan of action that she did not believe any engagement she might make would concern him one way or another. However, he surprised her by coming home for luncheon, and she paid him the rather empty compliment of consulting him.

"Sure, go by all means," he said more agreeably than he had spoken in some time. "By the way, I hear you made quite a killing last night."

"Well, I did have a good time," Ruth admitted.

"A good time! If the rumors that are going around are true, you were the belle of the ball. And I'm glad you went to the Revels with Clarinda. She's far and away the most stunning girl I've seen since I got to New Orleans. I rather think I ought to make a point of telling her so. I owe her an apology of sorts. I didn't even recognize her when she spoke to me in the Blue Room the other night, she's changed and developed so much since I was here last."

"I think she'd be very pleased if you told her you think she's stunning. Caresse says she's a great admirer of yours. And she asked me herself if I thought you'd have time for a dinner party. I didn't encourage her because I know how busy you are and—everything."

"Well, you showed your usual good sense. As a matter of fact though, I'd rather enjoy a dinner at the Darcoas'—or we might have them here, very quietly. Of course, I don't want to do anything Mrs. Lalande would interpret as a lack of feeling, at this time. But we'll see. Anyway, the Darcoa connection's a good one. It might even be . . . ."

Obviously the immediate success she had scored and her report on Clarinda were both immensely gratifying to him. She decided to take advantage of his unexpected good humor to ask him a few guarded questions.

"Please don't think I'm prying, Uncle," she began. "I'm not, really. But you did say—or rather Downes said—you were going to your room early Saturday, because you were so tired, and that you didn't want to be disturbed."

Foxworth's air of casual good humor vanished. "That's right," he answered curtly. And then, as Ruth hesitated, he asked, "Well?"

"I'm sorry if mention of it displeases you," she went on. "But it's only that Joe Racina and Russ Aldridge both know you weren't—in your room, I mean. And if you didn't mind, I would so like to be able to explain to them that . . . ."

"So far as that goes, I don't give a damn what either of them thinks. I certainly don't propose to justify my actions to them—or to any other Tom, Dick, or Harry who wants to poke his nose into what doesn't concern him."

"But honestly, Uncle, Russ wasn't prying. He wouldn't dream of . . . . I mean, it just happened that he was along. Of course, Joe kept on saying he knew you wouldn't be home, and when Russ bet him you were, he still wouldn't believe it.

167

And after that, when we found you really weren't here, he seemed to think you might be doing something you were trying to conceal."

"Well, I was. I do lots of things I don't want everybody in on. But strike Aldridge, by all means. I take back what I said about his sticking his nose into my business. It goes double for that long, lean clown of a newshound, though. If his poking around should happen to cause me any real annoyance, I'll find ways to take care of him. Small fry of his stripe never did bother me any too much. What the devil affair of his was it, or is it, what I do?"

"It was about some friend of his in Central America. I forget the name. And the merger with Trans-Caribbean, and all sorts of things like that. I didn't understand very well . . . . And if it hadn't been for what happened at the Lalandes' that same night . . . . It's just that I wouldn't want him to think—"

"That's enough, Ruth! I don't care to discuss it any further. So far as I'm concerned, Joe Racina can think what he pleases; if he makes himself too objectionable about what is strictly my business, he'll get hurt. He wouldn't be the first one to find out I'm not the sort of person to brook interference of that sort. For your own peace of mind, my dear," Foxworth went on, his tone losing some of its edginess, "don't you trouble that pretty head of yours about anything that went on at Richmond Place so far as I'm concerned. I don't know whether Odile killed herself or was killed. If she killed herself, that's that. If she didn't, the old nigger woman, Tossie, is already under arrest and charged with doing it. Which reminds me, I've got to get her a lawyer, the best one to be had."

He took a small leather memorandum book from his coat pocket, scribbled a notation in it, and restored it to its place. With the action, his earlier good humor seemed to return.

"That's that," he said with obvious satisfaction. "And, by all means, run along to your dinner. If, by any chance, your host indicates a desire to pump you about me or my business, let him know—from me—that he's fooling around with a buzz saw. And I think you'll find Sabin Duplessis—didn't you say he'd be there too?—lots of fun. You know I suggested him before as a possible squire for you."

Ruth refrained from reminding her uncle that, on this same occasion, he had lauded Joe Racina to the skies. She had learned, somewhat to her discomfiture, that the fact Foxworth voiced an opinion one day did not necessarily mean he would still hold it the next, and that it was unwise to confront him with such inconsistency. "Still wouldn't be a

168

bad plan—give Aldridge a run for his money," Foxworth went on. "Quite a chap, Duplessis, even if he does seem to be a little on the *précieuse* side. Sometimes you'd think he's the kind who'd go in for china painting and that sort of thing. But he's *muy hombre,* as they say down in Puerto de Oro— one of the few people I'd not want to tangle with unless I had to."

Judith had been right in saying that her little dinner would be entirely different from Orson Foxworth's, though it ended on a note which was no less ominous.

Even the beginning was different. Joe led his group straight to a small, inconspicuous side door, where no line was drawn up, and secured immediate entry. Then, without ceremony, he headed straight for the small plain room that he liked, where the round table, like those in the outer dining room, was unadorned except for a carafe in the center.

"Do either of you girls want cocktails?" he inquired. "We're going to have a good wine with our dinner," and as Ruth and Judith both shook their heads, he went on. "Neither do I, and you're just as well off without one, Sabin."

"That's what you think. But if you don't mind, I'll have a double Dry Martini . . . . Oliver's aren't quite up to Downes'," he said, turning from his host to his fellow guest, "but they're pretty fair, at that. You better join me. Don't let Joe bulldoze you."

"I shan't. But I shan't let you overpersuade me either," she retorted.

"Are you sure? Not about anything? Want to bet on it?"

He was quick on the uptake, she could see that, and she also saw what Caresse had meant in describing him as exciting. Without being handsome, he was extremely striking in appearance, slight and dark and given to quick sudden movements which had an almost uncanny grace. A small black mustache, hardly heavier than his eyebrows, followed the curve of his upper lip, and his teeth looked all the whiter by contrast. His face, like his hands, was tanned to a golden brown and he gave the effect of being still in uniform and still ready to take off for parts unknown at a moment's notice. He sipped his drinks slowly, meanwhile making delightful small talk and Ruth found his magnetism inescapable. Judith sat by, lovely and composed, taking no part in the lively dialogue, but obviously undisturbed by it, Joe, on the contrary, began to show signs of impatience.

"Look here, Sabin, that makes three doubles you've had

now," he said at last. "Let's get going on some food before you start looping."

He motioned to the slim mustachioed waiter, "Go ahead and bring in the shrimp aspic, Abraham," he ordered, rather shortly. Abraham bowed and hastened off, leaving the little room just as a bus boy entered it, bringing French bread, hot from the oven. Joe extracted one of the long, crusty loaves from its enveloping napkin and offered it to Ruth, who broke off the heel.

"Don't fill up on it," he warned her, as the others helped themselves. "You're quite welcome to it, you understand. But there's some real food on the way. Not the sort of plushy feast your uncle provided the other night, as Judith wrote you, Ruth. But every dish quite an achievement in its own way. ... I remember the first time I ever had this particular version of shrimp in aspic," he continued as Abraham reappeared and placed a glistening, ruby-colored serving before each of the diners. "I'd never been to Antoine's before, and I guess I'd looked forward to it more or less ever since I was old enough to realize that food needn't be just something to satisfy hunger. I was a cub reporter at the time, and Clark Salmon—he was city editor of the *Item* when I broke in— was decent enough to give me an assignment to cover some bankers' association dinner here. Honestly, I can still recall the sort of reverent ecstasy that followed the first taste of Antoine's shrimp aspic."

"Don't pay too much attention to Joe when he gets started on the subject of food," Judith said. "Or he won't get off it all the evening. He'll only go on to say how much better it is here than anywhere else in the world and start making invidious comparisons between Creole cookery and everything we eat in New England. I've heard all that hundreds of times now. I'd like to hear about something else for a change—the Twelfth Night Revels, for instance. Did you enjoy them, Ruth?"

"Oh, *yes!*" Ruth answered emphatically; and without further urging she gave an enthusiastic description of her first Carnival ball, ending with a glowing tribute to Clarinda. "When I saw her standing in the library, wearing that pink tulle dress, and all those camellias, I felt as if she'd stepped right out of a dream—a dream I'd never really believed would come true, though I'd hoped it would, for years. Of course, I like Caresse a lot too—I didn't think I was going to at first, but I do," she added candidly. "And I feel badly when I remember that, if she hadn't been in such dreadful

170

trouble, I wouldn't have gone to the ball with Clarinda. But just the same—"

"Just the same, Clarinda was your dream come true," Judith said understandingly. "I see just how you feel. But perhaps the worst of the trouble Caresse has had is over. Perhaps this wonderful opening in New York—" She interrupted herself to outline the offer from Haas and Hector to Sabin, who was now doing full justice to the excellent Chambertin, which had been served with the filets Marchand de Vin. "Have you seen Caresse since she talked with Miss Hickey?" Judith asked Ruth in conclusion.

"Yes. She came in yesterday morning and told me all about it. She's very hopeful that she can get off by the end of the week."

"Well, she can't," Joe said shortly. "I tried to tell her so Monday night, you may remember. I wanted to emphasize what I'd said at the table on the drive home too, but she dodged me. I reckon I'll have to corner her and talk to her in words of one syllable."

"Why?" inquired Sabin.

"Because—well, let's skip it. I was hoping we could get by without any reference to what happened the other night. We'd much better have stuck to the subject of food."

"What the hell," said Sabin, with a touch of impatience. "If we all sit around here bound and determined not to talk about anything connected with Odile, and worrying about whether some casual expression might remind us of her, it'll be one lousy party. We might as well be frank about it, and if any of us feels like mentioning it, go ahead."

"I suppose you're right," Joe agreed. "I know I can't help thinking about it. Probably none of us can. Speaking for myself, I keep wondering just what did happen to that poor girl. Toe Murphy's not the ordinary run of dumb cop. He's a college man—admittedly on an athletic scholarship, but even so, he's not just some precinct bully who was handed a uniform, a gun, and a badge on his ward leader's say-so that he'd make a good policeman. And he had a damn fine record in the FBI school. I heard about that while I was in Washington."

"As far as I could see, he wouldn't rate any Nobel prizes." Sabin put down his wineglass and spoke rather jeeringly. "I thought I was in for a rough ride, when he started to question me. As a matter of fact, he didn't seem especially interested in anything I had to say. He made me tell him about where and how I got that gun and why I gave it to Odile. Then he asked me what I'd done Saturday night, and I

171

told him I was too stinko to know. That was about the sum and substance of the whole thing."

"I expect he's waiting for the grand jury," Joe said reflectively. "That's what they're holding Tossie for . . . In this state you can't be tried on a capital charge unless the grand jury indicts you first," he explained to Ruth. "And of course they wouldn't call a special grand jury for something like this. So Tossie's just got to stay behind bars until the regular jury day. . . . All the same, Toe isn't the kind to go off the deep end. If he says Odile was murdered, he's got some reason for it. Sure, he might be mistaken. But it isn't just a wild guess he's grabbed out of the nearest hat. And for the same reason, I know he doesn't believe Tossie did the killing."

Sabin nodded.

"I know she didn't too," he agreed. "If Odile was killed, it was a man who did it."

For a moment, no one spoke. Ruth looked across the table and saw that Judith was watching Joe. But, for once, Joe was oblivious of Judith. He had been leaning forward on his crossed arms, in his characteristic attitude. Now, though his position did not perceptibly change, there was no longer anything about it that suggested pleasant relaxation.

"A man?" he asked quietly, almost casually.

"Sure, a man," Sabin continued. "I'd had an emotional jolt of my own Saturday night that started me off on a binge and took me uptown, downtown, all around the town—you know how that wound up. I don't remember much about what I was doing or where I was. But one picture stands out pretty clearly. That is the yellow block of a drawn shade in the window of Odile's room—the window opening on that screened patio. And there were two shadows on the blind, a girl's and a man's. The girl's shadow was Odile's. I mean, it must have been. I don't know whose shadow the man's was, but I naturally assumed it was Léonce. Anyway, it was a man. Nobody could have been mistaken about that. And while I was looking the two shadows came together and made one shadow. Maybe it was an embrace, maybe it was . . . ."

His voice trailed away into silence.

"Maybe it could have been a struggle?" Joe asked.

"I suppose so," Sabin answered absently. "I wouldn't know. The sight of those two shadows coming together and making one shadow drove me nuts. Of course, I'd been drinking anyway, so it isn't all too clear in my mind, outside of that one sharp picture. And the rest of the night's a blank.

172

I must have gone around from one joint to another, spoiling for a fight, and finally getting service. But I don't remember that part of it," he concluded, raising his glass again.

"So you don't remember anything that happened afterwards!" Joe snapped, his voice no longer indolent and casual.

"That's right .... Say! What do you think you're trying to get at?"

"Just this. You're my guest, and all that, but I'm pretty familiar with the layout at 84 Richmond myself. There isn't but one place from which you could have seen what you've just described, and that's from inside the walled garden beyond the patio. There's no gate in the wall, and it's high enough to shut out any view of the ground floor windows from the street. There aren't but two ways to get into that garden. One of them's through the house, the other by climbing the wall. So I'm asking you what the hell you were doing inside that walled garden on the night Odile was killed by a gun that belonged to you!"

11

How Joe and Judith Racina talked things through in front of a grate fire—

January 7, 1948

THE INSTANT of silence which followed Joe's challenge was surcharged with impending violence. But before this could burst into being, Abraham entered, proudly bearing a silver bowl, and somehow the gathering tension eased. Judith reached along the table and laid her hand on her husband's arm; he responded with a quick smile of reassurance. At the same moment Ruth turned to Sabin, who was visibly fighting for self-control, and disregarding his suppressed fury, deftly created a conversational diversion.

"*Brûlot!*" she exclaimed. "I was fascinated when I saw it being made the other night, in the big dining room, and I hoped Uncle would have some at his dinner too. But he didn't and I was a little disappointed. So I'm all the more delighted that Joe and Judith thought of it."

"I thought of it, but I took it for granted you'd have had it before, and I didn't order it," Joe told her. "We can still have it though—and we will. This is something else—a Jubilee."

Abraham had titled a cup of brandy into the silver bowl and Ruth saw that this held large dark cherries. Abraham ignited the brandy and stirred the mixture with a silver ladle. The blue flames leaped and danced until the juices of the simmering cherries were thoroughly blended with the seething spirits. At this point Abraham ladled them over rounded portions of bland ice cream, and, with a flourish, placed them before the silent diners. Then, with an expression of satisfaction, he quietly withdrew, leaving the door open behind him to facilitate his next entry. Sabin pushed back his chair, went to the door, and closed it with a crash. Standing before it, he faced Joe.

"Now we'll have an understanding, Racina," he said unsteadily. "And I mean now. Right now."

"Sit down, Sabin," Joe said, his tone quiet and casual again. "We'll have an understanding, but we'll reach it like ordinary human beings, and not like road company hams. I asked you a question that you'll have to answer sooner or later anyway, because if you've said too much in letting anybody know you were in that garden Saturday night, you've also said too little if you don't explain it."

"I'd like very much to see the collection of china in the corridor," Ruth suggested. "Perhaps if Judith would take me to look at it, you two men—"

"That's a nice gesture, but it's superfluous," Sabin broke in harshly. "If anybody's going to leave, I am. But not before I tell Joe that of all the swine I've ever encountered, he's the filthiest."

"You're going up in your lines, pal," Joe retorted. "Filthy cur is the word, not filthy swine. And you need a glove in your hand so you can strike me across the face and say something about pistols for two and coffee for one. For God's sake, Sabin, quit hamming. Somebody's been killed—remember? And out of a clear sky, you come along and announce you were on the scene, drunk as a fiddler's wench, at about the time the killing took place. What are we supposed to do next? Play gin rummy? I'm asking you what you were doing there?"

"And I'm telling you it's none of your business."

"If Odile was murdered it's everybody's business. You say you talked to Toe Murphy yesterday. Did you by any chance tell him what you've just told us?"

"That's no business of yours either. But just for the hell of it, I'll answer you. No, I didn't tell your friend Detective Captain Murphy anything about it. And what's more, I'll tell you why I didn't. Odile was killed by a man. I propose to find out who that man was, and when I do I'll kill him with my own two hands. You think that's hamming, too. You think I'm drunk again because I've had a couple of cocktails and a few glasses of wine. Well, I'm not. My mind's a lot clearer than yours. A lot cleaner, too. And if you'll follow me out—because I'm leaving here—I'll tell you what else you can do with your questions and rotten stinking insinuations."

"Mr. Duplessis," Ruth said gently. "I'm sure this is only

175

one of those misunderstandings that can easily be cleared up. If you'll just sit down so that we can all try to . . . ."

Mockingly, Sabin interrupted her. "Sorry, I really haven't a thing fit to wear. If I've said anything to offend you or Judith, please consider that I've apologized profusely. But also please remember that I wasn't the one who started this riot." He opened the door to the hallway. "As I said before, I'm not drunk. But I probably shall be in the very near future. Good night. I've had *such* a good time. You must come see me, real soon."

The door slammed behind him and he was gone.

"I sure do hand it to Ruth Avery," Joe told Judith after they had deposited their guest at her uncle's house and were headed home. "If diplomatic training can give a girl the amount of balance she's shown this last hour, I'm all for it. I hadn't supposed it would. I've seen something of those cookie-pushers and muffin-hounds in the crowd she runs with in Washington. And I had a pretty horrible moment, wondering whether she could take it, when I saw her confronted by a maniac who may or may not have just killed somebody, but who's certainly done a lot of other killing here and there in his time."

"In your scorn for the cookie-pushers and the muffin-hounds you're overlooking the fact that she's met a good many other types during the course of her stepfather's career," Judith retorted. "Including her stepfather himself. He's the one who's really set her standards, not the gilded youth from the obscure recesses of the State Department and the less exalted and more needy embassies. Sabin's certainly not her first sample of the Armed Forces; and most of them have done their fair share of killing."

"You're not mad at me by any chance, are you, Judith?"

"Of course I'm mad at you. It's all very well for you to step into the spotlight with your second-act climax; but how do you think I felt when Sabin went to pieces that way, raging and cursing and calling you a swine?"

"I hope you had sense enough to gather that he's an incurable romanticist, complicated by liquor. And his scenery-chewing sure laid an egg, as far as I was concerned. He capped the climax when he roared that the reason he hadn't told Murphy what he'd seen was because he was proposing to track down the killer himself."

"I suppose the kindest thing to say about him is that he's unbalanced."

"You ought to keep more up to date, m'love. 'Maladjusted' is the latest psycho tag line. It's a pip, too, because you can toss it anywhere. What you really mean though is that Sabin is nuts, to which I say, 'Amen!' But the question remains, how nuts? Enough to kill someone?"

"Not someone he loved! And Sabin did love Odile."

"What are you talking about? Not a day goes by that someone doesn't kill a sweetheart or an estranged wife on the theory that if he can't have her nobody else shall. But usually these apes give themselves up after they've finished the job, almost as if they wanted to make sure everybody knew what they'd done and why .... Tired, Judy?"

"Not a bit .... And I know what that's leading up to. So while you take Ethel home, I'll have a look at our hostages and get my knitting and a fresh package of cigarettes for you."

She laughed back at him as she got out of the car and, on the third try, managed to slam the door hard enough to engage the latch. Joe kept the motor idling. Judith let herself into the house and, after a few minutes, their faithful sitter appeared, bundled in a shapeless topcoat.

"You really needn't have waited, Mr. Racina," she protested, "you know I've only got three blocks to go."

" 'Tis a foul night for man or beast to be abroad, lass," Joe replied grandly. "Let the Farmer's Daughter bear you homeward on wings of exhaust gas. Hop in—but you'll have to slam that door pretty hard or it won't stay shut."

Years earlier, when its fresh luster was as yet unmarred by contact with the world, Joe had christened his car the Farmer's Daughter because of its intermittent but intimate relation with a traveling man—himself. Upon being questioned, he tried to explain this to the puzzled sitter in the course of their brief ride; then, having deposited her at the door of her boarding house, he turned back up Henry Clay Avenue and brought the Farmer's Daughter to a halt in a corrugated iron garage. Sidling out, he launched the usual struggle to bring the sprung doors of his garage into approximate register; the day when hasp and staple could be made to coincide was long since one with the ages and a bit of baling wire now effected a compromise fastening. Thoughtfully, Joe appraised its progressive inadequacy. The time was not far off when he would have to find a longer piece of wire.

Whistling cheerfully, he opened the back door, which Judith had unlatched for him. The kitchen and pantry were clean and quiet and, as usual, he made a mental comparison between the condition of Judith's domain and his own. Then he passed through the pleasant dining room to the book-lined study, where a fresh fire crackled cozily in the grate, and letting himself down into his special armchair, fumbled for a cigarette and grinned at Judith, who was already seated on the other side of the hearth. In the early days of their marriage, when Joe was eking out his newspaper salary by writing he-and-she romances for the pulps, he had fallen into the habit of working out involved variations on the boy-meets-girl theme by discussing his plots with his wife. Very often a casual suggestion from her had provided just the fresh lead he needed to give the shopworn sequence a new switch; and with the passage of years, his habit of talking things through with her had become more and more fixed. She realized this was what he meant to do now.

"If it were only a question of Sabin, and did-he-or-didn't-he, this conversation would be brief and simple," Joe said, without preamble. But he fell silent again and some moments passed before he added, "I suppose the first thing to do is to decide whether Odile's death was a murder or a suicide. And the hell of it is, they're both equally plausible. You can rationalize one as readily as the other."

"How?"

"Well, let's take suicide first. That girl didn't have just one good reason for it; she had half a dozen. Four, anyway. First, her realization that she'd be a hopeless invalid the rest of her days. That must have come as a terrific shock. You know how you used to wonder, back there in Walter Reed Hospital, whether you'd be able to face disfigurement."

"I couldn't have, if it hadn't been for you, Joe."

"All right, I'll accept that for this time, because it fits in with what I'm going to say next. Even if I do needle you now and again, you know I think the sun rises and sets on your head. But Léonce was two-timing Odile and their marriage had become a rather sorry mess. You weren't there the other night to see the bits of by-play between him and Caresse and the blaze in his eyes whenever she gave him the brush-off. It was plain as a pikestaff that there was or had been something between those two. Matter of fact, Caresse herself admitted Odile might have had reason to think she and Léonce were carrying on an affair."

"That would have been pretty sordid, Joe. Her own sister, in her own house!"

"I'll grant you that. But Léonce is a tomcat who thinks of himself as a sort of male Mata Hari—a man no woman can resist. I've heard you say he had a sort of dark magnetism about him. I wouldn't know about that. But evidently there was a hell of a flirtation going on; enough to give Odile the idea that she was being cheated and that she 'couldn't take it any longer,' as her note put it."

"If that were true I don't see how she could," Judith admitted thoughtfully.

"Glad you agree with me," Joe remarked, obviously encouraged to spin out his theories at still greater length. "Léonce was Odile's second reason. As to the third, I got the idea from some of Sabin's ravings tonight that maybe he and Odile suddenly began to realize, sometime in the course of the past few days, how much they still loved one another. Conceivably that might have been what brought on Odile's hysteria. They certainly had some kind of a definite understanding once, even if they weren't formally engaged. Then came the war, and of course Sabin volunteered right off. For one thing, it was the sort of exhibitionism that suited him so well—dashing off into uniform. For another, he has got guts, even if he does go in for Ming pottery and Huan jade or whatever it is."

"And while he was away . . . ."

"Exactly. Sabin was a touch too old, I gathered, to make combat aviation, and was assigned to army transport service when he applied for bomber training. It was just one of those things. They had lots of bomber pilots at the moment, I suppose, and needed some more transport fliers in a hurry. In the army you do what you're told. But he was never stationed at any one base—it was Iceland one day and Dakar the next, with a quick shift to Noumea, or wherever. Finally came the news that his plane had gone down somewhere between Calcutta and Kunming. Some top brass was with him, a couple of our generals and one Limey. So Odile thought he was dead. It isn't strange you never heard all these details. This happened while you were in Africa, or were still hospitalized."

"And about this time, I suppose, Léonce St. Amant came along."

"Right. Léonce, and what you call his dark magnetism, whatever that might be. Anyway, the girls went for him, and Odile was no exception. Most of the people who knew him figured that the only reason he settled down to marriage in such a hurry was that he thought the draft might get him after all, heart murmur or no heart murmur. And of course there were those who realized that Amélie and her two girls were all mighty well fixed, and that Léonce was marrying a damn good income, with a lovely and charming gal to go along with the bargain. I don't know, though. I think he loved her about as much as he's capable of loving any woman, and about as steadfastly. He was certainly a devoted husband for a while .... And then he slipped off to the old playboy routine of love 'em and leave 'em, wherever he could make a pass and get away with it. Later on, Odile's illness gave him all the excuse he needed to justify himself to himself."

"But somewhere along the line Sabin turned up again."

"In person. Harder and a bit drawn. Pretty bitter when he found out how things stood, of course. He's got plenty of money, left to him by some doting aunt. Sabin made no bones about the fact that if he ever got into another plane, that would be too soon to suit him. And so there wasn't really much to keep him occupied. He would see Odile from time to time, but always with others around; and there would be these occasional Saturday lunches and bridge fights at his studio .... There was one of them the day Odile was killed—or killed herself. We're still arguing that point, aren't we?"

"You are."

"All right, I am. Suppose, then, she found out that marrying Léonce had really been a ghastly mistake, not because of the way *he* acted, but because of the way *she* felt. Suppose she looked ahead and saw herself tied for life—a long life of invalidism—to one man, and hopelessly in love with another. Maybe that's what she couldn't take any longer. God knows it's a situation which has driven many others to suicide in the past .... Anyway, what it all adds up to is that if self-destruction is ever a reasonable act, Odile St. Amant had reasonable grounds and to spare for taking her own life. That makes it believable she did so."

"Unless it's even more believable that someone had a reason for wanting her out of the way."

"Who, for instance?"

Joe fairly shot out the question. But Judith's answer came like an answering shot.

"Her mother."

For a moment of electrified silence, Joe stared at his wife. Then he jumped up and came quickly to her side.

"That took me right between wind and water, Jude," he said. "It's so completely wide of the mark I've been shooting at. Whatever gave you the idea? I know you've never liked Amélie Lalande, but—"

"Never liked her! How could I like her? I've always known she was a shallow, heartless, scheming, catlike woman, that all the talk about her devotion to her daughters was just so much gush! You know her name has been linked with

180

Foxworth's for years and years, and there've been no end of theories as to why they didn't marry. One was that Foxworth isn't the marrying kind, whereas Amélie's precisely the sort of person who would insist on bell, book, and candle. Another was that Foxworth spent most of his time in and out of Puerto de Oro and that Amélie wouldn't have any part of burying herself down there."

With a hiss, a small jet of gas escaped from a lump of coal and took fire in a long bright finger of yellow flame. Judith watched it for a moment and then went on.

"But the day after Odile's death, Foxworth tells Ruth he and Amélie are to be married, which means they had been planning it before. Now tell me this: is it too unthinkable that Amélie had finally decided to count New Orleans well lost for love amid the breadfruit—and that then along came Perrault's verdict about Odile's condition? Wouldn't that mean the marriage would have to be indefinitely postponed, especially in view of Amélie's devoted-mother routine?"

Joe let himself down on the arm of Judith's chair.

"You know, you could have something there," he admitted thoughtfully. "Only if you follow that line of reasoning, you've got to include Foxworth. He couldn't abdicate from the empire he's built up in Central America. As long as he heads the Great Blue Fleet, his base of operations must be Puerto de Oro. He and Amélie couldn't take a hopeless paralytic into their tropic Paradise. Odile needed the care that couldn't be provided for her there, and, moreover, she's married to a fathead for whom Foxworth has about as much use as he'd have for an attack of amoebic dysentery . . . . So it's your hunch that after all these years everything was about to go right when Perrault steps in and, so to speak, forbids the banns."

"Yes, and that gives me another idea. In addition to everything else, Amélie might be saying to herself: 'You'd really be doing the girl a great favor if you killed her. You'd be sparing her years of wretchedness.' I don't say it's the sort of temptation to which she would yield. But human beings frequently do yield to temptation, beginning with Adam. And with Odile out of the way painlessly, quickly, and mercifully— Amélie could at last attain her heart's desire. There you are. She had the opportunity and she had the motive—the two things detectives are always talking about."

The glow in the grate fire was fading. Joe rose from the arm of Judith's chair and poked the coals; then he added a fresh shovelful from the scuttle on his side of the hearth and sat down again.

181

"Both of them had the motive and the opportunity," he admitted. "As I said before, you've got to include Foxworth. You know, you're pretty good at this, Jude. Any more suspicions, Miss Pinkerton?"

"No. I'll leave the rest to you."

"All right. Let's get on to the others. Léonce not only had the opportunity and the motive, but he's stupid. Remember how Tossie—no, you weren't there. I was though. I do remember, distinctly. Tossie swore she saw Léonce prowling around the hall that night. He might have been trying to sneak out of the house on some chasing expedition. He might have been on his way to or from Odile's room, despite the doctor's orders. He might have been making a play for Caresse, though God knows he wasn't getting any encouragement from that quarter while I was around. For that matter, her show of despising her brother-in-law might have been a case of protesting too much. Certainly he and she had just been in some sort of escapade that involved smashing up his car. It could have been innocent enough; also it could have been something else. Temptation could have been whispering to them too, saying the kindest thing anyone could do for that suffering girl would be to put an end to her wretchedness. And there you have it again—both of them with undenied opportunity, both of them with a conceivable motive, both of them tugged by temptation—and in addition, one of them stupid enough to do anything that buttered his ego."

"If stupidity is so significant, wouldn't that clear Orson Foxworth? He isn't stupid, whatever else might be said of him."

"Agreed. Only ruthless. How ruthless might be open to question. But he virtually underwrote the revolution down yonder in 1932 and he knew mighty well how much bloodshed that would involve. And he is the only one of those under discussion who prepared a careful and completely false alibi to conceal his whereabouts and his movements on the night Odile was killed."

"Why, you might say the same about Sabin! He needn't really have been blind drunk. The liquor on his breath and the way he acted would have been enough to back up his claim that he didn't remember anything. He could have been preparing an alibi."

"And that's another shrewd observation, m'love. In addition, Sabin was on the scene and he concealed the fact from everyone but us, to whom he admitted it without realizing what he was saying. A bullet from a gun he gave Odile earlier the same day took her life. He's maladjusted in any

182

case and frustrated in his love for Odile. He has a violent and ungovernable temper. He was subjected to twin temptations— if I can't have her, no one else shall; and again the old one—anyone who spares Odile years of invalidism is really doing her a kindness. Besides, let's not forget that whatever sent Odile into her wild hysteria was something that happened while she was with Sabin. That's a pretty formidable total, when you cast it all up on one balance sheet .... And yet somehow it doesn't ring any bells."

"If I had said anything like that, you would have been ever so superior about women's intuition."

"No, it's more logical than that. Sabin was the only one in the crowd who stood to gain nothing by Odile's death except the satisfaction of having removed her from another man's embraces."

"There's still another person you haven't mentioned."

Blankly Joe looked at his wife. Then his countenance cleared. "Vance Perrault? Yes, he had the opportunity. He could come and go as he pleased. And up to this moment, he is the last person definitely known to have seen Odile alive. But as Toe Murphy says, you start with somebody like that and then go back to find out who could possibly have seen her alive later. When you get to the one who really was the last person, you've got your murderer. In this case, any of the others could have seen her after Perrault left at ten-thirty or thereabouts. And when it comes to motive, we're stymied in his case. He had nothing to gain by her death. As for killing her because it would really be doing her a kindness— Perrault is the one man who wouldn't give in to any such temptation. Medical ethics are almost a phobia with him. And the big argument the medical profession advances against so-called mercy killings lies in the fact that a patient who is incurable today may be curable tomorrow through the discovery of some new drug or some new operative technique. Vance Perrault could no more commit a mercy killing than he could perform an abortion or endorse a patent medicine guaranteed to cure cancer."

"But I wasn't even thinking about Doctor Perrault, dear. It was Tossie I had in mind. She's actually charged with the murder."

"Oh—Tossie! I thought we'd written her off. Still, her fingerprints were on the gun. Also, Caresse said something when she and Ruth were here the day of the funeral about two blue silk pillows that disappeared from Odile's room. She insisted that Tossie must have taken them away, either just before or just after the old woman gave the alarm about finding Odile's body. I don't see the significance of that myself. I mention it only because I'm trying not to overlook a single detail. Anyway, according to Léonce, he had overheard Tossie say something to the general effect that she'd rather see Odile in her grave than have some strange nurse around. That's not very convincing as a motive, and Léonce isn't a very reliable witness, even though Tossie did admit having said something of the sort. Besides—Tossie's a simple soul. I don't think she'd feel like the others, that she was doing Odile a kindness in killing her to keep her from enduring years of invalidism. I think Odile's illness would only mean to Tossie that 'mah baby' would need her faithful old mammy more than ever. Which is what Tossie lived for. And it still stands that she couldn't have written that note . . . . Wait a minute! That note! Angels and ministers of grace, defend us! What a dope I've been! What an ape!"

For the first time Judith's nimble fingers stopped their deft manipulation of the large ivory knitting needles, and she let her hands fall idly to her lap. "Yes, dear?" she asked, smiling indulgently.

"Why it's like a neon sign in an otherwise dark street—and I missed it till this good minute. That note—don't you see? It wasn't necessarily a suicide note at all! Now get this, Jude. Here's the wording of it: 'Darling—I have tried to be a good daughter and a good wife, but I can't take this any longer. I love you. Odile.' "

"Yes, Joe. I remember it."

"Naturally, with her body lying in the same room, everybody thinks it's a suicide note. And Toe, realizing she didn't kill herself, decides it's a forgery, in spite of the fact that only one of four persons—namely, the supposed forger—would know it wasn't genuine, while three others, all of whom had seen her handwriting for years, hadn't the least doubt about it being authentic. Why? Because that's exactly what it was!"

"You mean she actually wrote it herself?"

"Sure as shooting. And it was a farewell note too. But not a farewell to the world. Which makes it obvious the note was addressed to her mother. So we make a fresh start from there and from now on I'm guessing. But it's the kind of guessing that makes sense. See if it doesn't."

"I'm listening hard."

"All right. Let's say Odile and Sabin make the mutual discovery they're still in love. And something, maybe a word or look from Léonce indicating he thinks Caresse is more desirable than his wife, proves to be the last straw as far as

Odile's concerned. It's borne in on her almost between two clock ticks that this tomcat she's married to is a total bust, dark magnetism and all, and that she's body and soul in love with a swashbuckling romantic who's remained faithful to her for years and years, even though she herself handed him a bum rap."

"Why do you always lapse into that police court jargon when you get excited, Joe?"

"Oh for the love of heaven, Jude, what difference does it make? I'll polish it up for you later. But get the picture: Odile's a square shooter, not a casual two-timing tramp; she won't continue to live with her husband and be unfaithful to him on the sly. But the doctor's just told her she hasn't much time left. So if she's to get any joy out of life before she becomes entirely helpless, she's got to make some kind of a quick decision. She's a practicing Catholic, therefore divorce is out of the question; but now that she knows in whose keeping her heart really is, she'll be darned if she's going to waste what little time she has left in sitting around the house and watching Léonce chase other women, especially her own sister. She'll have those few precious weeks or months of wonderful rapture to take with her into the dark future Doctor Perrault has shown her, and she'll do it honestly; namely, she'll become a fallen woman, an erring wife or what have you. Sabin is to come to the little garden at ten o'clock or thereabouts and they'll leave for no matter where."

"Joe, you're letting your imagination run away with you."

"Could be. But at least it checks with the facts as we know them so far and nobody else has come up with anything else that does."

"But the girl was found dead!"

"There were two unpredictable circumstances—Odile's own emotional condition, which made it impossible for her to stay on an even keel; and Doctor Perrault's return some two hours before he was expected for a second visit. Remember, he had said he'd come back again about midnight; but when he was out on another call in the same neighborhood, he came by at ten o'clock or thereabouts. So let's reconstruct the scene—and again I'm only guessing—something like this: the elopement is planned; Sabin will come by at whatever the hour is—say it's ten-thirty for the sake of argument; Odile will meet him and they'll go to Honeymoon Haven. But the surrender to authentic passion upsets Odile's tremulous nervous adjustment, which isn't too strong at best. She goes into that emotional nose dive, or hysteria, or whatever you choose

185

to call it, and Sabin has to bring her to the house in a condition of pretty complete helplessness. All right. The doctor comes, decides she must be quieted, finally gives her a hypodermic, and says he'll look in again about midnight. But the effect of the hypo is brief. In the light of her generally overexcited and overwrought condition it might well be. She comes out of the fog and finds the situation almost made to order. Everybody's been sent away by the doctor, Sabin can help her pack when he comes. So she writes her note. Not a suicide note, a note to her mother telling why she's running off with another man."

Joe rose, took hold of the poker, and stabbed with it at a large lump of coal until it shattered, bright flame enveloping its fragments.

"And then comes the second unpredictable," he continued, turning his back to the grate. "Doctor Perrault arrives about ten, finds Odile up and about, and this second frustration sends her into another and even more devastating spin. So he administers a second hypodermic, and this time he makes it a good one; she's back in a drugged sleep that he knows will keep her unconscious until morning. And that means, obviously, that when Sabin does arrive to fly away with her on wings of rapture, his signal is unanswered. Maybe he does see the shadow struggle or embrace that he told us about, or maybe he only imagined in his drunken state that he did see it . . . ."

"But he wouldn't have prepared for an elopement by getting drunk."

"You've got a point there, no doubt. But perhaps he thought from her earlier spell that the elopement was off anyway, and was out to drown his frustration. And in this drunken state he foggily remembers he has a date to be in that garden at ten-thirty, and that's why, drunk or not, he does show up. At least it's a possibility. But I don't doubt there could be half a dozen believable explanations for it. That's not what's troubling me. The thing I keep coming back to, now that I'm on this track, is the note. The note's gone. Vanished. As long as it was only a suicide note, its disappearance wasn't a matter of great moment. But if it wasn't a suicide note—if it was what I think it was—whoever's now got that note killed Odile."

12

How Caresse Lalande
purged her wardrobe—

January 8, 1948

"CARESSE! What do you mean by locking that door? Open it this minute!"

The command was repeated three times, with ever increasing asperity, before the girl to whom it was addressed paid any attention to it. At last she closed the lid of the suitcase which she was filling, added a plaid skirt to the pile already on the chaise longue, and shaking her disordered hair out of her eyes, walked towards the threshold.

"What do you want, *maman?*" she inquired, her hand on the latch.

"I'll tell you after you let me in. I've got to speak to you privately. And it's very urgent."

With her hand still on the latch, Caresse glanced around the cluttered room. The doors of the armoires and the drawers of the dressers were all open and wearing apparel of every description was scattered about. Caresse had on nothing but a very scanty slip and a pair of scuffed-out bedroom slippers. Briefly, she considered the advisability of keeping the door locked until she could claw some kind of a dress from the heap on the bed. Then she decided against it and turned the key. Amélie, clad in the deepest mourning, swept into the room.

She was still in deshabille, although some time had already elapsed since she finished consuming the black coffee, sweetened with saccharin, and the bit of unbuttered *brioche* which constituted her breakfast. But three days of intensive attention to her wardrobe had done wonders for it. The purple velvet robe had been steamed and carefully placed in a moth-proof bag for use a year hence, and the sweeping negligee she now wore was made of black crepe. Without Tossie's help she was unable to achieve the elaborate style of

187

hairdressing she preferred; but she had made the welcome discovery that a black snood set off the beauty of her blond locks as nothing else had ever done. A visit to the strongbox where she kept some of her more antiquated and less glittering jewelry had resulted in the extraction of a large onyx cross, suspended from a chain of onyx medallions, and wide onyx bracelets; so at this point not only her hair, but her neck and arms were somberly encircled, while long jet pendants dangled from her ears and the negligee was caught at the breast with a brooch of black enamel. She continued to carry a chiffon handkerchief, but this also had changed its character; it was now an enormous black square, edged with wide black lace, as if to indicate that nothing smaller or simpler would serve to dry her tears. At the sight of her daughter she gave a slight scream.

"Caresse! A *peach-colored satin* slip! How *can* you? And it isn't as if you didn't have plenty of lovely white crepe ones! They came at the same time with mine. I saw them."

"I'm saving those for New York. This old thing's good enough to pack in."

"I'm not talking about its age. Of course anyone could see that it's practically a *rag*! I'm talking about its *color*! Why, I no more could wear a colored slip or a colored nightgown or any other intimate garment in color now than I could—"

"I know. 'When Ah mourns, Ah, mourns.' But you didn't come banging on the door just to go over that again, did you?"

"Well, it's all part of the general picture. But I have lots of other things to say to you." Amélie glanced about, seeking a vacant chair, and finding none, moved the pile of clothes on the bed further to one side and seated herself in the space thus cleared. "First of all, I want you to understand that this New York plan of yours does *not* have my approval," she went on. "It's one thing to be connected through a radio program with a place like Clothilde Lafargue's Fashion Plate Dress Shop—Clothilde's never forgotten that she was Queen of Carnival and she's made it a strict rule not to have any one associated with her in its management who hasn't at least been a Maid in one of the more exclusive courts. But it's quite another thing to enter the employ of a New York department store, owned and operated by God knows who. I never thought I'd live to see the day when a daughter of mine, born and brought up as you have been, would lower herself to the commercial level. I never—"

"Yes, I know. In your day ladies never worked. That's the only way you've ever admitted that your day is past. However, it's something that you've admitted it at all."

"You don't need to be insolent, on top of everything else. You are the most selfish, unfeeling, heartless girl I ever saw in my life. Why, the very day of the funeral, you go streaking off for a walk with someone you never saw even a week ago, and end up at the Racinas', of all places, for supper! Judith Racina's never been halfway civil to me, though heaven only knows why she should think she's so much better than anyone else. She doesn't make any secret of the fact that her father's an ordinary farmer, and certainly her marriage didn't take her any higher on the social ladder. As you very well know, I like Joe; but after all, what's his family background?"

"I wouldn't know. But I do know that he's won a Pulitzer prize and that Judith has some kind of a military decoration for heroism. If anyone in our family's rated awards like that, I haven't heard of it."

"Don't you dare disparage your family. *You're* the first member of it to bring it discredit. And as if that walk and that supper party weren't bad enough, what do you do the very day *after* the funeral? Broadcast, as if nothing had happened! And go around making arrangements for Ruth Avery to attend a Carnival ball! You must have a crush on her, or something, the way you've taken up with her. I shudder to think how Clarinda Darcoa—all the Darcoas for that matter— must feel about it. They know as well as I do that properly grief-stricken people don't act that way. Carnival balls don't so much as *enter the mind* of anyone with a heart when there's been a death in the family."

"Clarinda's tickled to death that she's met Ruth so soon. Maybe you didn't know it, but she's crazy about *parrain*."

"What!"

"It's the Lord's own truth, as poor old Tossie used to say. He's been her dreamboat ever since she was a little girl."

"Much good it would do her! He didn't even recognize her when he saw her in the Blue Room the other night."

"He would the next time. Anyway, she's giving a big luncheon for Ruth tomorrow. And the whole Darcoa tribe is mighty glad that Clarinda and Ruth hit it off so well. Maybe you've forgotten that Clarinda's father is a director in the Trans-Caribbean Company—the crowd that *parrain* has been trying to make a deal with. Clarinda says her father's pleased as Punch at the way things are going, even if the other Trans-Caribbean big shots are taking it like a dose of medicine. And it happens that *parrain*'s pleased too. He told me so himself, when I went to hash over this New York offer with him. He talked to me quite a lot about Clarinda. Besides, he needed one more vote or stock control or what-

189

ever you call it and Papa Darcoa was hesitating. But now he and *parrain* are just like red beans and rice. It's a kick, isn't it? To find those two highbinders getting to be buddies, even if they don't come from the same side of the tracks."

Having made this confounding retort to her mother's accusations, Caresse opened the door and called to Lop, while Amélie was still regrouping her forces for rebuttal. The maid's prompt appearance suggested that she might have been lurking nearby, hoping for just such a summons. At all events, when she entered, her expression was one of eager anticipation. And this became even more marked as she rolled her large velvety eyes from one pile of clothing to another.

"You may have all the things on the bed, Lop," Caresse told her. "That is, you may take them away and divide them with Ona. Mind you don't try to play any tricks, though. I'll check with Ona later and find out whether you've been fair."

"Ain' gwine play no tricks, Miss Caresse. Ah done tol' Ona already you was a-fixin' to give us some of yo' pretty clo'es. Us'n mighty proud to git 'em, Ah kin tell you."

Lop reached over the bed and swept the clothing that lay there into her covetous arms. But the pile was too large for her to encompass easily. Two or three dresses eluded her and slipped to the floor. She laid down the others and bent to pick up the straying garments, gasping with incredulous delight.

"You given me yo' handsome green party dress, Miss Caresse? Sho 'nuff?"

"I don't care whether you get it or Ona. If it's the one you both like best, you'd better draw straws."

Staggering under the weight of her burden, but making continued sounds of ecstasy, Lop left the room. Although Amélie did not try to prevent this departure, she had now rallied sufficiently from the unwelcome news about the Darcoas to open another attack.

"You shouldn't have given that expensive dress to Lop, Caresse. There are any number of girls in your own set—"

"Oh, for the love of heaven, stop harping on 'my set!' You told me yourself, before I put that jade green number on last Friday, that no lady would ever wear anything so extreme. Since then Ruth's said so too—a lot more tactfully but a lot more tellingly. I got the idea all right. And I don't propose to have the girls in my set saying behind my back what you've said to my face. I can just hear them: 'Isn't that the sort of thing Caresse Lalande *would* choose? Of course, *I* wouldn't dream of wearing it unless I built it up with net. . . .'"

190

"Well, I'm glad you admit that much," Amélie replied, changing her tactics. "But evidently you haven't considered that if you go to work for this New York store you'll be called on to model all kinds of extreme styles and—"

"Ruth says I wouldn't. She says Haas and Hector are on the conservative side. And Miss Hickey told me the same thing."

"Well, you'd be modeling *colored* clothes, wouldn't you? Bright greens like that formal you just so foolishly gave away, and bright reds like that woolen sports dress you were wearing Saturday, and yellows and pinks and—"

"I suppose I should. I don't suppose I could specify that I'd model only dead black or dead white for a year and then drift gradually into soft mauve and dove gray. But if it'll make you feel any better, I'll agree to stick to mourning in private life—that is, modified mourning. I won't go around dripping with it, the way you do."

"Caresse, this is too, too much! *Dripping!*"

"Well, that's the way it looks to me . . . . See here, when you bull-dozed me into opening that door, you said there was something very urgent you had to discuss with me right away. And so far you've done nothing but gripe. If you've really got anything weighty on your mind, you'd better tell me what it is. I was trying to finish sorting out these things and get a head start on my packing this morning. You've kept me from doing that. But you can't stop me from taking a shower and getting into some clothes and snatching a cup of coffee and a sandwich—all within the next half hour. Because an hour from now I've got to be on the air."

"I intend to supervise the rest of your sorting and see to it that your colored clothes go to needy gentlewomen and not to flighty servants. And you might as well stop packing. Because I don't intend to let you go to New York."

"You don't intent to *let* me! I'd like to know how you can stop me!"

"You're only nineteen. You won't be of age for two years yet. If you won't listen to reason, I'll make you listen to the law."

Amélie rose from the bed and confronted her daughter triumphantly. "I suppose you thought if you went sneaking down to Orson's office and wound him around your little finger, you could get around me too," she said. "Well, you can't. In fact, you chose the worst possible way to do it. If you had any fine feeling you never would have consulted an outsider about a matter which no one but your mother has any right to decide. Your dear, dead sister wouldn't have done such a thing. She was a lady, in every sense of the word, and she considered me first of all." Amélie brought the chiffon handkerchief into play, but she did so briefly, aware that time was really pressing. "Odile carried forward all the best traditions of the family. She never would have gone alone to a man's office and—"

"I don't get this line about an 'outsider.' *Parrain's* been in and out of this house ever since I can remember. And you sure have always acted as if you thought everything he said was the law and the prophets. How was I to know you wouldn't think so this time? I supposed of course that if he said he thought it would be a good idea for me to take the job you'd agree with him. I thought that would be the very thing that would settle it."

"You did? Well, I should certainly like to know why! I'd like to know what right he has to advise you about anything."

"Well, since he's about to become my stepfather—"

"And who said that?"

"You told me yourself that—"

"I told you he was *urging* me to marry him and that I was thinking it over. After all, he's been in love with me for years. You know that. And out of consideration for you and your sister I've put him off, time and time again, just as I have dozens of other eligible suitors, because I didn't want to saddle you with a stepfather! Odile appreciated my devotion and my sacrifices, but all you do is to flout every reasonable request I make of you. If Orson is encouraging you in this line of conduct, I guess I'd better have a few words with him on the subject. I don't propose to have him defying my authority, especially when I have the law on my side."

With even more majesty than she had entered the room, Amélie swept out of it. Caresse glanced at the little clock on her mantel, and saw that its hands pointed to quarter to one. There would be no time for the shower now, or the sandwich either, and it was too bad, because both would have helped. She felt hot and dirty after her hectic attempts at packing; her temples were throbbing, her mouth was dry, and there was a lump in her throat. Unless she could pull herself together, her broadcast would be flat and colorless. And that would be disastrous, for Miss Hickey would surely be listening in. It had never been so important that her voice should "mike like a temple gong" . . . .

She decided to take the shower, even at the risk of shortening the customary tests before the broadcast actually began. Under the halo hat, her hair did not show very much, except for the bang; and in any case, the page boy bob did not require much attention; she could get ready to leave in short order. But she had not reckoned on a run in one of her sheer black stockings and the consequent necessity of rummaging for a fresh pair; nor on the fact that the zipper on her new handbag would catch halfway across the opening as she was trying to put clean handkerchiefs and a new package of cigarettes into it. She was next obliged to shake out her keys and money and compact and transfer them to another purse.

While she was frantically hurrying to complete this shift, a light tap at her door was followed by the entry of Lop.

"Lop, I honestly haven't a second to spare," Caresse told the maid before she could speak. "If you and Ona can't agree about the division of those dresses . . . ."

"Tain' a thing lak dat, Miss Caresse. Hones'. Us ain' gwine have ary word bouten dat. An' Miss Am'lie on de foam, so Ah cain' ask her. What must Ah do bouten dis here?"

She held out a small blue pillow trimmed with lace. With her hand on the zipper of the new bag, Caresse stood very still.

"Where did you find that, Lop?" she asked quietly.

"Ah fin' hit jus' dis ve'y minute in Mistuh Léonce room," the maid replied. "Hit was stuck in de co'ner behime de chiff'robe, on de flo', an' when'st Ah'se cleanin' up . . . ."

"You mean it was hidden there?"

"Ah don' know was it hid or not hid. All Ah knows is dere it was."

"Only *one* pillow?"

"Yas'm, Miss Caresse, dis de onlies' one Ah see, an' Ah done look high an' look low fo' de other one, after Ah see dis here'n."

For some moments, which she could ill afford to spare, Caresse considered the situation. If both the missing pillows had been found behind the chifforobe . . . . But as it was . . . . Finally coming to a decision, she ran the zipper along the upper edge of her bag to close it.

"Lop, don't say anything about finding this pillow to anybody," she admonished. "Not to anybody, you understand?"

Lop nodded vigorously. "Yas'm, Miss Caresse. Ah understan's good, an' Ah do jus' lak you say."

"I haven't time to think about this now. I'm dreadfully late. So listen: take that pillow and put it back right where you found it, and just exactly the same way you found it. Then later on, you and I can talk and I'll decide what's to be done about this. Will you do that, Lop?"

"Sho'ly, Miss Caresse. Jus' lak you tells me, dat's how Ah'm gwine do."

"Good. And now I must run. Remember, Lop: exactly the way you found it, and not a word to another soul."

The chimes announcing the first quarter after one greeted her as she ran down the stairs, and above them she heard her mother's voice at the telephone.

"I don't care how important that is, Orson, I know this is much *more* important. No, I *can't* wait until later in the day. I want you to come straight out here so that I can talk to you privately while Caresse is giving her program. It's very *urgent* . . . . Well, she says you told her to defy me, and if you did that you may as well understand . . . . Very well then. I'll expect you."

Caresse slammed the front door behind her. The shower had not helped much after all, except to make her feel cleaner. Her temples were still throbbing, her mouth was even drier, the lump in her throat was bigger than ever. It had honestly never occurred to her that her mother would resent Foxworth's advice. And as to that question of the law . . . . Caresse didn't suppose that *maman* really knew what she was talking about, but there was always the off chance that she might . . . . And now the discovery of one of Odile's missing pillows concealed behind the chifforobe in Léonce's room . . . . In her haste and dismay Caresse yanked the door of her convertible open and started to slide under the wheel before she noticed that Léonce was already in the driver's seat.

"You're a little on the late side," he told her. "I thought it might help if I drove you down to the Roosevelt."

"Get out of my car! You know I wouldn't ride with you if my life depended on it."

"Maybe not. But it isn't your life that depends on it. It's your job. And besides, I want a lift to town. My car is in the shop getting greased, so I took a taxi home for lunch. But I need the old jalopy to take your mother to the cemetery later this afternoon. What's more, I've got to talk to you. No fooling, Caresse. And you never give me a chance at the house. Be a good Elk and get in on the other side."

Caresse hesitated. She wanted to go back into the house and telephone for a taxi, but it was all too true that she was "on the late side." She walked around the car and climbed in beside Léonce, who quickly put it into gear. Then, without loss of time, he began to plead his case.

"Don't let's fight, *chére*. There's something I want you to know."

"Then it must be about yourself. And I can't think of anyone who interests me less," Caresse retorted.

"Please, darling . . . ."

"Oh for God's sake! . . . . And watch out for that bus! This time I can't afford to have you plow into the back of a truck. Not that I could afford it before. But it turned out to be a very useful eye opener, so I suppose I ought to feel grateful."

"You're making this hard for both of us, Caresse."

"Good!"

"Won't you please give me a chance? I don't mean just a chance to talk. I'll find ways of doing that, if I have to follow you to New York. I mean a chance to get back to where we stood before—well, before Odile—hell, you know what I'm trying to say."

"Of course I do. And Odile knew it too. That wouldn't have bothered me so much, I guess, if you'd been the kind of person worth going overboard for. Odile was old enough and pretty enough and smart enough to take care of herself. And she was on to you, all right. She told me so when . . . ."

Caresse checked herself abruptly, and fell silent.

"Yes?" Léonce's voice was mocking. "Was that by any chance Saturday night—after Doctor Perrault left?"

"After Doctor Perrault left? After . . . ." Recalling the little lace-trimmed pillow that had just been returned to its hiding place in her brother-in-law's room, Caresse broke into harsh laughter. "What a complete stinker you are, Léonce. And to think I ever fell for your so-called charm."

"I take back what I said about Doctor Perrault's leaving. I'm so upset I don't know what I'm saying or thinking half the time. I didn't mean that, of course. It just sort of slipped out before I thought. That isn't what I wanted to tell you. It's us, you and me, that I keep thinking about. Because what we meant to each other that afternoon, the way you felt about me and the way I felt about you, that's all possible now. And no sneaking off to a tourist camp, either. Of course we'd have to wait a year or so, for the look of things. But I'd do that—for you. No fooling, Caresse. You know I'm crazy about you. I won't so much as look at another woman, either. I'll settle down. Honest. If you'll just say that after a while, after the year of mourning's over, you'll marry me. . . ."

"You must have taken leave of what little sense you ever had. It's only a few days since you reminded me that divorce was out because we were all such good Catholics. Perhaps now *I'd* better remind *you* that you and I are quote within the forbidden bounds of affinity unquote."

"I don't know what you're talking about, Caresse. You've certainly got a new line."

"Well, I had an idea that sarcasm might be wasted on you. But I didn't realize I'd have to interpret Canon Law to anyone who quoted it himself only last Saturday. You were married to my sister, weren't you? In a church, by a priest? All right. You couldn't marry me without getting a dispensation and, under the circumstances, you'd find that rather difficult. Those old boys can be pretty hard-boiled. But even if you could get the Apostolic Blessing, I wouldn't marry you. Not if you were the last man on earth. That sounds trite. It probably is. But it's exactly what I mean."

"I don't believe it. I don't believe you can have got over caring for me so soon. And there must be some way we could get a dispensation. There must be somebody . . . . Look here, Caresse, I'm mad about you."

"Nuts! The only person you're mad about is yourself . . . . It couldn't be—or could it?—that you're so afraid of losing a soft snap in the way of free rent and so on that you enjoyed in *maman's* house as Odile's husband and that of course you'd have to give up now? Is that it by any chance?"

Léonce looked at her in smug triumph.

"Apparently you don't realize that under the community property law half of everything Odile and I had belongs to me, and that Odile had a tidy little fortune in her own right. Besides, she made a will leaving everything to me. So I'm not worried about finances. I only say that to show you I did mean what I told you about us."

"How did you know about Odile's will?"

"A stenographer in Narcisse Fontaine's office," Léonce began, heedlessly, "told . . . . I mean . . . . that is to say . . . ." He floundered helplessly for a moment, and then recovered his composure. "What I meant was that Odile herself told me she had gone to Narcisse Fontaine's office to have him draw up her will, leaving everything to me. And later on I happened to mention it to Mr. Fontaine, when he was passing an act of sale for me—"

"Or did you happen to mention it to one of his stenographers with whom you were whiling away the tedium of an otherwise dull evening? . . . . Well, here we are. If you'll drop me off at the Baronne Street entrance you can take the car around the corner to the Dixie Parking Lot. That's where I always leave it and they know me, so I won't need a check. And now that you've had your say, let me have mine. I hate and despise the very sight of you. If I thought you'd have a chance to keep on badgering me like this, I'd be the one to

196

go nuts. But three days from now, I'll be halfway to New York."

"Caresse!"

"Get lost, Léonce."

She ran across the banquette and passed quickly through the revolving door into the lobby of the Roosevelt, where the hands of an immense clock pointed inexorably to one forty-three. The elevator had never seemed so slow, nor the corridor to the broadcasting station so long. She was completely breathless when she finally slid to her seat at the microphone in Studio B, an unrehearsed typescript on the table before her. Through a glass partition she could see her director pretending to tear his hair over her last-second arrival. These theatrical gestures did nothing to restore her equanimity, and the typed sheet shook a little as she held it up and began to read from it. But she did her best to concentrate while maintaining a background awareness of the smooth uninterrupted sweep of a bright red second-hand around the dial of the studio clock. Without conscious volition she looked up. The director caught her eye and, notching a neat check mark on the script, first glanced at his stop watch and then tapped his nose with his forefinger. She nodded slightly, without interrupting the clear modulation and tempo of her diction:

"This week the talk of the town has centered on the Twelfth Night Revels, with special emphasis on the finder of the golden bean, Miss Lucille Bernard. Her regal costume of silver cloth and purple velvet, her sceptre of orchids, the traditional plume attached to her crown, have all received the attention which was their due; her bearing and beauty have been declared unsurpassed in the annals of the Revelers. But looking back through these annals, we find that, from the very beginning, the queens reigning on Twelfth Night have been the objects of spontaneous admiration.

"So today, in considering 'The Fashions of Yesteryear,' let us glance through some of the Revelers' earlier records. In 1887, Miss Leila Bohn, who two years earlier had reigned as Queen of Momus, drew the golden bean. She was a girl so truly beautiful, so genuinely beloved, that when her happy find was disclosed, every other girl in the group which had clustered around the giant cake, hoping that hers would be the supreme good fortune of the evening, forgot her own ambition and began to clap her hands, her delight entirely unclouded by envy. Miss Bohn accepted the acclamation with the ease and graciousness characteristic of this general favorite, and was a vision of loveliness in her dress of white

197

brocade, made with a front panel of pink satin finished with a garniture of pink roses and veiled in white lace. The bodice was pointed back and front and the low neck outlined by garlands of pink roses . . . ."

Suddenly Caresse realized in a vague sort of way that she had seen something out of the ordinary which she was unable to identify. At the next point in the script where a fleeting pause was indicated, her eyes passed over the director, who was still tapping his nose with his forefinger, to the glass partition which divided the watching public from the broad-casters. The sight of Joe Racina standing there, a thread of smoke spiraling from the cigarette between his lips, came as a distinct shock; but it did not break the continuity with which she continued to speak into the microphone:

"And now let us take a look at the queens who reigned over the Revelers at the turn of the century, for they too were lovely exponents of 'The Fashions of Yesteryear.' In 1900, Miss Evelyn Penn was gowned in pink taffeta, made with a bouffant skirt and cut with a low neckline bordered in pink brocade. Her mantle was of white brocade lined in satin and bordered in ermine, her crown a thin gold band with a sunburst of pearls centering around a diamond.

"The following year, 1901, Miss Elise Richardson was crowned by Miss Penn. Coincidentally, Miss Richardson was also wearing pink when she drew the golden bean. Her dress was pink organdy fashioned with a batteau neckline, bordered with three ruffles trimmed with ruchings of ribbon and lace insertion. A similar trimming was used on the full skirt. Her crown was the same as that worn by Miss Penn and her mantle of white satin trimmed in marabou.

"In 1903, Miss Alice Stauffer was the finder of the golden bean, and her dress was so striking that to this day it is well remembered by any number of admiring Orleanians. It was a Paris model, made of white tulle, embroidered in a ring design. About twelve inches from the bottom, the skirt flared suddenly and from there to the hemline was trimmed with bands of satin ribbon, in graduating widths. Miss Stauffer's white satin mantle was embroidered in small figures symbolic of the evening's design, which featured Pierrots and Pier-rettes. She wore a diamond star on her forehead attached to a golden fillet and carried long-stemmed American Beauty roses."

Caresse glanced towards her director, who was moving his right finger energetically along the circumference of an imag-inary circle and obediently she stepped up the tempo of her delivery. But she found that she was reading without hearing herself, because the active part of her mind was wondering why Joe Racina, who was known to have nothing but contempt for the broadcasting industry, had come to the studio. With an almost physical effort, she compelled herself to concentrate on the script again:

"In 1910, the queen was Miss Carrie Walmsley, who wore white satin heavily embroidered in gold beads, the decolletage of her dress outlined in similar embroidery. She also wore a golden fillet around her head, but to this was attached the single white plume which is now traditional. Though her mantle was of matching white satin, its embroidery was emerald green in color and its pattern one of fleur-de-lis.

"In 1921, silver tissue was the favored fabric, as it has been again this year. Miss Dorothy Clay wore a magnificent gown of the glittering material, which was doubly resplendent because of the iridescent sequins forming its panel. Her cloth-of-silver train was embroidered in a poppy design."

Only a third of a page more. The director was once again tapping his nose contentedly. And at last came the lines of release:

". . . . and so goodbye, until Saturday afternoon at this same time. This is Caresse Lalande thanking you for inviting her into your radio for another chat about Fashions of Yesteryear."

Caresse sat poised and silent. Beyond a third glassed-in partition she could see the announcer in his cubicle, though the words of his closing panegyric about The Fashion Plate Dress Shop were inaudible to her. She saw him strike a gong with a chamois-wrapped pestle, and turned her eyes toward the glass behind which her director stood. An instant later he drew a forefinger across his throat. Caresse breathed deeply and pushed her chair back from the table. Her microphone was off the air, and she was free to do what she pleased.

At once she hurried to the door, where a neon sign with the legend "on the air" had just blinked out. Joe Racina was waiting for her, smiling a bit sardonically.

"Highly edifying discourse," he observed. "Especially that part about how to achieve distinction in dress on so very little in the way of cash outlay. Not that you haven't a voice that's a honey. Only it's a shame to use it for hymning the glories of milady's lace-edged panties. Like using a Stradivarius to summon customers to a fish peddler's cart."

"Joe, stop making conversation. You didn't come down here just to tell me that. What's the matter? Has anything happened—anything bad, I mean?"

"Well, not necessarily. But if 'tain't bad, I might as well

tell you first as last that 'tain't good neither. How's about coming down to the bar with me, and having a drink while I tell you about it? I'm afraid you'll need one before you've heard me out."

"You know I can't do that."

"Since when? Why, I've seen——"

"Since I'm in mourning. No matter how I might feel about it, *maman* would pass out cold if some one told her—and some one would be sure to—that I had gone into a public restaurant, to say nothing of a bar, within a week of Odile's death."

"I'm sorry, Caresse. Truly. And I should have known better. But isn't there some place around here where we could talk—privately? That's what I really had in mind when I suggested the bar. Nobody listens to any one else in a place like that. It's the old idea of it being darkest right under the lamp. But the bar's out, of course."

"We could go into Ed Hoerner's office. He's rehearsing the 'In Old New Orleans' cast for their half hour show on Friday night, and that means he won't be using it for at least another twenty-five minutes."

"Good."

Joe followed Caresse down the carpeted hallway to the office in question and closed the door behind them. Then he said gravely, "You're in for a disappointment, Caresse. I said it wasn't bad news, and it isn't, really. But you may think it is."

"Do come out with it, Joe, won't you, please? I can take anything except this hinting here and hinting there business."

"Well, here goes then. You'd best forget all about going to New York with Miss What'shername—Hickey, wasn't it?— Saturday night."

"I won't forget it!" Caresse blazed. "And you can tell *maman* I said so! It was bad enough to have her call *parrain* about it. I'd like to know what she means by asking you to . . . ."

"Hold up, lady. Easy does it. Your mother hasn't said the first word to me about this."

"Well, she said plenty of them to me this morning. It was yaketa-yaketa-yak for hours, about how I was an unfeeling, undutiful, heartless girl, going off to New York at a time of mourning and what would people think. So naturally, I supposed that she'd called up the reserves by asking you to bring me to the point where I'd let her have her way. But I won't. I won't, I tell you." A note that was almost desperation crept

200

into her voice. "I've *got* to get away from New Orleans—and I'm going to."

"Again I'm telling you, honey: Easy does it. I don't know about your mother, but nobody else is trying to keep you here. Permanently, I mean. It's just a case of putting off your departure for a week or so. Ten days at the most."

"But I can't, Joe. Don't you see, I've told Miss Hickey everything was set—that I appreciated the opportunity—that I was ready to go any time she was. Now, if I have to tell her I've changed my mind, that I'll have to wait, that I can't even tell her when I *will* be able to come . . . . Can't you understand, Joe? If Haas and Hector get the idea that I'm the unreliable sort of person that doesn't know her mind from one day to the next, they'd probably call the whole thing off, and I'd lose this chance that means everything to me."

"I think you're working yourself up for nothing. Miss Doohickey or whatever her name is probably hasn't read anything about Odile's suicide. Even if she had read about it, the name Odile St. Amant wouldn't have had any connection with that of Caresse Lalande, so far as she was concerned. So why don't you tell her there's been a death in the family— tell her it was a suicide, for that matter—and that your mother is taking it so hard that though at first you thought it would be all right for you to leave, you now feel you ought to stay with her for a week or so longer, at least."

"I won't do it. Later on, perhaps. But those people aren't going to want anybody featured in their Salon Superbe that's been—that's mixed up in—that's had a lot of notoriety about—oh, for heaven's sake! You know very well what I mean. Don't just stand there as though I were talking to hear myself talk. And, if Mother didn't call you up as reinforcements, what business is it of yours whether or when I go to New York?"

"I'm not here to tell you whether or not you should go. What I'm trying to work myself up to tell you is that you can't go."

"Can't go? Can't? Who'll stop me?"

"Toe. Toe Murphy."

The girl's eyes widened in sudden panic. For a moment she peered at Joe defenselessly, as though in the realization that something she had dreaded was now inevitably upon her. Then she began to babble almost incoherently.

"Because he'd arrest me? But they can't do that, Joe. They've already arrested Tossie. That man said she killed Odile. I know she didn't. But he said so. You heard him

201

yourself. Joe, you mustn't let them arrest me. I haven't done anything, really I haven't. I know what. I'll leave tonight. There's a plane around midnight, a big plane that goes to New York. I'll telephone Miss Hickey and tell her—well, I don't know just what, but I'll think of something. I'm half packed already, it won't take me any time at all to finish. They mustn't arrest me, Joe. If they did and Miss Hickey heard about it, it would be the end. You will help me, won't you, Joe? Really, I haven't done a thing to be—"

"Check it, Caresse!' Joe rapped out sharply. The abrupt command seemed to recall the girl to herself, almost as though some physical impact had halted her speech. She looked at Joe uncertainly for a minute, shook her head, and spoke with almost complete composure.

"That was silly of me, wasn't it?" she asked. "I suppose I was hacked for a second. Go ahead, Joe. Tell me why Captain Murphy won't let me go to New York."

"It's kind of an involved story. There's no idea of an arrest or anything like that. The most he would do would be to put you under bond as a material witness for the grand jury, when they meet to determine whether they'll indict Tossie for murder. But he won't do even that, I can promise you, if you give him your word you won't leave for New York till he says it's okay."

"I understand. And of course I won't leave till then, now that you've explained. Because he would find some way to bring me back, and that would be the worst thing that could happen, wouldn't it? Worse than saying I'd have to stay with *maman* for another week or two, on account of a death in the family. But *why* is Captain Murphy going to insist on keeping me here?"

"Well, I tried to explain to all of you the other night how it is with Toe. He's no super-sleuth. But he notices little things and he never neglects any of them. Like those spots he saw on your dress the night Odile was found dead. Remember he asked you about them? And you said they were blood, from some sort of automobile accident—a collision with another car."

"But that was true."

"Sure it was. Only your car, the car you went downtown in, wasn't in the collision. Neither was Léonce's. Toe had them both checked that night. And since that time he's had the police files checked for accident reports. You know, there's a section of the ordinance that says you have to report any kind of an accident to the police if it happens in New Orleans."

"But this one—" Caresse began, and then stopped abruptly.

"Yes?" prompted Joe.

"Nothing. Only with all the excitement about Odile being sick when we got home, and—and what happened afterwards, it never entered my mind to make a report. Besides, Léonce was driving and it was up to him. And of course there must be lots of little accidents that never do get reported."

"Of course. Toe realizes that. But an accident that hurt someone badly enough to get blood all over a dress isn't that little, and so Toe thought that even if you hadn't reported it, the other automobile would have. Now there's a couple of things he wants to ask both you and Léonce."

"Such as?"

"Such as what was the license number of that other automobile. He says of course in a case of that kind everybody takes the other car's license number. And he wants to know whether either of you reported to your insurance companies, because that's something else everybody does, in order to let them know there might be a claim for damages. You or Léonce did get the other car's license number, didn't you?"

Caresse shook her head.

"I didn't," she admitted. "I don't remember Léonce doing it, either. The blood and all—"

"Well, you see, that's just it. Both you and Léonce did get mauled up some, and you told him yourself the spots on your dress were blood. And Toe said—"

Caresse stopped him with a swift gesture. Her expression had become one of cold resentment.

"Just how did you happen to be talking to the police about me in connection with this?" she demanded. "It occurs to me that none of it really concerns you. And if I lose my chance of getting to New York because of your prying, I'll—I'll—I'll never forget it, and I'll see to it that you don't, either."

"Don't be a child, Caresse. Try to understand that you're in trouble—at least, you may be in trouble; trouble big enough to make you forget petty spite about imagined affronts. Certainly I didn't pry into your affairs. I went to see Toe Murphy about something altogether different. Talking with Judith last night, I suddenly got a hunch that no one seemed to have hit on before. It looked very plausible to me. So much so that I went to police headquarters to lay the facts as I saw them before Toe. And they didn't concern you at all. They concerned some one else very much. But Toe wasn't impressed. He gave me and my theory a quick brush-off without saying why. And it wasn't till then that your name came into the conversation. And I wasn't the one who brought it up. Toe did."

"How did he find out I planned to leave New Orleans?"

"I told him that," Joe admitted. "Why not? You certainly hadn't indicated that it was a confidential matter. He was asking me about you and . . . . Well, if you must know, about you and Léonce. I told him I didn't think you were interested in Léonce, even if you had been flirting with him a little, because after all, you've been flirting with a lot of men. Besides you were so all-fired taken up with this job that had been offered you in New York that you couldn't see Léonce or any one else in New Orleans, except maybe your mother, with a spyglass. And that was when he said he didn't think you'd better leave town for a time."

"But why? I haven't done anything to be—to be arrested for."

"Try to look at it from Toe's point of view. I know that's a lot to ask. But put yourself in his place if you can. Odile's dead, and Toe is convinced she was murdered. He notices spots on your dress, and you say they're blood spots. They may have been there before Odile was killed. You say they were, because the blood was due to being hurt in an automobile smash-up that afternoon. But your car hasn't got a scratch, Léonce's car hasn't got a scratch, there's no report of a traffic accident to the police, there's no report to an insurance company by either side, no license number of the other car in the collision—and you still insist the blood on your dress got there during an auto smash-up."

"But it did, Joe. I give you my word—I'll swear to it on a stack of Bibles—I'll say it to the priest at confession. Those blood spots got on my dress in a traffic accident, early that afternoon, and before I even knew Odile had had some sort of attack and had to be brought home."

"Granting that every word you've said is gospel, how are you going to convince Toe Murphy? We're only supposing, mind—but suppose that blood on your dress hadn't been your blood, but Odile's—"

Her scream stopped him, and even in the split second before she recoiled, pressing the back of her hand against her mouth, he was struck by the difference in the quality of her outburst and her mother's. This was no wail penetrating a scene staged for the benefit of an onlooker, no shallow appeal for sympathy and consideration; it was a cry permeated with both terror and horror and it seemed to spring

204

straight from her vitals. There was something fearsome in its very spontaneity and its strength. It rang true. For a moment after she had silenced herself, Caresse stared at him with anguished eyes. Then she crumpled forward in her chair, hiding her face in her hands. With a pang of pity, Joe leaned over and put his hand on her shoulder.

"There," he said soothingly. "There. Don't, Caresse. I wouldn't have said that to you if I could have helped it. But I couldn't seem to make you see how serious this all is. I've got my own ideas of who either killed Odile—if she was killed— or knows more about how she killed herself than's been said to date. I'm sticking to that idea, too, no matter how dopey Toe Murphy thinks it is. And I've also got my own ideas about what you and Léonce might have been mixed up in. But that, as you pointed out before, is none of my business. When all's said and done, however, I'm not the one you have to convince. It's Toe."

"But you just said he wouldn't believe anything I told him."

"There's one thing he might go for," Joe said thoughtfully, after a reflective pause.

Caresse looked up at him with eagerly questioning eyes.

"It's that dress. After all, Doc Perrault said that when he examined you and Léonce, you-all were mauled up some, or words to that effect, but hadn't been hurt badly enough to need treatment. As I see it, then, there couldn't have been a lot of blood. A few spots, maybe. Whereas, if—but skip that. Suppose you bundle up that dress and let me take it to Toe Murphy, so he can examine it as much as he pleases. Toe's a reasonable guy. If it's just a case of a few drops here and there .... Good Lord!" he interrupted himself, as she suddenly looked up at him and he saw the color drain away from her face. "You haven't sent it to the cleaners already, have you?"

Her lips opened and closed soundlessly. But she shook her head and her eyes were wide with fear.

"Very well then. If you haven't done that, everything's all right," he said reassuringly. "I'll go home with you right now if you like and get the dress. I'll take it straight to Toe Murphy myself."

"You can't, Joe," she whispered, amost inaudibly. "I never could have worn that horrible dress again, no matter how many cleaners worked over it. When I finally got out of it, early Sunday morning, I burned it in my own fireplace before I got into the tub."

13

How Orson Foxworth played the
infatuated suitor at Amélie
Lalande's house—

January 8, 1948

NOTHING COULD have been less loverlike than Orson
Foxworth's frame of mind when he answered Amélie's summons. Her call had caught him in the midst of a conference
on a schedule of standards for determining the valuation of
the various vessels, wharves, conveyors, and other physical
properties of the Trans-Caribbean Company. The fact that it
got through to him at all was a source of profound annoyance, and he resolved to find some way of making Amélie
understand that business hours were sacrosanct and that she
would invade them at her peril. He would tell her this in
words of one syllable, four-letter words if necessary, and he
would do so coldly, tersely, and harshy. But he would make
her understand.

These resolutions took flight the instant he caught sight of
her. The portieres of the drawing room were still drawn
back, as they had been on the day of the funeral; from his
station by the hearth he could see her as she came down the
stairs and he realized immediately that she was no less angry
than he was. He knew her well enough to recognize that this
anger, unless it were appeased, might well jeopardize the
relationship he had so long sought to establish between them;
and he had no more idea of permitting Amélie to elude
him, at this stage of the game, than he had of allowing the
merger with Trans-Caribbean to miscarry. Later on those
high-hats who thought they could do all the dictating would
find out they had a bear by the tail; in like measure, Amélie
would discover that a demanding wife was not the type of

woman who could enslave him. But he would have to bide his time in both cases; for the moment, it behooved him to play the infatuated suitor as well as the tolerant tycoon.

Acting upon this unwelcome conviction, he advanced to meet her with outstretched arms and a fond smile. She did not appear to notice either, but closing the portieres, she swept past him towards her favorite high-backed chair, with the obvious intention of enthroning herself there before beginning her diatribe. He deftly blocked her passage, catching her lightly but lovingly around the waist.

"Let me go, Orson. I'm not in the mood for lovemaking. I've got something to say to you."

"And I'm here to listen. But you can give me a kiss first, can't you?"

"I haven't the slightest desire to kiss you. Or to have you kiss me . . . . You heard what I said, didn't you?"

Well, it was even worse than he had feared. He would have to move very cautiously. He released her, with just the right degree of reluctance, neither prolonging the embrace against her wishes nor terminating it with such abruptness as to leave any doubt of his own. He gave her plenty of time to seat herself, to arrange her draperies and to assure herself that her black snood had not slipped from its proper place. Then he came and stood before her, smiling indulgently.

"It's going to be mighty hard for me to keep my mind on anything except how lovely you look," he said. "But I'll try, because I know something must be troubling you terribly—something new, I mean. Tell me what it is and let me see if I can't help. I'm almost sure I can. I'm pretty good at helping."

"Very well. You can undo the harm you've done in encouraging Caresse to defy me."

"But I didn't know I'd encouraged her to defy you, darling. I thought I'd done exactly what you'd wanted me to do in urging her not to hesitate about taking advantage of a great opportunity."

"Then I can only say that you took a great deal too much for granted."

"Did I? I'm sorry. How?"

"Well, in the first place you shouldn't have assumed that you had a right to advise her. You and I aren't married yet, we're not even formally engaged. You'd better wait until we are before you interfere between me and my daughter—the only child I have left."

The black chiffon handkerchief was conveniently if somewhat provocatively placed. Amélie made effective use of it while Foxworth continued his argument.

"But darling, we're going to be married. The only reason we're not formally engaged, as you put it now, is because an announcement of that sort wouldn't be suitable, so soon after—that is, coming from a house of mourning. You told me yourself that we were 'solemnly betrothed.' You used those beautiful old-time words. And I didn't for a moment suppose I was 'interfering.' I supposed—"

"That's the second way in which you took too much for granted. You shouldn't presume to interpret my wishes until you've found out what they are. And it certainly isn't my wish that Caresse should accept a paid position from some common New York tradespeople, who'll probably require her to model chiffon undergarments and go to all the night clubs to show off their most immodest fashions."

"I assure you nothing like that will take place, Amélie. I think Ruth's already told Caresse that, if anything, Haas and Hector err on the conservative side. I've been acquainted with the firm for some time—it's a favorite with the *haut monde* of Latin America, and I don't need to tell you that the highborn ladies in those countries are not only very elegant, but very circumspect in matters of dress. Besides, I created an opportunity for a quiet talk with Miss Hickey, and I was very favorably impressed with her. She's a shrewd, efficient, reliable Irishwoman, with plenty on the ball. Caresse couldn't be in better hands."

"That's what you think. But I don't want my only daughter to have an Irishwoman for a boon companion and a bosom friend. That's the trouble with you, Orson. You never did realize the importance of good social position. I suppose it isn't strange, considering your background. But it's one of the things that's made me hesitate about marrying you—that's *still* making me hesitate. Because I do recognize its importance. And I intend to make Caresse recognize it before she ruins her life. I've reminded her that she isn't of age and that until she is, she can't leave home and take a position unless I permit her to do so."

Amélie rose from her chair, confronting her suitor with the same air of triumph that had marked her ultimatum to her daughter an hour earlier. But Foxworth was neither impressed nor cowed. Instead, he was struggling so hard to keep his temper that he might not have succeeded if a faint thread of amusement over Amélie's heroics had not woven its way through his anger. By making a great effort, he again manged to speak mildly and persuasively.

"My dear, I won't try to argue with you about my social position, though my sister, Muriel, might like to do so some day. However, I do know several presidents and premiers well enough to call them by their first names. Well, we'll let that pass for now . . . . At the moment, I think I should correct your impressions about your legal rights over Caresse —they might get you into trouble. Not that it's strange you should have been under a misapprehension. It's quite true she can't vote until she's twenty-one. However, according to Louisiana law, a parent can't force a child to remain under the parental roof after the age of puberty. And I think you'll admit Caresse reached that some time ago."

His tone had become almost playful. But far from being mollified by his manner, chagrin made Amélie all the angrier. He decided to resume the loverlike role he had attempted at the outset.

"Are you going to keep me on the carpet indefinitely, my dear?" he inquired, half-humorously, half-tenderly. "I've had a hard morning and I'm pretty tired. I'd really like to sit down. Only I'd be ever so much more comfortable on that nice big sofa than I would in one of these straight-backed chairs. And if you stay here, and I go halfway across the room, I'll have to shout to make you hear me. I don't want to do that. I want to whisper to you. Because I'm going to let you in on a state secret. That is, if you'll give me the chance. I want to tell you, before anyone else knows it, something that's tremendously important, about this morning's meeting."

Amélie hesitated. She was still outraged by the disclosure that the law did not conform to her wishes, but this grievance was being jostled out of the foreground of her thoughts by curiosity. Until now Foxworth had never voluntarily confided to her anything about the enormous manipulations that governed his Blue Fleet empire. What little she knew she had been obliged to extract from him piecemeal by persistent inquiries. Now he was actually offering to share his secrets with her. The temptation was too strong. She walked slowly to the sofa and did not repulse him when he followed and, seating himself beside her, again slid his arm around her waist.

"That's better," he said contentedly, "much better. Now I can really talk to you."

"Yes, but don't forget that's what we've come here for—so that you can talk, I mean. We didn't come here so that it would be easier for you to make love to me."

"It's a bit difficult to know just where and how to begin,"

he said thoughtfully. "You're a baby about such matters, thank God! But—well, let's get at it by going back to something you said a little while ago about my lack of background, and—"

Amélie made a little gesture of protest, but he caught her hand in his.

"No, no. I'm not bringing that up by way of complaint," he assured her hastily. "I'm using that as a starting point because it leads up to what's going on in my office right now. For years the big trade rivals between this country and Central America have been my own Blue Fleet and the Trans-Caribbean outfit—bananas, coffee, coconuts, land development, maritime shipping, and all the rest. Trans-Carib was the old, established crowd, doing business long before I came barging in. And while their headquarters were here and in Mobile, they still kept an office in Gloucester, because that's where they had started when Massachusetts was the center of all our country's shipping business."

He paused, a bit absently, as though his thoughts had left the ornate, over-furnished room on spacious concerns of their own.

"Well, those people had a lot of business ability in the Yankee Clipper days. They became the first real American aristocracy, where the what'stheirnames spoke only to the whozises and the whozises spoke only to God. And you had to be born into the Trans-Caribbean crowd. You couldn't work your way up, once they got the thing established as one of the world's big shipping firms. Which was all right, I suppose, as long as the old blood didn't run too thin; but run thin it did. And when you get to the point where you name a vice president in charge of traffic because his mother was a Van Gobbledygook, watch out."

Amélie started to speak, but again he waved her to silence. She would have resented this but for the drive of her curiosity, and the tingle of pride in the fact that Orson Foxworth was about to reveal himself to her not in the guise of a gallant, but as the builder of a new empire whose throne she was to share.

"Let me finish, Amélie. It will help you to understand some of the things about me that . . . ." He left the thought unspoken. "Maybe it was that family fixation or whatever you'd call it on the part of the T-C crowd that made things easier for me. I was a nobody from nowhere, as they saw it; the son of a small-town storekeeper in Kansas. I hadn't gone to the right schools or anything. What they didn't know was that I had it figured out when I was eight years old that if I

210

bought two bits' worth of raw peanuts and a nickel's worth of paper bags, and roasted the nuts in my mother's oven, I could sell the works for sixty cents that same afternoon. And they didn't know that there wasn't any real difference between my doing that and buying a carload of Florida oranges or Mexican pineapples and selling them for a profit; or that I'd come to New Orleans and buy a shipload of bananas, and distribute them along the inland towns, and that going on from there, eventually I'd buy ships of my own. And that because I wouldn't give a damn who or what a man's folks were, if he had the stuff that would help me to build a bigger and faster and more profitable fleet, I'd be shouldering my way into their bailiwick."

Again she paused, staring down at the carpet. Then he shook his head, like a suddenly aroused sleeper.

"I didn't mean to go into my life history," he said harshly, "but what you said about my background got me started. Because my idea always was the hell with background, it's only the foreground that counts. And that's made the real difference between the Trans-Caribbean crowd and my Blue Fleet. If they hadn't been so long-established without competition, they'd have been dead pigeons by now. As it was, they went down about as fast as I went up because practically everything I got I had to take from them. Now they're trying to get some of it back, and it's too late. They haven't got the stamina, or the brains, or the fight to do it. They've got too many socially correct vice presidents and executives that couldn't by rights make an honest living emptying wastebaskets. They can merge with us or they can go under. I won't stop what I'm doing, and they're on the losing end. If they keep on bucking me, it's only a matter of time till they hang a red flag out in front of the T-C Tower in Gloucester and the auctioneer starts asking what is he offered. But if they amalgamate with the Blue Fleet, we all make money. That's what I put up to them. I even by God offered to let the combined outfit keep the Trans-Caribbean name."

"No doubt, people who go in for that sort of thing would find everything you're telling me very fascinating," Amélie interrupted petishly. "But I must say I can't see any connection between it and what we were talking about. I mean Caresse, and your encouragement of her to disobey me and defy the family traditions. In spite of what you say, background has its obligations as well as its privileges. And no daughter of mine is going to flout either the one or the other. Do you mind explaining why you not only refuse to help me do my duty as a mother, but actually hinder me?"

He jerked away his arm and leaped up, so abruptly that she was genuinely startled. But her exclamation of dismay was cut short by his curt retort.

"If you'll give me a chance to finish what I was saying, perhaps even you would understand."

"Oh—then—I know it's unforgivably bold of me to question anything the great Orson Foxworth chooses to do, but *may* I ask you not to adopt such a tone in speaking to me?"

"Yes, you may ask. But now you'll listen! I've had my fill of your caprices and whims. I'm trying hard to believe that it's only because of the emotional strain you're still under that you're being so unreasonable, and that's why I've been acting like a pet poodle begging you to be nice to me. But there's a limit to everything."

"Indeed there is, and . . . ."

"For the last time of asking, will you let me finish what I started out to say?"

"Yes, if you'll say it like a civilized human being and not like a gangster."

"Very well. My dear Mrs. Lalande—yours of even date received and in reply, beg to state that the one condition I made in connection with the merger was that I was to be president, general manager, executive director, and all-round boss, even though the combination remained the Trans-Caribbean Fruit and Steamship Company in name, and the Great Blue Fleet ceased to exist—in name. Beg to advise further that this was the big stumbling block, the one thing their Board refused to consider, probably because I wasn't related to anybody's forty-second cousin. But I had figured that bunch of stuffed shirts would balk, so I had everything set to take them on a real hayride. I won't bore you with the details of the political setup between Puerto de Oro and Llorando. But the Trans-Carib stuffed shirts were about to lose the final round by an upheaval which would leave them without any connections in Llorando, and any time that happened they could kiss themselves goodbye, and I'd pick up the pieces for the first verse and chorus of a song."

"Orson, I repeat I'm not interested in anything at this moment but in keeping Caresse from taking a headstrong, wilful, and *ruinous* step."

"I'm coming to that, if you'll just let me. Where was I? Oh. . . . With all my lines laid, one of the stuffedest of the Trans-Carib stuffed shirts suddenly comes over to my side—body, boots, and breeches. Francisco Darcoa, no less. With the stock he controls and what I've been able to pick up very quietly, the merger's going through, and I'm to be president of an outfit that will practically control all East Coast shipping between us and Latin America. With my organization to run that combination it will mean money, power—hell, it will mean anything I want it to mean. And now as for Caresse . . . ."

"I was *really* beginning to wonder whether we'd ever get to my side of this."

He stopped his restless pacing, seated himself beside her, and slid his arm about her once more.

"I've seen this whole situation coming—the merger and all it would mean. Also what I could offer you after it was accomplished," he went on. "I wanted to be prepared for—well, for everything. And I acted accordingly. About a year and a half ago a very remarkable piece of property was put on the market in Puerto de Oro. It was originally the private residence of a Spanish governor, and it never went out of his descendants' hands. But the de la Torres to whom this *palacio*—and it's all of that—belonged have all died off except for Doña Caterina and for some reason this beautiful girl was determined to become a nun. So the property came up for sale, and I bought it, furnishings and all, just as it stood."

He paused long enough to give weight to his words. Amélie moved slightly so that she would be able to look at him while he talked, but she did not withdraw from his encircling arm or interrupt him.

"Just wait till you see it," he went on. "I meant to surprise you with it—that's why I haven't told you about it before. But I'm letting you in on so many secrets, I might as well let you in on this one too. The *palacio's* built in a hollow square. big enough to cover a whole city block, with an immense inner courtyard. There are a few surviving buildings of the same type—the Torre-Tagle palace in Lima, for instance, which belonged to relatives of these same people I'm talking about. But there aren't many such monuments to a lost civilization left, only a few in private hands, none that I know of, except this one, where there's been no division of belongings for centuries. Here everything's intact—paintings, silverware, porcelains, furniture, draperies, carpets, ornaments of every description—why, it's a treasure trove! Even the family jewelry's never been divided. There's a parure of emeralds and diamonds—tiara, necklace, earrings, brooch, bracelets, all complete—that one of the governors gave to his bride nearly two hundred years ago. Of course, I've got that in a safe, along with half a million dollars' worth of other gems. It's the finest collection of its kind I've ever seen."

213

Again he paused and this time Amélie made a vague sound, resembling a soft purr.

"You berated me for being away so long," he continued. "Well, the main reason that I was delayed—aside from all this rumpus with the Trans-Caribbean—was that I was putting this palace into condition and that it required pretty constant and watchful supervision. It was a treasure trove all right; but it was a crumbling one. Now it's been restored—and so skillfully that none of the solid new structure shows. That wonderful mellow look of antiquity which gave it half its beauty is quite unimpaired. But it's also the last word in luxurious living. For instance, the bathroom I designed for you has a sunken tub, big enough to swim in, and Pompeiian designs all around the walls."

Again Amélie made a little sound, less vague than the previous one. This time it distinctly bespoke startled admiration.

"That leads out of a dressing room with mirrored lockers all around it," Foxworth told her. "The locker space is new, but the mirrors are old—I had them set into beautiful paneled wood. You could hang up a hundred dresses without crowding them. I don't know whether a marble-topped *coiffeuse* would appeal to you—if it doesn't, that's easily enough changed. But of course all the floors are made from marble that was used as ballast for the Spanish galleons when they came over to take back treasure from the New World. And in this room the floor and the *coiffeuse* match. I think it's quite effective."

This time Amélie found it possible to frame actual words, or rather found it quite impossible to refrain from doing so.

"It must be beautiful," she said. "Simply beautiful. Why, Orson, I don't see how you could keep all this a secret so long! I should think you'd have been bursting with it. It's just like a fairy tale."

"I've only just begun," Orson Foxworth said exultantly. "The bedroom leading out of this dressing room has a complete set of the old gilded hand-carved furniture that's so hard to find. The draperies are pale blue brocade with gold and silver threads running through it, and the hanging lamps are solid silver. There's a Madonna over the mantelpiece that's valued at two hundred thousand—dollars, not pesos. . . . Well, perhaps I'd better not go on. I might never get through. There are forty rooms in the darn place, and every last one of them's got something distinctive about it. Besides, I haven't said anything about the patio yet—or the garden.

The garden's back of the house and just the same size. All in all, it's quite an establishment. Just the same, I haven't built it up with the idea that it was going to serve a large family. In fact, I've tried to make it a perfect setting for just one woman—one woman and her devoted lover. With a palace like that to live in, they could let the rest of the world go by."

He bent his head and, unrebuked, let his lips linger over the golden locks escaping from the black snood. Gradually they wandered across her brow and her cheeks and came to rest near her lips.

"When the house is still at night," he whispered, "we'll sit in the patio and listen to the fountain. And then we'll go upstairs—that beautiful room with the great azure and gold bed will be waiting for us. It *is* like a fairy tale, isn't it, Amélie? A fairy tale that I've had the power to make true. And we can be like the prince and princess in the fairy tale, living happily ever after, if we don't let anyone spoil all this for us."

"Why, who could spoil it when you've thought of everything, provided for everything?"

"Don't you think any third person would spoil an idyl like that? Can't you guess now why I was pleased that Caresse had an opportunity that would take her in a different direction—why that was something else I created, if you must have the whole truth?"

"You mean that you—"

"I mean I've known Rudolph Haas for years. All I did was to drop a hint. If Caresse hadn't been able to make good on her own, the hint wouldn't have had any weight. But as it was—"

"Then you deliberately planned that Caresse shouldn't go with us?"

"I wouldn't put it quite so strongly as that. But yes—I did rather hope, all along, she wouldn't. Not that I dislike Caresse. I'm very fond of her. You must know that. But as I've just said, she'd have been a rather intrusive figure on the scene I've just described. Not only as just a third person, either. You know how much male attention she always attracts. Why, if she were there, we'd have every rutting young buck from Tampico to Balboa walking bear and strumming guitars under our windows!"

"Oh, Orson, don't speak so coarsely! And don't—don't give me such awful shocks! How could I dream you'd planned all this? The palace and—and everything!"

215

"Why you were pleased as Punch about the palace not two minutes ago! What do you mean by 'everything'?"

"I mean you deliberately planned to get Caresse out of the way. Didn't you?"

"Out of *our* way. Yes."

"But even supposing that did work out just the way you wanted it to, wouldn't there . . . ."

"Wouldn't there what?"

"Wouldn't there still have been Odile?"

"If she hadn't—died? Yes, of course. But you must remember that when I came north, I didn't know there was anything the matter with Odile—or with her marriage. I thought she was a healthy, happy woman. There wasn't any reason for me to suppose that she had any special need of you, much less that she'd have any idea of coming to Puerto de Oro, except perhaps later on for an occasional visit—and I wouldn't have objected to that. I thought she and Léonce would go right on living here at Richmond Place—Caresse was the only one I considered in my plans for us."

"You say you didn't know before you reached New Orleans that Odile was sick or that Léonce was making her unhappy. I don't suppose you did. But you didn't know Caresse had a job, either. I distinctly remember that I telephoned you last Saturday morning—"

"Correct. But it didn't take me long, after you telephoned me, to get in touch with Rudolph Haas by long distance. And it didn't take him long to get in touch with Miss Hickey by the same means. She was in New Orleans already, poking around picture galleries; and she had already heard Caresse broadcast. All of which was a lucky break for me, the way I figured it. Because, as I said a few minutes ago, I meant to see to it from the first that she shouldn't come to Puerto de Oro with us. And you'll admit that there was a pretty good chance that she would have, if fate hadn't intervened, first in one way, then in another. If Léonce and Odile had been hitting it off all right, as I had every reason to suppose they were, they'd have been glad to have the house to themselves. They'd have felt just the same about it that I do and as I should think you would. They wouldn't have said this in so many words to Caresse, but they probably would have given themselves away, sooner or later. I happen to know that Odile felt pretty strongly on the subject, but she never said anything for fear of hurting your feelings. Of course, she wouldn't have wanted to hurt Caresse's feelings either, but after all a sister's rather different from a mother, and Caresse can take a hint. Eventually, she'd have felt in the way. Be-

216

sides, she probably would have liked the idea of a trip to Central America, just on its own merits. Most girls would. They think of it as exotic, romantic, and all the rest."

"Well then, you intended all along that Caresse wouldn't be coming with us, but you didn't actually begin to *plan* to get her out of the way until Saturday morning."

"That's right. I've said all of this two or three times now. I never realized you had to have things spelled out so thoroughly, Amélie. I thought you were rather quick on the uptake. And I don't care much for your expression 'get her out of the way.' You make it sound as if I wouldn't have stopped at anything to prevent her from going to Puerto de Oro; whereas actually I was doing her a great service."

"You didn't stop at anything to put through your deal with Trans-Caribbean. You've never stopped at anything to get what you wanted or to do away with what you didn't want. And you work terribly fast. You didn't know Saturday morning that Caresse had a job, and by Saturday afternoon you had all the wires pulled so that she'd get another."

"Correct again. I do work fast. And I'm not easily balked. But I don't get what you're driving at, Amélie. You've known me a long time. My methods aren't new to you. Or their results either."

"I'm not driving at anything. And I'm trying to keep from thinking. Perhaps that's what makes me seem so stupid, perhaps that's why I have to ask you to repeat what you're saying to me. I don't think—I won't think—but just the same—"

"Just the same *what*?"

"I don't wonder she can't put it into words. But perhaps she'll let me do it for her. I think I've caught her idea."

Foxworth and Amélie were both on their feet before Léonce had finished speaking from the threshold. He appeared quite unmoved by the charges of eavesdropping and sneaking which were hurled at him. He crossed the room unhurriedly and the look which he turned on Foxworth was insolent rather than intimidated.

"I haven't heard quite as much as I wish I might have from my vantage point in the hall," he said. "But I don't have the same trouble you do, Mr. Foxworth, in following my poor mother-in-law's agonized reasoning. This is what she was trying to say: 'You didn't want any interlopers in your tropical wonderland, so you found a way to get rid of Caresse in a few short hours. But there was still the unexpected problem of Odile. Well, you work fast, you're not

217

14

How Orson Foxworth
had a narrow escape—

January 8, 1948

NOT A few of the most significant experiences in Foxworth's tumultuous career had lacked all similitude to reality. But no hairbreadth escape, no amazing discovery, no precipitate victory had ever seemed to him so wholly unbelievable as the fact that, having desired Amélie Lalande for years and being at last on the very threshold of the nuptial chamber, he had by his own act rent the bonds which united them.

This unbelief had a twofold foundation: never before, in his entire life, had he stopped short of a coveted goal, much less deliberately turned away from it when it was actually in sight; and never, as far as physical charms were concerned, had Amélie seemed more seductive than she did when he flung himself out of her presence. Yet no power on earth could have forced him to keep his troth with her after the charge which had capped the climax of her denunciations; and no fairness of the flesh could have compensated, in his eyes, for her outrageous behavior, her shallow-mindedness and her ignoble soul.

He knew himself well enough to recognize that he was very angry and that his fury, in the truest sense of the word, might be blind; but despite his incredulous amazement over the outcome of the afternoon, he realized that he was at last seeing Amélie clearly. His pride was not galled because he had lost her; instead, his self-contempt was centered in the humiliating awareness that he had not previously recognized her for what she was. Of course he was by no means the first man who had been hoodwinked by superficial beauty, and he would by no means be the last. But Orson Foxworth was

219

not in the habit of making a fool of himself, even less of letting anyone else make a fool of him.

He was still seething with rage when he left the Lalandes' house; but he tried to rationalize the sequence of events, from the moment when Léonce slithered through the portieres, to the moment when he himself tore out of the front door. Because of Amélie's importunate message, Foxworth had left his office while many matters of great consequence were still pending; somehow he must cope with at least the most urgent of these before the end of the day—the definite conclusion of his agreement with Francisco Darcoa, for instance. That could not be put off. But in his own present state of turmoil, Foxworth knew he could not meet that calm, grave, and deliberate gentleman with any chance of fortunate results. He would take umbrage where no offense was intended; he would interrupt the quiet flow of the other's remarks with impatient questions; he would unconsciously raise his voice until he was fairly shouting in Darcoa's face. He knew his own failings as well as his own power, for just such departures from civilized behavior had—temporarily—been his undoing more than once in the past. This time he could not take such a risk. He must meet Darcoa in that aristocrat's own collected and measured way. Not the least of Foxworth's grievances against Amélie was that she had made this so difficult for the moment as to be almost impossible.

He had started his car mechanically and had almost reached St. Charles Avenue before he realized which direction he was taking or why. Then he decided to go further uptown and drive on, marking time, until he had regained his self-control. He swung into the slow-traffic lane and drove along at minimum speed . . . .

He had given Léonce short shrift, asking Amélie only one question—"Is that really what you were trying to tell me?"—before ordering her son-in-law from the room. She had faltered out a startled affirmative and Foxworth had said, very well, in that case he would like to speak with her privately for a few minutes; he would attend to Léonce later; meanwhile there had better not be any more eavesdropping. And Léonce had not even stood his ground; he had slunk away, after his brief moment of vain triumph, like a cur who knew he was in for a whipping, as soon as the master's hand was free to administer it . . . .

Now that Foxworth thought the matter over, he realized that it had not taken very much time to tell Amélie off either: not when you reflected that she had long been his beloved and was still his betrothed; not when you remembered that he had come obediently to her bidding only a short hour before; not when you considered that since then he had tried, with all the patience and wisdom he could summon, to clarify her bewilderment, to soothe her agitation, and to prove that he adored her . . . .

"So you think that I don't stop at anything—including the murder of a lovely and innocent girl—to get what I want? By the same token, I suppose you think I don't ever stop wanting anything I once coveted—including the possession of a beautiful and elusive woman? Well, you're wrong, Amélie, on both counts."

She tried to interrupt and expostulate. He cut her short.

"It's my turn to talk. And I don't think you'll find what I have to say hard to follow or tediously long this time. In fact, though I'm willing to go briefly into the reasons for my decision, if you want to have me, they won't alter the result of it. And I can put that into just one sentence: you and I are through, Amélie."

"You and I are—oh, Orson, how can you say anything so cruel, even in jest? When you know my heart's broken, when I've turned to you for comfort and support in my terrible sorrow, when—"

"You weren't jesting, were you, when you accused me of murder? Oh, I know—you didn't do it in so many words! And you got that sneaking son-in-law of yours to speak for you, so that you wouldn't have to say anything incriminating yourself. But that was what you meant just the same. And it isn't exactly my idea of a kind thing to say. If we're talking cruelly to each other, it isn't I who started it. As for turning to me for comfort and support, you didn't do that either. You got me here to rail at me and rebuke me. You're determined to have someone to ride, and now that you can't ride your daughters any more, you thought you'd have a try at me. It wasn't a very sound idea, but as long as you were going to have it, I'm glad you had it now. I can see that I've had a very narrow escape. As to your broken heart and your terrible sorrow—well, I guess we'd better skip that part. But I have ideas of my own about that too."

"Orson, you said that this time I'd understand, that you wouldn't have to explain. And I'm completely confused, I'm utterly crushed by every word you're saying. Here you and I have adored each other for years and now, on the very eve of our marriage—"

"What marriage? You've just reminded me that we weren't 'formally engaged.' You've told me I'd better wait until we

221

were before I 'interfered' between you and your daughter, before I 'presumed to interpret your wishes.' Well, I'm prepared to wait—indefinitely. Because there isn't going to be any marriage."

This time Amélie's interruption began with a long wail. But it finally ended in coherent speech.

"Why, I said we were 'solemnly betrothed!' "

"Yes, and in my ignorance I supposed that meant the same thing as being formally engaged. As I confessed to you, I never had much of an education, so I suppose my mistake was natural. Anyway, you've convinced me that I made one. You've shown me that I took too much for granted in assuming that a formal engagement and a solemn betrothal were one and the same thing. So I should think you'd be very much relieved by my positive declaration that I'll never make the same mistake again."

"If you had the slightest compassion for a bereaved mother—if you had the remotest inkling of what it means to be a gentleman—"

"You don't usually think of murderers as especially compassionate, do you? . . . . And though it seems rather anticlimactic to speak of gentlemanly instincts in the same breath, I must remind you that you weren't hesitating to become formally engaged to me merely because there had been a death in your family. My lack of background was another reason. Not a reason that you thought was good a long time ago—one that you still considered sound this very afternoon. And it *is* sound. I never pretended to be a gentleman. I didn't realize before that was your main requisite. I thought you wanted a man. And a lover. Of course, a legalized lover, but still—"

"Oh, Orson, I want you! I love you with all my heart and soul, I—"

"You haven't any heart and soul. Or much of any mind either. You've got a beautiful face and a beautiful body and that's about all. It isn't enough, Amélie. At least, it might be enough for a mistress. But it isn't enough for a wife."

She had taken the chiffon handkerchief from its hiding place in her bosom and was sobbing convulsively into it. Briefly, he realized that he was amazed because her sobs now left him unmoved, when only a few hours earlier they would have caused him acute distress. But he did not dwell on his astonishment and presently he forgot it, because there was so much else on his mind which was forcing itself into speech. He had told the truth when he said that the crux of his decision was contained in one sentence. But now he found

222

that his reasons were clamoring for utterance, that he would be choked if he did not voice them.

"I told you all along that we shouldn't be husband and wife, that we were only meant to be lovers. I tried to make you see that you needed a chance to go your way almost as much as I needed a chance to go mine. And you wouldn't believe me. You were affronted at my honesty. So, because I thought I had to have you, I finally asked you to be my wife. And what happens? Inside of a week you're telling me that I'm 'interfering,' that I'm 'taking too much for granted.' And at the same time, you're assuming that I ought to be constantly at your beck and call, that you can be as captious, or as shrewish, or as unreasonable as suits your mood of the moment, that you can even denounce me for murder—and have me take it! If I needed anything to prove my point, you've certainly handed it to me on a silver platter!"

"But I don't mean to be captious or shrewish or unreasonable! I didn't mean to denounce you for murder—that is, not really! Not seriously! It's just that I'm so overwhelmed with grief—"

"As I said awhile back, I think we'd better skip that part. I've tried hard enough, Lord knows, to believe that was all the trouble. I wanted to believe it, because I wanted you. I've tried to think of you as any halfway decent man ought to think of his future wife and generally does: not just as someone to share his bed and board; but his name, his standing, his problems, his hopes and fears. When I told you how I'd fought my way up the ladder, I wasn't bragging; I was trying to share my success with you. And when I told you about the merger, I wasn't gloating; I was trying to share my secrets with you. I was talking to you as if you'd been my wife already. I was paying you a lot bigger compliment than when I talked to you about the *palacio*. Because I would have set you up in that, if you'd have gone, without benefit of clergy. But I never would have given you a glimpse of what passes for my soul."

He looked down at her bowed head and her shaking shoulders, and again he was conscious of fleeting surprise. For he had no desire to put his hand on her beautiful golden hair or to encircle her slim waist with his arm.

"And you were just plain bored," he said so thoughtfully that, for the moment, his anger was engulfed in gravity. "You wanted me to get through my story, so that you could go back to your grievances about Caresse and her insurrection and about me and my presumption. What I told you didn't give you confidence in me; it didn't make you feel

223

proud of me. And I was so sure beforehand that it would. That's the sort of certainty a man feels about the woman he's asked to be his wife and who's consented—that whoever else doubts him, or fails him, she'll believe in him, she'll stand by him; that far from charging him with anything, she'll indignantly refute the least charge made against him by others. That's what he thinks she means when she tells him she loves him. He doesn't think she's just marrying him for his money or for—carnal desire. He never would have asked her to marry him in the first place if he'd thought that was all she'd mean. He'd have gone gunning for other things and he could have got them cheap. But he doesn't want anything cheap from the woman who's going to bear his name and who he hopes will bear his sons."

After that his fury had come back in full force and he had said a great deal more, most of which he knew, now that his anger was finally cooling, no man should ever say to any woman. He should not have said, for instance, that he had been mistaken in believing they could have been happy together even as lovers, that when a man came home after a hard day, he did not want to begin the evening with an amorous interlude; he wanted first of all to find a woman waiting for him who would give him a sense of peace and welcome, who would understand that he did not want to talk very much, far less go in for violent lovemaking, until he had had a good bath and a good drink and a good dinner in quiet surroundings. Amélie—so he told her—would have begun questioning her lover and nagging him and ordering him around before he was fairly in the house and no man who was worth his salt would put up with that .... He should not have said, either, That Amélie was probably too old to have a child and that he wondered why he had not thought of that, long before .... Most of all, he should not have said that people who lived in glass houses must not throw stones, that if he had not told her where he was last Saturday night, neither was there anything to prove she had not slipped out of her bedroom and into her daughter's. After all, she had been the one who kept saying, over and over again, "If it hadn't been for Odile ...."

No, he should not have said any of these things and, after a lapse of time, he would find a way of admitting this, indirectly, to Amélie. He had been inconsistent himself in lauding the blessings of domesticity when he had strained away from these for years; and it was beneath a man of his stature to fling a woman's age in her face, still more so to hint that she might have been guilty of a hideous crime—

especially when a similar charge, coming from her, had precipitated the break between them. For this was all it had done, he saw that. Sooner or later it would have come anyway. Her charge had not caused the break, only hastened it. He was thankful it had. And some day, somehow, he would make amends for his coarseness and his violence. He owed her that much. But never again should she influence his life, much less tamper with it. His first verdict was also his final one; he was through with her. As far as that statement went, he had nothing for which to apologize and nothing to withdraw . . . .

It was getting dark. He switched on the dashboard lights and saw that it was much later than he had realized. He had driven further than he intended. By this time Francisco Darcoa, in all probability, would have left his office, after vainly awaiting a promised telephone call for some hours; and even a man as habitually serene as he seemed, might very well be annoyed by such a breach of good manners and good business. And annoyance in that quarter was the last thing that Foxworth desired to encounter at this particular stage of negotiations. But for Amélie and her cursed importunities, the whole matter might have been settled by now! And he had been fool enough to think of her as a helpmate! No, not quite that much of a fool—he simply had not considered that aspect of marriage when he had asked her to be his wife. Belatedly, it loomed before him in all its supreme importance. Yes, he had certainly had a very narrow escape . . . .

It was a long time since the Darcoas had invited him to their house. During Carmelita Darcoa's lifetime, he had occasionally gone to their larger and more lavish parties; but he had never been a member of their inner circle; and since Francisco Darcoa had become a widower, he and Foxworth had met more often at downtown clubs and at large semi-public functions than in private houses. Now, after some reflection, Foxworth decided that, despite this lack of intimacy, his wisest course would be to stop off on Coliseum Street as he went downtown. The loss of a business day might be a serious one for him; in this case, his apology should be neither indirect nor retarded.

He swung his car around and drove rapidly through the fast-gathering dusk. The lights were just coming on in the houses along his way and, where the shades were up they had the pleasant and inviting look peculiar to the twilight hour. He could see small groups companionably gathered, visitors drinking coffee, returning fathers whose children were boisterously hailing them, husbands and wives exchanging the quiet, affectionate kisses which marked their reunion after a day's untroubled parting. For the first time since Ruth's visit began, he found himself rather hoping that she would be waiting for him in the library when he reached Toulouse Street. There was no reason why she should be; he had not suggested anything of the sort to her, and, indeed, he had probably made her feel that she was slightly superfluous in his busy scheme of things, that he somewhat regretted his impetuous invitation. He must try to be a little more considerate, for his sake as well as hers; she was kind and thoughtful and intelligent; perhaps in some degree she might satisfy his sudden yearning for companionship. Now that he had abruptly dismissed Amélie from his life, he felt incredibly lost and lonely. He did not want her back, he would not have taken her back at any price; but he must find someone to give him a new interest and a new stimulus. Success was not enough after all, nor even the power that came from it; they crowded his career without crowning it. Sex was not enough either; strangely, almost vengefully, it demanded a spiritual element to complete it. Religion, in the orthodox sense, meant nothing to him; though, largely from expediency, he had gone through the form of becoming a Catholic since making his headquarters in Central America; however afterwards, he had often remarked, rather boastfully, that he could not believe anything he could not explain. Unutterably, he now wished that he might have faith in something or someone, sufficient to carry him through this dark hour.

As he drew up at the curb in front of the Darcoas' house, it occurred to him that none of those he had passed seemed more inviting than this one. The ceiling light in the small square portico illumined its supporting columns and the white paneled door beyond, giving them a reflected radiance. The wide wings stretched out generously on either side, and though no one was visible at any of the windows, these too gave the impression of spaciousness and luminosity. A faint sound, like the distant tinkle of a guitar, and of a man and girl singing together, seemed to come from somewhere in an upper story. Foxworth paused by the front steps to look and to listen, his appreciation tinged with something very close to envy; while he stood, gazing at the welcoming door, it opened slowly and Clarinda Darcoa came out.

Evidently she was on the point of starting to a late afternoon party, for she was dressed as if for some festive occasion. Emerald green plumes swept gracefully across her glossy hair from the crown of her small sable hat; her close fitting jacket and full, ankle-length skirt were made of emer-eld-green velvet, sable-trimmed, and she was carrying a large sable muff. Framed as she was by the white columns, she might have stepped straight from a canvas by Goya; yet this exquisite picture seemed to have been mysteriously modern-ized by the hand of some still greater master.

The light which so generously illumined the portico shone less brightly on the approach to it, and, from her momentary hesitation, it was evident that though she could see a figure beyond the steps, she did not immediately identify it. Then she smiled and held out her hand.

"Good evening, Mr. Foxworth," she said in a voice which betrayed no surprise at his presence. "How kind of you to call! Won't you come right in?"

"But you were just going out," he remarked, coming for-ward a little. "And to tell you the truth, I wasn't intending to make a social visit. I want very much to see your father on a matter of great importance, and I'm afraid I've missed him at his office. I hoped I might find him here."

"He isn't home yet. But do come in and wait for him! I wasn't going out for anything important—just another cock-tail party. And I can go to that later—or not at all. It wouldn't matter in the least, one way or another."

"Then—thank you very much, I will come in. And perhaps I may use your telephone. If Mr. Darcoa hasn't come home, he may be waiting for my call downtown."

"I'm sure he would be, if he were expecting one from you. He'd understand that you'd been unavoidably delayed in some way. The telephone is in the rear of the hall, under the stairs . . . . Jephthah, show Mr. Foxworth where to go and then bring him into the drawing room."

She must have unobtrusively touched the bell, for the door had opened before she finished speaking and an elderly man-servant had stepped forward. With the ease and eagerness of an old retainer, he bowed, took Foxworth's hat and coat, and indicated the direction of the telephone. Then he withdrew to a respectful distance until the ensuing conversation was over, before stepping forward again.

"Miss Clarinda is waiting for you, sir. This way, to the right of the front door."

During the brief period of Foxworth's absence, Clarinda had removed her plumed hat, uncovering her lustrous black hair. She had also taken off her jacket, revealing the upper part of her green dress. It was made in drop-shoulder style, with short puffed sleeves. Between the glossiness of her hair and the brillance of her velvet bodice, her skin took on a

227

quality that was almost dazzling. She wore no jewelry and this lack of ornament did not in the least detract from her striking beauty; indeed, if anything, her neck and arms gained in effectiveness because their smooth expanse was unbroken. Yet, irrelevantly, Foxworth thought how greatly that magnificent parure, which the early Spanish governor had given to his bride, would become Clarinda Darcoa. The velvet dress proved the complete suitability of the gems' color; he could amost see the green fire of those matchless emeralds sparkling in her ears, on her fingers, and on her breast; they would fairly glow against that gorgeous skin. Impulsively, he wished that he might give them to her. Well, if the merger went through and his business relations with her father gradually developed as he hoped, perhaps, as an old family friend, he might be permitted to offer them to her as a wedding gift. For of course she would marry one day. The mystery—and the miracle—lay in the fact that she had not done so long since.

"I got through to your father without any trouble," he said, dismissing conjecture and recalling himself, though not without an effort, to the realities of the moment. "He had waited to hear from me, most considerately. But he suggested that I should now wait for him here, as he finally was on the point of starting home. I'm very much chagrined that I've put him to so much inconvenience already, and I don't like to think that his homecoming will be marred by a business discussion. But it is extremely important to me, and if you're sure that I'm not inconveniencing you too, by waiting—"

"I'm very sure. I told Jephthah, while you were at the telephone, that we'd have tea—unless I found you preferred something else. Would you? Of course, you can have coffee instead, or a highball or anything you choose. But I always think that in cold weather, there's nothing quite like tea in front of a fire, at this time of the evening. It's such a sociable drink and such a sociable hour, somehow."

"I agree with you. I'd much rather have tea than anything else. And I'm afraid you'll find that I do rather more than justice to it. I didn't have any lunch and I'm ravenously hungry."

"Oh, in that case—"

Clarinda moved unhurriedly from the room and during her brief absence Foxworth looked appraisingly about him. The house was high studded, like most buildings of its period, and the lofty walls were smooth and white, enhancing the effect of spaciousness. A few splendid old paintings were spaced at intervals and the heavily carved furniture and incidental ornaments harmonized with these; but they had been used selectively rather than lavishly. The draperies of gold brocade at the long windows and the matching upholstery imparted a quality of warmth which might otherwise have been lacking in the general effect; the burnished brass of the andirons reflected the flame on the hearth. Paper-white narcissi, blooming above the pebble-filled bowls in which their bulbs were imbedded, stood on the polished tables; yellow roses were skillfully arranged between the candelabra which flanked a small, silver-crowned statue of the Virgin and Child. Here, in this one room, was the very essence of old Spain, its austerity mingled with its splendor, its charm tempered by its dignity; but here too were freshness and vitality and fragrance, in the same measure that Clarinda herself embodied these attributes.

She came back into the room and seated herself on the sofa, her green skirt spreading fanlike around her. She did not explain why she had left, nor excuse herself for having done so; but Foxworth surmised that she had gone to give instructions for supplementing the light refreshments originally ordered. In a few minutes he made the welcome discovery that his guess was well founded. Jephthah came in with a silver tray equipped with a repoussé tea service and surmounted by a purring samovar; then he departed to reappear with a laden muffin stand. Tiny sausages wrapped in bacon emerged from one covered dish; light biscuits liberally stuffed with ham from another; piping hot cheese balls from still another. By the time Foxworth had done "rather more than justice" to this heartening fare, the void created by the missing lunch was amply filled. But it transpired that there was still more to come. Jephthah's next entry was made even more impressively than his previous ones: on a silver salver he bore an immense frosted cake, studded with crystallized fruit cut to simulate flowers; and finally, with something very like reverence, he set an antique decanter and some tiny matching goblets on the cleared tray.

"I was so glad to find that you took your tea clear," Clarinda told Foxworth. "We're just beginning to get our own shipments from China again, and sugar or lemon really does spoil that wonderful smoky flavor—while as for cream! Well, that's worse than mixing the very best Scotch with ginger ale. But now I'm sure you need a liqueur and this is old Armagnac. That's coming through again too. However, we still feel it's something of a treat, so I hope you will."

"I shall indeed. But no more of a treat than everything else about this delightful interlude."

He spoke with the utmost sincerity. He had been at the Darcoas' house for less than an hour, and yet, in that amazingly short time, he had ceased to be angry, ceased to be anxious, and ceased to be lonely. He did not overlook the fact that he had also been cold and hungry on his arrival and that these creature wants had likewise been assuaged; but they were dwarfed by the greater necessities to which Clarinda had ministered. He went on observing her, with closer and closer attention, and finally he asked her an extremely personal question.

"How old are you, Clarinda?"

She smiled in her slow charming way. "I'm just past twenty-seven," she answered, without hesitation.

"Twenty-seven!"

"Yes. It's a very advanced age, isn't it? My younger sister's been married almost eight years already and has four children. She was better at 'gathering her rosebuds' than I was. But after all, I do have my uses as a maiden aunt and as a dutiful daughter."

Foxworth laughed. "You don't look either part, as we generally visualize it."

"Then appearances must be more than usually deceptive. Lina and Dick live with us, and they're on the go most of the time, so they need a good nursery governess. And Father's never liked the details of household management, so since Mother died—"

"Do you mean to say you're responsible for all this?"

He looked around him with increasing amazement and admiration. Clarinda answered quietly, her tone tinged with amusement.

"Not the pictures and the furniture and the ornaments, of course. They'd all been in the family a hundred years or more before I was born. But their arrangement—yes, to a certain degree. And the flowers and food and little things like that—why, naturally!"

"They don't seem like such little things to me. You keep house for eight persons, including four children and—"

"Yes, but I've been very fortunate. I've never had any servant problem. And it's much easier for Dick and Lina this way. He was just a kid too, when they were married. And though he's a dear boy, he hasn't yet developed much faculty for making money. So you see . . . . They're very happy together. You might have heard them singing, when you came in. Very often they do at this hour, before they start out on a round of parties. Then generally, Father and I are alone for dinner. Of course, I still go to the Carnival balls and a few other big affairs. But when a girl's been out nearly ten years, they don't seem as exciting as they did at first. I was really envious of your niece the other evening."

"You gave her the time of her life. She's immensely grateful to you. So am I. If there were anything we could possibly do to show it—"

Like his previous comment, this suggestion was wholly sincere; but Foxworth instantly realized its complete lack of finesse. For the first time since entering the house he was uncomfortable; Clarinda was not the sort of girl for whom a man vaguely offered to "do things." But if his speech struck her in the same light that it had him, there was nothing in her rejoinder to betray this.

"Why, you have! You've sat with me for nearly an hour. I've always hoped that I could have a talk with you some day—I mean, at a party or something like that. But I never dreamed that I'd get a chance to sit by the fire and take tea with you, like this."

She raised her great dark eyes and Foxworth could see their look of unclouded candor. It would have been an insult to doubt that her sincerity was as great as his own.

"Most of the men I meet—well, they're like my brother-in-law, Dick Forrestal," she went on. "Just as nice as they can be. But—well, immature. Provincial. I don't know just how to put it, without sounding condescending or disparaging and I don't want to do that. But they just don't seem to have anything to offer—at least, anything I want. Oh, I don't mean materially! Please don't misunderstand me! Lots of them are quite rich, if that mattered, which it doesn't. Because, of course Father can give me everything under the sun I want, when it comes to what money can buy. And that doesn't seem so important to me anyway. But those nice boys don't say anything I'm interested in hearing, they don't do anything that rouses my admiration. They haven't much initiative. They're not out looking around for more worlds to conquer. They're satisfied with our own little world here in New Orleans. And I'm not—that is, not completely."

She paused, still looking Foxworth full in the face and when she went on, a note of anxiety had crept into her voice.

"I'm afraid I shouldn't have said that. I'm afraid you'll think I'm critical and opinionated and dissatisfied—just like a typical old maid! You don't know me at all, and I wouldn't blame you if you took it that way. But what I meant to say was, it's so wonderful to be with a man who discovers, who builds, who creates. Why, what you've done in Puerto de

Oro—what you're still going to do—it's what Cornelius Vanderbilt did in Nicaragua or Goethals in Panama! And you've given me a glimpse of it! I've never been so thrilled in my whole life as I have in this last hour!"

She pushed the tea table away from her and rose. Foxworth was already on his feet. For a breathless moment they stood close together, looking at each other, and Clarinda's candid eyes did not fall under Foxworth's piercing glance. Then suddenly his hands shot out and he gripped her arms hard just above the elbow.

"Clarinda!" he said hoarsely. "Clarinda—do you mean that? Because if you do—"

"Of course I mean it. And I'm not sorry I said it, either."

"Sorry! You'll never be sorry, Clarinda! Never, never, never!"

"Well, I'm the one to apologize now! I said, over the telephone, that I was leaving the office immediately and I thought I could. But just as I was starting out—"

Neither Foxworth nor Clarinda had heard a latchkey turn in the front door or noticed Francisco Darcoa's quiet entrance. But there was nothing in his manner, as he greeted his guest and kissed his daughter on the brow, to indicate that he had been either astonished or offended to find them standing face to face in an atmosphere supercharged with unleashed emotion. He invited Foxworth to be seated and, sitting down himself, drew Clarinda to the arm of his chair. For a few moments he chatted affably about inconsequential topics. Then he suggested that perhaps he and his caller might adjourn to the library for their business discussion. For the second time, Foxworth was on his feet before Clarinda could rise.

"Of course, if that's the best place for our talk," he agreed readily. "But I've nothing to say to you, Mr. Darcoa, that's private—as far as your daughter's concerned. In fact, if you're willing, I'd like immensely to have her present at our interview. It may concern her future as much as it does ours."

15

How Caresse Lalande and Joe Racina visited the show-up room for the afternoon session—

January 8, 1948

THE COMMONPLACE tides of workaday life were running their prosaic course when Joe Racina and Caresse descended the stone steps of the Roosevelt Hotel. Its very reality seemed unreal. Subconsciously, Caresse had felt that all the world must be aware of her calamitous plight. Yet the people around her acted as though nothing were amiss. The usual line was waiting to buy tickets to the Orpheum; customers were strolling casually into the nearby coffee shops; taxi starters were whistling their shrill summons; a traffic policeman was languidly waving a car away from a space that was closed to parking; and a matronly woman, her arms filled with shopping bundles, scolded a small child for not keeping place with her. Joe sensed what was passing through the girl's mind.

"The world has a way of not giving a damn about individual troubles," he told her. "If I stepped in front of one of these cars and was run down, people would go right on doing what they've always been doing, hurrying home to dinner, going to the neighborhood movie, having babies, cussing out the government, visiting the dentist twice a year, arguing at the bridge table and so on . . . . Oh, Judith and the kids would be unhappy for a while, of course, and a few of my friends would say, 'You never know when it's your turn, do you? Why, I was talking to old Joe only day before yesterday!' But by and large, the world would wag along as though Joe Racina had never lived or died."

Caresse smiled up at him rather wanly. The sudden surge

of resolution which had prompted her to accede to Joe's earnest proposal that she accompany him to police headquarters forthwith had subsided, and fear of the unknown ordeal that confronted her was taking its place.

"It's all very well for you to talk, Joe," she said. "You don't have to prove you didn't murder your sister. You don't have to keep thinking things like: 'Will they put me in prison if I can't make them believe me? Will they hang me?' And all the while I just know that if Miss Hickey finds out about any of this, I'll lose my chance; and if I can't leave with her on the Crescent Limited Saturday night, she's bound to find out about it, isn't she?"

They had come to the tiny, glassed-in cubicle which served the Dixie Parking Lot as an office, and one of the attendants had already hurried to bring her car.

"Don't forget about the rule that everybody's presumed innocent till proved guilty," Joe reminded her. "It's up to the authorities, not to you, to do the proving, and I'm betting they can't do it . . . . Here's your car, isn't it? Like me to drive?"

"Please. I'd probably run it smack into the nearest pedestrian."

Joe took the wheel and guided the car into Common Street. While they waited for the traffic officer's signal, Joe looked at the dashboard clock.

"Is that right? Five minutes to three?" he asked incredulously. "I had no idea we'd been talking that long. Maybe I should have telephoned Toe to let him know we were coming. He might be gone by the time we get there."

Nonetheless, he slowed to a decorous fifteen miles an hour in passing the cluster of towering Charity Hospital buildings, and again in going through a school zone. Thereafter, however, he sent the car along at a speed that was well beyond the limits fixed by municipal ordinance. "If a traffic cop stops us, the chances are I'll know him and can talk us out of a jam. I don't want to miss Toe. If we can get you squared away . . . . And like as not we'll have to hunt for a parking spot . . . ."

His apprehension on this score was groundless. As they approached the great gray stone pile of masonry which housed police headquarters, the criminal courts, the sheriff's offices, the jury commission, the city morgue, and the parish prison, another car was just pulling away from the curb. He maneuvered Caresse's roadster dexterously into the vacated space, and snapped off the ignition. Taking her elbow, he hurried her across the neutral ground to the opposite banquette, past the great bronze urns that flanked the granite steps, and through the ornamental bronze doors. Once inside, he turned sharply to the right along a corridor that extended the full block of the building's length.

"Through here!" he directed as they came to a plain, unmarked door, paneled in opaque glass. Before a desk near the window of a rather littered room, a bulky man confronted a typewriter, stabbing at the keyboard with thick fingers. His hat was pushed far back on his head, his coat was draped over the back of his chair, and he chewed vigorously at a frayed length of cigar. From the scowl with which he glared at the yellow paper in the typewriter, the set of his heavy shoulders, and the tense posture of his legs—which were poised as if he were about to hurl himself upon an adversary—it was obvious that the throes of literary composition were little to his liking. With a final thrust at the keyboard, he transferred his scowl from the paper to the newcomers. Then his expression relaxed, and he hastily removed his hat and dropped it among the miscellany of papers on the desk.

"Hiya, Joe," he said cordially. "Long time no see. What's up?"

"Hiya, Dan. I don't get around much any more, and that's a fact. Nothing's up. Nothing special, that is. I wanted to see Toe for a minute or so. Don't tell me he's gone for the day."

" 'Course not. He's down in the show-up room. Not much of a haul, today, so he won't be long. But you better go down and wait for him there. You'll likely miss him, if you stay up here, because most of the boys go from the show-up room right to their cars and beat it for their territory or their homes or wherever, depending what shift they're on. The show-up room opens right into the garage, you know."

"Say, that's an idea! Do you mind, Caresse? Or would you rather wait up here till the show-up's over, while I go downstairs and hang around to grab Toe when he's through?"

Caresse looked about the littered room in helpless bewilderment. "Oh, no," she said. "Not by myself. I won't mind what it is, if you're there." She took his arm. "Let me go with you, please, Joe."

"Surest thing you know. Why not? But let's not lose any time. Be seein' you, Dan. It's like old times to come back out here. Don't take any wooden pickpockets!"

They hastened through corridors, stair wells, and dark basement hallways to a dim recess where Joe unhesitatingly opened a door and motioned her to precede him. She did so, but drew back against him the instant she had crossed the threshold. Never before had Caresse Lalande even imagined such a scene as that of which she now became a part in the unlit room. Everything in it was painted a flat, dead black. Yet Caresse could see that the benches were occupied by bulky figures, silhouetted against a brilliantly spotlighted, elevated stage which ran the full length of one wall. Between the stage and the room, however, a taut screen of plastic extended from ceiling to floor, and what would have been the backdrop of the shallow, screened stage, had it been in a theater, was ruled off horizontally at half-inch intervals by white lines. The height of these lines above the floor, from five to seven feet, was indicated in numerals along a scarlet vertical line in the center. In the dim "auditorium," the only spot of light was the green glass of a reading lamp's shade, and the cone of radiance which fell from it to a lectern. Before this a large man was leafing through report sheets fastened to a wooden clip-board. Joe felt Caresse tremble as she shrank against him.

"It's nothing to be frightened about," he whispered to her. "The screen, for instance. It's just a contraption, devised so that the people on the stage can be seen without seeing anything of those who are looking at them. And the man by the reading stand is Captain Harry Gregson, one of the senior detectives on the force. The people who were arrested since the last show-up are brought out there one at a time, for everybody here to look at. Maybe there are some holdup victims among the detectives in the room here; if so, they've been called in to see whether they recognize any of these people. And the detectives know many of the prisoners by sight, so that if they try to lie and say they were never arrested before . . . ."

The clang of heavy metal indicated that a backstage cell block had been opened. As Joe and Caresse took seats on one of the benches, a corpulent, coatless officer, his round face heavily shaded by the wide brim of his hat, brought a garishly overdressed girl onto the stage and directed her to stand against the vertical red line. The floodlights were pitiless in accentuating the details of her appearance: the chemically bleached straw color of her coarse hair, the plucked arch of her eyebrows, the heavily plastered cosmetics, the sleazy plaid of her jacket and skirt, the cascade of pink ruffles descending along the front of her blouse, even the shoes with the run-down heels.

Bending over his lectern, Captain Gregson was reading aloud from the topmost report on his clip-board.

"Josephine Blue, twenty-four years old, 894 Iberville Street, booked in the third precinct—stand up straight, Josephine!—for soliciting. Arrested at the corner of North Liberty and St. Peter Streets, where she accosted Officers Melberg and Duval of the Vice Squad at 2:30 P.M. of this date. What's your real name, Josephine."

"You got my real name," the girl answered sullenly.

"Did you ever go by any other name? Ever use an alias?"

"Never."

"Where you from?"

"Detroit."

"Ever arrested here before?—and you might as well tell the truth, because we can check up on your answers easy enough."

"Yes."

"When, and what for?"

"Last October. I was grabbed on the numbers, and put in the ice house."

"How long did they keep you there?"

"Two weeks."

"And you haven't been arrested since?"

"Yes, a month back, for the same as today."

"Anybody else got any questions?" Gregson asked of the silhouettes in the dark section of the room. There was no answer. "All right, Josephine. You'll be up in night court tonight. And whatever they do to you, you'd better leave town and go back to Detroit when you get out."

The girl swaggered disdainfully off the stage. Caresse plucked at Joe's sleeve.

"Is that what they'll do to me if they arrest me, Joe? Will I have to stand up in front there and let these men stare at me, and answer questions? Oh, Joe, I'm sorry I let you talk me into coming here. Please take me away. What did that girl mean by saying they put her in the ice house for two weeks?"

"Don't be a dope, honey. This is for vagrants or habitual criminals—people like that. And the ice house is Tenderloin slang for the isolation hospital. The morals ordinance is Number 5112, so if anybody's arrested for violating it and is found to be diseased, and sent to the isolation hospital for treatment, they say they were picked up for the numbers and sent to the ice house."

"That's all of the women for today," Gregson announced. "Tell Johnny Meredith to get the men started in here."

A small, sallow, rat-faced individual shambled nervously to

237

the center of the stage. Little, beady eyes, deep in their sockets, darted apprehensively from side to side, as he brushed the back of a claw-like hand across colorless, almost grayish lips. In an effort to still the visible trembling of his knees he sought to smooth the rumpled and stained fabric of his trousers.

"John Zogelman, alias Monkey Joe, alias J. H. Bird," Captain Gregson was reading aloud. "Arrested for vagrancy by Officer Spalise this P.M. The said officer noticed above prisoner at Canal and Rampart Streets, and when questioned, the same could not give a good account of himself and was taken into custody and booked accordingly." He unclipped the report, and placed it, face down, on the growing pile of others which had been disposed of earlier during the show-up. "When were you arrested last, John?"

"Two years ago, in San Antonio. Honest, I ain't never been arrested here before, Cap. I wouldn't fool you."

"Did you do time?"

"Yeah. Seventeen months out of twenty-two. In Atlanta."

"What was it—muggles or junk?"

"Junk."

"Are you still on the junk?"

"I hope God paralyzes me on the spot if I am!"

Near Caresse and Joe one of the shadowy silhouettes leaned toward another and growled, "Listen at him. Look at those knees. Him off the junk? Why, he can't even turn his motor off, he needs a bang so bad right this minute!"

"If we give you hours to get the hell out of town, will you beat it and never come back?"

"I sure will, Cap. So help me!"

"Okay. I'll send for you after the show-up. And if you ever poke that puss of yours into New Orleans again, we'll throw every charge in the book at you. Take him away! Next!"

Three young men—one of them little more than a boy—walked to the center of the stage with a show of bravado which, in the case of the youngest one, was obviously feigned, but appeared to be real enough insofar as his two companions were concerned. All three were alike in that their hair was smoothly pomaded, and brushed straight back. The tallest of the three, who likewise appeared to be several years older than either of the others, drew a comb from his coat pocket and ran it through his hair, tapping it against his palm, afterwards, before replacing it.

Even Caresse could feel a sort of tension charge the atmosphere in the room, though nothing was said. In the

238

stillness, the youngest of the trio shifted nervously from one foot to the other. Both his companions cast a look of contempt at him. Unseen by the men on the stage, a tall, wide-shouldered figure rose from a bench on the far side of the room, and Caresse started, for as the figure approached Captain Gregson's reading lamp and was more clearly revealed by the light filtering through the plastic screen, she recognized Toe Murphy.

He and Captain Gregson engaged in an earnest, low-voiced colloquy for some minutes. Murphy turned to the dimness and beckoned. A smallish man rose and made his way uncertainly toward the lectern, joining in the low-voiced conversation. Caresse could see him nod vigorously in response to a question, and point unhesitatingly to one of the men on the stage. Then Murphy and his companion returned to their seats.

"Harold Brown, Sam O'Day, Leon Raichac," Gregson began to read aloud. "Arrested this noon, Brown and O'Day in a rooming house, 986 Camp Street; Raichac at his residence, 2377 Annunciation Street. Charged with D and S, when a pistol and seven cartons of cigarettes were found in the room of O'Day. What's your real name, O'Day?"

"O'Day!"

"Ever use any aliases or been arrested before?"

"Nope!"

In the shadowy show-up room another figure rose.

"He's a liar, Cap. I recognize him. He's been arrested at least once right here in New Orleans in connection with the burglary of that supermarket out on the Jefferson Highway about four-five years back, under the name of Duke Bohannon, alias Dallas Blackie. He jumped bail that time and forfeited his bond, to keep from going to trial. I ain't never seen the other two before, though."

Joe Racina leaned toward Caresse and whispered, "That's Frank Cassard. He's got a camera eye, just like his daddy, old Joe Cassard, used to have, and the same kind of sure-shot phenomenal memory. Other cities used to send here for Joe Cassard, when he was alive, to work at big crowds like national conventions, or a Eucharistic Congress, because he could pick a known crook out of a crowd so easily—and his boy's going to be just like him."

"How about that, O'Day?" Gregson asked. "Did you ever go by Bohannon like he says?"

"I ain't talking till I get a lawyer."

"Suit yourself. What about you, Brown or whatever your real name is? Where are you from?"

239

"I got nothing to say. I want a lawyer."

"And you—Raichac? How come you to be mixed up with these punks? You ever been in trouble before?"

The youngest one of the three prisoners made an effort to speak, swallowed convulsively, tried to moisten his lips with his tongue, and finally shook his head in the negative. Gregson turned to the spectators.

"Captain Murphy, you said you wanted to ask a question."

Toe Murphy rose.

"I sure do. And I'm asking Raichac. Were either of you or all of you out on the Gentilly Road on the night of January 2nd—last Saturday night, I mean?"

Raichac looked down at the floor without answering. The man calling himself O'Day, smiled triumphantly.

"Look son," Murphy continued, in a surprisingly gentle tone, "don't let those two bums kid you. They're not really tough. You'd see that in a minute if you could put me in a room with the two of them at the same time. They're the kind of trash that'll push kids around, or stick up a filling station when they're coked up. But we'll fingerprint them and mug them now, and we'll send their prints, pictures, and measurements to the FBI files in Washington, and two days from now we'll have the complete record on who they are and what they've done. And there's a gentleman right here beside me who's just identified all three of you, positively. He was in his car, right back of the service pumps at that filling station on Gentilly Road. His car was broken down and he had telephoned for a tow to bring him to town. That's why he was waiting there. He saw the whole thing. And the man you held up, he's here with me too. He can only identify one of you, the one who held the gun. But it's open and shut, son. And when those two hard guys see that we've got the goods on them, they'll spill their guts to us, trying to cop a short term for a plea, and chances are they'll try to put the whole blame on you. It'll be two against one, and where will that leave you? I've got a hunch you haven't been in trouble before. You don't act like it. And you don't know these punks. They're rats in their hearts. I know 'em, though. I've seen too many just like them. If you help us nail this thing down, maybe we can help you. I don't know. I couldn't promise you anything except that you'll get more of a square deal from us than you will from them. So if . . . ."

The boy straightened up and raised his hand, like a pupil trying to attract his teacher's attention.

"Okay. I'll talk." His two companions glared at him, and

Johnny Meredith stepped quickly out upon the stage. But Raichac was already giving them glare for glare. "Nuts to you!" he jeered. "You guys said we'd have a roll of jack like a saw-log; and what did we get out of that cash register? A lousy twenty-two bucks. I could a made more'n my share of that in a day's work on the docks, and I wouldn't a been in no jam afterwards, neither. Yeah, we stuck up the joint. Him"—he pointed to O'Day—"he was the one said it'd be a cinch, and for me to drive whilst him 'n' the other one went in. They said I wouldn't be taking no risks that way, and when the man come out they stuck a gun on him. While they was going through the joint, I turned the car around and headed her back to town with the motor going, and when they got through they ripped the wires off the telephone and we drove back to town. They said all they got was twenty-two bucks, but I got my own ideas about that, too."

"Okay, that'll do," barked Gregson. "Take him up to the office and let him dictate his confession to one of the stenographers, and sign it afterwards. You arresting officers fill out the charge form in the D.A.'s office. Next!"

There were only a few more prisoners. Two Negroes who had been arrested for fighting, half a dozen others who had been caught in a raid on a dice game. There was one swarthy seaman, a Panamanian, who had jumped his ship, and was claimed by the two representatives of the Immigration Bureau's border patrol who attended each show-up as part of their regular tour of duty. Captain Gregson turned the last of his slips face down on his lectern, picked up the stacked papers, tapped them edgewise against the top of the lectern to align them, and returned them to his clip-board. While he was thus engaged, the floodlights illuminating the stage blinked out, and the room lights were turned on. Caresse gasped as the stage vanished, and only the glistening outer surface of the plastic screen was visible.

The spectators had already risen, and were milling about. By twos and threes, they moved to the door, which was left open. Caresse could see them getting into waiting "prowl" cars. The room emptied rapidly, and was all but deserted by the time Toe Murphy, who had stopped to exchange a few sentences with Captain Gregson, approached them with a friendly word of greeting.

"I made you as soon as you came in," he declared, "and figured you'd want to have a talk about this and that. So I sent my partner on ahead. You might remember him, Joe. Terry Colvin. He was a rookie back in the days when you used to hang around here."

"Sure I remember him. Nice kid. But what we came out here for was to let Miss Lalande talk to you—and answer any questions you might want to ask her."

"Good. We can stay right here, if you'd like. It'll be more private than upstairs. The other boys are checking their assignments there."

"Oh, please, Captain Murphy. Not in this ghastly place. If you wouldn't mind. After what I saw and heard here just now, I don't think I could take it, really. I mean I could, of course, if I had to. But if you *could* let us go somewhere else . . . ."

"Sure. Why not? I can understand how you'd feel about it. We're so used to this routine—we have these show-ups every morning and afternoon—we don't think anything of it, any more. It's just a job of work, you understand. Like a doctor in an operating room. But I can see how you wouldn't want to talk in an operating room, either, if they'd just got through with the first operation you'd ever seen."

"Can't we go up to the second floor, Toe, to one of the court anterooms, where the witnesses wait to be called? There wouldn't be anybody there, this time of day."

"Nothing easier," Murphy agreed cheerfully, leading the way into the large basement garage. "We'll go down here and grab ourselves a handful of elevator. No use climbing the stairs when riding's for free."

Once they were ensconced in the small anteroom, and Joe had let himself down sectionally into one of the chairs, Murphy closed the door behind them. "Sit down, Miss Lalande," he said pleasantly. "Now, what can I do for you?"

"Why—that is to say, I thought—Joe said you wanted to talk to *me*."

Murphy looked inquiringly at Racina, who nodded. "I told her what you said, and why you figured the motor accident was a phony. Go ahead and ask her what you want to know."

"The main thing was about that dress," Murphy began. "I'd like a chance to go over that with one of our chemists, and . . . ."

"But you can't, Captain," Caresse explained with something like desperation. "I told Joe. After you left our house with poor old Tossie Sunday morning, and I went back to my room, I cut that dress up and burned the pieces."

"That's a big help, all right," Murphy growled. "I mean a *big* help. Mind telling me why you'd do a thing like that?"

"Yes, I mind," retorted Caresse with sudden spirit. "But Joe made me promise I would. I want to leave for New York

242

Saturday and, because it's so terribly important that nothing should interfere with my plans, I'll tell you whatever you want to know. About me, that is. And where I went Saturday. And about the accident. There was one, really."

"There wasn't any accident your car or your brother-in-law's was mixed up in."

"I know there wasn't. Léonce and I went for a drive in the country after my broadcast. Saturday afternoon, that was. He picked me up at the hotel."

"In *his* car?"

"No. In one of the used cars from the Voisin-Caprelle lot. It was a car with a Mississippi license. And we drove down . . . ."

"What was the idea of that?"

"It wasn't my idea at all. Léonce was the one who said his car might be recognized, or mine might, if we stopped and parked somewhere, or anything like that. And he didn't want any gossip about us taking a drive out in the country."

"Oh, that was the way of it, was it?"

Caresse looked down at her fingers. She clasped and unclasped them nervously, but though her voice was low, it was composed as she continued. "He—we, that is—felt that Odile was jealous, and that if she heard gossip about Léonce and myself, with all the trouble her sickness was bringing on, she might think . . . ."

"It's all right about that part of it," Murphy interrupted not unkindly, almost as though he were the one to find himself prey to embarrassment. "It's only about the accident I'm asking now. Was that before—or after—you stopped and parked or whatever it may have been?"

"Before we . . . . I mean, we did stop for a few minutes at the Pakenham Oaks and talked about—well, about Odile, and Léonce said . . . . I mean we were there only a little while, and then Léonce said . . . . or rather, he started the car and we drove on that gravel road toward Gentilly."

"The Paris Road. That's in St. Bernard Parish. And when you got to the Gentilly Road, you could turn back toward town and be coming toward New Orleans from the direction of Mississippi in a car with a Mississippi license."

Caresse looked appealingly toward the corner where Joe, sunk down in his chair, was fumbling out a cigarette. His face remained quite void of discernible expression. She turned to Captain Murphy angrily.

"Has Léonce been talking to you already?" she demanded. "Are you—that is, did he—"

243

"Miss Lalande, I've got news for you. If you think your brother-in-law was pulling a sharp dodge with that stuff, you need to be tapped for the simples. That's so shiny at the seams and out at the elbows . . . . But that isn't what I meant. If you got as far as the Gentilly Road, you were back inside the city limits of New Orleans. And that road's pretty well patrolled, day and night. So the chances of there being any real kind of auto accident without getting a report on it are zero-zero."

"But we didn't. That was what I started to tell you. It was on that gravel road, and not far from the oaks where we had stopped for a little while. A big truck was parked there, and Léonce wasn't watching. He piled the car right into the back of it."

"Remember whose truck it was?"

"No. I do remember though that the man said he was from some food-freezing plant not far from where we were. And when Léonce gave him some—some money to get his truck fixed he said one of the men at his place would straighten out the dents, and that he wouldn't even have to take it to a garage. And the car we were in, I suppose Léonce had that fixed by the mechanics at Voisin-Caprelle's. Because it was their car."

Captain Murphy pondered this thoughtfully, nodding the while, as though in agreement.

"That'd explain it all right," he said, musingly, at length. "Yes, sir. It sure would. In another parish, so it would be outside of our jurisdiction. And neither your car nor his, and no claim against anybody, if he paid off the truck driver, so there wouldn't be any report to the insurance companies, either. And the way I get it"—he looked at Caresse with something like approval—"I can see why you'd burn that dress. Yes, it all seems to add up, and make sense. Do you know, lady, I don't think that brother-in-law of yours would ever be one of my favorite people. You're dead wrong about his having talked to me. But he will. The more I think of it . . . ."

"I want to say something more, please, Captain Murphy. May I?"

"Sure. It's a free country. Shoot!"

"What I told you wasn't to get Léonce into trouble. I don't like him, and I told him this afternoon I despised the sight of him. But I wasn't trying to make you think worse of him. It was only because Joe said you wouldn't let me go to New York Saturday—"

"I haven't changed my mind on that, either. Not yet. It might be, though, that by Saturday . . . ."

"If you knew what it meant to me!"

"I do. But I've got a job to finish. Let's see, this is Thursday. Could be I'd have it wound up by Saturday, too. Yes, sir. Could be."

"I want to finish something, too. I mean, what I started to say about Léonce. Tossie said that he was walking around the house the night Odile died. Remember? Well, he was. But he wasn't trying to get to Odile's room. He—he was—he said he wanted to talk to me. That he had to talk to me."

"And did he? Talk to you, I mean?"

"Only long enough for me to tell him, through the door of my room, that I never wanted to lay eyes on him again as long as I lived, and that if he didn't go away I'd call *maman*. And it was after that Tossie saw him."

"Which still doesn't mean he couldn't have gone to his wife's room then."

Joe rose abruptly, dropped his cigarette to the stone floor, and ground it out with his foot.

"In other words, you persist in your theory that Odile was murdered," he said, "and that one of the people who was at the Lalandes' house Saturday night killed her. That means her mother, husband, sister, Tossie, and Foxworth. *And* Sabin Duplessis, whose gun was used to do the job and who, by his own admission, was inside that walled garden at a time when Odile was still alive. So—"

Murphy looked up from his chair, without rising.

"Quit fretting that master mind of yours about it," he said. "I got news for you, too. You heard me tell Miss Lalande just now I had a job of work to finish, and that it could be I'd finish it by Saturday night. About who did it, you can stop worrying, Buster. I can't prove it yet, and until I can, I'm not talking. And I'm not letting anyone who could help me do the proving out of my reach. But I know who killed Mrs. St. Amant. I've known it for two days."

245

16

How various persons visited the
tomb of Odile St. Amant—

January 8, 1948

AGAIN, WHEN they went out into the street, Caresse marveled that the workaday world should still be unchanged. The wintry afternoon was waning, and the stream of traffic had thickened; the pedestrians seemed more hurried and more purposeful, now that the business day was approaching its end, than they had earlier in the afternoon. Otherwise the general atmosphere, outside the Criminal Courts Building, was much the same as outside the Roosevelt Hotel; but this time the complete unconcern of the crowd affected Caresse differently: instead of dreading an awareness of her plight, she longed for some sign of understanding, some spark of sympathy. She did not fear curiosity and its consequences; she was appalled by preoccupation which amounted to callousness. Once more Joe sensed what was passing in her mind and tried to cheer her.

" 'Is it nothing to you, all you who pass by?' " he quoted a little grimly. "No, I'm afraid it isn't. But if they don't give a damn about you, you don't have to give a damn about them, either. There's a lot in that, you know."

"Yes, I suppose so. But we all need *someone* who cares."

"And sooner or later, we all find someone who does. Now there were a good many years, when I was knocking around and thought no one did. I used to get sort of sorry for myself, now and again, like the damn fool I was in those days. And then what happened? Right out of the blue, along came Judith. And look at me now!"

"I don't think I could wait for years and years for something like that to happen. I wouldn't have the courage or the endurance."

"Yes you would, if you had to. Besides, you won't have to

246

wait years and years. Isn't it Vance Perrault who's fond of saying, 'good old L.J.' gave up honking his horn in front of 84 Richmond Place because he couldn't stand competition in the Big League? And that this has left only eight or nine contestants still battling for the pennant?"

"There never were as many as that. And even if there had been, they were only also-rans. Only one man counted—and he doesn't any more. So you see—"

Her lower lip was trembling visibly, and her face, which had already been abnormally pale when Joe first saw her at the microphone, was now whiter than ever. She spoke with desperation.

"I might get to be just like those poor people we saw in the show-up room. They didn't seem wicked to me so much as lonely and lost. That girl—Josephine Blue—when she gets back to Detroit, won't she do 'same as today' mainly because she never had a real sweetheart? The pitiful little man who takes dope—why do you suppose he started? I'm lonely too, Joe. I feel completely lost."

"You're right, I ought never to have taken you to the show-up room. If I'd had any sense at all, I'd have known what it would do to you. But what you're saying doesn't make sense either, honey. You're not lost and you don't need to be lonely. What you need right now, more than anything else, is a drink. No, I haven't forgotten what you said about being in mourning. I don't mean a drink at a bar. I mean a Joe and Jude Special, right out of his own private stock and mixed by her lily-white hands. Climb into that car on the double. I'm taking you to Racina's Retreat as fast as I can get you there."

While they talked, he had been steering her adroitly in the direction of her parked car. She got into it without objection and sank back on the seat as if she were thankful for its support. She did not speak until they approached the turn which would take them in the direction of Henry Clay Avenue. Then she touched his arm lightly with her fingers and Joe realized that these were trembling as well as her lips.

"I'd like very much to have a Joe and Jude Special, a little later. But if you don't mind, I'd like to go out to Metairie first."

"Out to Metairie!"

"Yes. To—to our family tomb, I mean. You see, I haven't been at all since .... *Maman* and Léonce go every day, and every day they've tried to make me go with them. I didn't want to. I felt as if I just couldn't—with them. But I did

247

want to go when I could be there alone. And I know that Léonce and *maman* were going this afternoon as usual. In fact, Léonce told me so himself. But they always go early. They'll have left by this time. And I don't mind having you with me, Joe. On the contrary, it would be a comfort to me."

"All right, I'll take you tomorrow—late, so that you won't run into the bereaved widower and the heartbroken mother. I can see where they would get you down. But don't try to go today, Caresse. You've had all you can take, already."

"Won't you please believe me, Joe? I'll feel better after I've been, and—and said a little prayer by Odile's tomb."

Her earnestness was impelling. They were already crossing the Carrollton Bridge. Without further argument Joe turned sharply into Pontchartrain Boulevard toward the lake. Caresse did not speak again for some time and when she next touched Joe's arm, her fingers were steady.

"We must pass a florist's, somewhere along the way, Joe. If we do—"

"Sure. Craig's is right up yonder, across the road from the cemetery gate." He maneuvered his car around a traffic light standard, drew up at the curb, and reached for his billfold. "Get something for me too, will you, Caresse? Whatever you'd like best."

"Odile would have liked roses best—rather small, red roses, that looked as if they could have come out of our own garden, or some neighbor's."

"Then get those, by all means."

She was gone only briefly and returned laden with overflowing cornucopias, the crimson roses a mass of color above the crackling white paper. She was still very pale, but she was entirely composed again now, and belatedly she commented on a matter which Joe had been mulling over ever since they left Toe's presence.

"Captain Murphy said he's known for two days who killed Odile. Then why does he—"

"Well, he told us. He hasn't any proof yet. Besides, when he says he knows, that means he *thinks* he knows. But he and I don't see eye to eye on that."

Joe had started the car, but was obliged to drive back some little distance along the boulevard before he could enter a traffic lane leading to the massive, ivy-clad gate of the cemetery. Caresse continued her questioning.

"Do you think you know too, Joe?"

"Yes."

"Would you tell me?"

248

"No, Caresse, I couldn't do that—not yet. I'm like Toe, I've got to wait for proof."

"But you don't think—that is, you never believed that I—"

"Of course not. And neither does Toe. He didn't really think so before, but those blood spots and that unreported accident were bothering him. Now that you've explained—and it took real guts to do that too—I expect you haven't a thing to worry about. Bet you anything you like I'll be waving goodbye to you when the good old Crescent Limited pulls out Saturday night . . . . Now suppose you tell me whether you've got any theories?"

"Yes, I have." She felt a swift impulse to tell Joe about Lop's discovery of the little pillow hidden in her brother-in-law's room. Joe would understand, for when she and Ruth had visited the Racinas on Monday she had told him about those pillows and their disappearance. But just as swiftly, she decided to say nothing about it. Not that she felt bound to Léonce by any ties of loyalty. But her dislike of him had become so intense that she did not want her feeling about him to influence her judgment. "I guess I'd rather not say what my theories are, either," she continued. "It's queer, isn't it, Joe? Captain Murphy and you and I all think we know who killed Odile and I'd be willing to swear that none of us has the same person in mind."

"Chances are you're completely right about that," Joe agreed, bringing the car to an abrupt halt as the traffic light at the cemetery entrance changed. Then, after the necessary wait, he drove slowly through one of the great arches, past a grassy hillock topped by a bronze equestrian statue and along a broad central driveway.

"I'm counting on you to guide me from here," he said. "I'm not too sure of my directions, in this immense place."

"Your first turn is right here, into Metairie Avenue," she said, indicating a long oval stretch ahead of them. "It's uncanny, isn't it? I mean that the track where my grandfather and his friends used to race their horses should be the road leading to Odile's tomb?"

"It is strange. But the whirligig of time, you know," Joe answered, in a determined effort to keep the conversation as casual as possible.

"Yes, I know . . . . This *is* an immense place, isn't it? I heard someone say, the day of the funeral, that it was the largest cemetery in the world. Somehow that was one of the things that made me feel worst. Little cemeteries are friendly spots, sometimes. You can almost imagine you're at home in

249

them, with your own people. At least I always have, when I've been in the country, on All Saints'. But a great city of the dead, like this . . . ."

She looked away from him, gazing out at the seemingly endless rows of granite and marble tombs, stretching in all directions, suggestive of the tiny, close-crowded houses of a popular subdivision, but with the unmistakable difference which Caresse had tried to voice: in spite of its impressive proportions, perhaps because of them, the cemetery lacked the comforting quality of homeliness which the living would have given to the humblest habitations and which is not wholly lacking in many quiet country churchyards. A wintry wind, sweeping in towards the city from the lake, intensified the chill of the atmosphere. Above the sea of gabled and corniced roofs, the statue of an artilleryman, complete with stone linstock, seemed frozen at the post where he maintained unending vigil above the burial place of the Washington Artillery. Further up the avenue, a stonecutter was hunched before the smooth marble tablet which sealed a vault, his chattering air-hammer writing an additional entry beneath the roster of those buried within.

"Please turn here again, Joe," Caresse said in a hushed voice. "Our tomb is just a little way down this avenue and we can drive right up to it."

Following her directions, Joe brought the car to a halt beneath a Jerusalem thorn tree, whose slim, drooping branches, now bare of foliage, overhung the pediment of a minuscule Gothic chapel surmounting two terraced stages, each with its own carved railing. Flanking the steps that led up to the bronze doors, the rail of the lower terrace terminated on each side in a stone urn. At the rail of the upper terrace stood the stone figures of two angels, their heads bowed, their hands folded in perpetual prayer.

Caresse unlocked the heavy bronze doors and they swung inward, slowly and silently, to disclose the interior of a mausoleum which was not only a burial chamber, but a private chapel. Outside, though there was a chill in the air, this had an invigorating quality; within, the atmosphere was not only glacial, but stifling. The gold crucifix on the altar was flanked by gold vases and gold candlesticks, which shone dimly in the encircling gloom. The altar itself, as well as the reredos, the walls and the pavement, were all of lusterless white marble. The light which filtered in through the small, stained glass windows was transformed to a deep violet color and merged mystically with the engulfing twilight. On the wall at the right, the smooth surface was broken only by the plain lettering of names and dates and by the long lines which marked the divisions between the separate vaults. But opposite it, wreaths and sprays of flowers were propped against a still unlettered slab. None of these still retained their first freshness; many had already reached the stage of shriveled discoloration. Caresse looked at them with undisguised repugnance.

"What do you say we throw all this foul stuff away?" she asked Joe.

He shrugged slightly. "I wouldn't know whether it was according to Hoyle or not. But I will say it would make the place a lot less gruesome, from my point of view. There's something about dead flowers on a tomb—"

"Yes, at least the flowers ought to be blooming. If they aren't, there isn't anything to suggest eternal life, much less resurrection."

"A chapel is supposed to do that, isn't it?"

"Yes, it's supposed to. But this one doesn't—not the way it looks now, anyway. It gives me a creepy feeling. I'm going to see what I can do about it."

Together they gathered up the faded sprays and wreaths, carried them into the open and deposited them alongside the driveway of crushed shells. When the last of the debris had been removed, Caresse filled the altar vases and massed the rest of the red roses against the unmarked slab. Then she lighted the candles and looked toward Joe for approval. He gave it readily, almost heartily. The transformation she had wrought was astounding. The atmosphere of the little chapel was no longer stale and dismal; it was filled with fragrance, it glowed with radiance; even the quality of its cold seemed mercifully tempered.

"Do you see now why I wanted to come here alone, Joe?"

"Yes, I do. You've done wonders, Caresse. I'd never know it was the same place."

"Odile would have hated it the other way. And *maman* never would have let me change it, if I'd come with her. But it'll be too late for her to do anything about those filthy old wreaths, when she gets here tomorrow. And I'll be able to remember it like this, after I've gone away."

She looked around her, her gaze falling first on the inscribed slabs, then on the massed roses beside the one which was still unmarked, and, finally, on the altar vases and the altar lights. At last it came to rest on the golden crucifix, now softly illumined. She crossed herself and knelt, quite without self-consciousness; indeed, after some moments had

251

passed, Joe began to wonder whether she had entirely forgotten him. He had long since ceased to practice his religion in an orthodox manner; but he had never outgrown the ease in churchly surroundings which is second nature to those whose formative years have been spent among Catholics. It would have seemed natural to kneel beside her, whether he actually prayed or not; and, as a matter of fact, he felt he would like to pray, if he could. The little chapel had become less a place of death than a place of peace. There were few enough such places in a troubled world. Perhaps . . . .

He waited, hesitantly, unwilling to simulate a faith he did not feel, wishing that he were capable of losing himself, as Caresse had, in heartfelt devotion. Then the decision was wrested from him. Without warning, Caresse pitched over and fell unconscious at his feet.

He was still kneeling beside her, calling her frantically by name, when a shadow darkened the altar. Ashamed, and even more angry, because he could not instantly suppress the strange quiver of something very like fear which forked through him, he looked up to see Vance Perrault entering the chapel.

"You certainly have come at the right time, Vance," he said in a voice which he realized was completely unnatural. In his relief, it did not occur to him to wonder why the doctor should be visiting the tomb. "Something's happened to Caresse. She's had a hell of a day, and I'm afraid I'm mostly to blame for it." The doctor's deft fingers were already feeling the girl's pulse, lifting her eyelids, and rubbing her wrists, while with his free hand he raised her head and supported it on his left arm. "I went to the broadcasting station and gave her some bad news from Toe Murphy," Joe went on, speaking with less constraint. "Then I persuaded her to go to the Criminal Courts Building and have a talk with Toe. I think it put her in the clear, as far as he's concerned, so it has served some good purpose. On the other hand . . . . And then she insisted on coming out here. It's the first time since the funeral and of course—"

"You and Toe Murphy!" Perrault exclaimed scathingly. He was now doing some skillful kneading and presently he continued with less scorn, "Well, don't blame yourself too much. I have an idea you're not wholly responsible for this fainting fit. If you'll hold her, like this, for a moment, I'll get some aromatic spirits of ammonia out of my bag. I'm the old-fashioned type who always carries such things around."

He shifted the girl's dead weight expertly from his own support to Joe's and hurried from the chapel. He had hardly left when she stirred slightly and, instinctively, Joe tightened his hold and murmured her name reassuringly. Presently she opened startled eyes.

"Don't be frightened, Caresse," he said in a soothing tone. "You fainted, that's all. You know where you are, don't you? You wanted to come out to Metairie. Remember? And it was just too much for you. But you'll be all right in a minute. Vance Perrault came in right after you toppled over and——"

"Vance Perrault! What on earth is he doing here?"

"Why, I didn't ask! I suppose he felt, the way you did, that he wanted——"

"But he couldn't have got into the chapel if I hadn't been here! He doesn't have any key!"

"Well, probably he was merely intending to look around. Anyway, he's gone to get you some ammonia or something. He'll be right back."

"I don't want any ammonia. I don't need any. I'm still a little dizzy, but that's passing. If only everything didn't rock so."

She pressed her hand over her forehead and closed her eyes again. Then, hearing Perrault's approach, she sat up quickly only to find that she was thankful to lean back against Joe.

"Hello!" she said with an attempt at lightness, as Perrault appeared in the doorway. "You and Joe seem to have a typical Victorian female on your hands. Swooning due to tight lacing, no doubt."

"This isn't the time to joke, Caresse. And I don't mean because we're in a mausoleum, either. Here, drink this." He handed her a small glass, partly filled with a cloudy, spicy liquid, and, after looking at it rebelliously for a moment, she made a slight grimace and began to sip it. "How long is it since you've eaten anything?" he inquired, when she handed back the empty glass.

"Let me see. I had some dinner last night. At least, there was some dinner. But Ona was in a hurry, because her daughter was graduating from a 'beauty saloon' and she wanted to go to the exercises. Besides, I wasn't very hungry. Then I had coffee this morning around eight."

"And since then?"

"Well, I meant to have a sandwich before I started for my broadcast. But *maman* came into my room while I was trying to pack and we had an argument. She didn't want me to give away my clothes, and she didn't want me to go to New York, and by the time I'd convinced her that I meant to do both, whatever she said, I had to hurry right along to the studio. I just barely made it, too. And since then—"

"Since then I'm responsible. I can't tell you how sorry I am."

"Oh, Joe, don't say that! You've helped me a lot. I feel ever so much better than I have for a long time, even if I did faint. And that must have been just because I forgot to eat, like Doctor Perrault says. I'll go home and get some supper and then—"

"Wait a minute, Caresse. I don't think there's anything the matter with you except nervous exhaustion and lack of food. But I can't be sure until you've had a checkup. If your dizziness has pretty well passed, I'd like to have you get in my car with me and let me take you straight to the hospital."

"Well, my dizziness has pretty well passed, but I haven't the slightest idea of letting you take me to a hospital. If you're bound to examine me, you can do it tomorrow morning, at home. But I had a complete physical, to please you, only about a month ago, and none of your wonder-boys could find a thing the matter with me then. I'm not going to be mauled over like that again, right away, to please anybody. And I'm not going to a place where I'll be waked up, after an almost sleepless night, before daybreak, to have my face washed."

"Don't becloud the real issue, Caresse. There's friction between you and your mother and it's telling on you. When it comes to the point where she doesn't see that you have proper nourishment, then it's time a physician stepped in. Moreover, it's a strain for you to stay in the same house with Léonce after—well, after everything that's happened. A hospital isn't ideal, but, under the circumstance, I think it's the best place for you."

"If I do go to one, you'll find some excuse for keeping me there. And then *you'd* be the one to make me lose my job. I'm going to leave for New York Saturday night if I have to go to the train on a stretcher."

She was trembling again and her words were choking her. Joe, who had continued to support her, looked questioningly at Perrault.

"Could I suggest a compromise? Let me take Caresse home with me. Judith would be more than pleased; and in case you've forgotten, she's a crackerjack nurse. She'll put Caresse to bed and see that she has every care, including plenty of nourishment. And there'll be no face-washing before daylight either."

"Oh, Joe, I'd love to go home with you! You're an angel to think of it. If you're sure I wouldn't be too much trouble for Judith, with everything else she has to do—"

"Nonsense, she'd eat it up. Come on, I want to start getting food into you—not to mention that Joe and Jude Special. Okay, Doctor?"

"Well—I don't think it's altogether a bad plan—for overnight anyway. Tomorrow morning, we'll see. Do you think you can get to the car all right now, Caresse?"

"Oh, I can carry her! She doesn't weigh enough to notice."

"Phooey to you. I can walk just as well as anybody. Look!"

With surprising steadiness, she started towards the door. Then she turned back.

"I forgot. I have to put out the candles and lock up here."

"I'll do that for you. Just give me your key. I'll return it to you when I look in on you in the morning. And mind, you're to go straight to bed as soon as you get to Joe's house and stay there until I've seen you again."

"I promise. The key's still in the door. Just turn it and take it out when you're ready to leave."

She nodded and went down the marble steps without looking back. Once settled in the car again, she smiled up at him contentedly.

"Captain Murphy said he didn't think Léonce would ever be one of his favorite people, Joe. And I can see why. But do you know, you're almost my very favorite person?"

"If you're going to talk nonsense like that when you open your mouth, you'd better keep it shut."

She knew that praise really embarrassed him and, wisely, did not persist in it. But because her gratitude was clamoring for expression, it crowded out everything else she might have said. She sat silently beside him while they wound their way around the monuments and mausoleums, returning to the oval driveway which had been a race track, and following this past the big tomb of the Army of Virginia. Then Joe swung back toward the entrance, skirting one edge of a willow-bordered lake.

"I suppose you know this was part of Bayou Metairie once," he said, hoping to divert the girl's mind from her recent harrowing experiences. "Of course, it didn't have wishing bridges and what not across it then. Indian trappers and hunters used to paddle their pirogues in from the marshes to Grand Route St. John, bringing their alligator hides and

crabs and fish to the Old French Market. In those days.
..."

Suddenly Caresse touched his arm, not lightly and trem-
blingly as she had when they were on their way to the
cemetery, but in a purposeful clutch.

"Joe, did you see that car that just turned in at the next
avenue?"

"Yes, of course. What of it?"

"You didn't see who was in it?"

"No, I didn't notice. I was thinking about something
else."

"It was *maman* and Léonce."

"The hell it was! But I don't think they saw you either. Do
you want to go back?"

"It's the last thing on earth I want to do. Let's hurry, Joe,
and get out of the cemetery. If they did see me they might
turn around. And I was so sure I'd dodged them. I thought
they meant to come early. I wonder ...."

For a little longer she continued to puzzle over the belated
arrival of her mother and her brother-in-law, and once or
twice she looked back, to see if they were following. But Joe
must have been right in believing they had not seen her.
Their car rounded a corner and disappeared. Again she
leaned back contentedly beside Joe.

It was true that Amélie and Léonce were much later than
they had intended in starting for Metairie. The hour after
Foxworth's departure had been consumed in charges and
countercharges, tears and recriminations on Amélie's part,
and sullen silence, punctuated by sharp retorts, from
Léonce.

"Well, you certainly have completely ruined my life now—
not that I had much to live for after losing Odile! But at least
I thought I could count on Orson, whatever happened. And
then, just when he and I were ironing out our little difficulties, the kind that are bound to arise from time to time, no
matter how devoted two persons are to each other—"

"Ironing out your little difficulties! You were raking him
over the coals like crazy and he was taking it—up to a
certain point. But his patience was beginning to wear pretty
thin and no wonder. Then, when you accused him—"

"I didn't accuse him of anything at all, except of advising
Caresse about going to New York without first consulting
me. And I see now why he did that. He was perfectly
justified in doing it. But *you* came in at just the wrong
moment and *you* accused him—"

"To get you out of a jam. To say the words you were afraid to say yourself."

"I never intended to say them. Don't talk as if I'd put them into your mouth! You'd been hanging around in the hall, sneaking and spying—"

"I hadn't been doing any such thing. I'd been downtown to get my car, so that I could take you to the cemetery, and when I came in, there were you and Foxworth bawling each other out. I waited for a while, hoping things would quiet down, so that I wouldn't break in on a scene, and instead of that they got worse and worse. And then I thought perhaps if I put in my two cents' worth—"

"You thought! Thought! Well, now you'd better do some more thinking. You'd better think what kind of an apology you can make to Orson Foxworth so that he'll overlook your outrageous behavior. You'd better think what you can do to make up for driving away the man who's been devoted to me for years, just when at last we had a little happiness ahead of us."

There was really no logical reply that Léonce could make to Amélie's irrational tirade, and, after a time, he gave up all attempts to do so. But at last he reminded her that if they were to get inside the cemetery, let alone spend any time at the tomb, they should be on their way. After all, the gates closed at five-thirty . . . .

"Of course, if you don't want to go, that's all right by me. But I came home early because you said you did. I've got the flowers you wanted. You seemed to set such store by it—"

"And I'd like to know who wouldn't! That is, anyone with a heart! But I'm beginning to think that all men are heartless—all except my dear, dead husband! If he had only lived—"

"Good God, are you going to start in on him! After all, he died fifteen years ago, and it's at least ten since I've heard you mention him."

"I try to keep my sorrows to myself. But now that I'm completely bowed down by them—"

In spite of this annihilating statement, she did not look in the least bowed down as she swept out of the room in her usual imperious fashion; and when she rejoined Léonce, fifteen minutes later, nothing about her appearance suggested a crushed woman. For mourning became Amélie. From the brim of her veiled hat, to the tips of her suede shoes, she was somber elegance personified. Her hysteria had subsided, and she was now decorously, if rather reproachfully, grave. She acknowledged the remarks of her son-in-law with cold civility, but made none on her own initiative, in the course of their progress to the cemetery. Léonce, though still somewhat sullen, credibly looked and acted the part of the bereaved widower, bent on paying a sorrowful tribute to his lost love. Like many men inclined to overdress in public, his appearance about the house was likely to be slovenly; but he was now freshly shaved, his stiff linen was immaculate, and his black broadcloth meticulously brushed. From time to time he turned to make sure that the spray of lilies and gardenias was not dislodged from the back seat, and with persistent politeness he made appropriate suggestions.

"Have you spoken to Father Kessells about a second Requiem Mass? If I understood you correctly, you said you wanted to have another."

"I do, but I haven't felt equal to it yet."

"Would you like me to make the arrangements? I'd be glad to relieve you of any—"

"I said not *yet*, Léonce. When some of my other terrible troubles are behind me, I'll try to manage all the indicated proprieties without assistance."

"I'm only trying to be helpful."

"Then please drive a little faster. We've let the whole afternoon slip away, and if we're too late to show my poor, dead little baby one tribute of remembrance, I'll never forgive myself. Never!"

Obediently, Léonce increased the speed of the car. Behind the towering live oaks of Metairie Ridge, the sun was sinking in a welter of red and saffron when they entered the cemetery gates and swept on towards the Lalande tomb. As they came within sight of it, Léonce uttered a sharp exclamation. Amélie, who had just assumed a drooping posture of grief, looked up quickly.

"What's the matter *now*?" she asked irritably.

"The mausoleum's open! The candles are lighted! Someone is in there!" Then, halting the car, Léonce added no less excitedly, "Why, it's Vance Perrault, isn't it?"

Her son-in-law's first ejaculation had elicited a smothered scream from Amélie. Now she peered forward, and answered with gratified relief.

"So it is! Dear Vance! How like him to come here!"

"But why should he?"

"He was terribly fond of Odile. It isn't strange that he should want to visit her tomb, is it?"

"But how would he get in?"

"I don't know, but there must be some simple explanation,

which he'll probably offer. Don't ask him for one, as if you suspected him of being a grave robber."

There was no time for Léonce to make a suitable retort to this scathing admonition. He muttered something unintelligible under his breath, again glancing malevolently at the dim figure inside the mausoleum. Then he stepped soberly out of the car and, with an air of solicitude, helped Amélie to descend. She did not look up again, but raising her veil with one black-gloved hand, pressed the black chiffon square to her eyes and leaned heavily on her son-in-law while mounting the steps. At the entrance she paused.

"Vance," she murmured through the muffling fabric, "Vance, is that you?" And as Perrault turned and came slowly to the door, she went forward to meet him, and laid her head on his shoulder. "Oh, Vance, what a comfort it is to find you here! One of Odile's dearest friends! It would mean so much to her if she could only know, and I have a feeling she does. I'm doubly touched at your sympathy and thoughtfulness because not once since the funeral has her own heartless sister—"

Perrault put his arm around her. "Caresse has just left here," he said. "She isn't heartless, Amélie—don't make any mistake about that, just because she doesn't show her grief the same way you do. She's taking Odile's death very hard. She fainted away while she was praying before the altar."

"She fainted!"

The exclamation came from Amélie and Léonce simultaneously. Perrault included both in his answer.

"Yes. Fortunately, I chanced to arrive just after this happened and had suitable remedies in my car. But I'm very much troubled about her. I would have taken her straight to a hospital if she hadn't protested so vigorously. I compromised by letting her go home with Joe Racina!"

"You let her go home with Joe Racina!"

Again the exclamation was simultaneous and the displeasure of Perrault's astonished listeners was obviously mutual. The physician answered with a calmness which bespoke a trace of resentment at their attitude.

"I did. Joe brought her out here at her earnest request. She's very fond of him. And Judith's an excellent nurse. Caresse couldn't be in more capable hands. If you'll excuse me for saying so, I think she'll be much better off at the Racinas' house, where no one will find fault with her or importune her, than she would be at home. I promised to go see her the first thing in the morning, and of course I'll let you know immediately how I find her. But if she's going to

259

be in any kind of shape to leave for New York Saturday night, she's got to have some rest in the meantime .... Would you like me to leave now, so that you two can pray quietly by Odile's tomb? I take it that's what you really came here for."

This time the answers were not identical. Léonce muttered that it probably would be a good idea if he and his mother-in-law were left to themselves. Amélie, still clinging closely to Perrault, begged him to stay with her. Then, for the first time, her glance swept past him to the unmarked slab beyond the bronze door.

"All the funeral floral offerings have been removed!" she cried. "Even the governor's wreath! And the place has been loaded down with roses! Whoever dared .... ? Was it like this when you came here, Vance?"

"Yes, and I thought it looked beautiful—the way Odile herself would have wanted it. You said you believed she knew—well, I believe so too. And if she does, I think it would mean a great deal to her that someone—"

"It must have been Caresse! It's exactly the sort of thing Caresse would do—decorate a magnificent marble tomb with common little garden roses—*red* roses, of all things!"

"I don't think you ought to feel that way about them, Amélie. If Caresse put the red roses here—and probably she did—she must have had some good reason for it. And as I said before, I think the chapel's been made very beautiful. Shall we go in together, since you've been good enough to ask me to remain?"

"Yes, and I'll make a more suitable offering. Léonce, where are *my* flowers?"

"Oh, I'm sorry! I was so surprised when I saw—that is, I left them in the car. I'll get them right away."

He hurried down the steps, followed by his mother-in-law's contemptuous glance and Perrault's more reflective gaze. Though he had started for the cemetery almost as a matter of routine, without any special emotion, Léonce was now genuinely upset. He found it impossible to take Perrault's presence at the tomb as a matter of course; yet no propitious moment had presented itself for requesting an explanation. After all, as the physician had reminded them, he and his mother-in-law had presumably come to the chapel to pray; besides, it was getting late, and a good deal of time had already been consumed in a discussion about Caresse. This discussion had given him further cause for uneasiness. Caresse was not the sort of girl who fainted for effect, or for any other reason, unless she were genuinely ill. And if she

260

were ill, he was doubtless at least partially responsible. He *had* "badgered" her. She had besought him to leave her alone and he would not. The "badgering" had been really more than she could stand, in her exhausted and high-strung condition. Her statement that this was so had not been made for effect either. Insofar as it lay within his power to love any one, Léonce now loved Caresse—just as once, insofar as it lay within his power, he had loved Odile. The thought that he had contributed to his sister-in-law's indisposition distressed him acutely. The knowledge that she had gone home with Joe Racina distressed him even more. It was all very well for everybody to say that if anyone were really in love with his wife, for any length of time, Joe Racina was that man. Judging by his own experience, Léonce did not believe that any man was ever so much in love with his wife that he would be impervious to the attractions of a girl like Caresse. And Joe was not without certain attractions of his own . . . . Léonce St. Amant, going down the steps of the Lalande mausoleum, to get the flowers wherewith to decorate his wife's tomb, was suddenly consumed with fierce unreasoning jealousy . . . .

The chiseling sound of the stonecutter's air-hammer still chattered through the brooding silence, Léonce, his teeth on edge, walked up the driveway and tapped the artisan's shoulder.

"I say, old man, would you mind very much stopping that until I leave?" he inquired. "I mean, until *we* leave. My wife was buried just last Monday, and I'm visiting the family tomb, right close by here, with her mother. The poor lady's almost overcome, and I'm afraid this racket is making it all the harder for her."

"Sure thing, sir," the stonecutter replied sympathetically. "I wouldn't want to worry you-all like this. It's most too dark to go on, anyhow. I'll call it a day and leave things nice and quiet for you."

He rose stiffly and began to coil his air hose. Léonce nodded his thanks and, returning to the car, carefully lifted out the great sheaf of lilies. Then, mounting the steps again, he offered them mutely to his mother-in-law, hoping that the seething rage by which he was engulfed might be attributed to grief. Before accepting the sheaf, Amélie threw the heavy black veil back over the brim of her hat; then, cradling the lilies in her arms, she gazed sorrowfully upward and, for some moments, retained the arresting posture of a mourning figure, attended by praying angels in stone. At last, slowly and haltingly, she advanced into the chapel, with Léonce and

Perrault following in her wake and, bending over, deposited her lilies beside the unmarked slab, moving the roses to one side. Then, straightening up again, she drew from her handbag a rosary of black and silver, which Perrault recognized as a somber departure from the bright jewels which customarily served for her prayer beads. As he watched her, she pressed the crucifix to her lips. But instead of next kneeling before the altar, as he had expected, she again laid her head on his shoulder and burst into tears.

"Of course I did come here to pray beside Odile's tomb, just as you said, Vance," she sobbed. "But I'm so overcome with all my sorrows that somehow I don't feel as though I could. I mean, it would be terrible, wouldn't it, if I fainted, the way Caresse did? Of course, what you said about her was most upsetting. And then you know what I told you while Léonce was getting the flowers, about just having dismissed Orson Foxworth from my life. Oh, I know there was no help for it! He suddenly revealed himself as a violent, domineering man. I never would have had a moment's happiness with him, and so I told him we had come to the parting of the ways. All the same, I've loved him for years, and I can't get over loving him in one minute, so—"

"If you *are* going to do any praying, it will have to be right away," Léonce cut in unfeelingly. His mother-in-law's version of the scene with Foxworth did not astonish him; he knew she was not the type of woman who would ever confess that she had been jilted. Nevertheless, the effrontery with which she distorted the incident increased his general sense of futile rage. Léonce, after dropping rather jerkily to his knees, had crossed himself hurriedly, and after repeating two Hail Mary's parrot-wise, hastily rose again. "What I mean is, they close this place in just a few minutes now," he added.

"And if we got caught here, we might have to stay all night, mightn't we?" Amélie inquired, looking from one man to the other with a shudder. "In this cemetery, with thousands and thousands of dead people! Oh, I couldn't bear it! I'd die of fright. I'm sure there are any number of ghosts wandering around. Don't tell me I'm silly, don't tell me there aren't any such things. I know there are. We might even see Odile, all in white, with that red blood on her breast. O-o-h!" The words ended in a shriek, shattering the pervading silence. At the same moment a sudden gust of wind, sweeping in through the open door, blew out some of the candles. Amélie shrieked again.

"Take your mother-in-law away, Léonce. I'll put out the rest of the candles and lock up," Perrault said abruptly, repeating the promise he had already made once before that afternoon. "It seemed best for Caresse to leave her key with me, after her fainting spell. I'll see to everything."

With a degree of haste which contrasted strangely with the deliberation which had marked her entry to the tomb, Amélie permitted herself to be assisted down the steps and into the waiting car. Then she drew her black veil over her face again and huddled into the corner. Léonce cast a harried backward glance through the rear window. The bronze doors of the mausoleum still stood open and a slender thread of candlelight slid through them. But its rays did not reach far. In the gathering dusk, Léonce did not see Sabin Duplessis standing nearby, half-hidden by the immensity of an adjacent tomb.

17

How Vance Perrault made a promise to Caresse Lalande—

January 9, 1948

Without conscious effort, Judith Racina had managed to give a New England atmosphere to the Queen Anne house on Henry Clay Avenue; the bed-chambers, especially, were reminiscent of those on Farman Hill, where she had spent her youth. When she and Joe moved to New Orleans, she had brought some of her early belongings with her, partly because she was genuinely attached to them, and partly because her thrifty habits precluded the purchase of new furnishings when old ones were already in her possession; and strangely enough, instead of appearing incongruous in their alien setting, these fitted in as if they had been meant to go there. Exhausted as Caresse was, when she reached the Racinas' house, she was not oblivious to the quaint and restful charm of the spare room to which Judith unquestioningly led her.

"I'm going to bring you some hot milk," Judith told her. "Of course if it'll taste better to you with a little coffee in it, that's all right too. And I suppose it would."

"I don't really care, Judith. If I could just go to sleep—"

"You will, Caresse. You'll be asleep before you know it."

Judith opened a bureau drawer and took from it a clean white nightgown which smelled of lavender. She shook out its folds and laid it over the spool bed, which she had already turned down invitingly.

"We have so many unpremeditated guests that I always keep the main requisites for their comfort at hand. I think this is about your size. And you'll find new toothbrushes and several standard makes of soap and other toilet articles in the bathroom. Not that I'd bother with any of them just now if I were you. I'm just telling you so you can look for them later and take your choice."

While she talked, Judith had unfastened the zipper of her visitor's dress and motioned to Caresse that she should raise her arms over her head. Then, in the same matter of fact way, Judith had peeled off the other girl's thin black stockings and expedited the removal of her dainty but very scant undergarments. Caresse was clad in the cool, sweet-smelling nightgown and reclining at ease among the plumped pillows on the spool bed, almost before she had grasped the fact that she was actually undressed.

"I'll be right back with the hot milk," Judith told her, stooping to touch a match to the fire which was already laid on the hearth. Then she switched out the overhead lights and was gone. Only the little lamp on the bedside table was left burning. But by this and the flames which quickly leaped into radiance, Caresse could see the braided rugs on the floor, the bead pincushion on the dresser, the china dogs on the mantel. She closed her eyes and opened them again. This time she did not distinguish anything special; she was conscious only of the warmth, the cleanliness, the tranquillity—and then of Judith at her side again, holding a cup to her lips.

"I told you how easy it would be to drowse off. But try to drink this, Caresse, before you go to sleep. Because you really are pretty empty. I won't bother you any more. But I'm leaving a thermos bottle and some sandwiches where you can reach them . . . ."

It was three o'clock in the morning when Caresse wakened, ravenously hungry. The thermos bottle had chocolate in it, rich, hot, infinitely satisfying. She drank the first cupful in gulps; then she sipped the nourishing drink more slowly, until the bottle was empty. A large linen napkin, still slightly damp, unfolded to reveal as its contents tomato sandwiches, cheese sandwiches, sandwiches with a filling of rare roast beef. Caresse devoured them all. Then she went into the bathroom and turned on the water. Without difficulty she found her favorite soap, bath salts, dusting powder. She lay in the steaming tub and soaked until she was drowsy again. Finally she dried herself on the thick-piled towels and climbed back into the spool bed. While her bath water was running, she had replenished the fire. Now, contentedly and drowsily, she observed further details of her surroundings which, in her first exhaustion, had escaped her notice: the design of old-fashioned nosegays on the wallpaper; the patina of the hardwood floor; the framed crewelwork and samplers.

But she did not look at any of them for long. Presently she was asleep again.

The next time she wakened the room was full of sunlight. She jumped up and, crossing the floor, flung open the door into the hallway. A little girl, wearing a blue gingham dress, was standing near the threshold, clasping a dilapidated doll close to her plump little stomach. She was not a beautiful child, but she had appeal and individuality. The expression of her large gray eyes was disarmingly friendly and her hair, parted in the middle and gathered into two short beribboned braids, was fair and glossy. She regarded Caresse with grave interest.

"Hello!" she said softly, her pleasant little face brightening as she smiled.

"Hello!" Caresse replied, smiling too. "Are you little Judith?"

"No, I'm Jenness," the child answered. "There isn't any little Judith—only Danny. Daddy says perhaps there'll be a little Judith too some day. She hasn't got here yet though .... I didn't wake you up, did I?"

"No. I waked up myself."

"I'm glad," Jenness said with evident relief. "Because Mommy said I wasn't to make any noise and I tried not to. But she told me to stay outside your door and let her know when I heard something."

"It's very kind of you to have let me have such a nice long sleep. But perhaps you'll tell your mother I'm awake now."

"Yes, I will."

In a sudden burst of noise and speed, the little girl rushed down the stairs, shouting as she went. A moment later, Judith came to the foot of the banister and called that she would be up in just a few minutes—would Caresse please go back to bed and wait for her breakfast? She obeyed, willingly enough, but with the definite hope that she would soon see the little girl again; and when Judith appeared with a laden tray, Jenness was at her side, carrying with great pride and care a covered dish for which there evidently had not been room among the others. After her mother had set the tray down on their guest's knees, Jenness removed the lid, disclosing hot, sugared doughnuts, and with her pleased, rather shy smile, silently offered them to Caresse.

"I know there ought to be just coffee to begin with," Judith said, looking fondly down at the little girl and then at Caresse. "And don't feel you have to eat anything you don't want. But it is late and Jenness was sure you'd be hungry.

266

The doughnuts were her idea. So I added them to the diet list when everything else was ready and let her bring them."

"It was a grand idea. I am hungry," Caresse answered, pouring out the coffee and accepting one of the doughnuts. "But good grief, Judith! Cranberry juice—Scotch oatmeal— curried eggs—walnut muffins—"

"I said, don't eat any more than you want. I see you have made away with all the sandwiches though."

"Yes, and were they ever good! That hot chocolate and those big chunks of roast beef certainly hit the spot. I don't guess I've eaten very much lately. Not just yesterday but— well, for a week. Or slept either. I certainly slept last night though. What did you give me, knockout drops?"

"No," Judith said, laughing. "Hot milk, just as I told you. You were all in, Caresse. Do you really feel better now?"

"I'll say I do. I don't feel like the same person. I can't thank you enough for letting me stay here. But when I've got outside a small portion of this food, I'd better climb into my clothes and be on my way."

"You'd better do nothing of the sort. In the first place, you can't climb into your clothes, because I took your undies and stockings away and washed them and they're not dry yet. In the second place, Doctor Perrault telephoned, and when I told him you were still asleep, he said that was fine, he'd call again later, but that you weren't on any account to get up until he'd had a look at you."

"Which means he won't be in until late afternoon! As if I didn't know that old trick!"

"Well, it isn't such a bad trick. As an ex-nurse, I'm all for it. You're not discontented or uncomfortable, are you?"

"Discontented! After all, how comfortable can you be?"

Caresse looked from Judith, who had drawn up a Windsor rocker and was sitting tranquilly by the bed, to little Jenness, who, having assured herself that the doughnuts were appreciated, had settled down with her doll on the hearth and was playing some private and absorbing game.

"It's all beautiful," she said. "You'll never know what coming here has meant to me. But I mustn't impose on you. I know you have lots to do, with the housekeeping and two children and all. And I've got lots to do myself. If I'm going to be ready to leave tomorrow night—"

"I don't have lots to do. Elvira, my part-time maid, is here and she's looking after Danny—he's too obstreperous to bring into a sick room. No, sick room isn't the right word, is it?—I should have said any room that's meant to be restful. But Joe's lending a hand with him and Elvira's also getting

267

dinner. We have our big meal in the middle of the day, partly on her account and partly on account of the children. After dinner, I'll put them down for their naps and then I'll actually have time hanging heavy on my hands until they wake up again, because Joe will be starting a new chapter and won't want to be disturbed. Perhaps you'll let me come and visit with you. I'd like very much to do that. But I'm going to be stern about the doctor's orders. And honestly, Caresse, I think if you keep quiet today, you'll be in ever so much better shape to leave tomorrow night. Have you still got so much packing ahead of you?"

"No-o-o. I think I could finish it in a couple of hours—that is, if I could stick right to it without interruptions. But there's my Saturday program—"

"That's right. You will have to wind things up at the broadcasting station. But I still think you could get everything done tomorrow. I can come and help you with the packing. Perhaps if I were there, you could stick right to it."

"Perhaps."

Judith did not say anything more on the subject and neither did Caresse, but each knew that the other was thinking about Amélie and her unreasonable importunities. Following this train of thought, Judith eventually made a guarded reference to these.

"Your mother telephoned too, Caresse. And your brother-in-law. I told them both you were still asleep, just as I did Doctor Perrault. They suggested that you should call them back, but I said there wasn't any extension telephone near your room and that until the doctor had seen you—"

Judith looked over at the tray. Except for half a muffin and about a spoonful of oatmeal, it was very thoroughly depleted. She made no comment, but rising, lifted it up and spoke to her little daughter.

"Come, Jenness. It's almost time for you to get ready for dinner. And we mustn't tire our visitor."

"But you'll come back, won't you?"

Caresse stretched out her arms, and the little girl came over to the bed; then, in her shy, appealing way, she returned the kiss that was offered her before she trotted out of the room beside her mother, tightly clasping her doll. Caresse lay still, listening to the pleasant sounds that drifted up to her from downstairs—Joe's hearty laugh, a younger child's exuberant chatter, a tinkling dinner bell. After that she went to sleep again.

When she next woke, Judith was already seated beside her,

in the Windsor rocker, with knitting needles slipping back and forth between the fingers which, even when thus diligently engaged, gave no effect of haste or restlessness. Caresse watched her for a few moments without speaking, and Judith, though signifying with a smile that she realized her guest was awake, did not immediately speak either. When she finally made a remark, it served to intensify rather than disturb the general atmosphere of relaxation.

"I'm going to have even more time on my hands than I thought. Sabin Duplessis dropped in just as we were finishing dinner and had pandowdy and coffee with us. Now he and Joe are deep in discussion. That means Joe'll be later than he expected, starting his chapter, but he'll have to finish it anyway, no matter how long Sabin stays, because he's uncomfortably close to his deadline. I'd be sorry for the interruption to his work, except that I'm relieved that Sabin's come to see Joe. They've both got pretty violent tempers and they had one of their periodic quarrels Wednesday night. Usually these quarrels don't amount to much. But I was a little afraid this one would. Now I know they'll talk things through and be better friends than ever."

Her serene smile deepened. Obviously she had no qualms concerning the outcome of the discussion which was under way in the book-lined study and Caresse felt no curiosity about it. After another pleasant interval of silence she asked a casual question.

"What are you making, Judith?"

"Oh, just a baby blanket! I make one after another—there are always new arrivals coming along. In fact, they were coming along so fast, among our friends, when Joe and I were first married, that my own babies didn't get any—any that I had made myself, I mean. But I hope the next one will."

"Is there—at least, do you—? That isn't meant to be an impertinent question. But you sound so happy, Judith."

"It isn't an impertinent question and it's no wonder I sound happy, because I am. Joe and I—well, it's one of those things every girl dreams about and hopes for and at the same time doesn't quite dare believe in, because it seems too good to be true. Only it *is* true in our case. And yes, I'm just beginning to think—it's too soon to be sure, but I believe that perhaps .... We both wanted children, and it's another thing that seems too good to be true, having them come along like this. Jenness is four, Danny two, and now, if there's a new one .... It won't matter the next time, either, whether it's a girl or a boy, because we've got one of each already."

269

Her perfect contentment, her complete sense of well-being and fulfillment were manifest in every word she spoke. Caresse swallowed hard, trying not to let jealousy creep into her own renewed feeling of hopefulness and courage. But it seemed to her that Judith had everything—at least everything that mattered: a husband whom she loved and who loved her; two fine children and the prospect of another; a home that was not merely pleasant but happy; adequate if not ample means for every material requisite. She was not expensively dressed, but though her clothes lacked style, in the sense that they failed to represent the latest vogue, they had individuality and distinction. Apparently she did not go out very much, but this was undoubtedly less because her hands were busy with humdrum tasks, than because she found her life perfect and complete just as it was. Such a woman had little need of the outside world. Caresse did not trust herself to comment on anything Judith had said, so eventually she asked a question that had no bearing on it.

"I'm very interested in your little girl's name. I've never heard it before."

'That's not surprising. I've never run across it but once myself, outside of our family. I wanted to name my first baby for my mother, but her name's Serena, and Joe pointed out that Serena Racina would never do! It was he who suggested Jenness as a second choice. Several Farmans have been named Jenness. The last one was my sister."

"*Was?*" . .

"Yes, she's been dead six years. You were so young when it happened, you probably never heard about it. But it was quite a celebrated scandal at the time. She was very much in love with a man who wasn't worthy of her. And when she needed his support, he didn't give it to her. He let her stand trial for a crime for which he was indirectly responsible. The verdict was guilty and Jenness couldn't face imprisonment. She committed suicide."

"Oh, I'm so sorry! I shouldn't have asked! I wouldn't have, if I'd dreamed—"

"Of course you wouldn't have. I know that. And it doesn't hurt to talk about Jenness or even to think of her any more. If it had, I wouldn't have named my baby for her."

"You—you didn't mind naming your baby for—for a girl who'd been mixed up in some dreadful scandal?"

"No. I was glad to. I hoped, in a way, it would help to vindicate her. Because, you see, I know she wasn't really to blame."

"But you couldn't have felt the same way, could you, if Jenness hadn't been your sister?"

"Yes, I could have. At least, I hope so. I hope I'd feel the same way about any other girl. I mean, any other girl I was sure of."

For the first time, Caresse, who had been lying quietly back among the pillows, began to pluck nervously at the counterpane. Judith laid down her knitting.

"That's a nice old quilt, isn't it?" she asked. "The pattern's called the wedding ring design. My grandmother gave it to my mother when she got married. Then my mother gave it to me. Of course, I'll give it to Jenness some day. It'll never wear out—people really made things to last, in the old days! And we Farmans have always taken good care of everything we had. I'd like you to meet my people, Caresse. Don't you think you could go up to the farm once in a while? You can leave New York on a five o'clock train, at the end of a working day, and get to White River Junction by midnight. Father would meet you there and drive you the thirty miles you'd still have to go. And it's like a different world on Farman Hill."

"I don't find that so hard to believe. You've brought part of that world here with you to New Orleans."

Again Caresse looked gratefully around the peaceful room. She was profoundly moved. But her hostess, even more than her surroundings, was responsible for the healing balm which overspread her troubled spirit.

"I'll write Mother about you," Judith went on. "I'm sure you'll hear from her right away. Probably you could get off from the store to spend Washington's Birthday at Farman Hill. But in the meantime . . . . We've lots of friends in New York. There's Peter MacDonald, who used to be on the *Bulletin* in Washington with Joe. He's one of the associate editors of the *New York Enterprise* now. Of course, you might like someone a little younger for night-clubbing—Peter must be all of thirty-six or thirty-seven. But he can still show a girl a pretty tall time. And he's got no end of young reporters cluttering up his office who'd jump at the chance of taking you out."

"I don't want—" Caresse began. But Judith interrupted her.

"Of course you do. You think you don't now, because you're all worn out, because you've just been through a dreadful experience. But as soon as you're rested again, as soon as your job's given you a new outlook and a new interest, Peter and his cohorts will come in very handy. Joe's

271

going to telephone Pete and tell him to meet you at the train. It's pleasant, don't you think, when you get to a strange city, to find someone at the gate? And don't for a moment imagine the favor'd be all on one side. Any man in his senses would feel proud to be seen around town with a girl like you. You must know you're what's generally called a knockout. And as if the personal angle weren't enough in itself, there'll be a professional angle to your appearances pretty soon, that the papers will just eat up. Have you forgotten what Joe said about the Caresse perfumes and powders and lipsticks and so on? Those will be good for columns and columns of advertising, not to mention any number of feature stories. Why, with the right press agent, you could come pretty close to being the current rage in New York!"

"No, I couldn't. Not feeling the way I do inside, even if all the rest were possible. And it sounds to me as if you were just dreaming things up, Judith."

"I'm not dreaming things up. You ask Joe. And you won't feel this way inside, for long. Besides, there's someone else I've thought of, a young neighbor of ours who's just gone to Columbia. He's the most brilliant boy I ever knew in my life. Oh, he wouldn't do for a beau! But as you say, you don't want a beau quite yet and he could fill in the gap. You and he could go to Farman Hill together, and you'd get to feeling as though he were your younger brother or your wonderful second cousin, or something like that, in no time. I can just see it all working out."

Judith folded up her knitting and rose. Then she smiled down at Caresse.

"You wouldn't believe I'd ever really been a nurse if I didn't tell you that it's now time for your nourishment," she said. "So I'm going to get you some. Also, I think I'd better look in on Danny. He has a way of completely unbolting his crib, when he wakes up from his nap, if there isn't anybody there to stop him. None of us has ever been able to discover how he does it, so the only thing to do is to get to his room before he's fully conscious. I can hear Jenness singing, and that's a signal Danny's coming to. She's getting wonderfully helpful about all sorts of little things." Judith bent over and kissed her guest. "I've just had a thought," she said. "If there *is* a new baby and it's a girl, I think it would be wonderful for you to be her godmother, before you start being godmother to a lot of perfumes and things like that. Caresse Racina—there's nothing the matter with that for a name, now, is there?"

It was nearly five when Vance Perrault finally came to see Caresse. He found her fresh from her second bath, dressed in her second clean nightgown and propped up among pillows in immaculate cases. Jenness, her braids tied with crisp new hair ribbons, her plump person clad in white crossbarred muslin, was seated on a small three-legged stool at the side of the bed; she was listening, enthralled, to the story of "Goldilocks and the Three Bears," which Caresse was reading aloud from a well-worn book.

"You don't look like the same girl I saw twenty-four hours ago," Perrault informed Caresse. He had suggested to Jenness that probably Lucy, the battered doll, was in need of medical treatment, and that she had better go and prepare her patient for the doctor's visit, a hint she had taken in good part. Now, with his finger on his own patient's wrist, he regarded her searchingly.

"That isn't strange. I don't feel like the same girl," Caresse replied. "I don't know how I'm ever going to thank you enough for letting me come here."

"Well, don't try. I don't need thanks. I only need to be sure you'll be well enough to go to New York. And I think I can be now, thanks to Judith. I wish I were as easy in my mind about Tossie as I am about you. I've been to see her today, as you asked me to do. And she's eating her heart out in that jail. However, I'm going to make a point of seeing Orson Foxworth about her before night. I believe he can help me to get her released right away."

"He can do almost anything he puts his mind on."

"Yes. Yes, that's true. He's a very resourceful man. He gets what he wants in one way or another."

The doctor had continued his cursory examination while he talked. Now he smoothed out the sheet and stood up. Caresse saw that he looked extremely tired and, with swift sympathy, asked if he himself were feeling well.

"Oh yes. Run ragged, that's all," he answered readily. "The number of people who manage to get sick these days! But you're on the mend, all right, young lady. Get up and have supper with the Racinas, if you want to. I understand your host's complaining because he hasn't had a chance yet to give you one of those Joe and Jude Specials. I wish I had time to stop for one myself, but I've got to be on my way. Judith says she's offered to go home with you tomorrow and help you finish packing. That's a mighty good idea, Then suppose you let Joe take you down to the broadcasting station. After that, perhaps you'd like to look in on Ruth Avery to say goodbye to her—I'm sure she'd be glad to have you, unless she has something else planned. And then—well, the rest of the evening will probably take care of itself, one way or another, till train time. But if it doesn't, I think I've said enough to both your mother and your brother-in-law so that you won't have any more trouble with them—that is, if you make up your mind you won't let them get you down, whatever happens."

"I won't. I won't ever do that again, I promise you. But I'm not sure yet that Toe Murphy's going to let me leave tomorrow night. That's why I need some advice. Would you—could you—tell me what I ought to do about something that I know and Toe Murphy doesn't know?"

"Why, I could try, of course."

"I haven't told a soul about this yet, because I didn't know whether that was the right thing to do. And now I don't know whether the wrong thing isn't to keep it to myself. It's about the pillows. Odile's two baby pillows. They're gone."

Doctor Perrault looked at the girl searchingly.

"You—you mean the blue one, with lace? Were there two pillows like that?"

"Yes. And they were always on the chaise longue. But they weren't there when we heard Tossie scream, and we came rushing in to find Odile on the floor and—dead."

"Can you be quite sure of that, Caresse?"

"I think so. Of course, I couldn't swear to it. We were all so excited that I couldn't really swear to anything. But I remember one thing, and that is how *maman* threw herself down on the chaise longue and moaned and carried on. Well, I remember trying to make her more comfortable, because she was completely distracted. And I *do* remember being surprised that the pillows weren't where they'd always been. So, of course, somebody who was in that room between the time you were there and the time Tossie found Odile's body must have taken them. That was the time when they disappeared."

"Yes, obviously," Doctor Perrault agreed. "But what you say surprises me because—you say there were two of them?"

"Yes, two of them. Then just yesterday Lop found one of them while she was cleaning, and brought it to me."

"She—she found one pillow? One? Where?"

"In Léonce's room, hidden behind the chifforobe. I made her promise not to say a word about it. Then I told her to put it back exactly where she had found it. That was just before I left the house to do my broadcast. What I intended to do was wait until I got back, and then Lop and I would make a search for the other one. But I never did get back, and unless we can find the other one it wouldn't really mean that . . . ."

"It might not really mean anything if you did."

"I don't know. That's what troubles me. Léonce hated those two pillows for some reason, and was always badgering Odile to get rid of them. She wouldn't. That was one of the few things she stood up to him about. On practically everything else, she let him walk all over her. So if they had disappeared after we found her. I wouldn't think anything of it, except that Léonce had got his way about them at last. But they didn't. They disappeared before that. And they couldn't walk out of Odile's room. Somebody took them. Somebody was in that room to take them; and one of them turned up hidden in Léonce's room."

"But you didn't tell Murphy about this when you saw him yesterday afternoon?"

"No. I haven't even told Joe. I haven't told anybody but you. When I talked to Captain Murphy, I still thought I would be going home, and would look for the other pillow then. And I also didn't want him to think I was just telling him something so he would let me go to New York Saturday. I couldn't do that."

"No. You couldn't. And I'm very glad you didn't. The thing that is troubling you now is whether you ought to go to New York tomorrow without telling about it. I can set your mind at rest. You have told me. And if, after you leave, it seems to be indicated that Murphy should be told I will tell him. Do you think you can trust me to do that?"

"Of course, I can. You know how we always trusted you—"

"I hope I shall always deserve that confidence, my dear. And I can promise you something else, too, Caresse. Toe Murphy won't keep you from getting on the Crescent Limited tomorrow."

"How can you promise me a thing like that?"

"Well . . . . What if I told you I'd abandoned my first diagnosis of suicide and that I know who killed your sister?"

"I'm afraid I'd say I'd heard the last part of that just once too often. So I hope you won't say it. Because Toe Murphy's said it and Joe's said it and I'm tired of hearing it. Especially as I have some ideas of my own on the subject, which evidently aren't the same as either Captain Murphy's or Joe's and probably wouldn't be the same as yours. I'd rather not discuss it any more, if you don't mind."

For the second time that afternoon, a slight nervousness had crept into her manner. Perrault answered her soothingly.

"No, I don't mind. I was only trying to give weight to my words. But perhaps I don't need to. I've never yet broken a promise I made you, have I, Caresse?"

He smiled down at her in the kindly, paternal way which she had associated with him since her earliest childhood. Gratitude and affection welled up in her heart as she looked up at him, effacing her momentary disquiet.

"No," she said. "No, you never did. I don't believe you ever broke a promise in your life."

"You're right. But some of them have been pretty hard to keep. A good deal harder than this one will be."

He had taken her hand again, not like a physician examining a patient this time, but like an old friend revealing abiding affection.

"I'm thinking of going away too, Caresse," he said gently. "I'm rather tired, as you say. I've felt the need of a rest for quite a while. But as long as Odile depended on me . . . . My other patients don't matter so much. Except you. And tomorrow night you'll be on your way to another city, you'll find another doctor among all your other new friends. Well, God bless you, my dear child. And if I don't see you again, goodbye. You won't need me tomorrow and your day will be very full. Mine will too, so I think the chances are rather against it."

He kissed her forehead. She put her arms around his neck, hugging him hard.

"Goodbye," she said. "No other doctor will ever take your place—you know that. But I hope you do get your good rest. You sure do need it. And at least you don't have to worry that Toe Murphy will stop you from starting off."

"No, I don't have to worry about that. But you're not going to any more, either, Caresse."

"All right. I *am* taking your word for it. And thank you. Not just for sending me here, either, or for relieving my mind. For everything you've done and been to Odile and me all these years."

It was not until after Vance Perrault had gone and she was dressing, with happy anticipation of her evening, that Caresse realized she had forgotten to ask him to give back the key to the Lalande tomb.

18

How Sabin Duplessis and Ruth Avery learned more about the previous Saturday night—

January 9, 1948

THE ANTICIPATION with which Ruth awaited the arrival of Ellen with her breakfast had grown more and more pleasurable for, by the time she had been in New Orleans a week, the tray had become a dependable source of surprise. The superb specimens of Lady Hume's Blush with which it was invariably adorned had ceased to astonish her, though they had by no means ceased to delight her; but the camellias were now flanked by a variety of gifts from Sabin. In a way, she found these offerings even more intriguing than Aldridge's, which were always the same, even though she realized that Sabin's had far less meaning; that they were, as Caresse had put it, "merely a part of his technique."

The King's Cake had been followed by pralines in a box shaped like a miniature cotton bale and the pralines by a package of books, each with New Orleans as a setting. The candy and the novels had come accompanied only by a visiting card, with a brief greeting scribbled across it; but the fourth gift, like the first, had a note attached to it and Ruth read the note before she opened the present:

Dear Ruth—

"Please consider that I've apologized profusely." Yes, I know I said that before and that I was behaving disgracefully when I said it. But now I'm not only cold sober; I'm in anything but a mocking mood. In fact, I'm heartily sorry for all my misdoings and intend to lead a new life. And that isn't said sacrilegiously either. It's said with the utmost sincerity.

277

I don't know whether you believe me or not, but if you do, perhaps you'll prove it to me by giving me a chance to prove to you that I can act like a civilized human being. (Speaking of proofs, I'm still at large, which seems to indicate that Captain Murphy isn't interested in Joe's suspicions and that they may be dismissed as figments of fancy!) I'm sure you're invited to the reception at the French Consulate General this afternoon, in honor of a roving ambassador, and I believe you might enjoy it. I know how busy your uncle is, so I suppose the chances are about even that he wouldn't have time for a function that conflicts with office hours; and if my guess is a good one, I'd like very much to take you myself, if you'd permit me. In any case, if you're free for dinner, what would you think of going out to the Bar-None Ranch on the River Road? As early or as late as you like? I'll call for you on Toulouse Street if the reception's out as far as you're concerned, or if you'll go to it with me. On the other hand, if you're going to it with your uncle, we could meet at the Consulate General and proceed from there. The Bar-None's a 'different' sort of place, not a synthetic one either, but the real thing. And Ad Given Davis, the proprietor, is quite a character. He and his ranch are both worth your attention.

I understand you're lunching with Clarinda Darcoa today, so I'll call you around twelve-thirty for your answer. I know that once these dove parties get started, there's no telling when they'll end. So I might miss you altogether, if I didn't get hold of you first.

A los pies de Usted y hasta muy pronto, Señorita.

Sabin Duplessis.

"I beg your pardon, Miss Ruth. Mr. Aldridge would like to speak with you, if it wouldn't be inconvenient."

Absorbed in her note, Ruth had not heard Ellen's discreet knock or noticed her quiet re-entry. Now she saw that the maid was standing before her, with an air of patient resignation.

"Oh—I'm sorry, Ellen. Ask him if I may call him back, in about half an hour."

"He isn't on the telephone, miss. He's in the library."

Ruth glanced down at her wrist watch. It was not quite nine-thirty. *Something's happened*, she said to herself. *He wouldn't come to see me, early in the morning like this, without sending me any word beforehand, unless . . . .* She swung her feet out of bed, feeling for her slippers. Then she realized that she had not yet given Ellen any answer and that the maid's expression of patient resignation was becoming more and more marked.

"Tell Mr. Aldridge I'll be down in just a few minutes," she said. Then, as the maid turned to go, she added hastily, "Have you seen my uncle this morning, Ellen?"

"Yes, miss. He passed through the hall, on his way out, just a few minutes ago."

"He—he seemed to be feeling well, didn't he?"

"Why yes, miss, as far as I could notice."

"Well, tell Mr. Aldridge—"

"I was going to, miss, if you'll excuse me for saying so, when you detained me to ask about Mr. Foxworth."

Obviously Ellen was a little tired, and Ruth, who habitually meant to be considerate and pleasant in her dealings with servants, would have been sorry to feel that she was responsible for Ellen's attitude, if she had not been wholly preoccupied by more disturbing thoughts. She still did not feel entirely easy about her uncle's connection with the Lalandes, or about the movements relating to his business which he continued to guard as secrets; her first concern had been lest there were some new developments in either of these directions. But if he were taking his routine departure for the office there could hardly have been any untoward happenings along such lines—certainly nothing that would precipitate Aldridge's appearance at the house so early in the morning. This must mean that something else had happened; and once again the unwelcome vision of Roatan's dark caves rose before Ruth's eyes . . . .

The instant she saw Aldridge she knew that her second guess had been the right one. He looked very grave, graver than she had believed it possible for him to look, and instead of giving her some sort of merry salutation, he came forward and took her hand, holding it silently for a moment before he even spoke her name.

"Ruth," he said at last; and again, "Ruth." Suddenly she knew that she must help him.

"You've come to tell me that you're going away, haven't you, Russ?"

"How did you guess?"

"I think I've known you would, ever since Sunday. Even at the Twelfth Night Ball—"

"Yes, I realized you were worrying, that you weren't having the unmarred pleasure you had a right to."

So I wasn't wrong about the harmony of mind and spirit, she said to herself. *He was conscious of it too. At least I wasn't imagining that I meant something to this man—as much as he meant to me. I wasn't dreaming of an attraction just because I wanted it to exist. I've got that much to save my pride. But it isn't enough. I wanted so much more I thought I was going to have so much more.* Aloud, she said, forcing herself to smile, "But I did! I had a wonderful time! It was just that I—I seemed to know you were going. I could almost see those caves you were talking about. You said they were on an island off the coast of Honduras, didn't you?"

"Yes, that's right. On the island of Roatan."

Again he seemed unable to go on. It was strange that he should be so tongue-tied, this suave aristocrat. Strange that she should be the one who could manage to continue speaking, quietly and collectedly, in spite of her inner turmoil.

"It was all decided at that meeting you went to Wednesday?"

"Yes, that's right," he repeated, almost eagerly, as if he were grateful to her for helping him. "You remember I said, at the Morrisons', that Guy Welburn had everything all fixed, but that I was held up by a pamphlet the Foundation wanted. Well, Guy made a speech at that meeting and succeeded in convincing the Board that this expedition was about ten times as important as any pamphlet possibly could be—that my report on the Peten to the American Society covered everything I needed to say at the moment, just as I'd kept insisting myself that it did, and that a supplementary brochure, if the Foundation still insisted on having one, could wait till I got back. Guy finally made those old fogies see that the opportunity we've got right now may be the chance of a lifetime—funds and equipment both available, government friendly, weather conditions at their seasonal best—"

"When are you going, Russ?" But she knew that too, so she was braced for his answer.

"Why, I'm going today! That's why I came so early. I couldn't leave without saying goodbye to you and this was the only way I could manage." He looked down at his wrist watch, as she had looked at hers half an hour earlier. "I hardly had a minute to myself yesterday, with all the preparations to rush through, and I didn't want to write or telephone about a thing like this. I wanted to see you and explain. Of course I ought to have realized that you wouldn't be up, that you'd need at least fifteen minutes to dress. I meant to say all sorts of things to you. Now I guess I can't say any of them. I haven't allowed any too much leeway for getting to the dock as it is. I have so much stuff to take that a plane wasn't practicable after all . . . . So, if you'll just say you understand," he concluded, rather desperately.

"Of course I understand, Russ."

She was not at all sure that she did. She was trying hard to do so, but she still could not see why some rumors about ancient urns and codices should weigh so heavily in the balance when a man and a girl who had just discovered each other could have had a long succession of lighthearted days together. For the discovery *was* mutual. She must hold to her belief in that. If she didn't, she couldn't stand this parting. Besides, Russ expected her to say that she understood. So she must do that too . . . .

"I knew you would. I knew I could count on that. You're a great girl, Ruth."

She raised her head proudly, thankful that she had not failed him, thankful that she could look at him without the betrayal of tears. Those would come later, she would not be able to help that; but at least he would not see them, at least she could hold them back until after he had gone. And she would not have to face him, in this valiant way, for more than a minute. Presently he would take her in his arms and hold her close. He would not see her face then, he would only feel her lips. And when he kissed her, it would not matter that he had left so many words unspoken. There would be no further need of speech . . . .

For the first time, her guess was wide of the mark. He had continued to hold her hand while they talked and now he folded both of his over it and pressed it hard. Again he spoke her name twice, looking down into her eyes. Then suddenly he was gone . . . .

Some time after she went back to her room Ruth realized that though she had read Sabin's note, she had not opened his present. She untied the ribbons which bound it and folded back the tissue paper, disclosing a box of highly-polished ebony, inlaid with brightly tinted mother-of-pearl flowers. The box had a quaint lock and a tiny gold key. Ruth unfastened it to find two antique scent bottles, heavily encrusted with gold, imbedded in gold-colored satin. When she took out the stoppers, an unfamiliar scent, even sweeter and stronger than Clarinda's, was wafted towards her, and tilting one of the bottles, she let the perfume drop over her fingers and rubbed it behind her ears and under her chin. She was conscious of the heady scent as she slipped his message from the lining of the lid:

I hope this is your first whiff of Madera de Oriente *and that it will appeal to you as much as it has to many highborn Spanish ladies, among them the one who originally owned*

281

this outfit, namely Queen Isabella—I mean the second, not the first, the former, in my opinion, being a good deal the lustier lady of the two. (Instead of financing one man with her possessions, she succeeded in annexing a number who were ready to finance her with theirs!) You have probably heard that she was lightheartedly engaged in relaxing morals in (perennially) Sunny Spain while Queen Victoria was grimly reforming them in (erstwhile) Merrie England. Well, a little lighthearted relaxation never hurt anyone, and apparently Isabella realized that perfume does almost as much for a woman as it does for a flower. Is it too much to hope that Madera de Oriente released from her own flacons, will give you the same realization and help to dispel the slightly staid attitude for which the State Department is, no doubt, responsible? Or are you so completely addicted to Old English Lavender that you won't take a chance on the effects of something more potent?

In spite of herself, Ruth smiled a little as she read the note. It would have been daring enough under almost any circumstances; coming from a man whose beloved had been dead less than a week, it was nothing short of astounding. Ruth's intuition told her that an association with Sabin might well be as dangerous as it would be delightful; but she was in no mood to listen to the voice of reason; she was ready to welcome anything that assuaged her hurt pride, anything that might soothe her sore heart. When Sabin telephoned at half-past twelve, she told him she would be glad to have him call for her at five o'clock and take her to the reception at the French Consulate General; she would also be glad to dine with him at the Bar-None Ranch.

In the meantime, there was the luncheon at Clarinda's to get through somehow. Ruth dressed for it with unusual care and, after a critical inspection of herself in the mirror, applied more make-up than was her usual conservative custom. Then she put on a little extra perfume. But the morning's camellias were still on her dressing table. After a momentary hesitation, she pinned them on the blue mink cape.

Though she was not late for the luncheon, she found a congenial company already assembled at the Darcoas' stately house on Coliseum Street—a dozen pretty, pleasant young women, some of them already married, most of them in their early twenties. She soon discovered that she was not expected to contribute much in the way of conversation, but she found this freedom from responsibility a relief and listened with relaxed enjoyment to the agreeable chatter about Carnival, clothes, recent engagements, impending weddings, exciting suitors and adorable new babies, which constituted the general subject matter. She had met several of her fellow-guests in the call-out section at the Twelfth Night Ball and found that they seemed to regard her already as one of them. There were many cordial references to future occasions when they would all be together and Ruth knew that this luncheon would serve to establish her in a circle which would automatically interlock with many others. The prospect of such a whirl was far from displeasing to her.

Sabin had been correct in his estimate of the probable length of the party. The sherry, the canapes, and the conversation consumed more than half an hour, and lunch itself was a leisurely, expansive meal, unhurriedly served. After lunch came coffee, peppermints, and more conversation, and it was nearly three when the bridge tables were brought out. Then the girls took their places around these, and cards supplemented, rather than impeded, the flow of small talk. Both went on and on, and occasionally snatches of chit-chat from another foursome drifted towards the one in which Ruth was playing.

". . . . perfectly dreadful about Odile St. Amant. Do you suppose it really was a suicide?"

"Of course. What else could it be?"

"Well, I don't know, but I've heard rumors that poor old Tossie's been arrested for murder, even though there's been nothing in the papers about it."

"*Tossie!* Why, she adored Odile. If it wasn't a suicide I'd be much more suspicious that it was—"

"Sh-h-h! Don't say anything you wouldn't want Ruth Avery to overhear. Remember Orson Foxworth's her uncle and that he and Mrs. Lalande . . . ."

". . . . Well, it certainly was sudden. I called him up to ask him to dinner at the country club next week, and his houseman told me he'd sailed at eleven. You'd think he'd have had enough of these wild dashes by this time."

"Him and Byrd! But usually he doesn't act quite so much as if the sheriff were after him. You'd think he was actually trying to make a getaway. Now, if it had been Sabin Duplessis . . . ."

Eventually, after a stealthy glance at her wrist watch, Ruth took advantage of her position as dummy and went to the telephone. Mr. Duplessis was not at home, she was told by the servant who answered; but he could be reached at Uptown 9017. Hoping that she would not delay the game, Ruth hurriedly dialed the designated number. A male voice, which was certainly not Sabin's, but which seemed familiar, answered instantly.

"I was told I might call Mr. Duplessis at this number. Is he there? Would it be convenient for me to speak with him?"

"Yes, indeed. Just a second."

An instant later Sabin was on the line. She thought she detected a trace of tension in his greeting.

"Your butler gave me this telephone number," she said apologetically. "I hope it was all right to call."

"Of course. Unless it's to give me the bad news that you've changed your mind about our date."

The tension was already gone, the pleasant persuasive timbre sounding again. Ruth felt unaccountably relieved.

"No. But the party's still going strong," she told him. "I don't believe I'll have time to get back to Toulouse Street. Would you mind calling here for me instead?"

"Of course not. It's right on our way to the consulate anyhow. I don't see why I didn't think of suggesting that arrangement in the beginning. And I'd be delighted to have the chance of showing off before all Clarinda's friends."

"What do you mean, showing off?"

"Why, walking up to the door and asking for you. Casually explaining that I hate to interrupt, but that you've been kind enough to say you'd go to the reception with me, and as it's getting rather late .... Of course, I'd like to brag about the dinner too, if you'd let me."

There was no doubt about it, Sabin had a very engaging way of saying and doing things; and by the time he called for her, Ruth was growing a little tired of ultra-feminine chatter and was doubly ready to welcome stimulating male companionship. Sabin made an impressive entrance, laughed and chatted with Clarinda and some of the guests for a few minutes, and then bore Ruth triumphantly off. He made no reference to any appointment which had taken him out earlier in the afternoon and Ruth naturally asked no questions concerning one; but on their way to the consulate he paid her several suave but trivial compliments which she accepted lightly and a little evasively. At one point he sniffed, with evident appreciation.

"I'm glad you agreed with me."

"Agreed with you?"

"That perfume does as much for a woman as it does for a flower. You don't suppose I thought that nice smell

284

emanated from Lady Hume's Blush, do you? One of the reasons that I don't care for camellias is that they're scentless."

"They have other qualities."

"Yes. But I like something a little more heady. Don't you?"

"Ye-e-s. But not too heady. The perfume set's beautiful, Sabin. But you're not going to keep this up, are you?"

"Keep what up?"

"Well, you've gone from a King's Cake to a queen's casket pretty rapidly."

"Yes, and I have the bracelet of an empress up my sleeve."

"Just above your wrist watch?"

"For the moment. It wouldn't look badly just above yours."

"Perhaps we'd better discuss that some other time."

"By all means. I wasn't thinking of making it a conversation piece at the consulate. And here we are."

He turned sharply in at a short gravel drive, depositing Ruth under the porte-cochere while he went to park his smart gray convertible in the circular areaway beyond. Guests were already leaving and, for a moment, Ruth wondered regretfully if the bridge game had not robbed her of an experience which she would have enjoyed more. But when Sabin joined her and they went together into the cheerful, flower-decked house, she decided that they had arrived at exactly the right moment. The thinning crowd permitted a more definite impression of the people she did meet, and these were really her kind; the group was more sophisticated and urbane than any she had so far met in New Orleans. She found herself chatting easily in French and Spanish on a number of topics, the cocktail and sandwich in her hand merely accessories to a discussion of subjects that were genuinely interesting. It appeared that she and her host had mutual friends in France, that she was familiar with other countries whose consuls were among her fellow-guests, and that many of their opinions on topics of the day coincided with her own. The thought flashed through her mind that it was a pleasant change to take part in a conversation like this, instead of listening to one which was confined to Carnival; then, with her inescapable honesty, she realized that had it not been for the departure of Russ, she herself would have felt the balls to be supremely important. She must not let the "fruitful grape" of Twelfth Night turn bitter.

Sabin was evidently enjoying himself too. He sauntered

back and forth, effecting the introductions which led to the agreeable conversations, but not taking much part in them once they were started. He was obviously a center of attraction. Ruth noticed that every time he moved away from her, some other woman claimed him, and that while many of them were no longer young, they were almost invariably either strikingly handsome or very distinguished looking. He was not only affording ample proof that he could "act like a civilized human being" but that he had unusual power to arrest and hold the interest of anyone he chose to notice, even in a gathering as discriminating as this one; and his audience was by no means exclusively feminine. Grave-looking, graybearded men, formally attired and wearing the tiny red ribbon of the Legion of Honor in their buttonholes, were among his eager listeners; so were various others who, though younger and less learned of appearance, had the almost unmistakable attributes of culture, wealth, and achievement. Ruth did not need to be told that Sabin would have been *persona non grata* if his behavior were habitually incorrect, irrational, or even unconventional. And it was becoming increasingly easy to persuade herself that Joe rather than Sabin had been to blame for the scene that disrupted their pleasant dinner.

She had been at the reception nearly an hour before she saw anyone she had previously met. Then, after almost everyone else had left the pleasant drawing room, Vance Perrault entered it. He looked drawn and weary, and in the face of such evident fatigue, his presence at an official function with which he had no special connection seemed rather surprising. However, the liking she had immediately taken to him was now intensified by the realization that his feeling for Odile must have been paternal rather than professional and that her death had been a terrific blow to him. Tactfully creating a diversion in the dialogue with which she was engaged at the moment, Ruth moved unobtrusively in his direction, only to see that he had hardly greeted his host and hostess before heading straight towards her.

"Good evening, Miss Avery," he said, his pleasant smile briefly illumining his tired face. "I rather thought I might find you here this evening. I hope you're enjoying your stay in New Orleans."

"Every minute of it. At least, I would be, except for distress over the terrible tragedy that came so quickly after our first meeting."

"Yes. Yes, it is terrible. I don't know when the loss of one of my patients .... But we mustn't talk about that here. I do

286

want to speak to your uncle though, about poor old Tossie. Is he in the dining room?"

"No, he couldn't make it this afternoon. He left the house before I was awake this morning and sent word that he might be held up at the office till all hours. I don't know, but I can't help feeling that merger he's set his heart on may come off at any moment now. At all events, I'm trying not to bother him more than I can help. Sabin Duplessis very kindly offered to bring me to this reception."

Perrault glanced in the direction of Sabin, who raised his glass in a jovial salute. But the doctor hardly returned the convivial gesture and the shadow on his face deepened perceptibly.

"Well, that's a disappointment. To tell you the truth, I came here myself largely on the chance that I might catch him on the wing. I haven't been able to reach him by telephone and I want very much to get in touch with him. Would you be willing to give him a message? This is one of the few times I wouldn't trust that Admirable Crichton of his to recognize the importance of one."

"Of course I'll give him the message. If he hasn't reached home by the time I do, I'll leave a note on his door marked 'URGENT' in big red letters."

"Good. As I said, I wanted to talk with him about Tossie. Caresse went to see her on Tuesday and spoke to me about her afterwards with considerable distress. She's worried over the poor old creature's health, and she asked me if I wouldn't go to see her too. I've been so hard pressed that I couldn't get to it right away, but I finally went to the jail this morning on the way to my class at Charity Hospital."

"Is she really sick?"

"Not in the sense that there's a specific ailment calling for specific treatment. But in my opinion it's important to get her out where she can receive better care, better food, and above all, a bit of human sympathy. Tossie's incredibly old and feeble, she's grieving herself into complete debility; while they're treating her kindly enough, the one thing that has kept her going was the feeling that she was needed, that somebody wanted her. Without that, she's lost; and in prison she's without it."

"Poor thing. And Joe Racina is positive she had nothing to do with Odile's death."

"So am I. And I find it quite unbelievable that even Captain Murphy seriously thinks she killed Odile."

"And is that what you want me to tell Uncle Orson?"

"I understand that he has already engaged an attorney for

her, and I'm quite sure the police have no right to hold her unless they make some kind of formal charge against her. And they haven't done so. I checked on that myself. So your uncle's attorney, or the one he engaged, can make a formal demand on the police that they charge her or release her. I'm convinced something of the sort is necessary to save the poor old soul's life."

"Is it really as bad as that? I wish there were something I could do to help! But at least I can see that Uncle gets your message, Doctor Perrault, and I will."

"Thank you. I've been greatly troubled about Tossie."

As if his purpose in coming to the reception had now been fulfilled, Perrault wandered towards the door, stopping only to speak to the acquaintances who actually waylaid him. Sabin, who had made no attempt to join in the conversation about Tossie, promptly appeared at Ruth's elbow, as he had whenever there was a break in the dialogue or an empty glass required refilling. He had contrived to indicate that he would be glad to linger until the party actually broke up; but there were now unmistakable indications that this moment was impending. He and Ruth were among the last to leave and, pleased by her enthusiastic comments on the reception, he asked her whether a short run or a leisurely ride would best meet her mood of the moment.

"Why, I thought you'd already picked the place where we're going!"

"I have. But we can take the Airline and then cut across at St. Rose or we can go by the River Road. I believe that's what you'd prefer. Of course, it's so dark by now that you won't be able to see very much. But I think you'd get the feel of it and that you'd like it."

"I do too. Let's do that."

He nodded and guided the gray convertible through a succession of city streets to a palm-lined avenue. They had already driven for several miles further when the high curving network, forming the rail approaches of the great bridge over the Mississippi, loomed before them. Sabin swung his car halfway around the traffic circle; then it shot along a straight black-topped road. In spite of the darkness, the headlights picked up the lush vegetation and scattered buildings to a remarkable degree; then the levee came briefly into view, beyond the wide lawns of modest bungalows, spaced between yards where stacked lumber was drying and open meadows where cattle were grazing. At one turn some white tombs, rising from the tangled grass of a tiny cemetery which was flush with the road, stood out with surprising suddenness;

at another, the blare of juke boxes and the jangle of slot machines rushed through the open door of a crowded amusement center. Just beyond the second small town through which they passed, the road actually seemed about to run into the levee; then it lurched to one side, and still clinging to the sloping green bank beside it, went on and on, so close that the two seemed to remain part of each other.

Wisely, Sabin waited for Ruth to voice her impressions without questioning her about them. The speed of the powerful gray car had been checked and they were only creeping along. No other vehicles were in sight, no houses, no people—only the levee, rising between the black ribbon of the road and the wooded fringe of the batture. Ruth drew a deep breath.

"You were right, Sabin," she said. "I do get the feel of it. I even get the feel of the river I can't see. I wonder why no one ever told me before how marvelous all this would be."

"I've often wondered myself why more wasn't said about it. A song's been written that does justice to Ol' Man River. But no one's done justice to Lady Levee yet, as far as I know, in either song or story. But look at her lying there—slumberous, serene, veiled in mystery—"

"Why, Sabin, you could write that song yourself! Why don't you?"

"What's the use? I haven't any incentive."

For the first time he spoke jerkily, almost angrily, and at the same moment he put his foot on the accelerator. Instantly obedient, the gray car leaped forward again. Giant oaks bordered the highway on the land side now, their moss-draped branches overhanging the road, and neat white fences enclosing the fields beneath them. Again something white loomed up and Ruth saw it was a small grandstand, placed at one side of a riding ring. Behind the ring, a row of barns was dimly visible, and further along the road a tall ranch gate overhung by an ox yoke and topped by the sign of the Bar-None. Still driving rapidly, Sabin took the lane leading through this gate, and brought the car to an abrupt stop beside the flagged terrace of a long, low building which twinkled its welcome with cheerful lights. Instantly the front door opened, and a man of genial countenance and immense girth came forward to greet them. Sabin advanced, holding out his hand.

"Good evening, Mr. Davis. This time I've brought the loveliest lady of them all to Bar-None—Miss Ruth Avery."

"We're mighty glad to have you here, Miss Avery. And to see you again, Mr. Duplessis. The barbecued chicken you ordered is coming along nicely, but the last I heard, it wasn't quite ready. Perhaps Miss Avery'd like to see the palominos before you go inside."

"Would you, Ruth?"

"I would, very much."

She spoke sincerely enough; but her interest, as Sabin had foretold, was aroused by the proprietor of the Bar-None Ranch quite as much as by the establishment itself. Ad Given Davis was an arresting figure. He carried his great size easily, and his whipcord riding clothes and wide sombrero became him. So did his elaborate shirt, lavishly embroidered with horseshoes, horses' heads, and other symbols of his chief interests. On his cravat of spotted calfskin glittered a diamond stickpin; the emblem of a fraternal order, also done in diamonds, shone in the lapel of his coat; and diamond rings, some of them two-stoned, flashed from his fingers.

Leading the way past the ranch house, this extraordinary host headed towards a large barn at the rear. "I'm sorry about the mosquitoes," he apologized. "That's just one of those things. Not even the cold weather we had this past week seems to discourage them." He fumbled for a light switch, and with its click the interior of the barn was thrown into garish illumination, disclosing a wide central walk-way flanked on either side by stalls.

"The stallions are all kept in this barn," Mr. Davis explained, jangling a bunch of keys and selecting one. "We'll go see them in a moment. Maybe you'd like to look in here first, though." He swung open a door, revealing a square room with walls of polished wood which multiplied the overhead lights. Nearly covering these walls were innumerable red and blue ribbons, with an occasional purple among them; beneath these, on one side, hung a dozen bridles, heavily ornamented; while crowded together on the floor, several wooden "horses" displayed tooled leather saddles, elaborately adorned.

"Don't tell me that's all silver!" Ruth exclaimed breathlessly. Sabin and Ad Given Davis laughed.

"That's nothing," the big ranchman said. "Wait till I show you my real pride and joy."

Opposite the door stood a tall case not unlike an out-size telephone booth covered with black leather. Ad Given Davis opened a padlock and laid it aside. Then he folded back the hinged front and top of the box, revealing a saddle so heavily crusted with silver medallions and inlay that except for the seat itself its black leather was hardly visible.

"That's for the big shows, and for parades," he explained. "I had it specially made down in Mexico. Even the *tapideros* are ornamented to match. And over there is the bridle that goes with it."

"Surely you don't mean you actually use it—to ride on, I mean," Ruth marveled.

"You bet I do. I'll be using it next May when I ride Clipper of Bar-None in the inaugural parade at Baton Rouge."

"How do you know?" asked Sabin. "The election isn't till a week from Tuesday, and it's my guess there'll have to be a run-off after that."

"It doesn't make any difference who's elected," Davis grinned. "They'll ask the Bar-None to be represented in the parade."

"I expect you're right, at that," agreed Sabin. "A saddle with enough silver on it to pay off the national debt would make quite a flash at anybody's inauguration."

The next few moments were devoted to an exchange of pessimistic views on national and international affairs; but eventually Mr. Davis led them from the tack room, after directing a stableman to close it. They then walked from one spacious stall to the next, while he gave them the name and lineage of each heavily-muscled stallion, with special emphasis on both the ancestry and progeny of Stonewall Jackson, the prize sire, a gorgeous golden creature with a white mane and tail. A complicated brace of leather thongs held the tail queerly arched, and Davis explained that when this "tail-set" was removed for the great horse's public appearances, the proud carriage of the tail impressively enhanced the general picture he made.

"Of course, you understand that 'palomino' is a color, not a breed," Mr. Davis went on. "Strictly speaking, it's that of a newly-minted twenty-dollar gold piece. But you're allowed a slight departure from that. To be exact, a palomino may be either five shades darker or five shades lighter than standard. Clipper conforms exactly, and Stonewall's just a touch lighter. But it doesn't matter so much in his case, because he's a saddle horse, not a parade horse."

As he spoke he turned a valve to let fresh, cool water flow into the drinking bucket within the stall, and the stallion, stepping forward, lifted his velvet-smooth muzzle to the bars of the enclosure. Trustingly Ruth reached forward to pet him.

"I wouldn't do that, if you don't mind my saying so," the rancher cautioned her. "A stallion's temper's none too certain, and I don't know anything much more painful than a horse bite. But if you'll come with me I'll show you something you can pet to your heart's content."

Once more he led the way across a wide enclosure to a row of smaller barns. A stableman had already switched on the big floodlights in a building which contained a single series of stalls, as roomy as those in the big stable, but without bars, and with Dutch doors already open but for a single crosswise shelf. In the second stall a sleek chestnut mare was lying down, a leggy little colt beside her.

"It's the first foal of the season," Mr. Davis announced with almost paternal pride. "That was his daddy we just saw, and this youngster looks as though he'd be the spit 'n' image of him. He'll be five days old tomorrow."

The colt struggled to its feet and timidly, yet trustfully, moved around his mother's flank on legs that were still a bit uncertain. Spraddling out in readiness for instant flight, he regarded the newcomers with soft eyes, suddenly flailing a swift tattoo on either side of his rump with his fuzzy little bottlebrush of a tail. Then, one cautious step at a time, he approached them until he was close enough to nuzzle at Ruth's handbag. She lifted her hand gently and rubbed first his forehead and then his neck; and obviously, the foal enjoyed this. But presently he bolted to the protection of his mother's bulk, as though suddenly aware he had left the only secure haven he yet knew.

"God love its heart!" exclaimed Ruth. Then, turning to their host, she added, "I can't thank you enough for showing us all this. I wish my stepfather could see it. He's a great horse-lover too."

"Come back next May and bring him with you," the rancher urged her expansively. "You'll really see something then."

"Right now, though," suggested Sabin, slapping at his neck, "I think maybe we'd better retire inside the screens. These musk-eaters of yours have been fleshing their fangs on me about as long as I can take it, pal."

"By all means, Mr. Duplessis. You and Miss Avery go right ahead. I'll join you in a little while. Might as well take a good look around while I'm out here."

Sabin and Ruth crossed the lawn at something very like a run, and his firm hand at her elbow steadied her against the uncertainties of loose gravel and spike heels. On the screened gallery they paused momentarily for breath. It led directly into the bar, and from this opened a spacious room, already well crowded with diners.

"Your table is yonder by the window, Mr. Duplessis," a

white-jacketed waiter informed him, nodding toward a pleasant corner. "But your dinner won't be ready for about five minutes. If you'd care for a drink first . . . ."

Sabin glanced at the small, curving bar of light-colored wood. Only one patron was there, a stocky figure whose wide shoulders visibly stretched the striped fabric of his Basque singlet. A tan beret covered the rather bullet-shaped head, and dark glasses with wide tortoise-shell sidebars concealed the eyes. Beneath the cuffs of trousers which had obviously once been an army officer's pinks, the tips of astonishingly small feet, shod in mirror-polished cordovan, were barely visible. But even apart from the striking costume, something about this solitary patron drew Sabin's attention for a moment, before he turned back to Ruth.

"How about it? Do you care for a drink while we wait?" he asked.

"I believe not," she replied. "After all, I did full justice to the French consul's champagne. And if there's real barbecued chicken in prospect, I'd like red wine with it. Why don't we go out on the verandah—gallery, I mean—where we can see Lady Levee, as you call her, till they're ready for us?"

"Good deal," approved Sabin. "Might even see a shooting star and make a wish. Now, for instance . . . ."

"Hiyah, Sabin, y'old puddle jumper. How's for a drink before you go off into the wild blue yonder?"

Sabin whirled toward the solitary bar patron, who grinned at him, and as Sabin's look continued to be one of blank unrecognition, raised a stubby hand to sweep off the tan beret, and then to remove the dark glasses. This brought his features clearly into view, including a heavy greenish-purple contusion about his left eye.

"Dutch! Dutch Schaefer!" Sabin shouted jubilantly. "Ruth, this is an old army buddy of mine. Dutch, Miss Ruth Avery. Boy, am I glad to see you again! Why, I haven't laid eyes on you, in it must be more than two years now. Let's see, that was at Edinburgh airport in Trinidad, wasn't it?—the time we were looking for Bennie Molter, only he'd already been put in command of that fighter group in East Anglia?"

"In two years, did you say, my fine bucko?" asked Schaefer wryly. "Pleased to meet you, Miss Avery. Wait a minute . . . . Miss Ruth Avery? Orson Foxworth's niece?"

"I hope you're not disappointed," Ruth said pleasantly.

"Meeting you? I'd have to be blind, deaf, and dumb to rate *you* a disappointment. So you're the great Foxworth's niece, and . . . ." He turned abruptly to face Sabin, " . . . . and you haven't seen me since two years ago in Trinidad. Am I supposed to yes you on that, Fly Boy?"

"But it has been at least that long, hasn't it?"

Schaefer vouchsafed Sabin a quizzical glance.

"If you say so," he replied noncommittally, with a guarded glance at Ruth. "How's for that drink?"

Sabin shook his head and Ruth murmured, "Thank you, no," as Schaefer replaced the concealing dark glasses and wadded his beret into his hip pocket.

"Well, if you'll excuse me for taking mine—I've just found out I really need one." Turning to the bartender he added a crisp, "Bourbon and bayou water. One in one glass, one in the other." He tossed off the whiskey in a single gulp and followed this with a sip of water. "Two years is a right smart of a time, all right," he added to no one in particular.

"Look, Dutch, I don't get this," protested Sabin with a touch of irritation. "If I've forgotten where it was we met, I apologize, and all that. But it doesn't call for the kind of act you're putting on now. Where was it then? Karachi? Liberia? Guam? Sfax?"

"You mean it?" asked Dutch doubtfully. "Get me told, Fly Boy. I'm only trying to do what's right."

"Certainly, I mean it."

"Well, I knew you were teed up, but I didn't think it was one of these washout binges," Schaefer observed, taking off his dark glasses, and pointing to the contusion which disfigured his left eye. "You're the guy who hung this shiner on me, if you want the straight of it. Last Saturday night, in the Diamond Horseshoe. Tell me for true, now. You don't remember that we spent most of last Saturday night together?"

Involuntarily, Sabin shot a startled glance at Ruth. She met his eyes with complete composure. "Suppose I disappear for a while, and let you two talk this over," she said. "After all, it doesn't concern me, and . . . ."

"Please, Ruth! I'd much rather you'd stay, if you'll be good enough. Not that I blame you for leaving. Apparently, you and I can't sit down anywhere without having last Saturday night dragged into the conversation."

"I asked you whether you wanted me to keep my trap closed," Schaefer protested defensively. "I wasn't trying to spill what anybody could recognize for a mess of beans. You had a right to tell me to shaddup, if this has fouled things up."

Their waiter appeared at Sabin's elbow and murmured that dinner was served. He nodded. "Come eat with us," he urged

Schaefer. "We might as well wash this thing up. If you can help me get the straight of what I did last Saturday night and where I did it ...."

"Thanks, I've had my dinner. I was waiting around for Ted Marshfield of the Blue Fleet legal department to meet me here and ...."

"Well, sit with us, anyway .... You don't mind, do you, Ruth?"

"Of course not. Unless it's something you wouldn't want me to hear."

"In that case, let's go."

They threaded their way among the tables and Sabin murmured, "Ruth, if ever this miserable affair is settled, I'll make it up to you—the embarrassment I'm causing you, I mean."

"Embarrassment? Why, I know lots of girls who would get the thrill of their lives out of this."

The words were plainly meant to be reassuring and they were followed by spontaneous praise of the shrimp remoulade which had just been placed on the table. But the dinner was no longer the triumph Sabin had planned, and his dark mood was not lightened, even when Ruth reminded him he had told her they could make a wish.

"Here's my chance," she said. "This is the first time I've eaten shrimps fixed this way. And I wish—"

"I thought it was part of the deal that you've got to keep your wish secret in a case like this," Dutch Schaefer broke in. "Not that I'm any authority." Then to the waiter, "Bourbon and bayou water—a double this time—the Bourbon in one glass, the water in the other."

The shrimp remoulade had been followed by salad, served in wooden bowls, and this in turn by sizzling pewter platters of barbecued chicken with crisp batter-fried onion rings, corn fritters, and broccoli, before Sabin turned impatiently to Schaefer and said, "Well, what are we waiting for? Contact!"

"Beginning where?"

"You're the one that knows about it, I don't."

"Well, I had quite a session before I met you. But maybe that fits in, because that's what you and I were talking about," Schaefer began. He glanced once more at Ruth, apologetically. "If I talk about your uncle, it's only because I've got to. No harm meant."

She nodded. "I think I'll be able to take it."

"Well, I'm coming in on Canal Street when I bump into you," he said to Sabin. "It was right at Chartres Street, and

295

we had us a quick reunion. You knew me all right, and when I suggested going any place where they'd serve us some drinking whiskey, and having a celebration, you were right there with the big yes. Only you wouldn't walk down Chartres Street, because that was where the Third Precinct Police Station was. You said it was bad luck to pass police stations after dark and reminded me about the time in Recife when the *cuartel* was . . . . But I guess we can skip that part. Anyhow, you were all for getting stinko. You said you wanted to stay stiff as an oak plank for at least a month; nothing less'n that would satisfy you, and then we got to this first joint—I disremember the name of it."

"It doesn't matter, I suppose. What I want to know is: did we do anything outside of drink, or did I tell you anything about what I'd been doing earlier that evening?"

There was no mistaking the note of anxiety which had crept into Sabin's voice. Ruth sat very still, listening intently.

"No," replied Schaefer. "I did all the talking and made you a proposition; a halfway sort of proposition, anyway."

"What kind of a deal was it?"

"That's where Miss Ruth's uncle comes in. Leave me tell it my own way, like I told it to you, but without the trimmings, this time. There was a hen on. There might be till yet. That's what I'm waiting for Ted Marshfield to tell me tonight. It seems like Mister Foxworth was willing to pay heavy sugar for a couple of guys to fly some surplus C-47's down south to a new airport back of the Cerro del Hule Range, where there was an airstrip nobody else knew anything about, yet. You know how it is down there; you get a flat valley between two pretty steep ridges, and a half a dozen *mozos* with axes and saws can make you a damn usable landing strip in no time at all. If you could get a bulldozer in there you could do it in half a day; but of course there's no chance to get heavy machinery through the jungle on the ground."

"Sure; but what about us?"

"Well, all I knew was I was to go out to Bud Craddock's camp in Little Woods on the lake front, and wait. Okay. So I did it. Next thing you know, a guy comes up to me there and says he's the one who has the skiff, so we go down the steps from the gallery—Bud's camp is built way out at the end of a long pier. I get into the skiff, and this guy cranks up an outboard, and off we go to where a big yacht's riding at anchor. Only one other guy there that I knew, outside of Foxworth. That was Cecil Brewster; you might have run into him at Manos, where he based, most of the time. He was skipper of an LST. The rest were strangers."

"I think I remember the name, but don't know's I ever met him."

"All this hush-hush stuff was the tip-off to me, of course. I had an idea that any nice surplus C-47 we could set down on a hidden landing strip in the jungle would be armed after it got there. And there wasn't any part of Central America that'd be more'n a short hop from there. Especially the North Coast, and most especially that part of the coast near Llorando. You could drop a load of T.N.T. around there, and after that an LST full of tanks and half-tracs and whatnot wouldn't have any trouble waltzing right up to the beach. Then it would be bye-bye government, and hurray for our victorious liberator."

"But all those elaborate precautions!"

"Times has changed, son. The old gray *filibustero* racket ain't what she used to be. Remember Dick Corliss?"

"Sure."

"Know where he is now?"

"Around, I suppose. His folks live over at Pascagoula or somewhere on the Gulf Coast not far from here."

"He's waiting for trial on a charge of attempted breach of neutrality or something. Him and two big-timers from that shipyard they had here in New Orleans during the war. A full chicken colonel, Dick was, and now he's under glass, because they found out he was going to take an LST loaded with tanks and suchlike out of Gulfport, supposedly to British Honduras, on the dizzy idea that those tanks would be used as agricultural tractors. The G-guys they have now are a lot of sharp cookies."

"And we talked about that Saturday night?"

"Nothing else but. And you were all for it. You kept saying you wanted to get the hell away from this lousy dump of a town, and didn't care where, as long as it was far enough off to where people who talked about a levee would mean a reception. And you got to sounding off louder and louder about what a rotten deal New Orleans was for anybody, which didn't win you any applause, pal. And then you got to saying hurray for the revolution and where would we deliver the planes, till I got the worry-warts standing out on my neck like prongs on a hatrack, and when I tried to shush you down and the bartender said you couldn't have no more to drink, why the sociable started for fair. And that was where I got this shiner, compliments of you. If you ask me, you still pack a hefty wallop, son. At least when you're

297

rightly ginned up, you could sure win you some Golden Gloves."

"And that's all you know about what I did on Saturday night?"

"Ain't it enough for you?"

"Plenty!" There was unfeigned relief in Sabin's voice. "And I do mean plenty. Let me ask you just one thing more. What time was it when you ran into me?"

"Right about midnight or a little earlier. That chin-chin on the boat was finished about nine-thirty. Foxworth left in a speedboat without lights, so I couldn't tell which way he finally headed, but I expect it would be somewhere near the Yacht Club where a car could be waiting for him. My skiff put-putted me back to Bud's camp, and I figure it was ten-thirty by the time I got in, and that with stopping for a drink or so it was right onto midnight, time I got into town and ran into you."

"Well, that clears up one part of it for me," Sabin said thoughtfully, as though speaking to himself. "Little by little I might .... But hold on a minute. You said I'd made a deal to go in with you on this Llorando play, or whatever it is?"

"It's all right, son. I figured it was the liquor talking, and not you. Besides, I think the whole deal's off anyway. Like I told you, I'm waiting for Ted Marshfield to tell me about it out here tonight. Wonder what's keeping him?"

"Whatever he says, I think you'd be smart to cool yourself out of it, too. I remember now reading about Dick Corliss. He goes to trial next month."

Schaefer shrugged his wide shoulders.

"What the hell! You and I took bigger chances many's the time, and for less jack. And if I'm in trouble, I'll have company. Besides—" He signaled the passing waiter. "Bourbon and bayou water," he directed. "I wish that guy would show up. He's 'way past due."

The waiter returned with two small glasses on a tray. He was followed by a nattily dressed, slender young man, who wore a light topcoat, and carried a soft fedora hat in his hand.

"Isn't this Captain Schaefer?" he asked the stocky flier.

"It's not his brother, Mac," chuckled Schaefer. "You from Marshfield?"

"In a way I suppose I am," replied the newcomer affably. He reached into the breast pocket of his coat, brought out a small leather billfold and flipped it open to show the identification card held there beneath a celluloid cover. The flier gave a wolf-whistle. Ruth turned a glance of almost agonized

298

appeal on Sabin, who reached along the edge of the table to cover her hand with his.

"So Ted Marshfield brought you out here?" Schaefer was saying. "Well, now, whaddaya know!"

"Perhaps it would be more accurate to say that we brought him out. He's in our car."

Schaefer turned to Sabin and Ruth.

"Give a look," he said, jerking a stubby thumb at the young man with the topcoat. "A G-man, no less. Sorry to have to rush off like this. You must come see me some time." He addressed the newcomer. "Okay, Nature Boy. Leave us go."

The young man made no move.

"This gentleman and the young lady, are they in your—party?"

"Nope. Never a bit." He grinned at Ruth. "Not that you wouldn't make a grand-looking gun-moll, lady; but I guess that's only in the radio serials." To the agent he added, "Just some friends I haven't seen for two years. So let's quit standing around and wiping egg off our faces."

The agent gestured for Schaefer to precede him. Hauling the beret out of his hip pocket, the flier started toward the entrance, tossing a casual, "See you in the gumbo some time!" over his shoulder.

Without loosening his protective clasp on Ruth's hand, Sabin had risen too. Now he slowly reseated himself. She had continued to sit very still, listening intently, throughout the latter part of Schaefer's long talk with Sabin, and she had not stirred nor spoken, even after the appearance of the agent. Sabin looked at her with undisguised admiration.

"Good girl," he said slowly. "Of course, you're more than that—you're a grand girl. But it doesn't make me any too happy to keep putting you through these endurance tests, even if you do meet them magnificently. As I said a while back, I'll try to make all this up to you some time. But at the moment, you'd like to go home, wouldn't you?"

"Yes, if you'd like to take me. But if you feel as if you could go on with your dinner—"

"No, I'm afraid I couldn't. You'll begin to think that's another habit of mine—bringing meals to an abrupt end."

"You've got so many nice habits, Sabin—writing notes and sending presents and talking about places and people in a way that shows you know what they really stand for—the way you did about Queen Isabella, for instance, and about Lady Levee. I hope you'll still write that song."

"All right. I'll make a bargain with you. When this mess is

all straightened out, we'll come to see Lady Levee again and I'll try to write the song, if you'll help me. But now we're going to take the short cut back to town. I know just how you're feeling about your uncle, even if you're too good a sport to tell me."

As they went swiftly back to New Orleans over the Airline, he did not refer to the agent's disturbing arrival, nor to Schaefer's account of the portentous happenings on Saturday night. But he did talk to her about Schaefer himself, admiringly, almost defensively.

"Just in case you've built up any wrong ideas about Dutch, he's quite a guy, in the best sense of the word. You mustn't be misled by his tough talk. That's only his way of covering up a really sensitive nature. I was flying formation with him one time—just the two of us—when I was being checked out on the C-47's. He was my instructor and we were on instruments. Suddenly over the headset came the rolling verses of 'Ozymandias'—the whole works. You can't imagine how stately it sounded—'My name is Ozymandias, King of Kings. Look on my works, ye mighty, and despair.' And it was Dutch. He'd forgotten to turn off his radio. So he had me for his audience and when he finished, I gave him the big bravo, and was he ever boiling! Just to prove to me that he wasn't the sort of chap who recited poetry, he picked a fight with me that same evening; and that was the time he blacked one of my eyes, so if I hung a shiner on him the other night, it just evened the score.

"Then there was this other time ...."

Sabin spun out the recital of Dutch Schaefer's exploits until they entered the courtyard of Foxworth's house. Looking up, Ruth noticed the lighted library windows.

"Why, I believe Uncle's home now!" she exclaimed. "When everyone's out, Downes leaves just enough lamps lighted to make the house look cheerful and inviting—not an illumination like that. And if Uncle *is* home, then there's nothing more for me to worry about—not at the moment anyway. Won't you come in?"

"Thanks. But I'm sure you'd rather see him by yourself."

"No, I wouldn't. I'd really like to have you come. Of course, I want him to know what we've heard this evening and you could tell him so much better than I could."

"I doubt it. And I doubt whether your uncle needs to have anything about this night's doings blueprinted for him. Give him your own impressions; that's all he'll need and what he'll like best. And incidentally, if you feel it'll help at all to tell

300

him about Saturday night—my part of the bucket of blood, I mean—well, you're welcome to. It won't do me any harm. I thought perhaps I ought to clear up that point. Because, being the kind of a girl you are, you could be afraid it might, and in that case you wouldn't mention it."

"I would have been afraid, if you hadn't told me. Thanks, Sabin, for everything. And we have another date with Lady Levee. Don't forget that."

"Not a chance. If all goes well, we might make it some time early next week. If all doesn't go well, it'll just be a pleasure postponed, as far as I'm concerned. But 'What's to come is still unsure,' and generally speaking, I subscribe to the theory that 'In delay there lies no plenty.' What about you?"

"Well, I recognize the quotation, if that's what you mean. But I'm not in the habit of acting upon it."

"I didn't suppose you were. But I thought perhaps you'd make an exception tonight."

If Russ hadn't gone off the way he did, I'd put a quick stop to this sort of repartee, Ruth told herself honestly. *It always ends the same way.* But her lack of illusion did not prevent her from finding Sabin's approach extremely persuasive and its results unexpectedly stimulating. The kiss which inevitably brought their argument to a conclusion was light rather than intense; but if not actually loverlike, it was very far from being neutral in character and, a little breathlessly, Ruth eluded a repetition of it. Sabin made no effort to hold her against her will; at the same time, she knew that another night there would be no discussion. He would take his kiss for granted. And she could still feel the fire of the first one when she bade him a swift good night, her exhilaration not untinged by perturbation.

I mustn't forget to tell Uncle about Tossie, she said to herself, as she went in the door. *I'd better do that first of all. If I don't, I might forget all about it. There are so many more important things on my mind. That is, so many things that are more important to me. But that's supremely important to her. It might even be a matter of life and death.* She went rapidly across the entrance hall to the stairway, intent on reaching the library without a moment's unnecessary delay, but a radiogram, prominently placed on the hall table, arrested her attention. Strange that it should have escaped her uncle's notice, when he came in—it was probably very important; it might even contain further alarming news. She picked it up to take with her and saw, to her surprise, that it was addressed to her. Laying down her gloves and evening bag, she ripped it open.

YOU SAID YOU UNDERSTOOD. PLEASE PROVE IT BY TAKING FIRST POSSIBLE PLANE TO TEGUCI-GALPA AND MARRYING ME THERE. ANSWER BOTH CARE OF AMERICAN EMBASSY AND TO SHIP. ALL MY LOVE.

RUSS.

At first she stared incredulously at the words with such utter disbelief in their reality that she was only half aware of their significance. As she slowly grasped this, the impact of their meaning staggered her. She sank down on the stairs, her vision blurring, her hands trembling so that she could hardly hold the flimsy sheet of paper with its overwhelming message. Then she heard someone calling her, lovingly but impellingly.

"Ruth! My dear child, are you there?"

There was no mistaking the voice, the one that for years had been dearer to her than any other in the world. Still blinded by happy tears, she leaped to her feet and ran up the stairs. Before she reached the landing, she ran straight into the arms of Richard Huntington.

19

How Orson Foxworth explained
to Richard Huntington that
he was not in trouble—

January 10, 1948

SHE CLUNG to him wordlessly, so shaken by mingled apprehension, amazement, and triumphant joy that she was beyond
speech. Not only her thoughts were chaotic; she was in
tumult to the very depths of her being. The endearing voice,
the gentle embrace finally soothed her. She raised her head to
look at him and in his quiet face found the answer to her
first question.

"You've come on account of Uncle, haven't you, Father?"

"Yes. But don't be frightened, Ruth."

"Is he here?"

"No, he hasn't come in yet. But I'm not troubled about
that—it isn't really late. And I'll be glad to have a visit with
you before I see him. I've missed you very much."

"And I've missed you. Oh, Father—"

"Shan't we go into the library, Ruth, where we can sit
down and talk in comfort? I'd suggest a drink too. You look
to me as if you needed one."

"Perhaps I did before I found you. But now that you're
here, I know that everything's going to be all right. When
....? How ....?"

"About four hours ago, in an Army plane. Incidentally,
your mother's well and sends her love .... I had my own
reasons for feeling it would be just as well if I didn't announce my impending arrival from Washington. But I did
telephone from Moisant Airport. Downes answered and said
he was sure it would be perfectly convenient to put me up.

He's done very well by me, dinner and all, though he warned me beforehand that you and Orson were both dining out—he didn't know where or with whom in either case. I thought you might be together. But evidently you weren't."

"No. I've been dining at the Bar-None Ranch on the River Road with a most extraordinary man named Sabin Duplessis."

"You mean the flier?"

"Why yes! Do you know him?"

"Slightly. I seem to know a good many people, at least slightly, these days. And your uncle . . . .?"

"I haven't the remotest idea. Does it matter?"

"Not particularly. He'll probably be along presently and tell us himself, in any case."

While they talked, Richard Huntington had been slowly guiding his stepdaughter in the direction of the library, his arm still around her. When they reached it, he released her and drew her cape from her shoulders. Then he looked down at the envelope she was still holding.

"I see you found your radiogram all right. I propped it up for you myself, against that vase of camellias. I thought you might overlook it, if it were just left lying on the table. And I also thought that it might be important."

"It's the most important message I ever had in my life. I want to talk with you about that, too. Oh, Father, there are so many things I want to talk with you about!"

"Well, what do you want to talk with me about first?"

"This," she said, handing him the radiogram.

With the deliberation which characterized all his movements, he unfolded the message and read it. Then he replaced it in its envelope.

" 'Russ,' " he said. "That, I suppose, would be Russell Aldridge, the archeologist."

"Yes. Do you know him too?"

"Certainly. But my knowledge of him isn't as comprehensive as I thought it was. I didn't know he was in love with you."

"I didn't either. That is, I thought—I hoped—and then he went away."

"When did all this happen?"

"I met him—let me see—why, it was just a week ago tonight! Uncle gave a dinner at Antoine's. The next morning, Russ sent me flowers and that same afternoon he came to call. Uncle was out, as usual, so bye and bye Russ and I went dancing. Then Sunday, he took me out to Lacombe for the day. And Tuesday was the Twelfth Night Ball. Wednesday he

304

couldn't come to see me on account of that awful scientific meeting, and yesterday—no, it was just this morning, he went away."

"My information was even more incomplete than I thought. I didn't know you were in love with him. But you skipped Monday in your calender of events."

"Yes. I didn't see Russ Monday. That was the day of Odile St. Amant's funeral. Did you know about that? About—her— her death, I mean, and her mother and—"

"Yes. I know about it. And I want to talk to you about it—later. But let's stick to the subject of Aldridge for the moment. And as I said before, I think you need a drink. Let me fix it for you, and then we'll really get settled."

Huntington motioned toward one of the big armchairs by the hearth, and Ruth crossed the room and sat down, watching him while he measured and mixed the whiskey and soda. She had always looked at him with loving eyes, but never had he seemed more comforting, more dear, more necessary to her than he did as he stood there, wearing, with accustomed ease, the same beautifully tailored clothes which he had worn for some time already, and performing with simplicity the same sort of homely and heartening task, which she had seen him perform hundreds of other times. Her tension had eased, her fears had vanished; her tumultuous thoughts had become rational again; even her joy over the assurance of mutual love between her and Russell Aldridge had taken on a steadier and more tranquil quality. With a wonder which she had often felt before, she sought for the outward and visible signs of that inward and spiritual grace which Richard Huntington, by his mere presence, seemed to impart to his surroundings and share with everyone with whom he came in contact. He was not a handsome man, nor was his bearing impressive. He was a little too tall for his weight and though he had fine eyes, his features were otherwise unremarkable. Comparing him with the other men of whom she had recently seen most, Ruth realized that he lacked Foxworth's authority, St. Amant's magnetism, Aldridge's driving purpose, Perrault's humanitarianism, Racina's mental agility, and Duplessis' volatile charm. He was not the product of an older culture than the archeologist, nor did he have a more lofty sense of integrity than the doctor. Yet something set him apart, even from these. Was it a larger tolerance, a more profound wisdom, a greater understanding —or that indestructible faith in both God and man which his friends and enemies alike said would some time be his undoing?

She could not tell and she did not greatly care. Presently she ceased to speculate on the qualities which made him seem so outstanding and relaxed from the sheer gladness in his companionship. He handed her the drink which he had prepared for her, waited for her assurance that it suited her, and then, mixing one for himself, took a chair opposite hers. They had both sipped away for some moments before he spoke to her again.

"About Aldridge," he said at last. "The answer to that question is your first consideration. So it's my first consideration, too, though we'll have to go back to the subject of the Lalande family later. Well, you've waited a long time to fall in love, Ruth, and Lord knows it hasn't been for any lack of opportunity. I haven't tried to keep track of all your suitors, the way your mother has. I knew it wasn't worth the trouble. But I haven't forgotten that Greek attaché in Berne, or the Bolivian president's nephew, or that young Congressman from West Virginia—to mention just a few who've given me uneasy moments. However, I don't feel especially uneasy now. I don't know a single thing to Aldridge's discredit—quite the contrary. He's about as fine as they come. Besides, your mother's kept saying that if you didn't meet your fate in New Orleans, you never would, and I was inclined to agree with her. Now you have. That's what she hoped would happen, unless I'm terribly mistaken. She'll be very much pleased. And I don't need to tell you that whatever pleases your mother generally pleases me, too."

"You say you don't know anything to Russ' discredit. Of course, I don't either. I think he's—well, I think he's wonderful. But just the same—"

"Just the same he's very keen on his job. And it happens to be one that keeps him moving around to all kinds of strange places. Yes, that's true. I don't suppose you'd have chosen Tegucigalpa for a honeymoon, or that you'd look forward, with any great degree of anticipation, to moving from there to Cuzco and from Cuzco to Merida and so on—much less to bringing up a family under those conditions. However, you've been to all sorts of strange places with me, Ruth. And the stranger they were, the better you liked them."

"Yes, Father. But you shared them with me. And Russ—"

"Yes, I suppose Russ was so keen on this particular expedition that he started off, almost as fast as if he'd been shot out of a gun, the minute he found things were set for him to go. Without—well, without asking you how you felt about it, without apparently considering you at all. But you see, he took it for granted you'd understand. That shows how he felt about *you*. If he hadn't admired you tremendously, if he hadn't loved you very greatly, he wouldn't have been so sure he could count on you."

Ruth set down her glass and, taking one of the camellias from the vase on the end table by her chair, began to pull off its petals.

"Perhaps that's true," she said slowly. "But you know, Father, girls *like* to be considered. They like to be *told* they're loved. They like to be *shown* they are by—well, by affectionate actions." She swallowed hard and went on. "Besides, it isn't just a case of whether he can depend on me, is it? Isn't it also a case of whether I can depend on him?"

Her voice shook a little as she asked the question. But though Richard Huntington answered her gently, he did not do so evasively.

"Depend on him for what? I don't think you can depend on him to change his way of life or give up the great opportunities of his profession for you. I don't think you can depend on him to feel that because he's invited you to something like a Carnival Ball, he shouldn't take advantage of a chance to rediscover something no one's seen in hundreds of years. But the next question is, do you think you'd want the kind of man who would? Because he wouldn't be the same kind of a man, in other ways, that Aldridge is. And, as far as I can make out, he is the kind you want. I'll go further than that. I'll say he's not only the kind you want, he's the man you want. Isn't he? Because, if he isn't, I don't see the use in carrying on this discussion any longer."

"He—I—yes, he is."

"All right. I thought so. Then let me tell you the ways I think you can depend on him. I think you can depend on him to make you proud of him—both of his character and of his accomplishments. You'll never have to apologize for him, to yourself, or to anyone else. I think you can depend on him to share a very full, rich, adventurous life with you. Oh, I don't mean there won't be pretty hard periods of waiting around for him in hot mongrel ports and God-forsaken cities so small they're hardly on the map! He won't be able to take you with him every time he goes burrowing into a cave on some island or excavating some ruin in the jungle. But you can depend on him to come back to you every chance he gets. You can depend on him to make you feel that those mongrel ports and God-forsaken cities seem like home to him because you're there. Because I believe you can depend on him to love you—very sincerely, very steadfastly, very faithfully. I've never thought you had a jealous disposition. That's

307

one of the reasons I'm so fond of you. I haven't much more use for a jealous woman than for a stupid one—after all, they're sisters under the skin. But if the green-eyed monster is getting after you, at this late day, let me tell you something based on what I've observed over a long period of years: it's a lot better for a woman to be jealous of her husband's job than of some other interests he might acquire. And I don't think Aldridge is the type that's likely to acquire those. Especially if he's married to a girl like you."

Ruth was still pulling petals off her camellia. But she had almost reached the end. Speaking more swiftly than was his habit, Richard Huntington went on.

"I don't believe you can depend on him to remember your birthdays, or to notice that you're wearing a new dress, or even to kiss you, at all the indicated moments. But he'll remember other things, he'll notice other things, and when he does kiss you, it'll mean something. It won't be from force of habit, and it won't be just because of pleasant propinquity. He's asked you to marry him, Ruth. That one bare demand, coming from a man like Aldridge, is worth all the idle, empty compliments in the world. He's asked you to reaffirm your statement that you understand. He's counting on you to do it. You can't let him down, not if you're half the woman I think you are. If you aren't, if you don't believe what I'm telling you—stay in New Orleans and go on having pleasant outings with Sabin Duplessis and all the other personable young men— not that I think these outings would lead to anything you'd really be interested in, if the past is any indication of the future. So, if you are my kind of a girl, if you do believe me—how soon could you be ready to leave for Tegucigalpa?"

She could be ready to leave, she assured him, the next morning. But they were both agreed that it should not be as soon as that. Ruth's mother would want to go to Honduras with her—an embassy wedding would fulfill some of her fondest hopes!—and she must be given time to buy just the right wedding dress, just the right trousseau, before starting for New Orleans. Besides, Huntington would like to talk over final arrangements, by long distance, with the American Ambassador at Tegucigalpa, who had been a classmate of his at "the" University. If possible, Huntington wanted to give Ruth away himself; he would have to confer with the Secretary of State and perhaps even with the President to see if he could extend his absence from Washington. Then there were those other grave questions, which were responsible for his presence in New Orleans and which must be settled.

They were still talking the situation over, when Orson Foxworth, looking remarkably debonair, youthful, and sprightly, came into the library shortly after midnight. Well, this was a pleasant surprise, he said heartily, wringing Huntington's hand. An Army plane, eh? Why, if he had had any idea . . . . ! He and Francisco Darcoa had been deep in consultation at dinner time, and so Francisco had suggested . . . . Yes, a very fine old house on Coliseum Street. Not what you would call pretentious, but extremely elegant. Elegant was the right word for it, wasn't it, Ruth? She had been there to lunch herself, that same day. So she would know, he explained to his brother-in-law. Well, he had stayed for dinner, and then somehow the conference had gone on and on . . . . How was the reception at the French Consulate?

"It was very pleasant thanks, Uncle. Lots of people asked for you. And Doctor Perrault sent you a message about Tossie. He thinks it's imperative she should be released, on account of her health. He wants to talk to you and your lawyer as soon as possible."

"All right, I'll give him a ring right away—or maybe the first thing in the morning would be better. Did you enjoy the rest of your outing?"

"Well, I enjoyed the ride to the Bar-None even more than I did the reception. Sabin Duplessis is going to write a song about the River Road."

"The hell he is!"

"Yes, it's got a name already . . . . And we went to see the first palomino colt of the season."

"You did! How's my friend, Ad Given Davis?"

"He's fine. And we ran into another friend of yours, a man Sabin called Dutch. His last name's Schaefer. I never found out what his first name really is. He was at the bar, drinking Bourbon and bayou water."

"His first name's Aloys. And that's always been too much of a load. Well, so he was at the Bar-None too."

"Yes, he sat with Sabin and me while we had dinner. He said he'd had his already. But he and Sabin are old cronies— Joe'd already told me that. They'd run into each other almost everywhere else in the world, so neither of them seemed to think it was the least strange that they should happen to meet at the Bar-None Ranch."

"It isn't, at that. And I should think Dutch might have added considerably to the evening's entertainment, from your point of view. I don't know how Sabin would have felt about having him butt in."

"Oh, Sabin suggested that he should join us. They talked a lot about old times—also about an extraordinary outing they'd had together last Saturday. I got so excited, just listening to them, that I had quite a letdown afterwards. I was actually limp, by the time Sabin and I started home. And then I found Father here—not to mention a radiogram from Russ asking me to marry him. So all in all, it's been a pretty tall evening."

"You found a radiogram from Aldridge asking you to marry him!" Foxworth exclaimed, completely disregarding the rest of her remarks. "Why, you've only known him a week!"

"Yes, but I'm going to radio back saying I will. Then as soon as I've sent my message, I think I'll run along to bed. Father can explain to you about Russ—between us, the Assistant Secretary and I seem to have that situation pretty well in hand. And perhaps you'll explain to him about your connection with Dutch—from something Mr. Schaefer said, I gathered it was even more exciting than Sabin's. And I have a queer idea that one of the reasons Father's down here is because he'd like to have you tell him about it. But in any case, you don't need me around. I know you and he would rather have a nice masculine talkfest by yourselves. And besides, I'm really all in."

She kissed them both affectionately, picked up her various small belongings, and left the room, turning, just as she reached the door, to smile back at them. Huntington returned her smile, and, declining Foxworth's offer of a satiny perfecto, took a richly colored meerschaum out of his coat pocket and packed it carefully from a worn, chamois pouch. Then he tipped a paper spill to the embers in the fireplace and, with meticulous care, applied the wisp of flame to the tamped tobacco and puffed away for a few minutes in experimental silence.

"I don't know what you think of Ruth," he remarked, after he was satisfied that the pipe was drawing properly, "but I'm not only very fond of her; I'm very proud of her. Not many girls—at least not many I know—would have bowed themselves out of the picture as adroitly, or as gracefully, as she did just now. Of course, she'd have given anything to stay. And I think you'll agree, Orson, that it isn't characteristically feminine to leave a family conference without a hint from some male participant, let alone leaving it with such aplomb."

"I'll cheerfully concede that Ruth's a great credit to your training," Foxworth replied, himself lighting a perfecto. "But I don't know why she should have especially wanted to stay. And I think she was telling the truth when she said she was tired. There's no reason why she shouldn't be. She's put in a pretty full day."

"Just the same, she has the normal amount of feminine curiosity, in spite of that general superiority to most of her sex which I've just been praising. And she's worried about you, Orson."

"She needn't be. And I disagree with you there too. If she's actually decided to marry Russ Aldridge, her mind's on him, not on me. Do you really approve her rushing into a match like that?"

"Yes, under all the circumstances. I'll explain that situation to you, as I see it, later on, since she's asked me to. But first, if you don't mind, I'd like to hear the other explanation she suggested—the one about Dutch Schaefer. And when we understand each other on that score, there's still another matter I'd like to bring up."

"Well, I know Dutch Schaefer and he's really one for the books. I've had various dealings with him, off and on, just as Sabin Duplessis evidently has. They're not important—at least I don't see them that way and I don't believe you would. But they are rather complicated. Couldn't we postpone a discussion of them and of that other matter, whatever it is, until morning? I only ask because, like Ruth, I've had a rather rugged day and you must be pretty well bushed from your trip. Besides, now that you've finally got down here, I hope you're not going to rush right off again. I should think that tomorrow——"

"If I hadn't thought these matters were urgent, I wouldn't have asked the Secretary of Defense for his plane. And if he hadn't agreed with me, he wouldn't have been so ready to turn it over to me."

"This is the first I've heard about that Army plane being the Secretary's own—you must have spilled that part of your story to Ruth before I came in. All right then, let's have it. But perhaps we can save time if I tell you I think I know why you're here and why you don't want to wait until morning to talk to me about some trouble you believe I'm in."

"Perhaps. Suppose you do tell me. Because I do believe you're in trouble and I want to help, if possible."

"All right. You've been hearing rumors that something's about to happen down in Llorando, and that I'm behind it all. And you're going to tell me that the days of William Walker and Lee Christmas and the other gay old *filibusteros* are gone for keeps, and that I'm acting as though Taft were still president with Philander Knox as Secretary of State, negotiating dollar-diplomacy treaties all over the shop."

Momentarily Huntington's fine eyes twinkled. With practiced and affectionate ease, he wrapped the fingers of his right hand about the bowl of his pipe and pointed the stem at his brother-in-law.

"What if I did tell you that, since it happens to be true? We've come a long ways since the big powers kept gunboats around to scare some small government which might offend a foreign fruit company, mining syndicate, or what-have-you—though, at the same time, we were conveniently blind when a revolution against one of these same governments was financed in the United States."

"Well, what's all that got to do with me?"

"If you want the details, this is what it's got to do with you," Richard Huntington said quietly. He spread out the fingers of his left hand, and tapped them, one at a time, with the stem of his pipe as he enumerated. "You have two transport planes at Callendar Field in New Orleans, an LST loaded with tanks that are masquerading as agricultural tractors in Gulfport, a fleet of small, shallow-draft landing lighters in Wolf River, and a barge of aviation gasoline in the Intracoastal Canal near Morgan City. We've a pretty complete dossier on it all, together with ostensible destination, actual destination, and tentative schedules of departure. Central Intelligence has done quite a job, with the help of the FBI and local peace officers."

Foxworth laughed carelessly.

"Central Intelligence could have saved itself a lot of trouble, Richard," he retorted, "by asking me about those things. I'd have given them the facts. Apparently, you've no idea how easily a light tank can be transformed into a bulldozer or a tractor. If you put in an order for agricultural machinery these days, you'll wait at least nine months for delivery. Whereas we can bid in this government surplus and get delivery at once, convert it, and go to town half a year sooner than if we'd try to buy the stuff in the open market."

"And the landing craft? I suppose you've a plausible explanation for those?"

"Plausible or not, it's true. Those small landing boats will be the equivalent of one mobile conveyor dock at any new port we choose to establish. They can run right up onto a beach and back off. With tractors to bring the stems of

312

bananas down to the beach over roads our bulldozers will clear, and landing craft to lighter them out to the ships of the Blue Fleet, we can begin doing business in a tenth of the time—and at about one-tenth of the cost—that would be required for setting up a conventional port facility from scratch."

"Orson, you've never lied to me. So I take it for granted that what you tell me is literally true, as far as it goes. But you haven't said that's the only idea you had in mind, and I trust you won't. Because you did have another idea, and it's one you wouldn't have shared, cheerfully or otherwise, with our Intelligence Section. That idea was to oust the administration at Llorando, and to use planes, landing craft, tanks, and all the rest to do the job if need be."

"So you've come down here to tell me, in effect, to be a good boy. Richard, Richard, doesn't it strike you if that were my purpose, neither you nor the rest of the Literary and Needlework Guild in the State Department could turn me from it?"

The fine eyes were not twinkling now.

"I came down here, Orson, to save you from going to prison—if possible. That is where you were headed. That is where, quite conceivably, you are still headed . . . . No! Hear me out, please!" Huntington drew a slip of paper from a billfold and, consulting it from time to time, went on. "Tonight the following men were taken into custody by federal and local officers, working in teams: Cecil Brewster, arrested in Port Arthur; Vicente Gutierrez, arrested in Tampa; Aloys Schaefer, formerly a captain in the Army's transport corps, arrested in New Orleans—to be still more exact, in the last named case, at the Bar-None Ranch on the River Road, in the presence of my stepdaughter and her escort of the evening."

Foxworth laughed scornfully. "Of course, I'm extremely sorry that anything should have happened to mar an evening's outing for your stepdaughter, let alone her escort of the evening. I don't know that it did though. I think Ruth rather likes excitement and I know damn well Duplessis does. But why in hell should these men have been arrested? For violating the neutrality laws? Why, they'll be out by noon! Before noon, in all human likelihood. There isn't a ghost of a chance to make that charge stick against any of my men."

"You've seen to that, I assume. That's what you mean, isn't it? But they're not charged under the neutrality act."

"What other charges could possibly be brought?"

"One of them—and I think it's your friend Schaefer—is

313

charged with stealing an automobile and transporting it across state lines. You see, the car in which he came to New Orleans from Mobile the other day—Saturday morning, wasn't it?—belonged to some one else."

"Certainly. It was loaned to him by a friend. I happen to know the circumstances because Dutch asked me to arrange for the car to be returned in the event he were unable to drive it back before leaving for Puerto de Oro."

"Yes, yes. To be sure. You'd be genuinely astonished if I told you who loaned that automobile. For naturally, it's no trick at all to scrape acquaintance with a convivial, hail-fellow-well-met chap like Schaefer. And it didn't strike Schaefer as the least bit odd that a man he'd met only five or six days before should offer him the loan of a car. It's the sort of offer Schaefer himself would make if the circumstances had been reversed. But as soon as Schaefer had driven from Mobile to New Orleans, crossing two state lines en route, the 'friend' went to the Mobile police and reported the theft of his car. Schaefer won't be convicted, I grant you. We'll see to that. But he'll be under detention long enough, and securely enough, to satisfy what you called our Literary and Needlework Guild. Oh, quite safely, I can promise you. As for Brewster, he was arrested on a New Jersey warrant. I've forgotten the precise nature of the charge, for that really is a matter of no consequence. He's being held for extradition, and even if the charge is simply dropped after all the red tape's been unwound, a lot of time will pass in the process. If my memory serves me right, the third man, Gutierrez, was found with stolen property in his possession. Another recent friend, who was called out of town suddenly, asked if it would be all right to have his laundry delivered to Gutierrez, at his diggings, and held there till he returned. Quite a packet of valuables was concealed in that bundle of shirts. When the time comes, the friend will return, and prove Gutierrez completely innocent. Until that time, however, all those elaborate precautions to safeguard these adventurous souls against any charge of having violated the neutrality act will be as useful as an anchor to a drowning man."

To Huntington's surprise, Foxworth nodded with every evidence of lively approval.

"Somebody's been making brains for you boys up there," he said cordially. "Of course, it's illegal as all hell. Uncle Joe and his Politburo and the whole NKVD never pulled a gaudier set of frame-ups on the day before one of their fair, free, and democratic elections in Poland or Rumania. My compliments to you and the rest of the Guild."

For the first time, Huntington appeared to be puzzled. The glance he turned on Foxworth indicated some bewilderment.

"I confess that's hardly the reaction I expected," he said slowly. "We have your three key men in custody, and by the way, there are keepers on every item of what you were preparing to send out—the planes, barges, landing craft, and all. Your expedition really has been immobilized."

Foxworth laughed. "You keep talking about the expedition. I give you my word there isn't going to be any. If you and all the cloak and dagger boys had stayed in Washington, if Dutch and Brewster and 'Cente were as free as the birds this minute, there still wouldn't be any expedition. You've had all your trouble for laughs and nothing more. Just as a sporting question, however, what was the real idea of framing up those fancy charges?"

Huntington rose, walked to the mantel, and tapped the dottle from his pipe into the grate. "To avert the almost incalculable damage your expedition might have done your country. We've spent many years and billions of dollars erasing from the consciousness of Latin America the memory of the old filibustering days. And in many ways that was the soundest investment the United States ever made. It paid off! Think back to the middle nineteen-thirties, Orson. The Nazis moved heaven and earth to sell Latin America on the idea that we were still power-grabbing imperialists. But they got exactly nowhere. Why? Because those people knew us as good neighbors and trusted us."

"But what's it got to do with me? Even if I were bent on turning a bunch of crooked grafters out of office at Llorando by a bit of extracurricular direct action, and if those people found out about it, the worst they'd give me would be a medal and a statue in the *Plaze de los Leones*."

Huntington quietly brushed this flippancy aside.

"Suppose we stick to the point," he said. "What the Nazis failed to do, the Russians are trying to do now. They haven't as efficient a propaganda organization, of course, but they've got a bigger and more zealous one. You asked me why those three men were arrested on trumped up charges? Because if they had been brought to book for violating the neutrality laws, there would have been a great new grist for the Soviet propagandists. 'See? Isn't this just what we've been telling you?' they'd be saying all over Latin America, 'The *Yanquis* talk about being good neighbors and yet one of their big

315

capitalists was about to overturn a neighbor's government because it wouldn't make the concessions he wanted.' And then they'd claim their agents in this country had been the ones to expose the plot so that even the *Yanqui* government had to take cognizance of it. But now——"

"But now you can turn those boys loose, Richard. I mean it. You've been admirably frank with me. I appreciate it. I'm going to return that compliment by being equally frank with you. There's to be no coup against the Llorando crowd because none is needed. I've already got what I was after in the first place. I can use the boats, the planes, the vehicles, and the fuel for just exactly what I told you—the pursuit of peace, dividends, and happiness."

"I'm still afraid we'll have to keep your Three Musketeers where they are, for the moment."

"Not for this or any other moment. Here's the situation. The Trans-Caribbean and the Great Blue Fleet had come to the point where they couldn't continue as separate organizations. Shipping costs are going out of sight. Just by way of illustration, a common seaman is paid about two hundred and forty dollars a month these days, plus overtime, plus food, plus medical care and so on. Under these conditions, and duplications of our facilities and the necessary division of the field between us was ruining us both. I'd suggested a merger long ago. But they brushed me off, figuring that with the Llorando crowd to back them up and keep them going, they could outlast my Blue Fleet, and then take me over on their terms. I decided to do whatever was necessary to take them over on mine, which meant that I would be the directing head of the combined outfits. If it was necessary to break their hold on Llorando to do it, well and good. I'd at least give that country a decent set of officials in place of the most rapacious for-sale plunderbund that ever ran a government. Meanwhile, knowing how valuable their stock would be as soon as that merger was accomplished, I'd been buying up blocks of it, here and there, as the occasion offered. That part of it had been handled by several sets of brokers, so that there'd be no leak. Coming back stateside this last time gave me my first chance to check up on the totals, and bless Pat! if I didn't have enough of their stock so that if I could get any one of their three big stockholders to come in with me, we could have complete control between us, and vote the merger into existence without further ado. Well, I've got my one big stockholder. I've got Francisco Darcoa."

The glow of supreme satisfaction which had illumined Foxworth's face when he first came in and which since then had faded while he argued and expostulated, now returned to it. He smiled expansively at his brother-in-law.

"Francisco and I see eye to eye in this matter," he announced triumphantly. "I told you I'd been dining with him and his daughter. No, I'm not sure that I mentioned his daughter before, but she was there, too. She made some excellent suggestions. She's quite a remarkable girl, Richard. And incidentally, a very beautiful one. Well, you'll be seeing her for yourself—they're coming here for dinner tomorrow night. As for the merger, it's as good as accomplished right now. And once it is—well, we needn't go into that. So you've really had your trip for your pains, Richard. I'm not in trouble, I'm not facing the prospect of telling it to a judge, a jury, and ultimately to a penitentiary warden—and now I think we really can save the rest of the discussion till tomorrow. As for the boys, a night in jail won't hurt them. You can have the charges dropped in the morning, and they won't lose anything by—"

Huntington laid down his pipe.

"One moment, Orson. What you've said is pleasant hearing. So much so that I hate to be the bearer of grim tidings. But you must realize that these arrests alone wouldn't have brought me posthaste to New Orleans. Up to this point, everything we've discussed could have been handled—was handled in fact—from Washington. Let's see if I can put it to you without sounding too much like an ambitious *deus ex machina*. For I'm here to help you, in every way I can."

"Hell, Richard, I'm all right. Nothing to worry about, now."

"About the boys, as you call them. What I told you is quite correct. The federal agencies and local peace officers work in teams. We've been in touch with the New Orleans police, too. Because, you see, it might have been necessary to detain you, and we were more than a bit puzzled about what sort of charge we could bring against you. For obviously the kind we had used for your musketeers wouldn't do. So our people in Washington got in touch with a New Orleans detective captain, who had made quite a record when he went through the FBI School not many years ago. They knew him, d'you see, and that's how they found out that he wasn't the least bit puzzled as to a charge that could be brought against you."

Foxworth laid one arm along the ledge of the black marble mantel, as if for actual support.

"And this—this local man's name—?" he asked quietly.

"Queer sort of name. Don't think I recall a combination quite like it."

"Was it Murphy? Theophile Murphy?"

"Right. He offered to arrest you for the murder of a certain Odile St. Amant. And that was when I asked the Secretary if he'd send me down here in his plane. I didn't tell him about the charge. I only suggested it might be better if I were down here on the spot when things began to happen, so that, if worse came to worst, I could use our relationship to persuade you to see things from our point of view. But the first person I called on, after I landed, was Captain Theophile Murphy. He—well, he told me the whole story. He showed me just how reasonable he could make such a charge against you appear on the basis of the facts in hand. And—and—when I told him we were no longer interested in your detention he indicated that our interest, or the lack of it, was a matter of complete indifference to him. I gathered that some one—he didn't say who—was to be arrested on a murder charge today—Saturday. And that's what I had in mind when I said that if you were in deep trouble, I hoped I could be of help."

20

How Tossie Pride was released from the Orleans Parish Prison at noon—

January 10, 1948

THE NEXT morning, over a second cup of coffee, Richard Huntington brought his brother-in-law back to the unfinished topic of the previous evening's discussion.

"Mighty thoughtful of you, Orson, to remember that in my part of the world we don't regard a crusty bun and a cup of *café au lait* as any reasonable facsimile of a breakfast," he said. "My own kitchen staff couldn't have done better by those stewed kidneys and scrambled eggs. It amazes me no end that details like that don't escape you. However——! Let's get at the real business of the meeting."

"Meaning?"

"This murder charge that appears to be pending against you."

"And against half a dozen others. Can't we go on the assumption that I am *not* guilty? It would be easier for me to approach the topic from that point of view, since I'm in the best possible position to know whether or not I killed a girl of whom I was genuinely fond."

"Certainly, certainly. I know you're not guilty. However, Murphy remains to be convinced. Our problem is to show him that he's in error. Believe me, I had no idea when our people got in touch with him that we'd run into any such situation as this. Now let's go at this thing logically. What reason has he, or does he give, for including you among his list of suspects?"

"A rather good one, I'm bound to admit. You'll understand, I didn't want any one to know about a certain conference I scheduled for last Saturday night, when it still looked as though I might have to take direct action against the T.C. crowd and their little friends at Llorando. So I rigged up a rather elaborate set of precautions to keep my whereabouts secret. I sent word to Ruth I wasn't feeling fit, and that I was going up to my rooms to catch up on some badly needed rest. I made it very plain I didn't want to be disturbed. Then, after she and Russ Aldridge left, I had Downes let me out the rear entrance, and went on about my business."

Huntington nodded, finished his coffee, and brought out pouch and pipe.

"And then this girl—this daughter of your friend Mrs. Lalande—committed suicide," he said, "and they felt that was an emergency which would warrant them in notifying you, and you weren't at home .... And later on, of course, you couldn't tell any one what you really had been up to. Quite a situation!"

"Well, it was really worse than that. Ruth and Russ Aldridge ran into a chap named Racina . . . ."

"I knew him in Washington. Good mind. Nobody's fool. Made quite a name for himself since then, writing books and magazine articles."

"That's the one. I suppose he's all right if you happen to like the type. I don't, particularly. However, he's got a good many contacts in Latin America, and Llorando was full of rumors. One of his friends down there asked him to find out how the land lay. That prompted him to go out looking for me. No use rehashing all the details. He pretty shrewdly surmised what I really was doing at the time, and told Ruth. She's a loyal kid, and the upshot of it was that she offered to bring him here to the house and prove him wrong."

"And unintentionally proved him right. It must have upset her quite a bit, too."

"No doubt. But of course she was much more upset by the message about Odile's death. And naturally, when I did come home, and found her and Aldridge waiting to give me the news, I dashed straight off to Richmond Place, without stopping for explanations."

"That's understandable," agreed Huntington. "Besides, at that time you believed it was a suicide. Naturally, you wouldn't foresee any connection between your punctured alibi and a possible murder charge. However, that's a short horse and soon curried. Let's go see this Captain Murphy and put an end to it."

"I'm afraid it's not quite as simple as that, Richard."

"Suppose you leave that part of it to my judgment. Once I explain matters to him, I'll promise there'll be no more talk of charges, indictments, or what have you."

"I'd like to share your confidence. But apart from that, there's the matter of my own dignity to consider. I don't care to put myself in the position of asking a policeman if he'll be good enough to drop his charges—and incidentally, there are really no charges against any one except Tossie . . . ."

He stopped abruptly, staring thoughtfully at his breakfast plate. Huntington made a vague gesture of dismissal.

"That's nonsense," he declared cheerfully. "This is the sort of thing that doesn't call for ceremonial procedure. Technically, you're right, of course. You don't have to prove your innocence. Murphy and Company have to prove your guilt. But my daughter has just found the man she wants to marry; and since he likewise wants to marry her, I don't want her happiness at this time marred. Let's get this matter straightened out as fast as possible without taking your pride into consideration."

Foxworth brought his palm down on the breakfast table with a force that caused the cups to rattle.

"You've made a pun without knowing it, Richard. Suppose we do disregard mine. We've still got Odile's old nurse to consider. She's in jail, charged with Odile's murder. You may remember Ruth spoke about it last night. And her name's Pride. Tossie Pride. She had no more to do with Odile's death than I did. I'm convinced of that. And Vance Perrault is troubled about her. Says she's too old and feeble to be kept in jail and wants me to have one of our lawyers get her out. He doesn't believe she killed Odile either, of course."

"On what grounds was she arrested at all?"

"Her fingerprints were on the gun. It's a long story, and doesn't make any particular difference. But we will go see this man Murphy, just as you suggested, about getting Tossie released. We'll put it to him man to man, first, with Vance Perrault present to back up my statement about her health. Remind me to telephone Vance to meet us at headquarters. But first of all, I want to telephone Ted Marshfield, and have him get everything set, so that if Murphy won't see reason, Ted can get out a writ of *habeas corpus* or an *instanter mandamus* or whatever the hell it is. One way or another, we'll have Tossie out from behind the bars by noon. And in the meantime, since you'll be there anyway, if you want to bring up the subject of any charges against me, why I can't stop you. Matter of fact, we'll tell Perrault and Ted to meet us there at eleven, and we'll get there at ten-thirty. Then while we're waiting around for them, and griping because they're late, you can do your stuff—and I hope it works. Just between us, I'll be damned glad to be able to say to Clarinda

Darcoa—but that can wait .... Downes! Oh, Downes! Tell Arnaldo to have the car ready for Mr. Huntington and myself in fifteen minutes, and get Doctor Perrault on the telephone for me. Fifteen minutes give you time enough, Richard?"

"As a matter of fact, Captain Murphy," Richard Huntington was saying, "your only reason for entertaining any suspicions concerning Mr. Foxworth's connection with this lamentable affair is his failure, or his refusal—call it what you will—to account for his whereabouts last Saturday night. Am I correct in saying that?"

For some moments Murphy carefully considered Huntington's inquiry. The three men were seated about the desk of the detective chief, in the room to which Toe Murphy had ushered them on their arrival. ("The Chief was up to all hours this morning on an out-of-town case," Toe had explained. "He won't be down until later, so we can use his place.") The room was plain, but scrupulously neat, in contrast to the generally untidy appearance of the outer office. A framed set of resolutions from a Peace Officers' convention was hung on one wall. On the desk were a few souvenirs of past captures. A silver-plated dagger served as an envelope opener and this was flanked by a cigar lighter in the shape of an airplane propeller.

"Mr. Foxworth's lack of explanation was the main thing all right," Toe admitted, fingering the dagger. "But after all, there were others. That business of coming right into the house without knocking or ringing, for instance, and explaining that the door had been left unlatched, so that anybody could have gotten in. And then there was that story cooked up in advance, for what was bound to be a phony alibi."

"Well, Captain, I'm here to give you an account of my brother-in-law's whereabouts last Saturday night." Orson Foxworth suddenly sat up very straight in his chair. Huntington shot him a quizzical glance, withdrew from an inner pocket a folded sheet of paper, and having adjusted horn-rimmed glasses to his satisfaction, addressed Toe Murphy, with an occasional glance at the closely-spaced typescript.

"Here we are: Mr. Foxworth left his house on Toulouse Street a little before seven; specifically, at six fifty-eight P.M. He was driven to the mouth of Bayou St. John at the lake front, arriving there at seven forty-six, and was waiting in his car, which was parked off the boulevard until eight oh two, when another car drew up alongside. In company with Ted Marshfield, who had come in this second car, he entered a speedboat which had been moored to the seawall's extension into the bayou. This boat took off out into the lake, and arrived at the yacht *Myrtis II,* which Mr. Foxworth and Mr. Marshfield boarded at eight twenty-three, remaining there until nine twenty-nine."

He dropped the paper into his lap and looked full at Murphy. "I can give you the names of the other persons who were aboard, and who can testify to Mr. Foxworth's presence there, if it should be necessary to do so. One of them, Mr. Marshfield, who accompanied him aboard, but did not return with him, will be here in a few moments with Doctor Perrault in connection with the request for the release of Tossie Pride. You can confirm what I've just said from him, if you feel it's necessary to do so."

"So far as it goes, let's leave it stand. But I mean, so far as it goes," Murphy replied guardedly. "What about after nine-thirty? That's the important part."

"The speedboat left the *Myrtis* at that time, and returned to the mouth of Bayou St. John at two minutes after one. Mrs. St. Amant died sometime between the departure of Mr. Foxworth from the yacht *Myrtis,* and his arrival on shore at the mouth of Bayou St. John, where his car was waiting for him. It is your conviction that she did not commit suicide, but was murdered. Accepting your view that this was a murder, it was committed while Orson Foxworth was out on Lake Pontchartrain. Doesn't that fact render it impossible for you to entertain any further suspicions that he might have been implicated?"

"It might. But before we go into that, what's the rest of your report? And before you tell me that, let's get something else mighty straight. I take it that no one man was following Mr. Foxworth all this while, and that what you've got there is a combination of reports from several shadows. Right?"

"Of course. But it is complete. Except while he was in that speedboat, Mr. Foxworth was under trustworthy observation at every moment from the time he left his Toulouse Street home to the time he walked into the house at 84 Richmond Place where you saw and spoke to him. One man checked his departure from his house and followed him to the lake. No less than two of our men were aboard the *Myrtis II* as crew members, to check his arrival there, and to make voluminous notes of what was said and who said it. Two men were waiting at Bayou St. John for his return and followed Mr. Foxworth home. In other words, he was continuously under surveillance."

"Ver-ry interesting," commented Murphy, with a tart

323

smile. He had begun to play with the paper cutter again. "But there's a hole in it I could toss a locomotive through without touching the sides," he added.

"Just what do you mean, Captain?"

"Take a look at your own paper, sir. When did he leave the lake front, and when did he reach the yacht?"

Huntington scanned his memorandum.

"He left after Marshfield joined him at eight oh two—say it took them two minutes to get into the boat and start. That would make it eight oh four. And he arrived at eight twenty-three."

"That's about as I remembered it. Must have been a fast boat, at that. And now the second point. What was the timing of the return trip?"

Again Huntington consulted his typed report.

"Left the *Myrtis* at nine-thirty, arrived at Bayou St. John—hmmm! I get your drift, Captain—at two minutes after one."

"Sure you do," agreed Murphy complacently, laying down the paper cutter and lighting a cigar. "I'm surprised you didn't get it before. In other words, it took Mr. Foxworth not more than nineteen minutes to make the trip from shore to the yacht, but three hours and thirty-two minutes to make the same trip from the yacht to shore. Wouldn't you say that needed explanation—especially when, as you just took the pains to say, that's the period in which Mrs. St. Amant was killed?"

Speaking for the first time since Huntington began his revelations, Foxworth interrupted.

"Look here, you two," he burst out. "I can explain that. But I'll be damned if I know whether I want to. When it comes down to being spied on like that, I'm tempted to say the hell with it, and tell both of you to pop your whips. Only I'm warning you, I've got a couple of whips I can pop right back."

"Come, now, Orson," Huntington broke in pacifically. "I can understand your chagrin at discovering that you weren't outsmarting the department with your melodramatic rendezvous out in the lake. You buccaneers are all vain, and it hurts to find out that we knew about your elaborate little game from the first. But you should have guessed that much, from what I told you last night. And in this case, it's a good thing we were keeping track of you."

"It's not a good thing to find out the government's maintaining its own NKVD to spy on private citizens going

324

about their private business. There'll be more to this, märk my words."

"Surely, surely. But we can discuss that some other time, can't we? Meanwhile, if you do have any reasonable explanation of the difference in the time you took to go out to the *Myrtis,* and the time of the return trip, let's hear it by all means."

"It's something everybody that's ever had anything to do with speedboats ought to be able to figure out. They're the most temperamental gadgets in the world. And this one simply broke down, well out from the yacht and well out from shore. Svendson—he was the one that was running the boat for me—had the devil's own time coaxing it into action again. Some feed pipe was clogged. Since we weren't showing lights, he more or less had to take down the fuel line and put it together again by Braille."

"You'll concede that such a thing would account for the time lapse, won't you, Captain?" Huntington asked.

"Certainly—provided you'll concede that the time lapse also would have allowed Mr. Foxworth to run to the yacht basin at West End where another car could have been waiting; that he could have been driven in this car to 84 Richmond Place for a few minutes, and then back out to the basin at West End, and from there back to Bayou St. John by the same old speedboat. As a matter of fact, such a course would have brought him to Bayou St. John right at one o'clock, give or take a few minutes either way."

"But I tell you, we *were* stuck out in the lake with a clogged feed line!" Foxworth exclaimed.

"Tough luck that all this should have happened at the only interval when one or another of Mr. Huntington's gold-plated sleuths didn't have their eyes on you," observed Murphy, puffing away at his cigar. "Who was the man running the speedboat?"

"Svendson. Pete Svendson. But there's no use calling for him. He's on his way to Puerto de Oro right now. Naturally, I wasn't picking any old Joe Doakes for company last Saturday night. Pete's third officer on the *Bienvenida,* and she left port yesterday, on her regular run."

Murphy shrugged his wide shoulders. "You see how it is," he said to Huntington. The buzzer of the desk telephone snarled, and Murphy reached for it laying down his cigar. "Have 'em wait," he directed after a listening interval, and replaced the instrument in its cradle.

"Besides," he continued to Foxworth, "you did walk into

325

that house on your own, last Saturday night, you know. No knocking, no nothing, just opened the door and walked in."

"But I told you how that was," retorted Foxworth. "You had your own insinuations about a latchkey in my possession, if you'll remember. And I told you I had knocked and rung the bell, but received no answer. So I tried the knob and found the door off the latch."

"People were going in and out that door pretty busily from midnight on. Nobody else happened to find it off the latch," Murphy pointed out.

"I suppose not. After all, if anybody had answered my ring or my knock, I'd never have known the latch was off, either."

"And when I stepped out to see, the latch was on, good and tight," Murphy added.

"Naturally. Finding the door in that condition, I snapped the latch back on, when I came in."

Huntington had been listening attentively. Now he refolded his typed memorandum, slipped it back into his pocket, and rose.

"This sort of thing gets us nowhere, I'm afraid," he said. "And it wouldn't, even if we kept it up all day. Am I to understand, Captain, that despite my statement as to what Mr. Foxworth did last Saturday night, you decline to dismiss whatever suspicions you may be entertaining regarding his possible connection with the death of Mrs. St. Amant?"

Murphy nodded. "That's a broad-A way of saying it, but it gets the general idea across, all right," he conceded, relighting his cigar from the miniature airplane on the desk.

"In that case, there's no point in our staying here any longer, Orson, wasting Captain Murphy's time and ours. Shall we leave?"

Foxworth rose. "How long is this going on, then?" he demanded.

"If everything works out all right, no later than some time tonight," Murphy assured him calmly.

"Tonight!"

"Sure, why not? I already know who killed Mrs. St. Amant."

"Then why in the name of God must you wait?"

"Knowing and proving's two different things. Like I said, I already know. By tonight I'll be able to prove what I know—or else."

"In that case, why not put an end to these dramatics now?" Huntington inquired. "If you know who did kill Mrs. St. Amant, you must know it wasn't Orson Foxworth."

"Why? I just showed you a hole in his story—or yours—big enough to make room for a triangle murder and a couple of torso killings . . . . Hold on!" as Foxworth started to speak. "I'm not saying you did it. And I'm not saying you didn't. I'm not saying anything until I'm ready to sound off, except that I know who killed Odile St. Amant. Just to wrap this thing up, don't take any speedboat trips out in the lake today, Mr. Foxworth. I want you and all the others to be where I can get in touch with you-all tonight."

"It so happens that a number of those persons will be dining with me tonight. The only exceptions are the Lalandes and Léonce St. Amant who, because of their strict mourning will be at home, I suppose, and old Aunt Tossie . . . .! By George, that's what we came out here for! To see about having her released, I mean."

"Sure," Murphy said. "You told me that when you first got here. And I never said a word, did I? Because I knew you were after something else, too. If it had only been Tossie, you could have sent your lawyer out here to handle it for you. Anyway, he's here—your lawyer, I mean. Him and Doctor Perrault. They're waiting outside. That was what that phone call was. They'd just come in. But you could have saved them the trouble. I'll be glad to turn Tossie over to you. We're not interested in holding her any more. Just a second."

He disappeared into the anteroom, returning a moment later with Vance Perrault and Ted Marshfield, a hatchet-faced, stoop-shouldered man with keen eyes and a sleek head of hair.

"I'm having the old woman brought down now. It'll take about five minutes," Toe went on. "Do you want her to go with you, or would you rather have us send her somewhere?"

"Why, I hadn't thought of that," confessed Foxworth. "I suppose she'll want to go back to Richmond Place. That's the only home she's known since Amélie married. However . . . ."

"I'll take her there, if you'd like," volunteered Doctor Perrault. "It's more or less on my way uptown. That is, if she wants to go there."

"That's thoughtful of you, Doctor," Foxworth said in a tone that was plainly one of relief as well as of gratitude. He turned to Murphy. "I suppose that means that she, at least, is definitely off your list of suspects."

The big detective grinned.

"A matter of opinion, Mr. Foxworth," he said. "That takes it for granted she was on the list in the first place."

"In view of the fact that in my presence you arrested her for the murder, that appears to be a reasonable conclusion."

"Could be. But there's tricks to all trades. Running down murderers is one way of making a living, so that makes it a trade, I expect .... Anyway, here's old Tossie, herself."

The old Negress was standing on the threshold, her eyes downcast, her shoulders sagging, her hands shaking. In the maroon-colored dress—a castoff of Amélie's—in which she was incongruously clad and which was far too loose for her, she looked even skinnier and more decrepit than when appropriately dressed in a neat uniform. A shirt-sleeved, derby-hatted, squat deputy sheriff having bustled her into the office, handed Murphy a small printed form.

"On the dotted line, Toe," he said in a curiously hoarse voice. "Gimme the old John Hancock, willya? Got to have a receipt when I make a delivery." He laughed at the threadbare witticism, took the slip which Murphy signed, and shouldered his way out of the door. Tossie looked from one to the other of the men about her, peering through the moonlike lenses of her spectacles.

"Wheah you at, Mistuh Orson?" she asked. "De water dreenin' out my eyes so bad Ah sho cain' make out to see you. Wheah you is at, Mistuh Orson?"

"Here I am, Tossie," he answered kindly, rising and going closer to her. "Right here."

"Praise Jesus, suh, so you is," she whispered, shuffling into the room. "God'll thank you fo' takin' keer uh po' Tossie when she in such bad trouble. He sho'ly will. He gwine thank you better'n ever Ah kin. De res' de folks been mighty kind, too. Miss Caresse come see me, and de doctuh come see me, but you made 'em turn ol' Tossie loose, an' Ah ain' never gwine forget hit, no suh, not me!"

"Why, that's all right, Tossie. Don't get excited about it. As a matter of fact, Doctor Perrault—see him, over yonder?—is the one you ought to thank. He asked me to see what we could do about getting you out, and he's just offered to take you home in his car."

The old woman broke into a storm of sobs.

"Look lak ev'body too good to me," she wept. "Even in de jailhouse, dey done treat me fine, lak dey knowed Ah wasn't none dis Saddy night trash."

"Good girl. And Mrs. Lalande will make things easy for you when you ...."

"Suh, did Miss Am'lie say she want me back?"

"Why, no, not exactly. We haven't told her yet that you're

328

free. But of course she wants you. She's your white folks, isn't she?"

"No, suh. Not 'zackly. Not no mo', leastaways. Miss Odile ben my white folks fo' de longest. And now she done daid an' in heab'm."

"But I'm sure Mrs. Lalande would be only too glad to have you back."

"Please, suh, Mistuh Orson, wouldn't you take ol' Tossie home wid you? Ah's too feared to go back to dat house in Richmond Place. Dat man hate me so he gwine kill me down daid, too. I mean dat knivin'-hearted Mistuh Léonce. You seed him try to do hit de night Miss Odile got killed. De Cap'n seed him too. If Ah goes back to dat house wid no Miss Odile to took keer o' me, he gwine kill me down daid fo' true. But you's a good man, Mistuh Orson. Ah knows dat fo' a fack. You'll took good keer o' ol' Tossie, suh. You ever has. Why hit wa'n't no longer'n las' Saddy night you gi' me . . . ."

"Never mind, Tossie. *Never mind!*"

"But Ah does min'. Tell de troof an' shame de debbil, lak de preacher say. An' you's ever ben kin' as could be. Only las' Saddy night, when you gi' me dat ten dollars to lef' de do' off de latch fo' you, Ah say to mahse'f . . . ."

"What was dat, Tossie?" Murphy asked quietly, again laying down his cigar.

"He de bes' man ever lived," Tossie exclaimed. "God'll punish me bad if dat ain' de everlastin' troof. Las' Saddy evenin' hit was, he gi' me ten whole dollars to lef' de do' off de latch."

"The door at 84 Richmond Place?"

"Sho'ly, sho'ly."

"Thanks, Auntie. That'll be all for you. Go and sit down in the outer office for a few minutes, will you? And don't worry about what's going to happen to you. I'll arrange with these gentlemen."

He watched her thoughtfully while she shuffled away. Then, as the door closed behind her, he picked up the discarded paper cutter and looked at Huntington.

"Perhaps you'll add that item to the memorandum you're carrying around with you, Mr. Secretary," he said. "That is, unless Mr. Foxworth has something to say in the way of explanation."

"I told you once before this morning that I could explain, but that I was damned if I wanted to," Foxworth retorted explosively. "This time I'll go farther than that. I'll say I'm damned if I will. You claim you already know that Odile St.

Amant was murdered and who murdered her. If that means you 'know' I killed her, the only explanation I could give you of that senile old darky's remark wouldn't satisfy or convince you, any more than my statement about the breakdown of my speedboat satisfied or convinced you. And if you 'know' Odile was killed by someone else, it's none of your business what Tossie meant when she said I gave her ten dollars to leave the door of the Lalande house unlatched. And that's my last word on it, Captain Murphy."

Murphy regarded him with a blank unwavering stare. "Very well," he said tonelessly. "If that's the way you feel about it I'm willing to call it a day. Except that I'd be very grateful if you would take Tossie home with you. You needn't keep her there, if you don't want to—you can settle that part with her later, without any help from me. But Doctor Perrault can't conveniently take charge of her just now. Because I'm going to ask him to hang around just a little longer."

21

How Orson Foxworth and Amélie Lalande came to an understanding late in the afternoon—

January 10, 1948

NEITHER HUNTINGTON nor Foxworth spoke as they went along the bare corridors, through the ornamental doors, and down the endless steps of the Criminal Courts Building. Tossie trailed behind them, peering uneasily ahead of her and occasionally stretching out a shaking hand in search of support. Once or twice the two men stopped to wait for her, Foxworth with unconcealed annoyance, Huntington with unruffled patience. When they reached the banquette, Foxworth signaled to his Mexican chauffeur, Arnaldo, to help her across it and gave a few brief orders in Spanish. After Tossie was comfortably installed beside Arnaldo and the car was under way, Foxworth leaned forward and rolled up the glass partition dividing the driver's seat from the rear of the limousine. Having assured himself that he would not be overheard, he spoke bluntly to his brother-in-law.

"I suppose you're sitting in judgment on me again, Richard," he said. "I can't help it if you are. I'd had all I could take from Murphy. In another minute—"

"On the contrary, I think there was a good deal of sound logic in your retort to him. I did think you should explain to him about the breakdown of the speedboat. I'm glad you brought yourself to do it. But this other matter was entirely different. In the first place, as you pointed out, it's doubtful whether anything you said would have proved convincing to Captain Murphy. In the second place, the situation to which Tossie referred involved a lady. And naturally any gentleman—"

331

"I don't call myself a gentleman," Foxworth said harshly. "What's more, the 'lady' involved in this particular case has reminded me, quite recently, that I didn't have any right to. So I might not have as many scruples as you would, from that angle. However, I should like to make it quite clear that Mrs. Lalande has never been touched by the slightest breath of scandal. That's one of the reasons I saw red when—"

"I fully understand your feeling, Orson. But I hope you realize that I did not need your assurance that there is some perfectly simple explanation for Tossie's remarks, had you chosen to give it."

"Exactly. Its very simplicity is what would have made it unbelievable to a man like Murphy."

Momentarily, the rage which had consumed Foxworth when he left the detective's office flared again. Then he went on more quietly, but speaking with increasing earnestness.

"I'd like to have *you* know the whole situation, Richard. I think you're aware that, for some years, my footing with the Lalandes has been that of an intimate family friend. I've always been deeply attached to both girls—which is one of the reasons I'm all the more outraged by these baseless suspicions in connection with Odile's death. I've helped Caresse get this job in New York which means so much to her, though she doesn't know yet I had a hand in it. And, as I told Ruth on Monday, I recently asked Mrs. Lalande to marry me and return to Puerto de Oro with me. She hesitated, for several reasons, to give a definite answer, and perhaps I might as well admit that I hesitated quite a while before proposing to her. I've never thought of myself, until quite recently, as a marrying man. Well, day before yesterday we called the whole thing off by—mutual consent. I haven't told Ruth that yet. I haven't seemed to find just the right moment for it."

"If you'd like to have me, I'd be very glad to do so for you."

"Thanks, Richard. I would like to have you. In fact, I'd be very grateful if you would. There are—reasons why I don't like to discuss it with her. But about this latch business: it was just one of those jokes that get interwoven with the relationship between people who see a lot of each other and grow very fond of each other, in one way or another. You know the kind I mean?"

Of course. Every family has them. They're common among intimate friends too—sometimes between employers and employees who've been associated for a long time. They're always amusing, sometimes important, occasionally

332

almost precious—to the initiates. But they don't even make sense to an outsider or a stranger. That's the kind you mean, isn't it?"

"Exactly. Well, as I said, I was a pretty steady visitor at the Lalandes', and Tossie was tremendously interested in my courtship. Like most of her people, there's nothing she enjoys more than a love affair; the more intense, the better. In fact, I believe the reason she's always hated Léonce St. Amant is because she knew he neglected Odile—almost from the very first. If he'd been passionately devoted to her, Tossie would have reveled in it. This mutual antipathy wouldn't have sprung up between them. Because it is mutual—antipathy and fear too."

Almost as if aware that she was under discussion and pleased at the importance this gave her, Tossie turned around on the driver's seat and peered in the direction of the men in the tonneau. For a moment she blinked at them curiously. Then she turned around again.

"I haven't sized up St. Amant very thoroughly as yet," Huntington remarked. "And I'd like to. Because it seems to me—"

"Yes. I'd like to talk to you about that too. But first let me finish what I was saying about the latch. The more a story's interrupted, the more it loses its point, and that's especially bad if it didn't have much point in the first place. Well, as I was saying, Tossie was very much intrigued with my suit, but it worried her that I didn't get to be 'head beater' around the place. Have you ever heard the expression?"

"Yes, indeed. And I can see just how she felt about it. But we seem to be turning in at your courtyard. So I'm afraid you'll have to postpone your explanation about the door after all, to my very great disappointment. I was really immensely interested."

"It won't take me but a minute to finish. I'll tell you as soon as we get inside the house."

Unfortunately, he was not able to do so. Downes had opened the front door before Foxworth had finished giving directions to Arnaldo about Tossie and explaining to the old woman that the chauffeur would show her where to go and that he himself would see her later. Then strains of music from the drawing room proclaimed the probable presence of a guest, and Ruth instantly rushed out to meet her stepfather and uncle, hailing them both with excitement.

"Do come in and listen! Just last night Sabin and I talked about a song that ought to be written—a song called 'Lady Levee.' And Sabin actually sat down and wrote it before he went to bed—words and music both. He brought it around here as soon as he was up—which wasn't so terribly early, and no wonder! He's been playing it and I've been singing it with him. Oh—excuse me! But you did tell me you knew Sabin Duplessis, didn't you, Father?"

"I certainly did," Huntington replied cordially. "Captain Duplessis flew quite a group of us to Oran in 1942, when negotiations with Darlan were interrupted by the Admiral's assassination. You may remember, my dear—I didn't get home for Christmas, which was your chief grievance in the matter .... How are you, Captain?"

"Fine—and delighted to see you in New Orleans .... Good morning, Mr. Foxworth. I hope you don't object to a little chamber music?"

"On the contrary. It's a very pleasant change from the offensive talk we've just been listening to. Aren't you going to let the Secretary and me hear that song?"

"If you'd both really like to—"

Sabin reseated himself at the piano and permitted his fingers to wander idly over the keys for a few minutes. Then he slipped from random chords into delightful melody and presently he began to sing:

> Lady Levee, most serene,
> Sweet and slumberous of mien—
> Though his promises be fair,
> Of the river's song beware!

"Now the chorus, Ruth! You know that already."

With the same lack of affected hesitation which Sabin had shown, she crossed the room and stood beside him. They smiled at each other, in friendly understanding. Then Sabin gave an almost imperceptible signal and they sang the chorus together.

> Wild flowers of every hue,
> Verdant grasses cover you,
> Lazy cattle graze on you,
> Ardent lovers seek you too.
> But the river is a rover
> Do not take him for your lover,
> Veil yourself in mystery—
> Lead him to the open sea!

"Bravo!" Foxworth exclaimed. "That's got it all right!

You'll have to go out on the River Road, while you're here, Richard, and see what a swell job Sabin's done."

"I'd like to go out on the River Road, but I don't need to in order to find out that he's done a swell job. I know that already. And I'm not surprised. However, I want to hear the next verses."

"Thanks for the compliment, sir. Well, you asked for it, so here goes.

> Lady Levee, watch the course,
> Your suitor quickly shifts his pace
> And moves with stealthy, hidden force,
> While showing you a smiling face.
> Entwined about you with his might,
> His crest upon your bosom lying,
> He begs of you your troth to plight,
> But do not heed this tender sighing.

> Lady Levee, strong and fair
> Of the river's song beware!
> He'd destroy you to be free—
> Lead him to the open sea.

"I'm afraid that's all," Sabin said. "But I want everyone in on the chorus."

"I want to hear it all again," Foxworth declared heartily. "Anyone would enjoy a song like that. Look, Sabin, why don't you have dinner with us tonight? And let's sing it together then? Would you? The Darcoas and the Racinas are coming—hang it, I meant to ask Perrault too, but I forgot, I was so furious with Murphy. Well, Downes can telephone Vance's office and leave a message. How about it, Sabin? I want as many of my friends as I can get together on short notice to meet my brother-in-law."

"I'd be delighted."

"Good. We'll dine around seven, but I like to regard the cocktail 'hour' literally, so come early. Meanwhile, seeing Sabin reminds me, Richard: how about Schaefer and the others? Hadn't you better get on the ball and clear them to liberty and the pursuit of happiness? All you have to do is telephone your people to call off the dogs."

"I'll be glad to."

Huntington left the drawing room, and when he returned, the telephoning effectively concluded, Sabin had already gone and Downes had announced lunch. Moreover, it was evident, from the moment Foxworth and his guests took their places at table, that something had gone radically wrong in the kitchen. The first course was tomato juice, which had obviously undergone no transformation in the way of seasoning after being removed from the can and which was not even properly chilled. A passable steak came next, but this was served to the accompaniment of boiled potatoes and boiled Brussels sprouts. When a sago pudding with custard sauce made its appearance, Foxworth flung down his napkin and angrily demanded an explanation of Downes.

"What under the sun's got into Selina? I never saw such a meal on this table before, or on any other table in New Orleans, for that matter. We might as well be eating at some railway hotel in the Midlands."

"I'm sorry, sir, very sorry indeed. But you'll remember that Ellen and I do come from the Midlands. We've done the best we could, but of course we never pretended to know anything about cookery, either of us."

"Whoever asked you whether you did? I said, what's got into Selina?"

Downes coughed. "Well, she did stay long enough to get Mr. Huntington's breakfast. We managed to persuade her to do that. The stewed kidneys and scrambled eggs—there wasn't anything the matter with those, now was there, sir? But Selina came to work this morning with her head tied up in a big red handkerchief and she said her tooth was just killing her."

"Her *tooth*! Which tooth?"

"She didn't say, sir. And then presently she began to talk about a 'mis'ry in her spine.' When Ellen came down with Miss Ruth's breakfast tray, the sink was full of dishes and Selina had gone."

"You mean to say there's no cook in this house? When at least six extra people are coming in for dinner?"

"I'm very sorry, sir, I really am," Downes repeated ruefully. "I'd have told you at once, but Mr. Duplessis was here, and you were all in the drawing room and seemed to be very much occupied. Besides, Ellen thought that if she could suit you for lunch, possibly we could get along. But I can see—" Downes' eye fell sadly on the sago pudding, congealing in its custard sauce on Foxworth's plate. "I believe we can manage canapes and cocktails, sir," he went on. "But more than that I wouldn't say. And with such good restaurants in this city—"

"This wasn't the kind of a dinner I meant to give at a restaurant. This was the kind of a dinner I intended to have at home. As I told you before, I wanted you to use a lace tablecloth, the best china and the gold plate."

The ill humor which had been dissipated by Sabin's song had now returned in full force; and it was not improved by the disappointing tidings that the 1840 Room, which was always his first choice when dining at a restaurant, was unavailable for the evening. He himself talked with Roy Alciatore, but the proprietor of Antoine's, though calmly courteous, according to his wont, was nonetheless firm: he was very sorry not to oblige Mr. Foxworth; but some weeks earlier the 1840 Room had been engaged for this same night. Possibly Mr. Foxworth would consider taking the Mystery Room instead. It was not usually reserved exclusively for a small group. But Mr. Alciatore would be glad to make an exception in this case, in partial compensation for Mr. Foxworth's disappointment. And might he suggest *champignons sous cloche* to be followed by *pigeonneaux paradis* and *omelette soufflée?* Mr. Alciatore would check over the wine list with his *sommelier* in order to assure the best vintages . . . .

Yes, it would be a distinguished dinner, Foxworth admitted grudgingly to himself. But he would still be deprived of the opportunity to which he had so greatly looked forward, of presiding at his own table, in his own house, the first time that Clarinda Darcoa and her father dined with him, of setting forth, in their honor, his costliest porcelains and his unique service of silver-gilt which had reputedly come from the Winter Palace in St. Petersburg. Girls like Clarinda appreciated such accessories to fine food and relished it more when it was presented to them in trappings of this kind. As to Francisco, he might or might not be a connoisseur, though he probably was; but almost certainly he would consider an invitation to dine at a public restaurant less of a compliment than one to dine in a private house. And at the moment Foxworth desired to show Francisco Darcoa every compliment of which he was capable. Helplessly, he raged because his cook had chosen this day of all others to have a "mis'ry in her spine."

However, there was nothing he could do about it. If Downes had only told him early that morning, or if he himself had not been obliged to spend so much time at the Criminal Courts Building, he might have got in another cook. It was too late to seek one out now. Moreover, an enormous amount of work, which must be done before night, was still staring him in the face. Having spent at least twenty minutes in conference with Roy Alciatore, he decided not to waste any more time on the telephone. His guests would come to Toulouse Street that evening in any case. There would be time enough to tell them then that the dinner would be served elsewhere. He went into his study, slamming the door behind him, and flung himself down at his desk.

Staring moodily at the reports, financial statements, inventories, cost sheets, and other documents spread out before him, he felt a tremendous urge to sweep the entire mass into a heap and onto the floor. The mounting tensions generated within him by the day's events seemed to call for some form of physical release, preferably violent. He had hoped that, once closeted in his study, he could devote himself to drawing up a tentative outline of the merger memorandum which he and Francisco Darcoa would jointly present to the Trans-Caribbean stockholders at their annual meeting a fortnight hence. The absorbing task of laying the definite groundwork for such a coup should have enabled him to dismiss all lesser matters from his mind at the same time that it assuaged his irritation. But the work simply would not come to hand. It demanded close and undivided attention and he was completely unable to bring his faculties to bear on the intricate schedules of securities, physical assets, franchises, and international regulations.

He admitted honestly to himself that it was illogical for him to permit trivial annoyances, such as the ailments of a cook and the unavoidable change in plans for a dinner party, to deter him from the work that would put him at the head of a veritable empire. But perversely they continued to do so. There were disturbing interruptions too. Huntington had asked for the loan of a stenographer and when the young man arrived from the Blue Fleet office, he was shown to Foxworth's study by mistake. Ted Marshfield telephoned to announce the ratification of a mineral lease in the Yerba Linda Valley and request directions for proceeding further. Foxworth gave the indicated orders and went savagely back to his notes—only to find Theophile Murphy's level eyes staring up at him from the papers on his desk.

What did Murphy really know—if anything? Was it not a habit of the police to predict an arrest within twenty-four hours whenever they were confronted with an unsolved crime? Obviously Tossie was no longer suspected, or Murphy would not have released her. That left Amélie, Caresse, Léonce, Sabin Duplessis, and himself as those among whom the big, slow-spoken detective had come to a decision as to guilt or innocence. What were the factors which supported the presumption of guilt in each case? Or rather, how did these look to Murphy? For it was Murphy who had made the decision. Foxworth kept recalling Murphy's unwavering stare that morning, when he—Foxworth—had bluntly refused to

comment on Tossie's revelation about the unlatched door—
and tardily remembered that he had not explained this to
Richard Huntington after all.

He rose hastily, determined that this time he would permit
no interruptions to thwart his purpose of confiding in his
brother-in-law, disregarding the papers which fluttered to the
floor as a result of his hasty movement. But before he could
reach the threshold, a discreet knock presaged the entrance
of Downes.

"Mrs. Lalande and Mr. St. Amant are calling, sir," the
butler announced.

"What! Do you mean to tell me you let them in?"

"Excuse me, sir. You've told me that you were always
home to Mrs. Lalande if she telephoned, and since Mr. St.
Amant is with her . . . . I'm very sorry if I've displeased you,
but you've never given me any instructions to the contrary. I
showed them into the drawing room, sir. Do you wish me to
tell them that I was mistaken, that you were called out
unexpectedly?"

In spite of his impeccably respectful demeanor, it was
evident that Downes felt he had a grievance, and, under
normal circumstances, Foxworth would have admitted that it
was a just one. It had not occurred to him to tell his butler,
after Thursday's stormy scene with Amélie that, should Mrs.
Lalande telephone, he would be most appreciative if she
would leave a message, because he was in conference and, at
the moment, could not be reached. He certainly should have
done this. On the other hand, she had never before come to
the house on Toulouse Street as an uninvited guest. So it was
not strange that he had neglected to make provision for such
an unforeseen contingency.

"Tell Mrs. Lalande that I'm engaged at the moment, but
that I will join her as soon as possible," he directed. "And—
er—I realize that you were following such instructions as I
had given you, by showing her into the drawing room.
However, if she should call again—"

"I think I understand, sir. Thank you, sir."

Downes withdrew, without permitting a certain feeling of
smugness to reveal itself in his countenance until he had
reached the stairway. Meanwhile, Foxworth, glancing at his
wrist watch, picked up a large sheet of tabulated figures, an
analysis of cargo-handling costs, and selected certain items to
be entered on a memorandum pad along with the notation
that it was now three-thirty P.M. From time to time he
glanced at his watch again. When fifteen minutes had
elapsed, he rose, stepped to a large mirror over the mantel,

meticulously adjusted the knot of a cravat that stood in need of no attention, and with an uneasy glance at his reflected image, resolutely left the room.

There was not the slightest reason, he told himself, why he should dread the impending interview. The fact remained that he would have given almost anything he could think of at the moment, if he could have been on his way back upstairs, with the ordeal safely behind him, instead of on his way downstairs to meet it. His apprehension over what lay ahead was curiously like what he had often felt when he sat in an outer office, thumbing dog-eared magazines, and awaiting a nurse's summons into the presence of a dentist whom for too long he had neglected to visit. He could not help making the comparison; it was no less apt because it was ridiculous.

Now that his first anger against Amélie had cooled, now that the break with her had proved to be a relief and a blessing, he felt the aversion—instinctive with any decent man—to speaking harshly to a woman. And unfortunately, harsh language was the only kind that Amélie would understand, or at least admit that she understood, under such circumstances as these. At the door of the drawing room he paused, summoning all his will power; but nothing in his manner betrayed his perturbed frame of mind as he entered.

"Good afternoon, Amélie. Good afternoon, Léonce," he said, nodding curtly to each without shaking hands and feeling quite unmoved by the consciousness that Amélie was looking her loveliest. "This is most unexpected. I take it some emergency has arisen. What is it?"

"Oh, Orson! You didn't come near us or telephone us at all yesterday! I felt I had to see you, and Léonce did, too! Surely, you understand why!"

"I'm afraid I don't. Won't you be good enough to explain?"

"Well, of course, first of *all*, Léonce wanted to apologize—"

"For eavesdropping? Or for speaking the words you put into his mouth? I'm afraid I can't accept an apology very intelligently, let alone very tactfully, unless I know what it's for."

"I wasn't really eavesdropping, Mr. Foxworth," Léonce said with a show of great earnestness. "As I've already told my mother-in-law, I'd come home early because I'd promised to take her to the cemetery. Then, as I went through the hall, I heard you and her—well, talking. It didn't seem to me

340

the best moment to break in on your conversation. So I waited a minute, and—"

"It didn't occur to you that you could go straight on to your own quarters, I suppose, without coming to the drawing room at all? No, probably it wouldn't .... All right, you're not apologizing for eavesdropping, because you didn't really eavesdrop. So I take it you're apologizing for having accused me of murdering your wife. That's a rather grave accusation, especially coming from a man who's under suspicion himself in connection with the same crime. But we'll let that phase of the matter pass for the moment. And I think we'd better dismiss the whole question of apologies. So, if that's all you had to say—"

"But it isn't," Amélie burst out. "I mean it's all Léonce had to say, and I wanted you to hear it from his own lips. But I have something to say, Orson, and I'd rather say it to you alone."

"Very well. I'll be pleased to excuse Léonce."

Léonce looked questioningly at his mother-in-law, but she did not appear to see him. He realized, now she had accomplished her purpose of humiliating him in Foxworth's presence, that she was only too glad to be rid of him. As a matter of fact, he was only too glad to go. When the front door closed behind him, Amélie made an appealing gesture.

"Orson, you told me, the last time we talked together, that if I'd only come and sit down beside you on the sofa, we'd arrive at an understanding much more easily and pleasantly than we could otherwise. I'm going to quote your own words. If only you wouldn't act in this cold, unfriendly way, I'm sure our little quarrel—"

"We didn't have a little quarrel. We parted for good. Whether you believe it or not, it was painful to me, because I'd loved you for a long time. But that doesn't alter the fact that our parting was final."

"Oh, you *said* we were parting for good, but of course you didn't mean it! All lovers say things like that to each other once in a while and it just clears the atmosphere. Besides, now that I understand you were really acting for the best, as far as Caresse is concerned—"

"I'm sorry, Amélie, but you seem to be laboring under a complete misapprehension. I did mean what I said. And we never became lovers. I'm glad you understand about my attitude in regard to Caresse now, but I'm afraid that, otherwise, your understanding's very incomplete. Evidently I didn't

341

make my position clear when I said you and I were through."

"But you *can't* mean you don't love me any more! I'll apologize too, I'll do anything you say—"

"I don't want you to apologize. I don't want you to do anything except leave this house. And I hope you won't come here again. I hope you won't call me on the telephone. Because I wouldn't like to put you in the position of being told I wouldn't talk with you, or that I wouldn't receive you. And that's what would happen, Amélie, if you forced yourself on me like this again."

At last something he said had struck home. Looking at her horrified face, he felt a momentary twinge of compassion. Nevertheless, he pressed his point. If he had felt she was stricken by the loss of the man she loved, he might not have been able to do it, but he knew she was only overwhelmed by the loss of an emerald parure, of a fabulous *palacio*, of untold wealth and power.

"I asked you to be my wife," he said harshly. "I did it unwillingly, but I did it. If you'd accepted me, unconditionally, I'd have stood by my proposal, even if I regretted it. But you didn't. You wouldn't. You hesitated because 'I had no background.' You told me I hadn't the slightest conception of a gentleman's instincts. You felt I 'took too much for granted.' You resented my 'interference.'"

"How can you be so cruel as to remind me again of all those awful things I said when I was so crushed by sorrow that—"

"Because you force me to. It isn't pleasant for me to do it. But you didn't say those awful things to me in sorrow. You said them to me in anger and resentment. And over what? Something that couldn't have come between us for an instant if you'd loved me or even been capable of loving me. That released me from my obligation. You're not my future wife. You're not even my friend. Friendship can be a pretty strong bond between a man and a woman sometimes—almost as strong as love. But it has to be founded on mutual interests, mutual understanding, mutual respect. We haven't any mutual interests. We don't talk the same language. You've lost my respect. To sum the whole thing up, you forfeited my friendship at the same time that you killed my love. And you can no more bring that back to life than you can bring Odile back to life."

"But we all fail each other sometimes, Orson! I did fail you, I admit it. I did forfeit your friendship. But I'll win it back. You'll see! Just give me time. I *can* resurrect your love—that doesn't die like—like a person. And when I've proved that it doesn't, you'll ask me again to be your wife and I'll say yes, without any conditions, without any hesitation, without any resentment."

She tried to throw her arms around his neck. He caught hold of her hands, but there was nothing loverlike in his grip.

"You won't do anything of the sort," he said. "And I'll tell you another reason why. I didn't intend to, I didn't choose to, but you've made it impossible for me to do anything else. For the first time in my life, I'm really hoping to get married. I'm not sure that I shall, because I can't be sure this woman with whom I've fallen in love will have me. I realize I haven't much to offer her. I realize I'm not worthy of her. And I can't ask her whether she'll have me until this terrible mystery which has involved so many people, myself among them, is completely cleared up. But if she'll accept me, when I do ask her, I'll be the happiest man on earth. If she'll only tell me that she'll consider me, I'll know I have a great deal to be thankful for. And feeling as I do about her, I believe it'll be plain, even to you, Amélie, that there's no room for another woman in my life."

22

How Orson Foxworth gave a dinner at Antoine's on Saturday—

January 10, 1948

WHEN Foxworth came up the stairs Ruth was just replacing the hall telephone on its cradle.

"Caresse called up," she said, "and did she sound happy—almost as happy as I feel! They were simply wonderful to her at the broadcasting station—told her they were sure she'd make a great hit in New York, wished her all kinds of luck, said her programs here had been such a success that they were going to get someone else to carry on along the same lines, though they'd never find another voice like hers, not in a million years. And Toe Murphy had telephoned *her*—said there was no reason as far as he was concerned why she shouldn't take the Crescent Limited if she still wanted to. If she still wanted to!"

"Well, I'm glad she's had a break—very glad. I've never been quite as fond of Caresse as I was of Odile, but she's a very attractive girl just the same."

"Yes, she is. And do you know, I shouldn't wonder if she grew to be more like Odile, as she gets older. Anyway, the point of her telephone call was that she's all packed now, and that she'd like to come down here and say goodbye to me. She's going to have dinner with Miss Hickey before they take the train."

"Why not ask them both to join our little party?"

"Of course I'd love to, but I didn't feel sure you'd want them. In fact, I was a little guarded about encouraging Caresse to come here at all. I said I didn't know just what

344

your plans for me were, the rest of the afternoon—that I'd call her back."

"I appreciate your thoughtfulness, Ruth, but you needn't hesitate to see Caresse whenever and wherever you like, as far as I'm concerned. When you get right down to it, I imagine her break with her mother will be just about as definitive as my own. Has your father told you . . . . ?"

"Yes, Uncle, he has. I hope you don't mind if I say I'm not sorry."

"Not in the least. But we won't stop to talk about it now—in fact, I'm not sure we'll ever need to. It's a closed chapter. Well . . . . From what you say it's evident that Caresse wasn't planning to linger around Richmond Place, now that her packing's done. Go ahead and call her back. And get in touch with Miss Hickey direct. She'll feel it's more of a compliment if you do. Say we'll start cocktails early, around six-thirty, so that they won't have any feeling of rush. Antoine's isn't the kind of food to gulp down. And be sure to tell Caresse we'll be in a private dining room. I don't believe she'll hesitate to go to a restaurant, if she knows that."

Decidedly, Foxworth's mental comparison between his interview with Amélie and a long-delayed visit to the dentist was more apt than he had believed at first. He now had very much the same sense of escape, of well-being, and of good will towards the world that he had often experienced after hearing the welcome words "Well, I don't seem to find anything else, Mr. Foxworth." Even his grudge against Toe Murphy was less bitter, now that he knew Caresse, at least, was freedom bound; after all, a detective had to do his duty, as he saw this . . . .

Miss Hickey and Caresse would both be delighted to come to the house for cocktails and go on to Antoine's afterwards for dinner, Ruth reported a few minutes later. Studying her radiant face, Foxworth remembered her remark, "Caresse sounds as happy as I feel." He was not, as a relative, given to much demonstration of affection, but now he caught her to him and kissed her.

"You're starry-eyed all right," he said half-humorously, half-tenderly. "Incidentally, I don't suppose you neglected to tell Sabin Duplessis your good news."

"Of course I didn't. I told him even before he had a chance to tell me about the song. And this afternoon he's sent me a perfectly beautiful present with a note that's a masterpiece, even for him."

"Good .... I suppose the Gulf's been strewn with radio-grams, going in both directions, all day."

"I wouldn't say strewn, exactly. But of course I got an answer to my first one and then I did send another, after I talked with Mother, early this morning, and that's been answered too. Mother's invited to the White House Monday and she reminded me that was a *command*. She isn't exactly pleased at so much haste, but I finally persuaded her that she could get the Constellation down on Tuesday. That means we can be off for Tegucigalpa on Wednesday, and everything's arranged for a wedding at the Embassy. It's all right for Father too. He got hold of the Secretary of State while—while you were in the drawing room."

"Obviously his conference was pleasanter than mine. I always said Richard was born under a luckier star than I was," Foxworth observed a little drily. "Well, I'm glad everything's coming along so nicely. I wish you'd tell me what you'd like for a wedding present, Ruth. Oh, not this minute! Think it over. But I want it to be something handsome too, something that would have lasting value and give you lasting pleasure. As I've said before, I'm delighted that you and Aldridge have hit it off so well, I certainly am. I don't mind telling you now that I rather hoped from the beginning—but I'd better not say any more, or you'll accuse me of being a scheming old matchmaker. I confess I didn't think things would move so fast—that's the only reason I asked your father if he really approved of having you rush off in this way. But matters of this sort do come to a head pretty quickly sometimes."

"They do, don't they?" Ruth murmured.

Foxworth shot a searching glance in her direction, but there was nothing in her happy and candid countenance to suggest an *arrière pensée*. "I might even fly down to the wedding myself," he went on. "Perhaps we could make up a group."

"That would be simply wonderful. If you did, you'd ask the Darcoas, wouldn't you? I mean, Clarinda's so lovely, she'd make a great impression at the Embassy; and besides, she's been so good to me."

Again Foxworth shot a searching glance at his niece and again her expression reassured him. "Why, yes," he said. "I do think it would be a good idea to include the Darcoas in such a group, if we make one up. Of course, it's too soon for me to tell yet whether I could get away or not. But Clarinda *has* gone out of her way to be pleasant to you, and I know you'd like to return her courtesies, if you could. You might

346

even ask her to be your maid of honor. Besides, she would make an impression at the Embassy, as you say. As far as that goes, she'd make one almost anywhere." For a moment he seemed to be turning certain matters over in his mind, and Ruth, who had learned that he did not like to be interrupted at such times, waited without impatience for his next remark. "Before we begin to make plans for Honduras, except in a casual way, I suppose we ought to complete our plans for tonight," he said finally. "So I've been giving some thought to the table arrangement, especially since the addition of Miss Hickey and Caresse will make ten of us."

"There'll be eleven if Doctor Perrault comes, won't there?"

"Yes, that's true. But I haven't heard a word from him yet, so I can't take his acceptance for granted. And I certainly shan't ask an extra woman, who might or might not fit in, just on the chance that he'll be there. We'll wedge him wherever it seems best if he does show up .... Well, I started to say that of course, under normal circumstances, it would be natural for you to act as my hostess. But your father should be seated according to protocol, quite aside from the fact that it would give me great pleasure to show him such a compliment. And I can't very well put him at *your* right hand! So, all things considered—"

"You thought of asking Clarinda to be your hostess? That's a grand idea! Father'd be perfectly delighted, I'm sure. Have you worked out the rest of the seating?"

"No, not yet. Shall we do it together now? Miss Hickey at *my* right, I think. That might be a tactful move. And perhaps Judith Racina at my left—I don't care too much for her husband, as you know, but I'm bound to say she's a very fine woman. And then—"

They sat down at the long library table together, spread out a sheet of paper, and made small circles on it, labeling and re-labeling these, after the habit of party-givers from time immemorial. When Foxworth expressed himself as completely satisfied, Ruth offered to write the place cards, and her uncle went off to dress, humming a little under his breath, and leaving her still engaged with her pleasant task. Huntington, who had spent the latter part of the afternoon in his own room, dictating to the borrowed stenographer, looked in on her just as she was stacking the cards and wrapping the seating plan neatly around them, ready to check back once more when she reached the Mystery Room.

"I might add a little postscript to the story you told, at

347

Uncle's request, while Uncle was having his *mauvais quart d'heure*," she remarked demurely. "You may remember I said, in response to one of your remarks, that it had struck me as significant, rather than accidental, when he didn't put Mrs. Lalande at the head of his table last week. Well, now it strikes me as significant, rather than accidental, that it's just where he's put Clarinda Darcoa."

It was time for them to dress too, so they did not discuss the possible significance of the move for long; and when they met again, half an hour later, in the drawing room, they found that Orson Foxworth was there before them and that Downes and Ellen were already making the final preparations for the reception of guests. Then, almost immediately, Miss Hickey and Caresse were announced.

Ruth had already formed a mental picture of Haas and Hector's capable representative, and she was instantly aware of its accuracy. Miss Hickey was a middle-aged woman with abundant, well-dressed hair of somewhat neutral shade, a ruddy face so pleasant and alert that her pug nose did not detract from it, and an erect, well-controlled figure. She was wearing a black velvet dinner dress with a flat scalloped overskirt and fastened up the back with small black velvet buttons centered in scallops. It was becoming, appropriate, and severely stylish, and her evening bag and slippers had obviously been made to match this model from the Salon Superbe, to which, in all respects, she was a great credit. Without either effusion or restraint, she greeted her host, acknowledged his presentations, and accepted one of Downes' famous Dry Martinis from Ellen's efficient hands. Then she stood by, watching with a satisfied expression, while Caresse held the center of the stage.

Vance Perrault had told the truth when he said the day before that she did not look like the same girl he had seen twenty-four hours earlier. The succeeding twenty-four hours had made an even greater change in her. The dark circles had disappeared from under her eyes; her color, though not really rosy as yet, had regained some of its fresh look, and the very absence of extravagant make-up enhanced its clarity. Her expression had changed too, and, looking at her, Ruth recalled the opinion she had expressed to Foxworth only a few hours earlier—that in time Caresse would resemble her sister more than she did her mother. The promise of this altered resemblance already showed signs of fulfillment.

Besides these physical changes, Ruth was quick to notice others. It was hard to believe that the girl who had reveled in

348

the near-nudity of the jade green "formal" only a week earlier would now conform so meticulously to the tenets of conservative taste. But Caresse had not only made a great effort in this direction herself; she had also received the benefit of expert and affectionate co-operation. The Fashion Plate Dress Shop could not hope to compete with the Salon Superbe; but its directress, Clothilde Lafargue, and her various managerial associates—each of whom, as Amélie had reminded Caresse, had been at least a Maid in one of the more exclusive Carnival courts—had taken pride in giving their protégée a royal send-off. After all, they had discovered Caresse Lalande—her exceptional grace, her flair for style, her remarkable radio voice. They did not propose to have her start off for New York with apologies for her appearance, nor to arrive there with the prospect of being confronted with glances of disparaging appraisal. So they had invited Miss Hickey to visit The Fashion Plate Dress Shop with her. The results of the ensuing conference had been extremely happy, both tangibly and intangibly, and Caresse now bore witness to its outcome. No one but an expert in such matters would have guessed that her dull black taffeta had cost only a fraction of the amount invested in Miss Hickey's lustrous velvet. It too was wholly appropriate and vastly becoming; and if its style was not severe, this was only because a severe style would not have suited Caresse. On the other hand, the bouffant bustle, accentuating her small waist, the short cap sleeves, revealing the whiteness of her arms, the round, rather high neckline which gave only a glimpse of the soft skin below her throat, the close-fitting, unornamented bodice—all these suited her to perfection. She came forward with that glad assurance peculiar to the normal feminine human being who knows that she is perfectly dressed for some special occasion, and who also rejoices in the knowledge that everyone who looks at her is doing so with admiration not untinged by astonishment.

"I've had the most exciting day!" she said, confirming the good news she had given Ruth over the telephone. "One mad rush, but I've loved every minute of it. And what do you think? Just after I talked to you, Ruth, Joe's friend, Peter MacDonald, called me from New York—I mean telephoned, just like that, as if it hadn't been long distance at all! He said he'd be at the train to meet me Monday morning, and he'd checked the reservations Miss Hickey had made for me at the Plaza with the reservation manager, and everything was all right. Of course, it would have been, since Miss Hickey made them, but just the same, it was nice of him to do it, wasn't it? And he said he wanted me to have dinner with him Monday night, that is, unless Miss Hickey'd made other plans. But she said to go right ahead, I couldn't be in better hands. It was swell of Joe to take so much trouble for me, wasn't it?"

"Yes, it was. And you can tell him, right now, how much you appreciate it."

In her eagerness to do so, Caresse could hardly wait until Joe and Judith, who had entered the drawing room just as she finished speaking, had made the first indicated rounds. She embraced them both, with impartial affection; but it was obviously Joe with whom she was most preoccupied. Although she drew him slightly apart from the others, Ruth could not help overhearing part of her eager recital.

". . . . and when Captain Murphy checked on my story, he found I *had* told him the truth. You know I said that horrible old truck was operated by a food-freezing plant near the Paris Road. Well, Captain Murphy sent someone to the only place of its kind in the neighborhood, and the driver, as well as the man who repaired the damages, confirmed every word I'd spoken. Oh, Joe, I can't thank you enough for making me go to see Captain Murphy! I can't thank you enough for everything!"

"I wish you wouldn't try. It makes me feel silly as all get out. Not that I could possibly be more pleased that everything's turning out so well for you, Caresse. But incidentally, I think there are two or three other factors which influenced Toe's decision. Maybe Sabin will tell us something about that when he gets here. Meanwhile, what do you say we flock along with the others? I've hardly spoken to Mr. Huntington yet, and he's one of the few men in high office that I can really go for in a big way."

"Oh, I'm sorry! I didn't mean to drag you off like this. But such a load has been lifted from my heart, that I have to talk to someone about it."

Her radiance was contagious. Everybody was conscious of it as she chatted first with one and then with another, while Miss Hickey continued to watch her with attentive and approving eyes. When Sabin arrived, he gravitated quickly to her side.

"No cocktail?" she inquired, noticing that his agreeable and effortless small talk had none of the usual accessories except a sequence of cigarettes. "Not even one of these super-dupers? Are you going to drink to me only with your eyes?"

"Alas, yes! And without even the hope that you will pledge with yours."

The pleasant badinage continued for some time. Sabin made no reference to Toe Murphy and Caresse did not miss it; she even forgot Joe had said that further explanations of her freedom might be forthcoming. It was a good moment just as it was . . . .

The good moment lengthened into a good quarter hour. There was no lack of ease among the guests, there were no awkward pauses in conversation. But Ruth saw her uncle looking surreptitiously at his watch and went over to him.

"I asked Downes just a few minutes ago," she said. "There still hasn't been any word from Doctor Perrault. Of course the office is closed but Downes called the house and the maid said he hadn't come in yet. Downes left a detailed message about joining us at Antoine's in case the doctor couldn't get here for cocktails. Do you want us to try the Doctors' Exchange, too?"

"No, Vance is always like this—uncertain of his plans up to the very last. I told you not to worry about the seating plan. He probably won't show up at all. Anyhow, we won't wait for him. But I am beginning to be concerned about Francisco and Clarinda."

As if his words had summoned them, they appeared in the doorway. Ruth had not met Francisco Darcoa before, and as she went forward to welcome him and his daughter, she had the same strange feeling of suddenly finding the clock turned back which had so dazzled her when she and Aldridge first wandered around Jackson Square. For Darcoa appeared to personify less the greatest single power in a modern shipping company than some grandee of the past—even no less a person than Don Andres Almonaster, the most spectacular Orleanian of his period. As for Clarinda, it took no effort at all to visualize her as Doña Micaela, the daughter of Don Andres, and later wife of the Baron Pontalba. Clothes alone could not have created the strong illusion of ancient grandeur. Part of it came from the man's looks, distinguished rather than handsome. His face was too long, his forehead too high, his lips too thin, his beard too pointed; yet the whole effect was one of infinite stateliness. Part of it came from his manner, dignified rather than cordial. He bowed without shaking hands, he spoke quietly, he smiled very little; yet again the whole effect was one of infinite courtesy. Ruth did not try to analyze the effect produced by his daughter. But more than ever she was conscious of Clarinda's fascination as the newcomer moved among her fellow-guests, a high comb crowning her glossy hair, an exquisite painted fan held lightly in her tapering fingers.

The Darcoas singled out no one for special attention as they circled the room, sipping their cocktails sparingly but with no lack of graciousness. After the first welcoming words, some time passed before Foxworth was able to arrest Clarinda's attention again, without doing so obtrusively. When his chance came, he spoke first of all, apologetically, about the change in plan for the dinner.

"I can't tell you how sorry I am. Especially as it must seem to you inexcusable. You told me the other day you never had servant trouble."

"But I also told you I realized my rare blessings in that respect. And I did not mean to imply that there had never been sickness in my staff. After all, servants are subject to human ailments, like the rest of us. I'm only sorry the poor woman is ill."

With something of a shock, Foxworth realized that he had not thought of Selina's illness as a condition calling for sympathy, but rather as an annoying handicap to his own convenience and pleasure. The slight pang of guilt which he now suffered, as a result of Clarinda's words, spurred him on towards making a suggestion based on an idea which had been slowly forming in his mind all day, but which, without her comment, he would have hesitated to put into words.

"I'm afraid I haven't given the matter much attention. I'd looked forward so much to having you dine in my house, Clarinda."

"Perhaps you could ask me again some other time. And if you did, I should accept."

There was no coquetry in her manner of speaking, but the slight indication of archness, mingled as it was with candor, had a very appealing quality.

"You're asked already," he said quickly. "And—thanks, Clarinda, for taking it this way. No matter what you say to save the situation, I know that, in the last analysis, the head of a household, like the captain of a ship, is the one who's really responsible for the way it runs."

"But perhaps you have too many responsibilities. If the captain has to be on the bridge, he does not try to supervise the galley at the same time. He has someone else do that for him."

Again the quality of her speech was wonderfully heartwarming. Foxworth went on with less and less hesitation.

"I have been rather crowding the calendar. And circumstances over which I've had no control have crowded it for me still further. Now just today—"

"Yes?" inquired Clarinda, opening her fan and looking at him encouragingly.

"Well, today, with the help of my lawyer, I succeeded in getting a poor old colored woman out of prison. She ought never to have been put there in the first place. She was Odile St. Amant's nurse and later her maid. Perhaps you've heard something about that tragic case."

"You're not talking about Tossie Pride?" Clarinda asked, ignoring the last remark.

"Yes, I am. Do you know Tossie?"

"Why, all of us know Tossie! She helped at our birthday parties and at our debuts. Every girl in our set feels that she has a claim on her. If I'd only heard—if someone had only told me—I'd have gone to her at once."

"Well, now she's here, at least for the day, but I don't know just what to do with her afterwards. She begged us not to send her back to Mrs. Lalande's. She's afraid of Léonce St. Amant—ridiculous of course, but there it is."

Clarinda closed her fan. "If you will let me, I will come to see Tossie directly after Mass tomorrow," she said. "We generally go to the Cathedral at ten. That would bring me here a little after eleven. And with your permission, I shall ask Tossie to go home with me, for an indefinite stay. Of course I know Ruth would show her every kindness. But what is this rumor—pleasant for her though disappointing for us—that Ruth will be here only a few days longer herself? And probably Tossie would feel more at ease with someone she has known since birthday party days. Yes, I feel sure our quarters are the logical place for her. You agree with me, don't you, Father?"

Foxworth, absorbed in his conversation with Clarinda, had not observed the approach of Francisco Darcoa. But his daughter seemed to take both his presence and his approval for granted. They looked at each other with affectionate understanding.

"My daughter and I generally agree," Francisco Darcoa remarked, addressing Foxworth. "So I have no doubt we shall in this case. But I must confess I did not hear all of your conversation with her. I have been having an intensely interesting one myself, with the Assistant Secretary of State. It seems at one period in his career he was stationed in Sevilla. He knows many of our relatives there. . . . You will enjoy talking with him about them, I am sure," he added, speaking to Clarinda. "It seems you are to have the privilege

353

of sitting beside him at dinner. I consider that you have been given a place of great honor."

"As Father has just said, he and I nearly always agree," Clarinda told Foxworth, opening her fan again.

There was, after all, not the slightest awkwardness in shifting the party from the Foxworth drawing room to the Mystery Room at Antoine's. As the pleasant, easy transfer took place, Orson Foxworth wondered why he had ever imagined there would be. Awkward situations did not arise, much less prevail, in the presence of persons like the Darcoas and Richard Huntington; such persons knew how to surmount these. And so, to do her justice, did Ruth. She went ahead with the Racinas and was waiting to greet the others as they arrived. The floral decorations and the menu had both been checked and the place cards were all in proper position when Foxworth himself entered the Mystery Room. Miss Hickey and Caresse had followed Ruth and the Racinas with Sabin, and finally he and Richard Huntington and the Darcoas had all gone together. It seemed so natural an arrangement to everyone that there had been hardly any discussion about it. After all, a host could not usher the last of the guests from his own house and also welcome the first ones at a restaurant. And Foxworth knew that Ruth would do that for him, very graciously and competently. Yes, Ruth was a credit to her upbringing, and Aldridge was a lucky fellow to have won her so easily and quickly—Foxworth hoped the archeologist realized his good fortune. For Ruth was very attractive too. Attractive was the right word. Attractive and intelligent and well poised and pleasant and dependable and sincere. These were all good words to appy to Ruth. But she was not enchanting or queenly or glorious. In short, she was not like Clarinda.

He looked across the long table towards her now—that ivory satin she had on—it had something of a bridal look about it. But of course, when she married, she would be much more gorgeously attired—she would wear fabulous laces and wonderful brocade. Tonight, for the first time since Foxworth had closely observed her, she had on jewelry. Not much. Only a large, old-fashioned brooch of seed pearls, fastening the fichu at her breast, and long pendant earrings to match. They were quaint and charming, they became her, like the high comb in her hair and the painted fan. But he still would not be content until he saw her wearing the parure of emeralds.

She had made no answer to the remark, "Perhaps you've

heard something of that tragic case," which had been half statement and half question. Instead, she had gone on talking about Tossie. But she must know—how much or how little he could not guess, but certainly something. For New Orleans was now, inevitably, seething with gossip nonetheless virulent because it was suppressed. Along the wharves, in the cotton and coffee exchanges, at the public bars and private clubs, over bridge tables, among quiet family groups, men and women were talking about the strange and sudden death of Odile St. Amant and exchanging opinions as to where the responsibility for it lay. Clarinda Darcoa could not possibly have escaped hearing some of these discussions, and she must have weighed the pros and cons in the case. She was an intelligent girl, a thoughtful girl. She could not have dismissed such questions lightly from her mind, and there was no sound reason why she should suspect him less than any of the others involved in "the tragic case." The idea that she might suspect him of murder was abhorrent and the more he dwelt on it, the more dreadful it became. It took all his will power to continue casual, cordial conversation with Miss Hickey and Judith. Then, reason gradually reasserted itself. Clarinda had spoken in admiring terms of his achievements, she had welcomed him at her fireside, she had accepted his hospitality and told him she considered it a privilege to act as his hostess. These were not the words and acts of a woman who suspected a man of a crime; they were the words and acts of a woman who regarded him with trustful affection. Suddenly, something he had said to Amélie forced itself to the forefront of his mind: "There's a sort of certainty a man feels about the woman he's asked to be his wife and who's consented—that whoever else doubts him or fails him, she'll believe in him, she'll stand by him; that far from charging him with anything, she'll indignantly refute the least charge made against him by others. That's what he thinks she means when she tells him she loves him." He had not yet asked Clarinda to marry him, she had not yet told him she loved him. But inexplicably he was assuaged and uplifted by this very certainty. . . .

"Ruth says you've written a wonderful song," he could hear Judith Racina saying to Sabin Duplessis, who sat on the other side of her. "You're going to sing to us sometime this evening, aren't you?"

"Yes, if you all really want me to. But it's nothing except pitter-patter. When I think of the stuff Joe turns out—"

"It *is* good, isn't it? And I believe this new book is going to be the best yet. I wish he didn't have to write under such dreadful pressure though. If he could earn enough so that we'd be a little ahead of expenses, he could take things easier. But at least we don't have to worry about being abreast of expenses any more. And we've got everything else—"

Foxworth considered Judith's words. Here was a woman who had been scarred by a frightful accident, so that she could not even dress like other women, who was tied down by small children and heavy housework, who lived a secluded and uneventful life, but who felt she "had everything" except complete financial security and who took this disadvantage in her stride—because of her happy marriage. Irrelevantly, Foxworth wondered whether she had been Racina's first love or he hers and decided that both contingencies were unlikely. Yet if his conclusion were correct the fact that there had been other men in her life or other women in his had not affected their harmonious relationship. Foxworth had been telling himself, with anxiety, that Clarinda must know he had been for years Amélie Lalande's declared admirer and determined suitor and wondering whether this would make a difference to such a girl. Listening to Judith, looking at Judith, he was suddenly encouraged to believe that it would not, though he hoped Clarinda was unaware that for a long time his suit was not characterized by what were generally known as honorable intentions. On this score, he felt less concern than on some others: men did not go courting to houses like the Darcoas' unless marriage was their end and aim, and therefore she would not readily assume that it might not always be their end and aim elsewhere, under somewhat similar circumstances. Caresse, for instance, would probably be much more apt to guess something of the sort than Clarinda, though she was so much younger. He was glad propinquity would no longer enter the picture, as far as Caresse and Léonce were concerned. Not that he supposed it had ever been a really dangerous factor between them. Still, only a week before . . . .

"Oh, thank you, Mr. Secretary," he could hear her saying to Huntington now. "Of course, I'd love to. I didn't realize Washington and New York were so close to each other, honestly I didn't. Why yes, any week end—"

Yes, any week end Caresse could fly down to Washington, and Richard and Muriel would put her up at "Tradition" and would see that she met all the right people and did all the right things. Caresse was out of the woods and into the clover, and he did not begrudge her any aspect of her bright future. But inevitably, it was his own future which concerned him most—his own and Clarinda's. Even supposing all the barriers which he had visualized between them were nonexistent, there were still other impediments which Foxworth could not dismiss easily from his mind; on the contrary, they seemed to loom larger and larger before him, as he continued to regard her across the long table. His Catholicity was merely a matter of expediency; hers the very essence of the faith of her fathers. She would be quick to feel the difference. . . . He was almost old enough to be her father; and though those twenty years of difference in their ages might not matter so much, at the moment, they could matter a great deal in time to come. Not to him—he could ask for nothing more rewarding, in his decline, than close communion with such a woman as Clarinda would become in her ripening years. But what about her? When she reached the most glorious period of her Indian summer, the winter of old age would have already set in for him; and whether it would be one of sparkling snow and bright sunshine, or one of frozen ground and bleak winds, no one could foretell. Would he be justified, even if she were willing, in binding her to a potential weakling or wreck? For whatever he became, she would remain bound to him. Her traditions, her character, her religion, would all compel her to regard marriage as an indissoluble bond. Once her being was merged in her husband's, it would be forever. Could he, in fairness to her, ask her to be his wife, knowing that her promise, if she gave it to him, would be for all time . . . .

"I'm terribly intrigued with this room," Miss Hickey was saying. "That is, I don't know why I should find it so attractive, because it's rather plain, isn't it? There's nothing particularly distinctive about it, except the signed photographs of presidents and other celebrities and the sawdust on the floor. But somehow it gets me. I don't understand though, why it's called the 'Mystery Room.' Can you tell me, Mr. Foxworth?"

"I can," Joe Racina broke in, as Foxworth hesitated. "I had it from one of the old-timers on the *Item* when I was a cub. And as a matter of fact, it's about two mysteries, not just one. Roy's father, Jules, happened to pick up a painting one time in a barroom on St. Charles Street. The place was being sold out. It was a picture that intrigued Papa Jules no end, because to the unschooled eye of innocence it seemed to be just a portrait of an old, baldheaded man's profile. But if you looked closely, you saw that it was also the painting of a very nude girl. That was considered risqué stuff in those days, it seems—"

"I've seen copies of that picture in France, myself," Miss Hickey exclaimed, chuckling. "It's a very well-known work of what may loosely be described as art. A chap with a very high forehead, heavy eyebrows, and so on."

"I wouldn't know," Joe replied. "I never saw it. Anyway, as I heard the story, Papa Jules got no end of innocent fun out of bringing people to this room and displaying the mystery of his painting. Sarah Bernhardt called him a wicked old boulevardier when he brought her here after one of her performances of *L'Aiglon* .... And of course, in time the room where the mystery picture was hung became the Mystery Room."

"But you said there were two mysteries," Miss Hickey reminded him.

"I'm coming to that. Papa Jules was gathered to his fathers, and his son, Roy, the one you've met tonight, took over. And not long after that the mystery painting disappeared. I tell you, it was a sensation. So far as New Orleans was concerned, the theft of the Mona Lisa from the Louvre was a Saturday night police court case compared to the theft of the Mystery Room portrait. And the mystery of that picture's disappearance is still unsolved, though I've my own ideas about it. I think some member of Papa Jules' family was sincerely shocked by that picture, and made off with it."

"And quite right, too," said Judith. "I never could see anything amusing in such things."

"Bravo, *Señora*. Well spoken!" added Francisco Darcoa. "I am happy to know I am not the only one who finds vulgarity offensive."

"There I go, opening my big mouth again," grinned Joe, without abashment. "Fortunately, Judy's around to bring up the family's average of respectability. I've an interesting theory about that sort of thing. It has always seemed to me—"

Joe broke off and looked up. The door of the Mystery Room had opened, and Angelo Alciatore was entering with a long envelope in his hand.

"Pardon me for interrupting," he said. "But this envelope was just brought to the door by a cab driver, with instructions to deliver it straight to Miss Lalande."

"For me?" exclaimed Caresse. "Why who on earth .... I mean, there's no one who knew where ..."

"Better open it," counseled Foxworth. "I know you ladies take a delight in wondering who sent you a letter, a telegram, or a gift box, when all you need to do is to look inside."

Caresse tugged at the flap of the envelope with trembling fingers. "I can't imagine . . . ." she said, still uncertainly. "There's something hard in here. Like a coin." Slowly she ripped the envelope along one edge and shook it. A small metallic object fell out, tinkling sharply against the edge of her plate before it came to rest on the snowy tablecloth. "Why, it's my key—the key to our family tomb in Metairie!" she whispered. But Sabin and Joe had both heard her and had both risen.

"Is it from Vance Perrault?" Sabin asked, in a shaky voice.

"Isn't there anything else in that envelope besides the key?" demanded Joe. "A note or a message or something?"

Caresse pushed the torn edges of the envelope apart. Inside was a smaller envelope. She drew it out, slit it open, and took from it several folded sheets, covered with small, neat handwriting.

"'*Dear Caresse,*'" she read aloud in a wondering way. "'*I did not forget to give this key to you yesterday, as you probably thought I did. I knew I should want to use it again myself. But now that my need for it is past—*'"

Sabin interrupted: "Mr. Foxworth, would you excuse me? I'm sorry to run true to form like this, breaking up dinner parties. But I must get to a telephone at once."

"Why, of course. Only—"

The words were spoken in the direction of Sabin's vanishing figure. A hush had fallen on the room. No one was eating or drinking or speaking. Again Foxworth regarded Clarinda across the long table and found her eyes meeting his, quietly, trustfully, reassuringly. Caresse leaned forward and spoke appealingly to Joe.

"Do you know what this means too?" she faltered.

"I'm afraid so," he said with unwonted gentleness. "If I were you, Caresse, I wouldn't read the rest of that letter until you get on the train. I assume it's Perrault's confession."

"*Perrault's confession! About what?*"

The exclamation came simultaneously from several directions.

"About Odile."

"*Odile!*"

Again the exclamation was general. Joe looked at Foxworth.

359

"Is it all right for me to explain here?" he asked. "I think I can, if you're willing."

"Certainly. That is, if—" His searching glance shifted from Clarinda to her father. "Of course you have heard about the strange death of Odile St. Amant, Francisco," he said steadily. "I realize that it's been a major topic of discussion in New Orleans for a week now, with the question, 'Was it murder or was it suicide?' uppermost in everyone's mind. But perhaps you didn't know the police had reached the conclusion that it was murder and that they have regarded half a dozen persons, Sabin Duplessis and myself among them, as suspects."

Only half-successfully, Miss Hickey smothered a startled exclamation. But it did not sound shocked; it sounded incredulously thrilled. At the same moment, Francisco Darcoa answered his host with unruffled dignity.

"I've heard of the case, naturally. But I have not paid the commotion about it the tribute of much attention. I have not heard mentioned the charges to which you refer. If I had, of course I should have indignantly silenced the speakers. One does not permit one's friends to be slandered in time of trouble."

"Thank you, Francisco. For—for saying that. For—for feeling that way." To his infinite embarrassment and surprise, Foxworth found himself so much moved that it was hard for him to speak. "All this evening," he went on with difficulty, "I have been sitting among my guests wondering if I would be arrested for murder in their very presence. I spent over an hour at police headquarters this morning and, when I left, it was with the conviction that Captain Murphy was determined to hold me guilty of that crime."

"Well, stop worrying about that right now," Joe said quickly. "If I hadn't been pledged not to say anything until Murphy gave the word, I could have relieved your mind two hours ago." Suddenly the tension around the table slackened. The atmosphere of the room was still one of excitement, but it was excitement mingled with relief and curiosity, instead of with shock and amazement. Miss Hickey gasped again and this time her smothered exclamation betrayed something very like eager anticipation. For years she had been an avid reader of detective stories; never in her wildest dreams had she dared to hope that a mystery would be unraveled in her actual presence instead of through the printed pages of a book. Now such a breathtaking experience was obviously impending. "Sabin and I were with Captain Murphy just before we came to your house, Mr. Foxworth," Joe went on. "He told us he had been in touch with the *Bienvenida* by

360

radio, and that her third officer, a man named Svendson, I believe, had completely corroborated what you said about the breakdown of your speedboat. That put you in the clear. Besides, he already knew it was Perrault. But Murphy made us both promise to keep mum, because Perrault had somehow managed to give the police the slip this afternoon and—"

"You mean he had been arrested and had escaped?" Huntington inquired.

"Not exactly. But he had been under surveillance ever since he left headquarters this noon. Sabin knows more about that aspect of the case than I do, because he's been following Perrault around himself for a couple of days. So I better let him give his own version of what happened when he comes back. But you remember, Caresse, that when you and I went to Odile's tomb on Thursday, we found Doctor Perrault hovering around there and—"

Caresse nodded, her eyes filling with tears. Foxworth glanced at her and was conscious of momentary regret that these painful memories must be awakened. But he did not look at her for long, and though he was listening to Joe, he was thinking of something else at the same time, while he gazed at Clarinda again. *When you and your father come to get Tossie after Mass tomorrow,* he was saying to himself, *I'll ask your father if I may call on him again, about another matter of great importance. And he'll say, why certainly, and the sooner the better, if it's really urgent. What about this afternoon? So I'll come at your pleasant teatime, Clarinda. I'll ask for his permission to address you. And he'll give it to me. By tomorrow night you and I will be—formally engaged. For you'll say yes when I ask you. I know that already. And since I do know it, since you'll make me the happiest man in the world, I'm not going to let any of the obstacles and impediments I've been worrying about stand in my path. Some of them have been swept aside already, right here in this room. Not the handicap of age, unfortunately. There's no way of getting around those twenty years. But the religious handicap is different. I couldn't help feeling the force of your faith if I were married to a woman like you. I'll make you see that, because of you, Catholicity will no longer be merely a matter of form to me. And there's bound to be some handicap in every marriage. Perfect conditions don't and can't exist, in marriage or any other relationship, because the human element, itself imperfect, is insurmountable. But I'll sweep away all the other obstacles. I'll make you the happiest*

361

of women and you'll forget the one impediment I can't overcome.

".... Well, Sabin was hovering around too," Joe was saying. "You didn't see him and neither did Perrault. Neither did I, for that matter. But he was lurking behind another tomb, nearby, watching everything that happened. He and Murphy had got their heads together that morning about one discrepancy in Doctor Perrault's story. And they had agreed that Sabin should keep an eye on the doctor wherever he went and whatever he did. You remember how Murphy kept insisting, from the beginning, that when you're trying to find out who did a killing, it isn't a matter of reading up on strange poisons or analyzing cigarette ashes or looking for secret panels in the wall. It's a matter of listing everybody who had an opportunity to do the job and then of finding out which one of those who could have done it might have a motive for doing it."

"But Doctor Perrault—" interrupted Judith.

"I know. There didn't seem to be any motive and Toe couldn't find one. But he still thought there might have been one he hadn't discovered, and he went on narrowing down his field to the last person who'd had the opportunity to do the killing and the last one who'd seen the victim alive. He grew more and more certain this was Perrault. So—"

The door of the Mystery Room opened and Sabin came in, quietly reseating himself between Judith and Caresse. This time it was Ruth who leaned forward to ask an eager question.

"Have you been talking to Captain Murphy on the telephone?" she inquired breathlessly.

Sabin nodded. "He's just got back from Metairie. He'd been stymied for a while, because the two detectives who'd been following Perrault reported that their man had disappeared. He left his car parked outside the hospital and never came back to it. So Murphy first sent out an all-station message to have him picked up. But nothing happened. Then Toe began to think over what I'd told him last Thursday night—about seeing Perrault come out of the Lalande tomb alone, locking it up after him and putting the key in his billfold. Toe followed a hunch and beat it out to Metairie. It was quite a while before he could get hold of anyone with authority to let him into the cemetery. Because it was closed for the night by that time, of course. But once the gates were open, there wasn't any more to it. At the Lalande tomb. . . ."

23

How Vance Perrault passed the hours between eleven in the morning and sundown—

January 10, 1948

THE BLANK unwavering stare with which Toe Murphy had been regarding Foxworth relaxed into something very like a grin when the door closed behind the shipping magnate and the Assistant Secretary of State. Toe shook his head and jerked a thumb in the direction of his departing visitors.

"Look at that man Foxworth's back," he said to Perrault. "Must be what they mean when they talk about high dudgeon. Mulish old coot, isn't he? After all, how stubborn can you be? Wonder what he's got in that hard head of his right now?"

"I think I can make a pretty close guess," Perrault replied. "There's really no secret connected with what Tossie meant when she talked about leaving the door off the latch. It's just a joke—a gag, I suppose you'd call it. It's been going on for years. He's always ragged the poor old creature about what a heartbreaker and a sinner she still was, and told her he knew how many nightwalking bucks were still coming to see her—and also which ones had luck and which ones didn't. And she's always come back at him by saying he didn't have enough gumption to do more than 'drap his wing' when Miss Am'lie was around; and she'd offer to leave the door off the latch for him so he could 'really get to be de head beater aroun' de place.' Of course, he always tipped her pretty lavishly, and it got to be a standing joke between them that he gave her these tips as an inducement to leave the door of the Lalande house unlatched for him. That was really all there was to her remark."

"Yes? Why didn't he say so then?"

"Because you insisted you knew who killed Odile St. Amant. And, just as he said, if you 'knew' Foxworth had killed her, you wouldn't have been satisfied or convinced by that explanation. On the other hand, if you 'knew' some one else had killed her, Tossie's reference to getting ten dollars for leaving the door unlatched wouldn't matter, one way or another."

"Well, I'm willing to grant there's something in that line of reasoning."

"Thanks. In view of it, maybe you'll entertain another suggestion, namely, that Odile did kill herself. The suicide note was completely genuine. I'd stake my reputation on it."

"There's no way of proving that now, though, is there? Some way that note disappeared. And I have my own ideas how and why."

"If you're thinking of Mrs. Lalande, whom you practically accused of forging it, you can dismiss that as of right here and now."

"So?"

"Quite so. I took that note myself, deliberately, in order to conceal it."

"That's interesting to hear. Why?"

"Because Odile could not have been buried in consecrated ground with the rites of her faith if she had been a suicide, and I didn't propose to have that added to her family's grief. Since you were convinced it was a murder and said so, I slipped the note into my bag. Father Kessells was satisfied it was not a suicide. At least, he had no visible evidence that you were wrong."

"Then suppose you let me have the note now. There's no further purpose in concealing it."

"I wish I could, Captain. But it's no longer in my bag. I was careless enough to leave it there several days, and I must have laid it aside somewhere, or dropped it. But no harm's been done. It wouldn't mean anything to whoever found it. There was nothing to connect it with any special person. It wasn't even addressed to any one by name."

"Did you know that Joe Racina has developed a theory of his own about Odile's death?"

"Yes. He came and told me about it of his own accord."

"It's his idea that whoever took that note killed the girl who's supposed to have written it."

"That's right. And mine is that she killed herself, and yours is that someone murdered her and that you know who did it."

"As a matter of fact, it won't be much longer before I can prove it. Like I said, it was an amateur job. Whoever forgot that the absence of powder burns is a dead giveaway would be bound to overlook something else, and it was just a question of figuring out what that something else was."

"And would you object to telling me who——"

"Who killed her? I expect to tell everybody. But in my own good time, which is when I'm ready to make an arrest. That's not for yet. Like I just said, though, it'll be soon."

"But you did ask me to wait. Was there some question you wanted me to answer?"

"There was—and is. It might help a lot if you'd answer it now."

"I certainly will, if I can."

"Then here goes: who was the patient you were called to see last Saturday night, about ten o'clock, when you decided you might as well drop in at the Lalandes' on your way home, instead of waiting until around midnight?"

The doctor put his hand first in one pocket and then in another, only to withdraw it empty each time. "I'm sorry," he said. "I must have forgotten to bring my call book with me this morning, and I don't remember, offhand."

"Couldn't you telephone your office from here, right now, and get the information? I suppose you relay all your own entries to your receptionist or your medical secretary, or whoever it is who looks after the office appointments and makes out your bills."

"Yes, I do, and I'd be happy to telephone, Captain Murphy, if this were any other day. But I don't have office hours on Saturday. And it happens that Miss Vincent, who keeps track of all those things you mentioned, is out of town for the week end. If she weren't, I could call her at home. Of course, she doesn't take records there with her, but she's got a good memory—a good deal better than mine, which is beginning to fail me in my old age."

Doctor Perrault smiled, rather ruefully, but Murphy did not return the smile. "The fact that this patient you visited Saturday night must have been someone who lived in the neighborhood of the Lalandes' wouldn't recall the name to you?" he persisted.

"No, it doesn't. I suppose that sounds rather strange to you. But my practice is very large, and most of it is in the uptown area. I make more than fifty calls in that section of the city each week. It would be impossible for me to carry them all in my head."

"But you will make an effort to find out to which particular house you were called on Saturday night about ten o'clock, one week ago?"

"Of course."

"And you will let us know, so that we can verify the fact that you really were called there?"

"Naturally. As a matter of fact, I will go to my office now and see if I can find the notation among Miss Vincent's records myself. In that way I may save you some time. And of course, I'll locate the call book, sooner or later too."

"Thank you very much, Doctor Perrault."

"And that is all, Captain?"

"Yes, except that you will be—well, under observation. I mention that only because of the possibility that you might not drive to your office. If, for example, you should head out toward the Airline or any of the other highways leading out of the city, you would be stopped and asked to return."

"May I ask why you adopt this course instead of arresting me out of hand? After all, you could hold me until you got in touch with Miss Vincent yourself on Monday. So why the delay?"

"Because I would look almighty silly if it turned out I was mistaken. There is always a chance of that. And if I arrested a highly respected physician on a charge of murder of which he was innocent, where do you think I would land? .... Unless, of course, you were to confess here and now how you murdered Odile St. Amant."

Doctor Perrault looked thoughtfully at the broad-shouldered detective for a moment. "In view of what I have seen of you and your methods, Captain Murphy," he said very earnestly, "I don't expect you to believe what I am about to say, namely: I swear by all that you and I both hold dear and holy that I am not guilty of murder. Under the circumstances, your reluctance to arrest me is quite justified. But that did not restrain you from arresting Tossie a week ago, did it? Because you knew the poor soul had no recourse ...."

"And her fingerprints were on the gun. Remember?"

"Your release of the old woman just now shows how much importance you attach to that fact. That's what prompted me to ask why you didn't arrest me."

"I wasn't taking any chances when I arrested Tossie. I don't do things that way, Doctor. I'm not even taking chances by failing to arrest you. You'll be under observation from now on, wherever you go and whatever you do."

Doctor Perrault shrugged his shoulders. "That's as may be," he said. "Good day, Captain."

"I'll be seeing you. And thanks for not putting on a big

indignation scene. If you come up with the address of the patient who called you at ten o'clock last Saturday night, and that part of your story is verified, you'll have any apology you want to ask of me."

Murphy wheeled around in his chair, signifying that the interview was over. Perrault walked with composure from the office, through the anteroom, and into the long corridor. He glanced from side to side as he strode towards the central door, in the manner of one profoundly interested in the world about him. At the top of the steps he paused for a few moments, slipping on a light overcoat and drawing on his gloves. Then he went to his car, unlocked it, slid behind the wheel, and drove, unhurriedly, uptown to the Healers' Building, where his own office was located. As he surrendered his car to the attendant at the garage entrance, he saw that an automobile with a red-lensed spotlight, which he had already observed in his rear-view mirror, was pulling up at the curb nearby. He shrugged his shoulders again and, entering the ground floor drug store, joined a group of fellow practitioners at one of the black-topped refreshment tables for coffee and conversation. When the group disbanded, he made his way to a rear door near the elevators and was taken swiftly up to his seventh-floor suite. Letting himself in, he went through the reception room and passed the cubicles, equipped for treatment and examination, to his private office. Then, without pausing in front of the filing case where Miss Vincent kept the records, he seated himself at his desk and dialed his home.

"Mr. Foxworth telephoned," his housekeeper informed him promptly, "to invite you to a dinner in honor of the Assistant Secretary of State. He will expect you at six-thirty or thereabouts tonight, at his home on Toulouse Street, if you can make it. But Mr. Foxworth said it wouldn't be necessary to notify him. If you can, he will be delighted; if you can't, he will understand."

"No other messages?"

"Yes. Mrs. Osborne telephoned to tell you she was not feeling quite so well today. There were no serious symptoms, she said, but she would feel easier if you could look in on her."

"I'll call her back and tell her I'll make it some time this afternoon. But if any other messages come in, have them relayed to Doctor Sullivan. Say you're not sure when you'll be able to reach me."

"Very well, sir."

He hung up the receiver, leaned back in his chair, and

drummed on the desk in front of him with his fingers. He had spoken sincerely when he told Caresse that none of his patients mattered to him as much as Odile; but there were several who mattered greatly. He had visited one of these, a little boy by the name of Tony Carr, before going to the Criminal Courts Building that morning. Tony, who was now six, had been very badly scalded by boiling water when he was about three. The burn was on his neck, and when the scar tissue formed, it was no longer possible for him to lift his head to an erect position. In order to overcome this deformity, a series of skin grafting operations had been undertaken; and, during the long painful process, Tony and Doctor Perrault had become greatly attached to each other. The child shrank with terror and dread from the specialist, Doctor Bryan, who performed the operations; but the family physician was always able to reassure and comfort the little boy. No one else could make an impression on his infantile mind; yet somehow Doctor Perrault had succeeded in convincing him that, if he wanted to hold up his head like his brothers and sisters, he must be a good soldier and obey orders. The final stage of the treatment was now in progress; Tony's arm had been in a cast for about six weeks, in order that a tube of skin could be transferred from the arm to replace the scar tissue of the neck.

"And the next time you come, the little flap you've been telling me about will be there, all ready to use, won't it?" Tony had asked eagerly. "Honest Injun, cross your heart and hope to die?"

Perrault had turned away from the thin, huddled little figure on the bed. He simply could not meet those big eyes which looked up at him so imploringly, yet so trustfully, from the pale, peaked little face.

"The flap will be there, Tony," he said. "All ready to use."

"But Doctor Bryan won't take hold of me until you get here, will he?"

It was a dreadful sin to lie to a little child. Such a lie could undermine a child's faith in mankind. Yet, when he left the Carrs' house that morning, he had told Tony that no one would touch him unless he, Vance Perrault, were there to make the pain easier . . . .

Now he knew he would not be there. And here was this message from Bertha Osborne. Bertha, who came from Brattleboro, Vermont, had been very much alone in the world. She was a teacher at Newcomb with a master's degree from Bates and a doctor's degree from Radcliffe; but her natural habitat was the New England scene, and she had not made friends easily in the strange southern city to which her work had brought her. She had found no congenial groups with which she could go sleigh riding on wintry Saturdays and no Congregational Church where she could attend services on Sundays. She regarded Catholicism as idolatry and Carnival as an exhibition of puerile extravagance. Creole gumbo gave her indigestion, and from the first of May onward, she suffered acutely with prickly heat. She went about her teaching capably, methodically—and miserably. Then, at some tepid collegiate reception she met Lloyd Osborne, who taught anthropology at Tulane, and it was a case of love at first sight for both. They married almost immediately and were blissfully happy together.

Bertha was already thirty-five, Lloyd forty-one; for three years, to their great mutual disappointment, their marriage was childless. Then, to their mutual joy, Bertha disclosed that she "had expectations." She accepted all the discomforts of a complicated pregnancy patiently and philosophically and underwent a long labor heroically. Then, two days after its birth, her baby died of an intracranial hemorrhage. The blow was a prostrating one. It was months before Bertha recovered from it, either mentally or physically; and, as she and Lloyd both told him, it was doubtful whether she would ever have done so without the skillful, devoted, and understanding care of Vance Perrault. He became their friend as well as their physician; next to the Lalandes' pretentious house there was no private home at which he spent so much time as at the Osbornes' plain little apartment. And finally, one evening when she opened the door for him, Bertha confronted him with an expression in which incredulity was mingled with joy.

"I can't really believe it's true," she told him. "I've been so sure it couldn't be that I haven't spoken to you about it before. I thought it was just—well, change of life. But yesterday, and again today, there's been a—a little fluttering. I haven't forgotten the feeling. I think it must be the quickening."

Perrault examined her and confirmed her hopes. Then, within a few weeks, he was obliged to tell her that they might be thwarted after all; miscarriage was obviously impending. He ordered her to bed and saw to it that she stayed there, under opiates. For weeks it was touch and go. Now, at last, there was every indication that she would carry the child full term—at least there had been when he saw her, just the day before. But here was this message from her. With an effort, he dismissed the thought of Tony, reached for the telephone, and dialed again. Bertha's anxious voice came to him over the wire.

"I've been having pains all the morning, Doctor Perrault. Not bad ones. Just little sharp twinges."

He asked a few quick questions, told her that he would be with her in fifteen minutes, and cautioned her that meanwhile she was, on no account, to move. He picked up his hat and bag hurriedly and left the office without even glancing about him. The elevator was delayed in arriving, and he rang for it impatiently several times; it seemed fantastic that it should make so many stops before it finally deposited him on the ground floor. Then he found the garage attendant lounging around the parking space, chewing gum; the idea that a physician might want his car in a hurry did not seem to enter the man's thick head. When Perrault spoke to him sharply, the attendant simply stopped chewing and stared at him in astonishment. After all, Doctor Perrault had never spoken to him that way before, so his dumfounded state was not surprising. But Perrault was exasperated by it. In his exasperation, he failed to notice whether the automobile with the red-lensed spotlight left the curb at the same time he did. But when he was halfway to the Osbornes' apartment he remembered about it and looked again in his rear-view mirror. The police car was still close behind him.

To his immense relief, he found that Bertha Osborne had overestimated the possible significance of the little sharp pains. He gave her a hypodermic and told her that, as a precautionary measure, he thought there should be a nurse in the house for the next few days. He would see about getting one right away. If the pains persisted, it might be well for her to move to a hospital, where she could be under constant observation by an interne in whom he had great confidence. For the first time since he had known her, Bertha Osborne showed signs of being unreasonable and rebellious.

"I don't want to go to a hospital. I want to stay at home where I can be with my husband. And I haven't confidence in any interne I've ever seen yet."

"I'm only trying to take every possible measure to safeguard you, Bertha. I know how much this baby means to you—and to Lloyd. After all, it isn't as if you were in your twenties or even in your thirties. This is your last hope."

The words, meant as a warning to her, rang in his ears as a rebuke to himself. This *was* her last hope, and she was counting on him to see that it was not a vain one as well. She believed that, with his help, she could get a living child into

370

the world. Deprived of his help, she might lose the belief and thus possibly lose the child. He had not forgotten her abysmal despair when she had lost the other one, despair from which no one except himself had been able to raise her. He made sure, by telephone, that a reliable nurse would be at the apartment within the hour, stayed by Bertha until she had fallen asleep, and gave careful directions to Lloyd, who had just come in and who was sitting dejectedly in the living room, his head bent, his arms hanging loosely at his side. But again Perrault went away overwhelmed by a sense of guilt. Was it not as wicked to refuse to give life as it was to take life? He thought it was . . . .

He was not far from his own home, and he decided that he would go there next. Not that many matters there required his attention; he had already destroyed his personal papers, made proper provision for the disposition of his library, and prepared a detailed schedule of instructions for the care of his patients. But when he had gone to his silent office in the Healers' Building, it was with the idea of writing a letter in the solitude which this afforded; and because of the summons from Bertha Osborne, that letter was unwritten. However, he should be able to command the same amount of seclusion in his own study. Still followed by the car with the red-lensed spotlight, he drove the few intervening blocks. His housekeeper, Mrs. Noney, a capable, comfortable-looking woman, saw him as he came up the walk and opened the door for him.

"Have you had lunch, Doctor Perrault?"

"Why, no, I haven't. But I'm not hungry. And I have to go right out again. I've just come in to a dash off a letter."

"Well, let me bring you a glass of milk and some sandwiches on a tray. You can eat the sandwiches while you write and it won't take a second to swallow the milk."

He saw that her feelings would be hurt if he refused outright, so he dropped the subject and went on to his study. Taking a sheaf of paper from one of the drawers of his desk, he adjusted it with precision on the writing pad before him. Then, removing a gold-banded fountain pen from the marbled jade of its holder, he held it poised as though waiting for a more just alignment of his thoughts. Finally he began to write, and the words flowed smoothly from under his moving hand:

Dear Caresse—
  I did not forget to give this key to you yesterday, as you probably thought I did. I knew I should want it again myself.

But now that my need for it is past—or rather, now that I know it will be by the time you receive this letter—I am sending it back to you: sending it with my thanks, because you have made it possible for me to unlock a door which would otherwise have been closed to me and the opening of which means everything to me.

With my thanks goes my love, as I think you know. For now that Odile is dead, I love you more than anyone else in the world. And because my love for you and my love for her have been interwoven so many years, I feel you are the one to whom this letter about her should be sent.

This very morning I swore to Captain Murphy that I had not murdered Odile. And I spoke the truth. For murder carries with it the essential element of malice—"malice aforethought" is the legal phrase. And there was no shadow of malice on my soul when I killed Odile. She would have understood this had she not been so nearly dead by her own hand that she could not grasp what I was trying to tell her. But it was through my own unforgivable guilt that she had the means of taking her life.

A week has now passed since I killed her to save her from committing this terrible sin and to save myself from betraying all the ideas which have guided me throughout my career. You do not understand either, Caresse? Well, I must try to make you do so.

As I look back, I realize that perhaps I should not have told her that her illness was incurable. For who knows? Even tomorrow, some scientist may make a discovery that will do for palsy what vaccine has done for smallpox and penicillin for pneumonia. That is one of the reasons why our profession—and the law, too, for that matter—forbids us to take life under any circumstances. If I had left her a single ray of hope, perhaps she would not have been so obsessed with the conviction that she was a burden to everyone she loved. And yet such a ray might have been as deceptive and as disillusioning as a mirage. Every day physicians must make the difficult decision between false hope, which will give way under the impact of reality, and harsh truth, which, however somber, will endure. May God forgive me if I made the wrong choice!

Mrs. Noney entered the room, bearing a well-laden tray. The tall glass of milk and the plate of neatly trimmed sandwiches were supplemented by an appetizing salad. Without disturbing anything on the orderly desk, Mrs. Noney put her tray down on a small table, which she drew within easy reach of the doctor. Then she stood silently beside it until he looked up.

"I've done what you told me about the messages," she said. "Relaying them to Doctor Sullivan, I mean. Except for one. I'm sorry if I didn't use good judgment. But I thought perhaps I ought to tell you about that."

Doctor Perrault replaced his pen in its holder, doing so without obvious impatience. "All right. What is it?" he asked.

"Miss Wilson, Mr. Stafford's nurse, has just called. It seems he's a great deal weaker. And he's been asking for you."

"Your judgment was good, as it usually is, Mrs. Noney. Call Mr. Stafford's house and say I'll be there sometime this afternoon. And thanks for the lunch. It looks delicious."

He picked up his pen again and tried to resume his writing. But the words which had flowed so smoothly at first now came haltingly; he could no longer focus his thoughts on them. He had succeeded in dismissing Tony Carr and Bertha Osborne from his mind. Now, with the message from Horace Stafford, they were both recalled to him and, in some ways, this latest appeal was the most moving of all. He and Stafford had been friends all their lives; they had gone to the same school and the same college; they moved in the same social circles and belonged to the same clubs. For years, it had been their habit to play golf together every Saturday afternoon. Then one day Stafford collapsed on the course. When Perrault examined him the next day, this lifelong friend proved to be the victim of leukemia. The progress of the ailment had been retarded by X-ray treatments, but Stafford had grown steadily weaker, and of course the golf games had long since been a thing of the past. To compensate for their loss, Vance Perrault had made it a practice to drop in on Horace Stafford regularly every Saturday afternoon. Today he had completely forgotten about it. Whatever else he left undone, he must manage to see Horace that day. Impelled to speed by the realization of the flight of time, he picked up the pen again.

I had given Odile a sedative, as soon as I first reached your house. But its effects had not been as tranquillizing as I hoped. You have already heard me say this in the presence of everyone who was in the drawing room last Sunday morning. However, I did not tell any of you something which was far more significant: that Odile had begged me to "put her to sleep so that she would never wake up" and that when I told her this was impossible, she burst into uncontrollable weep-

ing. I should have left the house immediately then. But I did not. I went into the bathroom, closed the door behind me, and deliberately washed my hands. I was perfectly well aware what Odile might do in my absence, and when I returned to her room, I found that my guess had not been wide of the mark. Glancing at my bag, I saw that my hypodermic kit was missing. Of course I knew that she must have taken the morphine tablets too, and hidden them.

She pretended to be drowsy at last, and I pretended to believe this. I can only plead—not in extenuation, for there can be no question of my guilt—that I was not thinking rationally, because I was so deeply moved by the realization that I had deprived her of all hope for the future. And so I left her, knowing what she planned to do and leaving her the means with which to do it. Furthermore, instead of telling your mother or Tossie to watch over her, I told them on no account to enter her room. And I said I would return at midnight, by which time I knew she would be past mortal help.

I went home and sat down to a dinner table where I could not eat. I tried to check on the cases which were in real need of care and found that I could not give any of them proper attention. But finally, after several hours, I began to think clearly again, to understand that I was responsible for the mortal sin which Odile was about to commit. And I knew that whatever else might happen, I must take that sin from her and upon myself.

I got into my car again and drove recklessly through the night, praying that I might not be too late. When I arrived at your house, I told your mother that I had been called unexpectedly into the neighborhood, and thought I might as well look in on Odile then as later. The other patient was, of course, entirely fictitious.

When I reached Odile's room I saw that only a miracle could restore her. I did my best to rouse her. I gave her a powerful stimulant, I lifted her out of bed, I tried to force her into walking. But her breathing grew slower and slower, more and more shallow. I lowered her unconscious form to the floor and administered artificial respiration. But I could see from the pallor of her lips, from her failing breath, that it was all useless.

Since that night I have heard, in a roundabout way, that Sabin Duplessis insists he saw the shadows of a man and a woman against the window blind. This must have been while I was trying to force Odile to walk. When I finally realized it was too late to save her in that way, I also knew there was

374

only one other way to take the sin of self-destruction from her: I must kill her while she was still alive.

I knew about the gun Sabin had given Odile. It was one of the things she told me at the time of my first visit, when the sedative I administered failed to take its full effect. At that time I had not yet realized the depths of her despair. While I felt quite certain her poor hands were too weak and too palsied to master the mechanism of loading the wicked little thing, to say nothing of pulling the trigger, I deemed it best to make assurance doubly sure, by dropping the package into my coat pocket. Do not attempt to reconcile this instinctive action on my part with what happened later. I suppose that, so long as I did not know she had taken the morphine from my bag, I could persuade myself that I had done all that was necessary by putting the gun beyond her reach. What a pitiful evasion! What a weakling I was!

The gun was still in my pocket, and I recall feeling a morbid gladness that I had not left it somewhere. For, if I had administered another dose of poison, there might be some doubt about which injection had killed her. But there could be no doubt about a bullet. I took the tissue-wrapped package from my pocket, removed the ribbon and paper, and slipped the magazine into place.

And so Odile did not commit suicide, dear Caresse. Her soul does not have that sin upon it. She was still alive when I pulled the trigger. She was killed by my hand, not her own. And because I took certain precautions, no one in the house heard the shot. Furthermore, I had slipped a rubber glove over my hand before I opened the package, so there were no fingerprints of mine on the gun. The fact that I overlooked the matter of powder burns is of no importance now.

If Tossie had not disobeyed my instructions about going into Odile's room, she would never have been placed under arrest. No doubt the poor old creature picked up the gun unthinkingly when she found it on the floor beside Odile, and that is how her fingerprints happened to be on it. Naturally, I could not rest until I secured her release, and I did not succeed in doing that until this morning. It has been a dreadful week. For of course I have had to live with the knowledge that some other innocent person might be charged with the commission of the deed which was mine alone—Sabin, Léonce, Orson Foxworth, even your mother or you, my dear. Yesterday, at the Racinas' house, I learned from Joe of your confession to Murphy about your outing last Saturday. I knew Murphy would find out you had told the truth and that he would never hold you after that. So I was able to assure *you that he would let you leave for New York tonight. And this morning, at the time of Tossie's release, I learned from Murphy himself how much he knew or guessed about my own actions. And this knowledge will clear all the others under suspicion. This being so, I can seek release myself. With one mortal sin already on my soul, why should I hesitate to commit another? Why should I endure imprisonment or face an executioner when the eternal sleep sought by Odile is so easy and so sure?*

Mrs. Noney had come into the room again. She glanced at the untouched tray, but made no comment on it. Neither did she make any move to displace it. This was not the first time she had seen Doctor Perrault neglect his food because of his absorption in the task at hand. However, after the task was finished to his satisfaction, he generally remembered to eat.

"I've had to use my best judgment again," Mrs. Noney said. "It wasn't about a patient this time. That is, the young lady *is* one of your patients, but she isn't sick at the moment. As far as I can gather, she's feeling pretty good."

Doctor Perrault looked down at the letter which he was on the point of signing. "Was the young lady Miss Caresse Lalande, by any chance?" he asked.

"Yes, sir. She said to be sure and tell you that you'd kept your promise. And that she hoped she'd have a chance to tell you herself how happy she was about it, because she understood you and she were both invited to the same dinner party. And then she added, 'By the way, tell Doctor Perrault that the dinner's been switched to the Mystery Room at Antoine's. The guests are going to meet at Mr. Foxworth's residence for cocktails, as planned, but then they're going on to the restaurant. It won't matter which place he meets us.' Would you want me to call her back for you, sir? Or to telephone Mr. Foxworth's house for you? I haven't done that either, because you haven't told me yet—"

"That's all right, Mrs. Noney. I'll take care of that matter myself. And your judgment was good again. It happens that I was just wondering where I could be able to reach Miss Lalande at dinner time."

He folded the sheets which lay in front of him and placed them in an envelope, sealed it, and put it in another, which he addressed without sealing. Then he put this in his pocket, together with a small supply of extra stationery. Mrs. Noney was still standing beside the untouched tray. He picked up the glass of milk and emptied it, almost at one draft. Afterwards he bit into a sandwich.

"Delicious!" he said. "I'm afraid I can't stop for the salad now if I'm to see Mr. Stafford before I go to the hopsital— I've got to get there this afternoon too for—for an emergency. But I still think you make the best salads, Mrs. Noney, of anyone in New Orleans. Don't you forget I said so, either."

"Thank you, sir. You may be sure I shan't."

Fortunately, Horace Stafford, like Bertha Osborne, lived only a few blocks away. As Perrault drew up at the curb in front of his friend's house, he could see the invalid lying in bed, near the window, looking out towards the street. So poor old Horace had actually been watching for him! It meant as much as that to have him come. He went rapidly up to the sickroom and grasped the translucent hands lying on the counterpane.

"And you thought I wasn't coming!" he said, in playful reproach. "Why, Horace, you ought to know me better than that! It's—let's see, how many years since we've missed our Saturday date?"

"It wasn't that I didn't think you'd come, Vance. It was just that I thought you might not come quite soon enough. I can't help having a feeling—"

The feeble voice trailed away into silence. The tired eyes closed. Vance Perrault looked up at the nurse who was standing nearby and shook his head.

"Well, you see I did get here," he said cheerfully. "And you mustn't give way to those feelings. They're just part of your symptoms, due to weakness. I think perhaps you need a new tonic. I'll send you something that will pep you up."

The translucent hands moved again, ever so slightly. The tired eyes half opened.

"If I could just be sure you'd be here, Vance, when—at the end. It isn't as if I had a wife and children. Or anyone else who cares. But our friendship—yours and mine—has always meant a lot to me. Well, you know how I feel. No use to say any more about it."

For the third time that day, Vance Perrault looked away from pleading eyes. For the third time the conviction that he was dealing a deathblow seized hold of his mind. Perhaps he could take a chance. He could not wait for Tony's operation, he could not wait for Bertha's baby; in this case, however, it might not be a question of days, or even hours, but of minutes. He glanced at his wrist watch. Well, there was no help for it. He did not have even minutes to spare now.

He drove off, along the familiar route to the Riverside Hospital, parking his car in the space reserved for staff members, behind the big brick building. As usual on Saturday afternoon, the lot was practically deserted. But as he entered the service door of the hospital, he saw the automobile with the red-lensed spotlight, which had been steadily following him, drive in and stop close to his own. Once more he shrugged his shoulders slightly. Then he went on to the Physicians' Room and called the Toye Cab Company.

"This is Doctor Perrault speaking. Can you have a limousine at the mortuary entrance of the Riverside Hospital in ten minutes?"

"You said a limousine, sir?"

"That's right. For my own use. Thank you very much."

He sat down at a small table, drew the additional stationery from his pocket, and began to write again, with even greater haste than before:

Dear Captain Murphy:

You were quite right about the powder burns, of course. But I was less than five feet away when I pulled the trigger. It was necessary to muffle the sound of the gunshot. Odile was already unconscious. I pressed a small, lace-covered, silk pillow against her breast, held the muzzle of the gun to it, and fired. The gun was small and the sound would not have been audible beyond her room. I don't suppose it really matters, but I stuffed the pillow into my bag and took it home, where I destroyed it.

Faithfully yours,
Vance Perrault.

He scrawled Murphy's name across his extra envelope and placed the note in it. Then he sealed it and put it in his pocket, beside the one he had written to Caresse, and, picking up his bag, walked down a long hallway to the Pathology Department and through a succession of adjoining laboratories to an inconspicuous door that opened on the silent mortuary. Stationing himself beside a window, he waited until the limousine for which he had telephoned drew up at the entrance through which the bodies of the dead were taken. He got into the car and gave a swift direction to the driver. The man nodded and they immediately sped lakeward, coming only once to a stop: before a florist's shop where Doctor Perrault descended, returning with an armful of small red roses. There was no other halt until the car, having passed through the massive archway of the Metairie gates, drew up before an ornate tomb where two stone angels stood with heads bowed and hands pressed together in perpetual and changeless prayer.

378

Perrault mounted the stone steps and unlocked the bronze doors of the tomb. Then he withdrew the unsealed envelope from his pocket, slipped a small key into it, fastened the flap securely and going down the steps again, handed it to the driver.

"You needn't wait," he said. "Someone will be coming for me. But I'd like you to take this envelope to Antoine's Restaurant and deliver it to either Mr. Roy Alciatore or Mr. Angelo Alciatore in person. The lady to whom it's addressed won't be dining there until about seven-thirty, and I promised her the contents should reach her safely this evening. It's very important, as she's leaving the city tonight. So I'd be much obliged if you'd take the envelope to the restaurant about eight." He reached into his pocket again and drew out a crisp bill. "Is this enough to cover the charges?"

"Oh yes, sir. Thank you, sir. It's more than enough. Can I help you take in the flowers?"

"No, thank you. Just hand them to me, will you? Those and my kit."

Perrault accepted the great armful of red roses and his small black bag. The driver resumed his seat, touched his cap and drove off through the early winter dusk. Perrault mounted the steps once more and, entering the tomb, arranged the flowers with great care beside the unmarked slab and took a hypodermic syringe, already filled, from his bag. Then he knelt before the altar and prayed.

"For this and other mortal sins and for all sins of my past life, I ask forgiveness, Father."

Envoi

I

March, 1948

"AND to think I was so fortunate as to get this charming house, without the slightest effort or delay, when *everyone* says there isn't a *thing* to be had in Washington. Of course, the Assistant Secretary of State used his influence, and we all know what *that* is! Even so, if Mrs. Deering hadn't wanted to go to New Orleans for Carnival and the Spring Fiesta and hadn't mentioned the matter to Mrs. Huntington at that White House luncheon—"

Amélie Lalande looked about her with unconcealed satisfaction. Although she had been in the smart maisonette on Massachusetts Avenue only two weeks, she had contrived to give its drawing room much the same atmosphere as that of her house on Richmond Place. She had brought with her all the decorative family photographs in silver frames, all the small lace-covered pillows, much of the bric-a-brac, the cabinet containing the regalia of a Carnival queen, and the portrait of herself in full evening dress. ("Rented houses are always so *bare* looking," she explained to Muriel Huntington, when the laden van from New Orleans arrived. "I feel I owe it to myself and to the new friends who'll be coming here to make the place where I'm living look *homelike*.") All the photographs of Odile were flanked by bud vases, each containing a single white rose. The photographs of Caresse had orginally been relegated to less conspicuous places, but these were so outstandingly ornamental that someone kept picking them up with interest and moving them forward again. The caller of the moment, a portly, sleek-headed man, whose formal attire was accentuated both by the flower in his buttonhole and by the pearl gray spats in which his rather thick ankles were encased, had just been doing this very thing. He kept inspecting them through his monocle, while giving vent to murmurs of admiration, voiced in an unfamiliar tongue. Amélie had found it necessary to take steps to recall her own charming presence to the forefront of his consciousness.

"And it's so kind of Richard's and Muriel's friends to regard me with such sympathy and understanding," she went on. "I know you all realize how much I appreciate your attitude, Count. Coming here as I did, a complete stranger and in deep mourning . . . ."

She drew a black chiffon handkerchief from the bosom of her black lace teagown and made brief but effective use of it. Her caller, resuming his seat on a chair adjacent to Amélie's sofa, leaned forward and possessed himself of her hand, again murmuring something that was unmistakably admiring. Amélie did not repulse or rebuke him.

"You have no idea how I look forward to your visits," she said softly. "When Muriel offered to give a dinner for me, of course I told her that I couldn't think of letting her do anything like that, for six months at least—well, three months anyhow. But when she said just a few close friends, for Sunday supper, I felt that was different. I thought my dear daughter herself would have wanted me to accept."

"Of course she would have," agreed the count, gently stroking the pretty little hand he was still holding.

"And Muriel selected those few guests with such wisdom. She seemed to divine exactly which persons, out of all her immense, distinguished acquaintance, would be most congenial to me. Then she seated you beside me. And you asked if you might call. And every few days since then, at about this same hour—"

"I should have come every day if I had not feared you would consider me intrusive—presumptuous," the count assured her. "But if you would permit me—"

"If I would permit you! But I would welcome you. Surely you know that! Surely you know that between us there can be no question of intrusion or presumption."

"Then from now on, it shall be every day. Dear lady, if you but knew how happy—how honored—I am by such marks of favor from you!"

He was still holding her pretty hand a willing captive. Now he raised it to his lips and imprinted on it a long kiss, nonetheless ardent because it was respectful. When he finally released it, Amélie drew a deep breath and again put her handkerchief to her eyes. Then she looked away from him and spoke with unconcealed emotion.

"I try to keep my troubles to myself," she said brokenly. "But you have made me feel that you would be willing to have me unburden my heart to you. Am I mistaken?"

"You know that you are not. You know that I should regard your confidence, like your company, as a great honor."

She sighed again, still more deeply this time. "Then perhaps you will understand the extent of my affliction if I tell you that when I came to Washington I was crushed, not only by the death of my beautiful young daughter, but by another loss, which, in a way, was even harder to bear."

The count moved from the chair adjacent to Amélie's sofa to the sofa itself and slid his arm around her yielding waist. "Tell me about it," he urged. "You will feel better afterwards."

"It was not another loss by death. But many tragedies are greater than that," Amélie said, so dramatically that the ancient cliché took on fresh vitality. "For years, a certain man had been my persistent suitor—"

"A certain man! Many, I am sure!"

"Ah, but it was different in this case! For I returned his affection—or rather, the affection he expressed. The others did not matter—I am not one of those women who can give her heart easily or often."

"Indeed, no."

"And, for a long time, after the death of my husband, I lived a life of complete seclusion. Our Creole customs of mourning—you have no idea how strict they are! And then there were my two little daughters. All my love was lavished on them. But finally—"

"Ah, finally—"

"I consented to marry this suitor to whom I have referred. And then, for the first time, he revealed himself to me in his true colors. He was domineering—violent—almost abusive. I was obliged to dismiss him from my presence, to tell him that I would never see him again. The shock of this parting and the reasons for it prostrated me. That was why I felt I must leave New Orleans, why I must have a compete change of scene. My second loss came, you see, while I was still overwhelmed by the death of my daughter, when I did not have the strength to endure it."

"There, there. If you will lay your head on my shoulder, and allow your pent-up sorrow to find release, you will see that afterwards . . . . Not that you should grieve for the loss of such a scoundrel. You should be thankful you have escaped from the fate of becoming his wife. For you will find another man more worthy of your love. Who knows, perhaps before so very long? And meanwhile—"

For a few moments Amélie continued to sob unrestrainedly, her head sinking lower and lower on the count's shoulder and finally seeking repose on his breast. Then, with an obvious effort, she raised herself and looked at him with a brave smile.

"Meanwhile, I have your friendship, which has done so much to restore my faith. And a precious, precious memory to sustain me—a memory which I shall always treasure. The man I thought I loved was unworthy of me, it is true. But my sweet, lovely daughter returned my devotion in the fullest measure. Even when she knew she was dying, she wrote me a letter. 'Darling,' it said, 'I have tried to be a good daughter—I love you.' Could any mother ask more than that her child's last earthly thoughts should be of her?"

II

April, 1948

Russell Aldridge had found a house for Ruth to live in where he could occasionally join her during the intervals of his work in the caves of Roatan. It was a little stone house on a hillside, a few miles south of the Choluteca River. In front of it was a garden, whose low stone walls followed the contours of the hill. It overlooked the airport and the dusty white road leading into Tegucigalpa. Ruth spent a great deal of time sitting in the garden, where she could watch the arrivals at the airport—the Pan-American planes and the Taca planes and the military planes of the government. On Fridays and Saturdays she watched more intently than at other times, because if Russ could get away to spend the week end with her, he would be coming in from La Ceiba or Tela or Puerto Cortez. He had no way of letting her know beforehand whether he would be coming or not. She had to sit and wait and hope. If he were not there by dark, she would know he had not been able to get away. Then she would leave this walled garden, overlooking the airport, and, passing through the little stone house, go to the smaller garden in the rear, where Teresina, the cook, would be stirring something in an iron pot over the open hearth made with clay cooking tiles. Ruth would tell Teresina that the *patrón* would not be there after all and that she herself would just have something on a tray. She had no trouble in making Teresina understand her; she had spoken Spanish all her life. But at first she had to be careful about remembering not to pronounce "z" like "th," as she would have done in Spain, because in Honduras this would have been regarded as an affectation.

Although she watched the airport intently on Fridays and Saturdays, on other days she was diverted by many other sights. Early in the morning there were always barefoot women, wearing loose white dresses and black *rebozos* wound tightly around their throats, plodding patiently along to market, each with a basket filled with produce on her head—eggs, peppers, avocados, mangos, pomegranates. And there were always half-grown boys, clad in open jackets and baggy trousers and broad hats of plaited palm straw, with long poles over their shoulders and half a dozen fowl hanging by their feet from the ends of the poles. Occasionally mule trains would pass by, the men who drove them carrying drinking gourds slung over their shoulders and sheathed machetes at their belts. And all day long oxcarts with disk wheels of solid wood would go creaking along.

From her walled garden, Ruth watched all these with fascination. Then she would look farther away, across the valley, past the airport, to the saw-toothed crests of the mountains and the gaunt radio tower projecting skyward from one of them. And when the blue-black thunderheads of impending showers blotted these from view, she would look back again at the garden, her gaze wandering contentedly from the croton bushes with their scarlet leaves, to the wild tumble of bougainvillea vines with their magenta blossoms, and to the tall coconut palms.

Of course she was not alone all the time. There were frequent visitors from town—the American Ambassador and his wife and other members of the Embassy staff; representatives of the great American oil and fruit and rubber companies, with their families and their visitors. She went into town to see these people too, driving the smart new Cadillac her uncle had sent her. But somehow she did not seem to care much about the endless bridge games, the interminable hours spent over long drinks, and the round of parties which crowded the lives of most members of the American Colony.

Sitting in her walled garden, one Saturday afternoon, watching the planes circling slowly down to earth and wondering, as each came into sight, whether Russ would be on it, Ruth marveled that this was so. Her friends—both the friends of her former life and the new-found friends in Tegucigalpa—often told her that she had been everywhere, seen everything, known everybody. This was not strictly so, of course. But it was true that her life had been extraordinarily full and varied. Looking back, she thought of her presentation at the Court of St. James's—of her private audience at the Vatican—of Imperial garden parties in Japan—of dinners at the White House and at the Elysée Palace. But though she did so with the consciousness that these and other such experiences had added to the rich pageantry of her life, this was without regret that the pattern was simpler now. It had grown almost unbearably complicated before she left Washington; and then had come that fantastic week in New Orleans, permeated with romance, yet touched by tragedy. When she looked back on that period, it seemed farther away than any of the other experiences she was casually recalling. Only the fact that from this strange extravaganza had emerged the glad reality of her marriage brought it back to her with clarity and reassurance.

Sitting very still, she thought also of the wonderful sights that she had seen in different parts of the world—the Great Wall of China sprawling over space—the Alhambra when the moon was bright—the harbor of Rio shimmering in the sunshine—the mystic bridges at Isfahan—the jewel-like windows of the Chartres Cathedral—and looked again at the saw-toothed mountains and the dusty white road and the tangled bougainvillea with no consciousness that they suffered by comparison. She thought, too, as she watched the circling planes, one of which might be bringing Russ home to her, of the other men who had wanted to marry her—the Greek diplomat, the Bolivian tin magnate, the West Virginia Congressman of whom her stepfather had spoken; also of others, about whom he had said nothing, possibly because he guessed nothing, more probably because he cared nothing. Her mother would have considered almost any one of these a "brilliant match." With any one of them she would have continued to live the sort of life she had always lived, enjoyed the same privileges, beheld the same wonders. But it would not have been the same. For she would not have seen them with Russell Aldridge, and he was the only man who had ever really mattered.

That, of course, was the answer, she reflected. If a woman—a normal, unremarkable woman, with no deep religious conviction that earthly joys were not for her, no great philanthropic purpose, no extraordinary talent clamoring for expression—did not have the man she recognized as her own, nothing else actually counted. There might be compensations for this lack. But as she herself had once read, in a book written by an author as wise as he was disillusioned, "A compensation is something which does not quite compensate." And something which did not quite compensate would never have satisfied Ruth. Only Russell Aldridge could have done that. If the Honduran hillside had been, instead, a valley in Vermont or a plain in Kansas, the answer would have been the same. Even when he was not there, she could be content, since she knew that sooner or later he was coming. She had learned how to wait. She was waiting now.

It would have been a thousand times better, of course, if instead of watching alone until the quick tropical night engulfed her, she had seen Russ driving up. If he had slammed the door of the car which had brought him from the airport and come quickly up the hillside and taken her in his arms. If he had sat beside her in the walled garden eagerly telling her everything he had done since he last saw her. If he had read aloud to her from some book which they both loved, and sat opposite her at the little feast which she and Teresina had planned with such care. If he had listened with her to the chorus of the tree frogs and the slow creak of the windmill and the distant tinkle of a guitar. If he had lain with her in the wide bed which seemed so empty and so commonplace when he was not there, but which, with his presence, became the magic setting for shared confidences and shared raptures .... Yes, if all this could have happened, it would have been a thousand times better.

In spite of her patience, in spite of her contentment, a pang of pain stabbed at her vitals as she thought of all the endless days and nights, still ahead of her, when there would be no spiritual and physical communion with the man she loved. Momentarily, her envy of those women whose husbands were always with them, thrust through her like a sharp knife. But the envy did not last, nor the pain. Those other women did not have her man, the only one she wanted. And the days and nights when she did have him made up for all those when she did not.

Besides, her need of him would not always be like this. When they had been married longer, when she grew older and steadier, the nature of the need would change. It would not be a desperate yearning of the flesh, as well as the spirit, only a tranquil quest for a kindred heart and mind. And he would need her more too, in the same way. They would not be separated so much. Instead of the hillside for her and the caves for him, there would be a home they could share all the time. In Virginia? In New Orleans? In some unknown part of the world? That, she told herself, as she had done so many times before, would not matter . . . .

Well, the last plane had come in, and Russ had not been on it. A gay crowd had been out from Tegucigalpa that afternoon, but her guests had left earlier than usual. Several of them were going to a dinner at the Peruvian Embassy, all of them to a dance at the country club. Teresina had served planter's punches and gin rickeys and sandwiches, and then she had gone back to the open hearth in the rear garden to lean over the clay tiles, peering into a pot containing a savory mixture, which she was solicitiously stirring. Ruth went through the house and spoke to her from the doorway.

"The *patrón* will not be coming tonight, Teresina."

The *criada* stopped stirring the mixture and shook her head. *"Qué lástima!"* she said sorrowfully.

"Yes, it is too bad . . . . I don't want any dinner, I ate so many sandwiches while we were having our drinks. *Buenas noches.*"

She turned and went back into the house, mindful that Teresina was still looking after her, shaking her head sadly. It was almost dark, but Ruth could still see to undress without lighting a lamp. She slipped out of her clothes and slid in between the hand-woven sheets of the big bed and lay very still.

"Next week," she told herself resolutely. "Next Saturday night at this time . . . ."

III

May, 1948

On her wedding day Clarinda Darcoa waked very early in the morning.

Not that she had passed a troubled or restless night. To be sure, she had gone to bed rather late, for she had given a party in honor of her twleve bridesmaids at the house on Coliseum Street, while Orson Foxworth was giving his bachelor dinner at Antoine's. But these late hours had been the exception rather than the rule for her. Throughout her engagement, she had calmly insisted that she did not intend to wear herself out with a senseless round of festivities. She had seen too many prospective brides do that, with the result that by the time their wedding days arrived, they were mentally and physically exhausted. She intended to be feeling and looking her best when hers arrived.

She had held firmly, though pleasantly, to her resolution, and she had done so in the face of considerable argument from the countless friends who had besought her to "make just this one exception." But her father had upheld her from the beginning, and, almost from the beginning, her fiancé had done so too. For, with customary candor, she had told Foxworth that she wanted and intended to save herself all unnecessary fatigue and excitement—for his sake as well as hers.

"I hope you will come to see me every day at teatime," she told him. "That will be our hour together, and no one shall intrude on it. Of course, I do not mean that we shall never have more than an hour alone—perhaps some days you can come a little early, and if you can, I shall be overjoyed to see you. I am sure you know that. But you will be busy during the first part of the day and so shall I. You have your merger to complete, your preparations for another long absence from New Orleans to make. And I have a large wedding for which to get ready—oh, such arrangements are not made in themselves, I am sure you know! In the evenings, my father will wish for conferences with us—with you about the merger, with both of us about the wedding. Then there are my sister and her husband and their children—I shall not be seeing them again for a long while. Naturally, I wish to have as much time as possible with them. I must show Lina, gradually, how to take over the reins of management here, so that no one will be any the less comfortable after I have gone. Shall we say that twice a week, at the outside, we will dine with friends or invite friends in to dine with us? And that the rest of the week we will keep for ourselves?"

"If 'ourselves' meant just you and me, Clarinda, you know I'd be only too happy. But business all day for me! Household duties all day for you! And family dinner every night except when there are guests!"

"It will be just 'ourselves' after we are married, *querido*. And we will have that hour at teatime. Will you not at least try my way first? Because afterwards—"

"Well, afterwards?"

"It will be all your way, of course."

She looked at him with the same admiration, affection, and confidence with which she had always regarded him. But now he was conscious of other qualities merging with these: of ardor mingled with the tenderness, of devotion mingled with the wonder, of a trustfulness that transcended all false shame.

"All right. We'll try it your way," he said.

It had been his pride, until very lately, that he had never followed any woman's lead, that it was always easy enough to make them follow his. Now he found that he took pride in following Clarinda's. Not because she was demanding or unreasonable or domineering like Amélie; but because she was steadfast and dignified and—modest. The beautiful old-fashioned word came back to him, with renewed force, every time he saw her. After the door of the drawing room closed behind him, she always advanced to meet him, raising her face to his kiss; but he knew that she did not expect this to be intense or prolonged, that she would have been both surprised and resentful if he had attempted a passionate embrace. Sometimes when they were talking together, she slipped her hand into his, and when they were in company, she always took his arm and remained close at his side. But she never proffered a caress of her own accord, and finally he asked her why she did not.

"Do you really want to have me?" she asked.

"Certainly I do."

"Now? Before we are married?"

"Of course. We're engaged, aren't we?"

"Yes. We're engaged. And I'm not so old-fashioned that I don't think a girl should show her affection for her future husband or so ignorant that I don't know that most girls are—shall we say more demonstrative than I am? But somehow—"

"Yes, Clarinda?"

"Well, men and women both have their own prerogatives,

388

don't they? For instance, it is the man's prerogative to propose marriage. I think he does a woman a great injustice if he fails to tell her he loves her, if he doesn't give her the chance to decide whether she wishes to accept him or not. Because the decision is *her* prerogative. One is as important as the other. But they are not the same, any more than men and women are the same."

"I see what you mean. And I agree with you. But after he has proposed—"

"After he has proposed, it is still his prerogative to take the initiative; by showing his fiancée his affection in all sorts of ways that he could not have done before—by constantly seeking to be with her, by giving her presents for her personal adornment, by saluting her as his future wife."

"And you feel her prerogative is still one of accepting or declining?"

"Yes. And I think if she must err, it should be on the side of restraint. Because, if his love for her is intense, her fiancé will never err on that side. And someone must remember that there are periods when moderation has its merits."

She smiled with the slight archness which he had already found so beguiling on several occasions. Clarinda was quite right: an accepted suitor seldom erred on the side of restraint, and personally, Foxworth was finding it harder and harder to do so. At first his admiration for her, though genuine and profound, had been sufficiently objective to temper his ardor. He had visualized her as the poised and gracious hostess in his *palacio*; as the beautiful woman trained in the tradition that wives should be compliant no less than captivating; as the dignified consort for the ruler of a great empire; and as the devoted mother of the heirs for this domain. But he had not considered her primarily and personally as his good companion, his prudent counsellor, or his dearly beloved. He had never before thought of a woman as a companion or sought one as a counsellor; and he had assumed, for years, that Amélie was his beloved. Now he found that the quiet hours, at the close of his driving days, which he spent at Clarinda's side, were among the most restful and the most fulfilling that he had ever known. He discovered that he wanted to ask her opinion, and that having secured her advice, he nearly always wanted to accept it; and to his increasing surprise, he realized that Amélie had never been his beloved in the true sense of the word. What he had groped towards hitherto was merely the shadow; what he had now was the substance. The revelation of all this was well nigh overwhelming.

With his awakened consciousness cane a greater and greater eagerness to realize all the benefits and pleasures which might result from the amazing turn of events. He remembered how he had dreaded the telephone messages with which Amélie had constantly besieged him; now he kept urging Clarinda to call him, only to find that this was one of the few points on which she was adamant: she would be delighted to hear from him at any time, she assured him; but she could not bring herself to risk disturbing his well-earned rest or intruding upon business matters. So he formed the habit of telephoning her twice every day, first to say good morning and ask if there were anything he could do for her, and later to assure himself that nothing had arisen to interfere with their afternoon's appointment. He showered her with presents of every description, and tried, by indirect as well as direct means, to discover any wishes of hers which might be fulfilled. And he thought of her constantly. Not only with impatience to possess her, but also with infinite tenderness, infinite respect—and infinite gratitude.

He had often wondered whether he succeeded in making Clarinda understand how completely she now dominated his existence. When she said, "If a woman must err, it should be on the side of restraint," smiling in her slow, charming way and adding, "There are periods when moderation has its merits," he knew that she had understood all along. The knowledge, far from offending him, gave him a strange new sense of gladness. He awaited with pleased anticipation her further remarks on the same general subject.

"That is one of the reasons why I suggested limiting the amount of time we should spend together—besides the more practical reasons of which I spoke," she went on. "But it was not the reason I suggested that our engagement should last for several months, instead of only for several weeks, as you urged. I suggested that because—"

"Yes, Clarinda?" he said again.

"Because it is natural for me to approach a great change—to prepare for a supreme experience—gradually. You see all this—I mean lovemaking—is entirely new to me. So perhaps I do not view the situation rationally. But I do know that each time I feel your fingers resting in mine, I am happier than I was the time before, that each time you kiss me, it means more to me than it did the time before. I already place my hand in yours instinctively—you know that because I do it, and you must have felt, from the way I do it, that the act is natural and spontaneous. But it does not yet seem natural for me to take the initiative in an embrace. So I have preferred to wait until it did. I knew it would before long. And it has seemed to me that if we tried to crowd such joys too closely together, or to anticipate their logical sequence, we would miss a development in mutual love which we would never find again."

He was profoundly moved, as much—though in a different way—as when Francisco had said one does not permit one's friends to be slandered in time of trouble. There was certainly something about the quiet, old-fashioned manner in which these Darcoas expressed themselves . . . .

"I think I understand," he said slowly. "I realize that courtship isn't merely an expedient designed to flatter a woman's vanity, that she needs time—at least, if she's the kind of woman you are—to prepare for a great change and approach—well, what you call a supreme experience. I see she'd miss something important if she didn't have this period of preparation. And though I wouldn't have believed it beforehand, I'm beginning to realize that the man she's going to marry would miss something too. But once they are married—"

He stopped short, realizing that whatever else he might add would be both inept and indelicate. But while he was grappling with this problem, Clarinda herself solved it.

"I told you that if you would let me have my way at first, afterwards it would be all yours, didn't I?" she asked softly. "Well, now I'll tell you something else. I know that whatever you want, I'll want too. Partly because you do want it—if a woman really loves a man, that's what she thinks of first, isn't it? What will make him happy, what will give him fulfillment, I mean. Not what *she* wants—that is, not primarily. But if they both want the same thing, if they're mutually happy and—and desirous, then their marriage is a still greater success, isn't it? And we will be mutually happy, our marriage will be a great success. I thought I wasn't ready for any more joy—yet. But you've given me such gladness, just since we began to talk, that I realize more than ever how much we want and need each other."

He had been on the point of leaving her when he asked her why she never kissed him on her own initiative. They had already risen and were standing in front of the fire. Now, when she looked up, she put her arms around his neck and drew his face down to hers.

"Dearest," she murmured, with her lips against his. "Did I really say something that made you afraid I'd be a reluctant bride? Why, what I've been trying to tell you all this time was that I knew I wouldn't!"

And now it was her wedding day and she had wakened very early in the morning. For a few minutes, she lay still, looking around the room in which she had slept alone for the last time. It was a pleasant room, permeated with pleasant memories, for she had always been happy in it. But the moment had come to leave it, and she did not dwell on memories long. She reached for her bell and almost instantly Tossie came in and stood beside the bed and peered at Clarinda through her moonlike glasses.

"Mah goodness!" she exclaimed. "Effen you don' look fresh as a rose, Miss Clarinda! Mah po' baby, when Ah went into her room on her weddin' day, she was so puny lookin' Ah suspicioned she hadn' slep' none and Ah knowed she'd been a-cryin' an' a-cryin'."

"Well, I certainly haven't been crying and I've slept soundly for more than six hours. But we mustn't waste time talking about it, must we? Because presently I want you to help me get dressed. That is, you'd like to, wouldn't you? Of course, Mariana will want to help too."

Mariana had been Mrs. Darcoa's maid, and, until the arrival of Tossie, she had served Clarinda in a similar capacity. But she had been greatly moved by Tossie's story as told her not only by Tossie herself, but by Clarinda and Foxworth, and she had gladly consented to share her pleasant tasks with Tossie during these final months before the wedding. Of course there was more work than usual, with the big reception in prospect and presents piling in every day, so Mariana's duties were increased; and Tossie was still surprisingly deft around a bedroom. Besides, Mariana did not want to leave New Orleans, and Tossie was enchanted with the prospect of going to Puerto de Oro and assuming a position of importance among the servants at the *palacio*.

Dwelling on this gratifying prospect, she drew Clarinda's bath and sprinkled fragrant salts in it; then she and Mariana were both waiting when Clarinda came out from it, wearing her lacy step-ins and brassiere. She liked to pull on her stockings herself—seams never *felt* straight, whether they were or not, she said, when somebody else did it for her; but because she knew it would please them, she held out a foot to each of the old women when they knelt beside her with her white satin slippers. Then, after her hair was dressed, she let them spread open her slip and drop it carefully over her shoulders, so there would be no danger of disarranging the smooth coils. And at last came the magnificent wedding dress of the old brocade and the long veil of rosepoint lace.

At least, as far as Mariana and Tossie knew, that was

what was to come last. But Clarinda had a surprise for them. She opened a drawer, and took from it a box covered with turquoise-blue velvet. And then she pressed a little spring, and the lid flew open and inside .... But the two old women were both blinking so, and exclaiming so, by this time, that they couldn't rightly see what was there, except more diamonds than all the other ladies they'd ever served had possessed, put together, and those glittery, green stones, em'ralds, is that what you called 'em, dozens and dozens of them—well, maybe hundreds and hundreds.

Clarinda lifted the ornaments out, one by one. First she put on the necklace and waited a minute and then she put on the earrings and waited again. She looked at her reflection in the mirror of her dressing table, and then, as she dislodged the brooch from the white satin in which it was imbedded, for the first time her fingers trembled a little. She clasped them in her lap to conceal this and gave a quiet order.

"I think you'd better call Miss Lina to help me now. I don't dare put on the tiara or have either of you do it. We might tear the lace. And, after all, that's got to be saved for the brides in the next generation."

Tossie tittered. "You thinkin' bouten de nex' gen'ration already, Miss Clarinda? Miss Lina's young ones, dey's all boys. Dey ain' gwine need no weddin' veils."

"Well, we'll hope I'll have boys and girls both," Clarinda informed her. "Anyway, we've got to take care of the veil. Go call Miss Lina."

Tossie went, holding her hand over her mouth and laughing behind it. So she might be making baby blankets after all—blankets and jacquettes and bootees. Fortunately, no familiarity with the climate of Puerto de Oro clouded her vision; this was one of unalloyed joy throughout the day. She and Mariana and all the other servants in the Darcoa household had seats reserved for them in a rear pew at the Cathedral. (So did Downes and Ellen and Arnaldo and Selina, for that matter, but this meant nothing to Tossie.) She saw the Archbishop in full pontificals and the golden ornaments on the high altar and the light, like a great glory, shining on it from above. She saw the pages and the flower girls, all dressed in spotless white, and the maid of honor and the twelve bridesmaids, gowned in iridescent splendor. She saw Miss Clarinda go up the center aisle on her father's arm and come down it on her husband's arm, a vision if there ever was one, what with that radiant look on her face and all that brocade and them rosepoints and them diamon's and them green stones. Poor Miss Odile, nothing at her wedding had compared with this. And Tossie could see it all clearly, because she was not crying copiously, as she had been before. Not that Miss Odile hadn't been a real lady too, and a beautiful bride. But that knivin'-hearted Mistuh Léonce she had married—Tossie had hated him from the beginning. Now Mistuh Foxworth, he was diff'runt. He was a good man. He took care of Tossie for true.

Tossie's frame of mind was doubtless rendered the more rosy because she not only served champagne during the course of the reception, but had taken a sip herself, every time she carried the tray back to the kitchen to be refilled. By the time she reached the flagship of the Great Blue Fleet she was in a truly beatific state. Her own clean little cabin filled her with satisfaction. She was tempted to linger in it after she had unpacked her modest belongings—somewhat less modest, be it said, than when she had entered the employ of the Darcoas. But she knew that her duty lay with her white folks. Timorously, she made her way to the magnificent new bridal suite. When she knocked at the door, she found that Miss Clarinda was already unpacking her own belongings and her bridegroom's.

"Hit ain' fitten you should be doin' all dat hard work," Tossie protested. "Jus lea' Tossie 'lone an' she'll have everythin' fixed fo' you, Miss Clarinda. You lay down an' res' you'se'f. You's had a hard day, same as every bride has an' de end ain' yet."

Clarinda hung up the suit she had been in the act of putting on a hanger when Tossie entered—a suit of fine shantung, belonging to her husband. Then she sat down in one of the big chairs of the flower-decked parlor of the suite, which Foxworth had so carefully caused to be prepared.

"Listen, Tossie," she said. "You and I are starting out to a country that's new to us both. We've both got to learn new ways. I've always had someone to draw my bath and hang up my clothes and straighten up my room for me. But that was before I had a husband. I have an idea that when a lady has a husband, things are different—or at least that they ought to be—in every country. I'll send you word, in the morning, when I need you. But I don't need you now. I don't need anyone except the new boss man. Good night."

For a moment, Tossie stood blinking at Clarinda from behind her moonlike glasses. The bride still looked fresh and rosy, as she had when she first waked up that morning; and there was nothing to indicate that she meant to undertake much more unpacking and arrangement. She had already removed her print ensemble and was clad only in a white chiffon nightgown and a white satin negligee. Tossie regarded her with admiration mingled with understanding.

"Ah wouldn' want you should tire yo'se'f wid mah work," she said. "But mebbe yo' right. Mebbe you won' need anythin' mo' till de mornin' hours."

Without further comment, she started for the door. There she almost collided with Foxworth, who had just been talking with the Chief Steward, voicing a decided preference for a table for two, rather than for seats with the Captain. Tossie bobbed respectfully.

"You de head beater now all right, suh," she said deferentially. "An' you don' need to lea' me no ten dollars for to make sho de do' unlatched."

He gave her twenty-five. She had never had so much money in her possession at once, in her entire life. She counted it, over and over again, with satisfaction, until she fell asleep. But she also remembered that she must look to her supply of knitting needles right away, and make sure she had enough wool, pink and blue both, so that either way . . . .

Clarinda was much later in falling asleep. When dawn came, she still had not told her beads, and never, since she was a little child, had she gone to sleep without doing that. But though she had her rosary entwined among her fingers, she could not seem to say any of the customary prayers.

"Hail Mary, full of grace, the Lord is with Thee," she began, over and over again, very softly, so that she would not disturb her husband, who was slumbering beside her. Yet she could not complete the simple formula. At last she gave up trying and instead whispered the words which sprang from her heart.

"Blessed Mother, grant that I may never fail to meet my husband's need, and grant his heart's desire. Not because that is my duty as his wife. But because with all my heart and soul and mind I love him."

IV

June, 1948

The car was an old model, but it had been waxed and polished to a brief renaissance of gloss. Bird-note squeaks were audible from springs and body-joints when it passed over any unevenness of paving. Close scrutiny would have revealed that at least one of the fenders had been crumpled and later straightened by a not too meticulous artificer. It bore a Mississippi license.

As Léonce St. Amant swung past the fenced ruins of the former Delaronde home, where General Sir Edward Pakenham had breathed his last in 1815, he brought the rejuvenated vehicle to a halt at a stile leading to a stately allee of great, moss-hung live oaks.

"Don't you think," he said smoothly, "that this job's a real bargain? You've seen her in action now. Plenty of pick-up, good rubber, good brakes, new rings—"

"But, Daddy, I don't want to buy no car! What's the big idea?" his companion protested in a thin, high voice which was almost a whine. She was a tall, lean girl, with a mop of coarse, henna-colored hair hanging loose around her shoulders, and a round, bold face heavily overlaid with make-up. In slavish acceptance of a fantastic passing fashion, she was wearing gold sandals and clutching a gold evening bag, though otherwise her dress carried informality to the extreme limits of shabby slacks and a rather soiled shirt.

"I assured the office that I was showing this car to a prospect who had asked for a demonstration," Léonce said with a smile. "And I'm a man of my word." He bent his head toward her, pushing aside the henna-colored hair and brushing his lips along the curve where neck and shoulder merged. "Remember what else I told you, honey?"

"Uh-huh," she agreed, and giggled. "Gee, you're cute. You're not like some, that just put their paws on you and say let's go, babe, let's go. You're—you're diff'rent. You're cute."

"You're different, too, sugar," Léonce murmured. "You seem to understand me."

"Do I? Honest?"

"Honest. And it's pretty tough when people don't understand you. When I saw you behind that counter yesterday I said to myself: 'Now there's a girl that would understand me.' And so when you said this was your afternoon off ...."

"Gee, you're nice. You say the sweetest things."

"I could say sweeter ones than that, if we weren't out here where everybody's passing all the time."

The girl giggled shrilly.

"Well, what we waiting for, Daddy?"

Léonce jammed his foot down on the starter, and, as the old engine throbbed into noisy life, swung the car around the fenced ruins and along the graveled Paris Road toward

396

Gentilly and a tourist court, which he would thus approach from the east.

There was one rather dreadful moment. At the point where paving and gravel intersected, a road repair crew was busy. Just as Léonce slowed down in obedience to a "Men At Work" marker, one of the laborers sent his pneumatic drill chattering harshly down into the tough concrete. At once there rose before Léonce the memory of his last visit to the quiet tomb in Metairie. A stonecutter had been painstakingly chiseling the surface of a blank marble tablet which sealed off one of the vaults, and the chatter of the compressed-air chisel had been so nerve racking that Léonce asked the man to stop until after his departure.

ODILE ST. AMANT, DAUGHTER OF CENAS AND AMÉLIE LALANDE, BELOVED WI—

That was all that had been cut in finished form. Faintly outlined against the blue-gray marble by guide line scratches were still the letters:

—FE OF LÉONCE ST. AMANT. BORN, MARCH 26, 1922. DIED, JANUARY 3, 1948.

HE GIVETH HIS BELOVED SLEEP.

As he spelled out the faint letters, he thought again of the note Odile had left. "Darling," she had written in that shaking, tremulous script, "I have tried to be a good wife and a good daughter, but I can't take this any longer. I love you. Odile."

Yes, she had loved him. She had told him so over and over again; it was not strange that he had been in her thoughts at the very last—

But then, she had never understood him.

V

July, 1948

In one respect, Judith had the same viewpoint about a dwelling place as Ruth: it did not matter to her where or what this was, as long as she shared it with her husband. But whereas Ruth did not qualify this feeling in any way, Judith's attitude of mind was affected by one special consideration: All the Farmans, as far back as anyone could remember, had been born on the Hill and buried on the Point; she insisted upon going back to the farm for her confinements.

Joe had never made any objections to this stipulation. He was genuinely fond of Judith's parents, and he had always fitted with remarkable ease into the neighborhood where they lived. To be sure, he had passed some extremely uncomplimentary remarks about the New England climate in March, when Jenness was born, and some which were downright profane, in January, when Danny was born. Cara, he remarked with a grin, was much more considerate. A New England July really had something to commend it; and Judith, feeling that this admission represented a signal victory for her, refrained from remarking that a New England July had a great deal to commend it, after six weeks of New Orleans' weather in which the thermometer had never dropped below ninety in the afternoons.

They had agreed to call the new baby Cara, but she was duly entered in the old family Bibles as Caresse Lalande Racina. The name stood out strangely among the other entries. Besides the ponderous illustrated Bible in the West Parlor, there was a "Cottage Bible" in two volumes on the little table that stood between the windows in the East Chamber, beneath the picture of "The Young Mother" representing a comely matron and a pretty little girl, both wearing their hair in a very quaint and charming fashion. The "Cottage Bible" did not contain the Apocrypha or maps or an index; but it had pages designed for recording births, deaths, and marriages, just as the big one did, and Joe had written the baby's name in it himself, when he had gone back to the East Chamber after Judith had wakened from her first long, refreshing sleep, and Doctor Barnes had come and gone, saying everything was fine, and little Cara was cosily tucked into the hooded cradle that stood within easy reach of the big bed. Then Joe had stood for some moments turning these pages of records and studying them with interest, just as he had two years earlier when he wrote in the name of Daniel Farman Racina, and four years earlier when he wrote in the name of Jenness Farman Racina.

"I might want to use some of those names in a story some time," he explained to Judith. "There are lots of them that I've never seen anywhere else—like Jenness, for instance." But Judith knew this was not the only reason that he stood turning the pages of the old Bible. She knew that he was pleased and proud to have his children's names entered there, that Farman Hill and all that it stood for, was beginning to mean almost as much to him as it did to her.

He had finished his new book early in February, and its selection by a leading book club had insured a sufficiently large sale so that he felt justified, as Judith had so long hoped that he might, in driving himself a little less hard. He had written a series of articles for *The Saturday Evening Post* during the spring, and a few incidental ones for other magazines. But he had not begun a new book as soon as the last one was finished, the way he had for so long, and now he was taking a real vacation—if looking after two young hellions, while their mother was in bed and their grandparents vied with each other in spoiling them, could, by any stretch of the imagination, be called a vacation, he told Judith, with a gesture of mock despair. But he did not say it until she was strong enough to take it in the way he meant it, and to respond with spirit that he might call Danny a hellion if he wanted to, but that Jenness was a sweet-tempered, quiet child, who never made the slightest trouble for anybody, and who certainly did not take after her father. If Cara proved only half as easy to manage . . . .

Joe went over to the cradle and looked dotingly at Cara, and Judith knew he was dying for an excuse to pick the baby up. But she was slumbering peacefully, and it was nowhere near feeding time, and Judith continued her observations by saying if he had such a high regard for discipline, he had better let sleeping infants lie, and sit down quietly himself and tell the news, instead of prowling restlessly around the room.

"There's all kinds of news," he said, lowering himself, in his usual sectional fashion, into a Windsor rocker and fumbling for a cigarette. "The most important, as far as we're concerned, is that my masterpiece has hit the best seller list in both the *Times* and the *Trib*. Not very far up, but it's there. And it couldn't possibly have got there any sooner, with the book sections made up three weeks in advance, the way they are."

"Why, Joe, that's wonderful! Have you got the book sections there? Show them to me this minute!"

"Can't I ever satisfy you? Here you were just telling me to sit down—"

He grinned and lumbered across the room to the four-poster bed, pulling some tear sheets out of his pocket as he came. Judith took them from him and began to read them with avidity.

"I don't call the masterpiece so far down," she said. "Tenth in the *Times* and eighth in the *Trib*—that's wonderful for a start. Next week it'll be higher and next month—why, Joe, it might even go to the top of the non-fiction!"

"Could be—and who'd 'a' thought it, five years ago? It still gives me a feeling of retarded panic when I think about the shoestring we married on. If it hadn't held—"

"But it did. And if it hadn't, we'd have found some way to tie a knot in it and make it do until we could buy a new one.

We don't come of the kind of stock, either of us, Joe, that's afraid of getting married on a shoestring. We don't come of the kind of stock that's afraid of anything. We always know we can pull through somehow . . . ."

She had continued to look, with triumphant eyes, at the best seller lists while she talked. Then she laid these down beside her on the counterpane and picked up a third tear sheet.

"What's this? Another one already, Joe?"

"Hell, no! I didn't mean to show you that one. Give it back here."

"I shan't do anything of the sort. Don't grab at me like that. If you do, we might start a regular fist fight, and I don't suppose I ought to go in for anything like that, just yet."

He knew that she should not, and he also knew that she was quite capable of doing so, if he tried to snatch the extra tear sheet from her. Holding up one hand, as if to ward him off, she began to read from a United Press Dispatch:

"DRUG IS FOUND HELPFUL TO VICTIMS OF PALSY.

"Pittsfield, Mass. (U.P.) Benadryl, medicine which has brought relief to many a sufferer from hayfever and hives, now is helping patients with shaking palsy, known medically as paralysis agitans or Parkinson's disease.

"Its successful use on 10 patients is reported by Dr. Joseph Budnitz of this city in the New England Journal of Medicine."

Judith laid down the tear sheet and looked up at him. "So if Odile had just had the courage to hold on a little longer—" she said slowly.

"Yes, that's it—the courage or the will or the incentive. Pretty grim, isn't it? Of course, the piece doesn't say this drug is a positive cure. But it does seem to give relief, it does seem to promise improvement. It's exactly the sort of thing Perrault had in mind when he spoke of a possible correlative for vaccine and penicillin. It's also exactly the sort of thing he meant when he said he shouldn't have taken away all hope from Odile."

He turned away abruptly and looked down at the cradle. This time he did not wait for an excuse to pick the baby up. He did so easily and capably, keeping one big hand firmly behind the small wobbly head. Cara opened her small pink mouth and yawned expansively.

"She's starving hungry," Joe announced. "Look at the way she's trying to find something to eat. Well, I can't help you out myself, honey, but I'll sure see you get what's coming to you." He smoothed down her clothes and put her on the bed beside Judith. "Go to it, young lady," he admonished. "You heard what your mother said—you've got to fight your way along and you can't fight if you don't eat. Remember that the Farmans and the Racinas don't give up. They pull through somehow."

VI

August, 1948

"Hello, Caresse!"

"Oh, hello, Peter!"

It was inevitable that Peter should recognize the girl's voice when she answered the telephone because no one else lived in the apartment which she shared with Miss Hickey, and Miss Hickey, in spite of all the years she had lived in the United States, still spoke with a slight brogue. But the fact that Caresse instantly recognized Peter's voice was more noteworthy. A great many different persons called her, both at the Salon Superbe and at the apartment, about all sorts of things: her broadcasts, her modeling, her incidental trips, her personal engagements; and, from the nature of her work, most of these calls came from men. But she had never once made a mistake when she said, "Hello, Peter!" She would have known his voice anywhere in the world.

"Sorry, but I've been held up at the office. I won't be able to call for you."

"Why, that's all right. Is dinner off too?"

"Lord, no! I got to eat, haven't I? You got to eat, haven't you? No reason why we shouldn't eat together, is there?"

"Not as far as I'm concerned."

"Good. But it will have to be late. And I've had a pretty rugged day. If it's all the same to you, let's make it some place where I don't have to dress. What about Giovanni's, around eight forty-five?"

"I'd like that. I'll be there."

"So will I. 'Bye."

Caresse was used to telephone conversations like this now. At first she had been slightly startled at the way in which Peter MacDonald took it for granted that she would get to and from restaurants, theaters, and even dances by herself, and that she would be prepared to go to them in either street clothes or full evening dress at a moment's notice. But she had long since ceased to be startled, and lately she had begun to realize in a vague but by no means displeasing way that Peter's seemingly casual attitude was actually complimentary. He took it for granted that she did not need explanations about the exigencies of a journalist's life, and he also took it for granted that she could adjust herself to these without undue effort. To a lesser degree, she told herself rather proudly, it was something the way Russ Aldridge felt about Ruth Avery. Only in her case there was no question of a love affair or anything like that; she and Peter were just two people who had exciting jobs and liked to talk to each other about them. And since the *Enterprise* had tickets at its disposal for all the theaters and horse shows and society benefits, somebody might as well use them.

Since she had so much unexpected time on her hands, and since she would be wearing a short dress, she decided to walk to Giovanni's. When Peter telephoned, she had already transferred her "mad money," her cigarettes, and her compact to her evening bag; now she shifted them all back again to the bag from which she had just taken them. She wrapped her white grosgrain slippers carefully in tissue paper and returned them to the shoe rack in the rear of her closet and removed some black kid pumps trimmed with small kid rosettes which were very trick indeed. She replaced her white marocain crepe dress in its long cellophane bag and took a black faille tailleur from its hanger. When she had previously heard from Peter, at four, he had told her they would be dining on the Starlight Roof at the Waldorf, and she had prepared accordingly. Now she prepared all over again. As she did so, the thought flashed through her mind that if he had only told her about the change of plan a little earlier, she could have accepted the invitation from Harry Holcomb, the director of her radio program, to have a cocktail with him at the Ambassador after her broadcast. There would have been plenty of time, since she was not dining until so late and Harry was good company too. But the thought carried with it no reproach for Peter.

Thanks to daylight saving, it was still bright and pleasant when she stepped into the street, and she decided to walk down the Avenue. It was only a short distance out of her way, and she still took unbounded pleasure in lingering before the shop windows, looking at beautiful luggage, beautiful linens, and beautiful lingerie. She liked to imagine herself traveling, as the representative of Haas and Hector, with such luggage; spreading a table, at which she would entertain distinguished guests, with such linen; and wearing such lingerie as the foundation for the creations of the Salon Superbe.

She also lingered before the windows where baby clothes were displayed, and never let a week go by without sending something to her god-daughter, of whom she was inordinately proud. But otherwise, clothing—except underwear—did not intrigue her much, because none of it that she saw displayed elsewhere could compare, in her opinion, with that which she modeled herself at the Salon Superbe. But she paused before the window displays of dresses and coats too, regarding them with a critical and appraising eye; there was always the chance that she might get an idea which could be turned to good account. She had made two or three sketches, as a result of just such careful observations, and Annabella Avila and Miss Hickey had both praised them very highly. The sharp eyes of Madame Avila and her associates missed very few innovations, and in many cases they inspired these. But no one was infallible. It paid to watch out.

When it came to sheer pleasure, Caresse got the most out of her stops before the windows where jewelry was displayed. Not costume jewelry—she was rather scornful of that. If clothes were really well cut, of fine materials, they did not need a lot of jangling bracelets and metal chains and fancy clips to set them off. But a string of pearls—that was something else again. The heroines in Mr. E. Phillips Oppenheim's novels, of which Miss Hickey had a complete set, and which Caresse was reading with great thoroughness, were almost invariably described as wearing "black dresses of restrained elegance with a single string of pearls." Caresse now had the black dresses of restrained elegance, but the single string of pearls was still far beyond her reach. She had confided her longing for it to Miss Hickey, and Miss Hickey had applauded her taste and added that there were so many "simulated" pearls, not to mention "cultured" pearls on the market now, which only an expert could tell from real ones, that she did not see why Caresse did not wear those, and added that the Salon Superbe would be delighted to furnish her with a strand of her own choosing. But Caresse had colored a little and said, well, she appreciated Miss Hickey's offer very much, but she had sort of made up her mind that she would like to buy the pearls for herself, and she had taken a queer aversion to any kind of an imitation of a real thing; she thought she would just wait; perhaps, if the Caresse Products were a success . . . . So she was waiting, but in the meantime she stopped and looked at all the real pearls which she saw displayed on Fifth Avenue.

When she reached Fifty-fifth Street she turned east and went past the St. Regis and a number of very smart shops; then she crossed Madison and entered a tall plain house with small white pillars in front of it and the name "Giovanni" inconspicuously displayed on one of these. The house did not look much like a restaurant outside; indeed the Little Club next door, with its doorman and its awning and its big plate glass windows, was far more exotic in appearance. Caresse had been there too—in fact, she had been to nearly all the best restaurants in New York by this time. But she was still very much pleased when Peter suggested that they should go to Giovanni's.

The English basement opened upon a small foyer, where tables with red and white checked cloths were grouped companionably around the bar, and a narrow space in the rear provided for a cloakroom and dressing rooms. Both the barman, John, and the checkroom girl, Joan, greeted Caresse cordially, and John suggested a Manhattan. Caresse thanked him, but shook her head.

"If Mr. MacDonald isn't here yet, I think I'll ask Giovanni if I can't go upstairs and see the baby for a few minutes."

"Sure. He'll be pleased to have you."

The proprietor, clad in black trousers and seersucker jacket, was standing at the top of the narrow stairs leading to the two dining rooms. He also hailed Caresse with great cordiality.

"No, Mr. MacDonald didn't get here yet. But I got the corner table reserved, the one you like, where you can see the garden," Giovanni indicated the choice spot, with a jerk of his head and, as he did so, the maître d'hôtel, Angelo, came rushing from the rear, as rapidly as if in flight from some unwelcome pursuit. He stopped short at the sight of Caresse, grinning expansively, and disclosing white, widely spaced teeth.

"I got Asti Spumanti nice and cold already," he informed her. "You want to see?" Then, without waiting for an answer, he ducked under the counter running through the narrow passageway, between the front and rear dining rooms, and dragged a silver cooler into view, withdrawing, sufficiently to reveal its label, an inviting looking bottle from the ice in which it was imbedded. "I know what you like, Miss Lalande."

"You certainly do. I never told you but once that I liked Asti Spumanti and ever since then you've had a bottle on ice for me every time I've come here. . . . By the way, have you some other name besides Angelo? Because I associate that name with Antoine's, my pet restaurant in New Orleans where the maître d'hôtel is named Angelo. And this is my pet restaurant in New York, so I'd like to associate a special name with you."

"Thank you very much, Miss Lalande. My second name is Cafueri."

"Cafueri? Then perhaps I could call you Cafu?"

"Most happy, Miss Lalande. Anything else I get ready?"

"No, thanks. I think Mr. MacDonald will want to order the rest of the drinks with the dinner, when he gets here."

Still grinning, Cafu plunged forward again, with even greater rapidity than before, as if the enemy were now in still closer pursuit and he must make up for lost time. Giovanni remained at the top of the stairway, welcoming all guests upon arrival, signaling to waiters, indicating tables. But meticulous as these attentions were, he contrived to give both his other patrons and Caresse herself the impression that she was singled out for special courtesies.

"You wait a minute. I take you up to my apartment in the elevator. The boy, he won't be in bed yet. My wife, she let him stay up late because he took such a long nap this afternoon."

"I told John I'd like to look in on the signora and the bambino if Mr. MacDonald were delayed. But here he is now."

Peter was just coming into sight along the dim well of the stairway. He nodded rather casually to both Caresse and Giovanni, but in spite of its nonchalance, the greeting did not seem to lack courtesy.

"Hello, Caresse .... You got my message all right, did you, Giovanni?"

"Yes, Mr. MacDonald. You see—"

This time Giovanni did not indicate a table. He led the way to it himself. The cushioned seat which surrounded the corner was extremely comfortable. Beneath the open window at its rear, a tiny garden, with bright-colored flowers clustering around a miniature fountain, was pleasantly visible. Caresse looked down at it with the same amazed appreciation which she had felt ever since first seeing it; she still found it hard to understand how a real garden could have been created in a nook of this sort and how it could give an effect of such refreshment and beauty. Peter did not look at the garden. He had laid down a long roll of brown paper which he had been carrying and was studying the menu with attention.

"I suppose you want hors d'oeuvres with special emphasis on the jellied clams, Caresse," he remarked. "But I think I'll have minestrone. What do you recommend next, Giovanni?"

"Scaloppine. Most delicious."

"Scaloppine it is then. And broccoli hollandaise. And a green salad."

"And a side portion of gnocchi," Giovanni said, writing busily.

"That'll do to begin with. We can decide the rest later. And of course we'll start with Manhattans, double for me, single for Miss Lalande. And let her keep her horrible sweet Asti. I want a good sound red Frascati."

Giovanni withdrew, still writing on his little pad. Cafu, now dashing towards the kitchen quarters, made a hurried detour.

"You want that window shut, Miss Lalande?"

"No, thanks. I like it just the way it is."

The Manhattans arrived, dark amber-colored, full flavored, delicately frosty. Behind the tall Italian who presented them on a small tray, trudged a shorter, stockier man, propelling a two-tiered table laden with glass containers variously heaped with Russian salad, celery root, artichoke hearts, deviled eggs, eggplant mixed with tomato, anchovies, sardines, olives, pickled onions, cole slaw, diced beets—and the jellied clams which represented the supreme achievement of the restaurant's hors d'oeuvres. Caresse, sipping her cocktail, designated one dish after another until her plate was heaped. Then, with obvious regret that there was room for no more, she attacked the array before her with healthy appetite.

"You act like a starving Armenian," Peter told her. "When you get to the point where you feel you can hold out for five minutes or so without any danger of collapsing from malnutrition, I'd like to show you something."

"All right, as soon as I've finished these clams. I don't notice that you're letting your minestrone get cold before you gulp it down."

Peter muttered something unintelligible and went on eating his soup. But when his plate was empty, he pushed it away and reached for the long paper roll which he had been carrying and which he had laid down on the seat beside him.

"Like to have a look at the Sunday magazine section for September twelfth?" he inquired, in his usual casual way.

"Would I—oh, Peter, you don't mean they got it in after all? They said not possibly, until the nineteenth!"

"A few well-chosen words will work wonders, even in the advertising department," he informed her loftily. "But I had hard work getting hold of this advance copy—that's what held me up. Here you are—hot from the press." There was

406

always some reason why Peter had been held up—some reason which, when tardily disclosed, made Caresse glad that he had been. She was thankful now that she had said nothing about the nuisance of changing from one outfit to another, doubly thankful that she had not mentioned the date with Harry Holcomb which she had missed. "Of course, you saw the proofs at the Salon," Peter went on. "But I was surprised myself that they came out so well. And Annabella made me swear not to let you know that they decided to change the layout to a center spread."

He handed Caresse the brown roll. She tore off the wrapping, spread the magazine out on the table and began to turn the pages with impatient fingers. A man at one of the center tables nudged his companion and said, in a stage whisper, "See that girl in black over by the window? That's Caresse Lalande, the latest radio sensation. She models for Haas and Hector too, and I understand they're planning to get out a new line, named after her. The man with her is Peter MacDonald, one of the associate editors of the *Enterprise*. They're here, there, and everywhere together these days." Peter looked towards the speaker, and something in the newspaperman's face silenced the other quickly. Caresse had not even heard him. She had reached the center spread and was staring incredulously at the brightly colored pages.

"There's a feature article too," Peter informed her. "Go on, turn a few more pages. We thought of making it the lead, and then we decided it would be better to have the ad come first, it's such a knockout."

The tall waiter had brought in the scaloppine, the broccoli, and the gnocchi. Peter dug into his and ate calmly and comprehensively; Caresse did not even see the plate in front of her. Giovanni, watchfully circling the room according to his habit, came and stood beside the table, looking reproachfully from his favored patron to her untouched food. But Peter made a slight movement and said something under his breath in Italian, and Giovanni answered understandingly and went away. A moment later Cafu came tearing up with the cooler and a wire stand, and began to turn the bottle with its famous label round and round in its bed of ice.

"You want your Asti now, don't you, Miss Lalande?" he inquired. "All nice and cold. You see—"

"Pour it for her anyway," Peter suggested. "And I've changed my mind. I'm going to have some too, after all. This is—well, it's turned out to be sort of a special occasion."

The maître d'hôtel did not connect the magazine lying on

the table, beside the neglected dinner plate, with Mr. MacDonald's words. "A special occasion" in which a beautiful girl and a personable and prominent man were jointly concerned had only one meaning, in his experience. But he hastened to bring a second champagne glass and to fill both to the brim.

"I want to congratulate you, Mr. MacDonald," he said heartily. "I give you my best wishes, Miss Lalande. I hope you be very happy."

"I am—oh, I am, Cafu!" Caresse exclaimed. "I've never been so excited about anything, never in my whole life." She had glanced up briefly, to acknowledge the maître d'hôtel's salutation; but now she looked down again. And, as she did so, she seemed to see not only the brightly colored pages which were actually spread out before her, but a certain string of pearls on a black velvet bust, which had held her fascinated gaze an hour or so earlier.

Still laboring under a misapprehension, Cafu had sped away again, this time to fetch Giovanni. Peter signaled to the tall waiter that he might as well remove the untouched plate of scaloppine. Caresse, unaware that it was gone, began to talk enthusiastically.

"You must get lots of extra copies for me, Peter," she said. "I want to send them to everyone I know—I mean everyone who had faith in me, who felt sure I was going to succeed. Mrs. Lafargue and all her assistants at The Fashion Plate Dress Shop. And the boys at the broadcasting station— I mean the one in New Orleans. And of course to Joe and Judith Racina and Russ and Ruth Aldridge and Sabin Duplessis and to my *parrain*."

She had told him about all these people in the course of their outings together. In fact, she had told him an astonishing number of things about herself, about her family and her friends and her work, about Odile and Vance Perrault. Peter was a very good listener. He said it was pure selfishness on his part, that he never knew when he might hear something that would make a good story. But Caresse did not think of it that way, any more than Judith thought of it that way when she saw Joe looking at the entries in the old family Bible. Caresse liked to talk to Peter, not only because he was a good listener, but because he was her kind of a person.

"I'll make a note of the fact that you want to buy out the edition," he told her. "Of course I don't know whether the boss will let you or not, but I can always ask him. And while you're making out that list of yours, what about putting down the name of your friend Captain Toe Murphy? He believed in you, didn't he? I think he ought to be one of the first to have a copy."

Giovanni had approached them again. This time he had poised above one hand an immense circular plate surmounted by a creamy, molded dessert, quivering above the orange sections which encircled it. In the other, he carried a large serving spoon.

"The Asti is on the house," he announced expansively. "But please to take some of this bavaroise with it, Miss Lalande. It is not just a specialty of the house. It is my own invention. Most delicious."

VII

September, 1948

Leaning back in his chair, his feet cocked up on the slide of his desk, Toe Murphy pursed his lips and shrilled the familiar two-note cadence of the wolf whistle. Dan Gallian looked up from the "Wanted for Bank Robbery" circular over which he had been poring.

"What the hell?" he demanded. "Is it June busting out all over this late in the year?"

Captain Murphy passed an open copy of the *New York Enterprise* Sunday Magazine across the desk to him. "Give this slick chick a look," he invited.

Gallian scanned the center double appreciatively. "Slick chick is right," he agreed. "But what am I supposed to do about it?"

"Don't you remember that little number?" prompted Murphy. "You mean to say you forgot a looker like that?"

Again Gallian scanned the Haas and Hector advertisement. "Caresse Lalande," he murmured. "Caresse Lalande. I'd ought to remember that name. Leave me think—hey! I got it. Wasn't she mixed up in some dizzy murder or suicide or something uptown somewhere? Sure she was. I haven't thought about that one in it must be six-seven months. Last January, wasn't it?"

Murphy nodded, "That's the one. Out on Richmond Place. Foxworth, the number one guy of the Blue Fleet was in it up to his ears for a while. Course he's the Number One Double A guy now since the Trans-Carib merged with the Blue Fleet and he married Francisco Darcoa's daughter. And say, she was another looker, all right. But in those days Foxworth was just one more suspect, so far's I was concerned."

"I got it now," Dan interrupted with animation. "Some

409

doctor knocked hisself off in one of the tombs out in Metairie, and left a full confession in a letter to this same Caresse number. Well, whaddaya know." He gazed at the Haas and Hector advertisement with increased interest, and sustained admiration. "Slick chick is right," he repeated.

"Hand back that paper, will you? I could go for another look at it too. And to think the smooth number sent it to me herself, with a hot little note."

"Want to show me the note?" Dan inquired.

"Not a chance! What's the point? Anyway, we were talking about this loony doctor. He left a confession, all right. But he needn't have. I had it pinned on him, no matter what he did. Only one thing I was wrong in. I figured a note this gal—the one that was murdered, I mean—had left behind must have been forged, seeing as I knew it wasn't any suicide. I made that in one look at the body when I saw there wasn't any sign of a powder burn. So naturally, I figured out somebody else must have written what was a sure enough suicide note in her handwriting. But it turned out later she wrote it, right enough. She had tried to kill herself, you see, and she was getting away with it, when this doctor friend of hers figured he was to blame for the whole thing, and to save her from having the sin of suicide, put a bullet into her while she was dying."

"I remember," Dan said. "Any guy'd do a thing like that couldn't of had all his marbles, I always figured."

"Well, I wouldn't go so far's to say that," Captain Murphy mused, thoughtfully regarding the toes of his shoes. "This Caresse Lalande—the girl the ad is all about—let me read the letter he wrote her, and, besides, he wrote one to me. And if you put yourself in his place, somehow the two letters make sense. I mean, once this dead girl that he killed had set out to commit suicide. On account of he had told her she was a hopeless case from some kind of paralysis. Naturally, no suicide really makes sense. I know that, same's you do. Not to mention it being a mortal sin. But it was a queer thing about that case. There were at least five people actually might have killed her—killed this Mrs. St. Amant, I mean."

With unconcealed interest Dan waited for Toe to go on.

"It's been a long time already and some of it I don't remember as well as I might," Toe said pensively, fingering the magazine. "But there was her husband, a trifling no-good two-timer, who was making passes for Caresse, the dead girl's sister; there was a loose nut by the name of Duplessis, that had been halfway engaged to the dead girl before she

410

married this two-timing St. Amant. I hear he's flying for some oil company down in South America—Duplessis, I mean. And there was Mrs. St. Amant's mother—a bird-brain with nothing but the original sand between the ears, but plenty of looks. And there was an old nigger mammy, I forget her name. And even this sister—this Caresse that's up there in New York knocking 'em dead now."

"That's a lot of people," murmured Dan.

"And of course there was this doctor. Vance Perrault," Murphy continued. "Funny thing, I never figured him at all, first off, even if he was the last person who would admit he saw this Mrs. St. Amant alive the night she was killed. He was the only one I couldn't figure out a motive for."

"But still and all you say you had it pinned on him, even if he wouldn't of confessed," Dan pointed out.

"That's right," Murphy agreed. "But it took me damn near a week to work it out. You see, Dan, every one of those people had a chance to do it, and every last one of them had what could be a motive for doing it. Every one of them had a motive, I mean, for which somebody right in this town had done a murder since I've been on the force. St. Amant, the husband, was making passes at the sister, for one thing. For another, checking up on him, he was spending more dough than he was making, being a high-octane chaser, and his wife's death would mean a sweet chunk of money for him. And living in the same house, he could have pussyfooted into his wife's sickroom and killed her as easy as damn it. Duplessis was a reckless devil, an army flier, crazy about the gal, sore because she'd married this St. Amant punk while he was in the service. Besides, it turned out he had climbed a wall to get into her room the night she was killed. He was stewed to the gills when he did it, too."

"What the hell would he climb that wall for?" asked Dan with a great show of naive innocence.

"Why, I wouldn't know, Mr. Gallian," Murphy replied in mincing tones. "Anyway, he claimed that when he saw there was a man in the room with her—saw it from the shadow on the blind—he climbed right back out again. I didn't say yes or no or kiss my foot to him about that part of his story at first. But it turned out to be true. And just to make the case real good, this Foxworth had been messing around with some kind of a revolution—I never did get the straight of that, but the FBI did—and he had cooked up a phony alibi for himself that covered the identical hours when this girl must've been killed. A sweet mess, if you'd ask me."

411

"But some of those people you could brush off your vest right away, couldn't you?"

"Not right off. Except for the mammy. I knew she could never have forged that suicide note. So I pinched her for the killing, right where everybody could see me do it, figuring maybe whoever really killed her would feel safe and get careless. On general principles I wrote off the girl's mother, mostly because she was the kind that wouldn't have touched a gun with a ten-foot pole. You know what I mean?"

"Sure!" Dan nodded vigorously.

"I never did really think the sister—this Caresse number here—was the one; but she had some blood on her dress, and the damnedest cock-and-bull story about an automobile accident that she and St. Amant were in together. The net on the whole thing was I couldn't make up my mind about her till one day Joe Racina—remember him? He used to hang around here a good deal years ago when he was on the *Item*. Anyway, he brought the Caresse gal out here after selling her on the idea of spilling everything she knew. That put her in the clear. But at that, she didn't tell everything. She knew one thing about her brother-in-law she kept to herself. It was about two pillows; but let that go, because it turned out that what she knew didn't really figure."

"That's as clear as muddy dishwater," objected Dan.

"Okay, okay. It doesn't signify. Anyway, by that time I had my sights on Doctor Perrault. This Sabin Duplessis had come to me with the story about what he saw on the blind. Somehow, I believed him. It sounded right. And later when I checked up on the times he'd been seen downtown, at this bar and at that, I proved it was right, because he couldn't have been where he was, and where plenty of witnesses saw him, and still have seen the girl alive after Doc Perrault saw her. This Duplessis had a letch to kill whoever murdered his honey-pot, and he'd been following the Doc around. Well, instead of making his regular rounds, visiting patients, going to the hospital and all such as that, he found the Doc driving out to Metairie Cemetery and hanging around the tomb where this Mrs. St. Amant had been buried. Spending hours out there, day after day. And when he told me that, I thought to myself, sure enough, there's our pigeon."

"And he was," added Dan sagely.

"Yes, but I still couldn't figure out no motive for him. So I had to go about taking care of the other suspects just the same: Foxworth and his phony alibi, St. Amant who was a wrong guy with a motive and an opportunity; and—just to

412

overlook no bets—my volunteer assistant, Sabin Duplessis, in case he might be putting on an act."

"They do, lots of times," admitted Dan. "Why, I remember when . . . ."

"Leave me finish, Dan. In the middle of it all, up pops Mr. Joe Racina with the idea that the suicide note wasn't a suicide note, but just a farewell message from a young married woman that was gonna run off with another guy. It's his idea that whoever has the note, killed the lady. And on the heels of that some hotshot from Washington comes down and furnishes Foxworth a complete, double-welded copper bottom alibi; a square one, this time, with a jillion G-men to back it up."

"That still leaves St. Amant and the Doc, doesn't it?"

"Correct as hell. It was bound to be one of them, and there's a way of proving which. Doc Perrault has got one soft spot in his story of what he did that Saturday night when the killing took place. He said the reason he went to this house in Richmond Place at ten o'clock instead of at midnight, was another patient in the same neighborhood had called him. So I put it up to him to name that patient and have the patient verify it. If he came through with the name, I knew the killer would be St. Amant. But if the Doc couldn't name the patient, I had him nailed down. Just to lay a good foundation, I told first one and then another of everybody mixed up in the case that I already knew who the killer was. It wasn't really a lie, either, because I did know it was either St. Amant or Perrault."

"Since when did you get so particular about telling a lie to a suspect?" demanded Dan indignantly. "Who you trying to kid?"

"Okay, skip it. It turned out I was right, anyway. Because when the Doc heard me ask him who his ten o'clock patient was, you could actually smell the stink of guilt on him ten feet away. I wasn't taking any chances. I pinned a couple of guys on him to follow him that day wherever he went. It happened to be a Saturday, and he gives me a song and dance about having lost his call book and his receptionist being out of town for the week end, and he will give me the name come Monday. And I'd have had the cuffs on him if those two clabberheads that was supposed to keep him in sight hadn't let him give them the slip at Riverside Hospital. You just can't make brains for some guys. They actually waited an hour without knowing their pigeon was flying. Then they telephoned me and, remembering what Duplessis had said about where this Doc had been spending most of his time, I beat it out to the cemetery. By the time I got hold of the manager and had the gate opened, it was all over. The Doc had put the needle in his arm and was dead as a beef."

"But leaving a confession," Dan reminded his colleague.

"Right," agreed Toe Murphy, bringing his feet to the floor. "Come on, let's go downstairs. It's time for the afternoon show-up. I guess I'll take this paper along with me. I might get a chance to look at it again."

"And you might give me a chance to see the note that came with it, too," Dan reminded him.

VIII

October, 1948

Sabin eased back the throttles of four mighty motors, and listened for the familiar "Wheeeee!" that accompanied the lowering of wing-flaps and landing gear. Behind him, in the electronic maze that filled the cabin, the torpedo-shaped "bird" whose eye could peer twenty thousand feet beneath the surface of the earth had been reeled in and nested. Automatic cameras, dials, and recording graphs were switched off. Seven hundred square miles of subterranean landscape had been mapped since the aerial magnetometer crew he piloted had taken off that morning.

Valbuena Lake, already dark within its walled crater, slid beneath him. Ahead lay the narrow strip of cleared jungle that was the airport. The plane itself seemed weary as at last it touched the ground and rolled to a halt. Sabin released his safety belt, unclipped his earphones, hung the head-set on an instrument knob, and turned to his co-pilot with a relaxing sigh.

"Another day, another dollar; a million days, a million dollars," he said. "Let's go, Dutch."

"Okay, chief. My mammy done told me there'd be times like these."

They followed the magnetometer staff, with its record rolls and its film cans and charts, while the ground crew swarmed over the big plane to prepare it for the morrow's exploration flight. Passing the radar mast, Sabin looked up. Within a few minutes now, the tropic night, whose abrupt descent had the effect of a curtain dropping between the earth and the sky, would close down.

In the cramped hutment he shared with Dutch Schaefer the two men shed their flying gear, showered, shaved, and donned slacks.

"I still think it's the nuts," Schaefer observed as they walked down a steep trail from their quarters to the mess hall for supper. "I mean this business of going two miles into the sky to look five miles under the ground."

"There's no other way this kind of country could be explored for oil," Sabin reminded him. "It's a damned useful job. When you think of what the world's up against in the way of petroleum needs, it's an important one."

"It's a job, anyway, and it takes you up into the open air," grinned Schaefer. "No G-guy comes and taps you on the shoulder for doing it, either. Remember that time at the Bar-None Ranch, when Uncle put the finger on me while I was talking to you and some gal?"

"Yes. I remember. Sometimes I think all that business happened to somebody else—in some other life. And then again it seems like something that was only day-before-yesterday. Funny, what?"

"Yeah. Funny. But everything's funny, when you get right down to it. I remember you saying one day in New Delhi, I think it was, that after the war there wouldn't be money enough to hire you to put on a parachute and even taxi a plane up and down a runway. And now you're out every day, flying this look-see baby of ours over terrain that's got me telling my beads and living a better life."

Sabin shrugged.

"Back in those days I figured I'd have something real to live for, I guess. Could be I'll get to the point where I see it that way again. But right now—" He left the sentence unfinished. Dutch shot him a swift and understanding glance.

"Right now, like you say, it's a damned useful job that somebody's got to be doing and it might as well be us. I never did hanker to be the hottest pilot in the world—just the oldest one. With luck, I'll make it yet."

Afterward they left the mess hall, whose windows cast a friendly glow into the warm night where the fireflies seemed to be dancing among the low-hung stars.

"It kind of gets you, at that, don't it?" Schaefer mused. "Think I'll take a run to town tonight. The military band'll be giving a concert in the plaza. How's for siding me?"

"B'lieve not."

"Aw, come on! Do you good to hoist a couple of veeskie cocktaileys. No binge, I promise you. Just enough to let down the hammer."

"I'm not in the mood, Dutch. I'll turn in early. This flying over jungles where, even if you walked away from a crash there's no place to walk to, takes it out of you."

"Okay, Skipper. You are the captain of your soul or what have you. Me, I'm going to see if Lucita'd like to let me make a little time tonight. See you tomorrow in the wild blue yonder."

"Hasta mañana. Vaya con Dios."

"Suene con los ángeles, caballero."

Sabin watched Dutch scramble for a foothold on the already overloaded jeep as it set out on its jouncing traverse of the rough trail to Valbuena. Softly whistling a chorus of "Lady Levee," he turned uphill to his hutment, smiling at the thought of what Dutch would have remarked if Sabin had said he had a date for that night, too.

Settling himself in a canvas deck chair on the hutment's tiny porch, he looked serenely out over the mirror of Lake Valbuena to the distant crests beyond, faintly silhouetted against the vague radiance of the sky. Then he reached into his pocket and took from his billfold a scrap of paper—the tiny note which had fluttered to the ground from Vance Perrault's bag, when the doctor rummaged hurriedly through it to get a restorative for Caresse. Perrault had not seen it fall; but Sabin, watching from behind an adjacent tomb, had noted where it lay. He had waited until the doctor was gone, and then he had picked it up and kept it. He knew that this note had been meant for him and no one else—the note which began with the word "Darling" and closed with the words, "I love you. Odile."